PRAISE FOR CAROLI

'T _____ turner. Unreliable na_____ s mean
yo _____ know where you stand until it all builds to a richly
satisfying climax. A fantastic psychological thriller.'

—John Marrs

'Brilliantly gripping and deliciously creepy. Make sure you clear
your day as you won't be able to put *Silent Victim* down!'

—Sibel Hodge

'Dark, shocking and utterly compelling.'

—Mel Sherratt

'This lady writes compelling, atmospheric, unputdownable
psychological thrillers.'

—Angela Marsons

THE
PERFECT
MOTHER

ALSO BY

CAROLINE MITCHELL

Individual Works

Paranormal Intruder
Witness
Silent Victim

The DI Amy Winter Series

Truth and Lies
The Secret Child

The DC Jennifer Knight Series

Don't Turn Around
Time to Die
The Silent Twin

The DS Ruby Preston Series

Death Note
Sleep Tight
Murder Game

THE
PERFECT
MOTHER

CAROLINE MITCHELL

THOMAS & MERCER

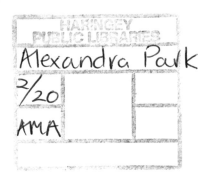
This is a work of fiction. Names, characters, organizations, places, events, and incidents are either products of the author's imagination or are used fictitiously. Any resemblance to actual persons, living or dead, or actual events is purely coincidental.

Published by Thomas & Mercer, Seattle

www.apub.com

Amazon, the Amazon logo, and Thomas & Mercer are trademarks of Amazon.com, Inc., or its affiliates.

ISBN-13: 9781542016643
ISBN-10: 1542016649

Cover design by Tom Sanderson

Printed in the United States of America

For Isaac

With what price we pay for the glory of
motherhood

—*Isadora Duncan*

PROLOGUE
ROZ
2019

I gently rubbed my stomach. It was hard to fathom that behind the wall of expanding flesh beat the heart of my little girl. She was more than an accidental pregnancy. She was keeping me alive.

If only I had listened to Dympna when she warned me that I was making a mistake. Tears welled in my eyes as I thought of my friend, so many miles away. How different my life would have been if I had taken her advice. Guilt sucked me in like quicksand, dragging me down until I could barely breathe. Was it the lure of New York that first drew me in? Or the empty promises that were made? I wiped away my tears with the back of my hand. How could I have predicted how this was going to turn out?

'It's OK,' I whispered to my unborn child. 'I'll keep you safe.'

I reined in my thoughts in case my baby sensed my fear. There was movement as she pressed against my ribcage. The thought of her entry into the world was making me sick with nerves. It was not the prospect of giving birth that worried me; it was what would happen the second she was born. I pressed my hand against my mouth to stem the scream building in my throat. *Keep it together.* My self-preservation depended on me being calm, focused and ready.

A door slammed on the floor above and a muffled argument ensued. I knew it was about me. My accommodation was luxurious, but not soundproof, and I had learned a lot about the people up there. Slowly, I crept around the apartment and fetched a chair. As I dragged it to the air vent, its legs scraped the wooden floor. I bent my knees as I stepped up on to it, trying to hold it still. It was risky, but this was the best place to hear what was going on above. Holding my breath, I listened for key words. They thought I couldn't hear them, but I knew what they were capable of. I snuffled through my congestion. The air was too dry, too cold, and goose bumps rose on my skin. The argument descended into soft murmurs. A decision had been made.

I climbed down from my chair, every nerve-ending tingling as adrenalin coursed through my veins. It was now or never. Footsteps crossed the floor above my head. My hand trembled as I reached for the knife carefully hidden beneath the folds of my maternity dress. It was small but sharp enough to pierce skin. What choice did I have? My heart reverberated against the wall of my chest and my breath came in short, quick gasps. They were coming.

There wasn't a second to waste. I tiptoed to the side of my wardrobe, my fingers clasped tightly around the knife. The lift whirred as it escorted its passengers to my floor. A ding signalled that they were here. I held my breath as the lift doors slid open.

It was time.

CHAPTER ONE
ROZ
OCTOBER 2018

'How far apart do your legs have to be for a thigh gap?'

Wearing her tightest skinny jeans and vest top, Dympna surveyed herself in the full-length mirror in my room. I lay stretched out on my bed, my head too full of my own worries to pay much attention.

'It's gone. It's definitely gone,' she moaned, mourning the loss of that all-important space between her thighs. 'I mean, look at me, I'm a whale!'

She was not a whale. Red-haired and feisty, she was beautifully rounded, and I envied her curves. We had been friends ever since she shared her sandwich with me in school at the age of four. People said we made a striking pairing – her with her red hair, me with my white-blonde locks tumbling past my shoulders. Rhubarb and Custard, they called us, after the sweets. We were never apart. We moved on to secondary school, sat through mass for an hour in church every Sunday and both got housekeeping jobs in the same Jurys hotel. It was a natural progression for us to share a flat; but the rent in Dublin was astronomical compared to my hometown in Ferbane, and I didn't have the heart to tell my best friend that I had just lost my job. If only that's all it was. There was far worse on the horizon for me. My stomach rolled over as the implications punched me like a fist to the gut.

'You're grand,' I said, taking a slice of pizza from the box on the bed. Another wave of nausea hit me as I nibbled on the crust. I'd barely been able to eat since I'd discovered the news.

'I suppose you're right.' Dympna sighed, my mattress bouncing as she plopped down beside me. She grabbed a slice of my pizza. 'Besides, the curvy look is in. Kim Kardashian's bum is twice the size of mine.'

'Then you've got some ground to cover. You'd better finish the lot.' I laughed as I spoke, but I was numb inside. Dropping the pizza slice back in the box, I realised I couldn't cope with it on my own. 'Oh, God,' I gasped as a lump rose in my throat. 'What am I going to do?'

Dympna's mouth dropped open and she froze mid-chew.

Dympna was always the strong one. After her family moved to Dublin, she encouraged me to go, too. She'd got us our flat, organised our jobs, even learned how to drive. I, on the other hand, was creative, scatty, and too impetuous for my own good. But I had grown up since moving in with her, and developed a routine. Now here I was, drowning in guilt, trapped in a no-win situation. Panic consumed me as I cried like a child, big fat sobs clogging my throat.

The takeaway box slid to the floor as Dympna wrapped her arms around me, and I realised her slice of pizza was sticking to my hair.

'What is it? What's wrong?' she demanded, squeezing tightly. I garbled that I needed some air to breathe. Dympna had always been a hugger. It was her answer to everything. She even hugged a teacher once when she broke down in class. *Hug now, ask questions later.* It was lucky that she was a girl. It's true, though, it *did* make me feel better. But by now my hair smelt like yesterday's cheesy feast. I noticed from the corner of my eye that some of my blonde strands were streaked tomato red.

Disentangling myself from her grip, I prepared to give her the news I had not yet come to terms with myself.

'I'm pregnant,' I blurted, unable to look her in the eye. I stared at my chipped nail varnish as I waited for the telling-off. The last thing I needed was a lecture about contraception. It had been a one-off; I'd been too drunk to exercise any form of self-control.

'Merciful hour!' Dympna had picked up the term from her mother and it was usually reserved for catastrophic news. She looked at me with complete and utter shock. 'When? Who? How far are you gone? Are you keeping it? What about your mam and stepdad . . . Do they know?'

Her questions fired like bullets, making my head spin. I consoled myself that at least she had not asked the question I dreaded.

'Who's the father?'

There it was. My chin wobbled as my tears threatened to overflow again. At least if I was sobbing, I couldn't be expected to respond, but I knew Dympna would keep digging away until I did.

'It was a one-night stand,' I said, grabbing a tissue and blowing my nose. 'And before you say it, I know. I was drunk and stupid, and the condom must have split.'

'And you weren't on the pill?' was Dympna's instant response. 'Are you nuts?'

Dympna's judgemental words made me feel even worse. I was not the type of person to sleep around. I was feeling lousy because I was struggling financially, and when he said he'd help out, well, I melted. It was a long time since any fella had cared about me like that. But my friendship with Dympna meant more to me than anything. She must never find out who he was.

'If I wanted a lecture, I would have told my mother.' I sniffled. Another person who could never know.

'Sorry.' Dympna's forehead scrunched as she tried to work a way out of this mess. 'What are you going to do?'

I delivered a weak smile, twisting my tissue, now sodden with tears. I had thought about nothing else since a home pregnancy test confirmed my worst fears. Aged twenty-four, I was old enough to raise a baby, but I wasn't ready to be a mother. I wanted to travel the world, to draw on my experiences and create portraits of the people I met. My artistic nature made me long for adventure. I wanted a life outside Ireland and the bubble I grew up in.

Dympna looked at me hopefully. She'd love nothing better than for me to keep the baby. We'd had several conversations about what kind of strollers we'd buy when we became mothers one day. Dympna wanted something modern and snazzy, while I mused about owning a Silver Cross pram. But it was *her* dream to have kids sooner rather than later, not mine; her relationship with Seamus had gone from strength to strength in the last six months. The last thing I wanted was to put some poor unfortunate baby through a childhood like mine.

'I'm not getting an abortion,' I said, clearing my throat. That much I was adamant about. I had nothing against women who chose that path, but I had sat through too many 'burn in hell' Sunday sermons to consider it an option for me.

Dympna nodded knowingly. Father Vincent had put the fear of God in her, too. It was a spittle-laced subject the Catholic priest was terrifyingly passionate about.

'So you're keeping it?' Her face brightened. 'We could rear it together. Like in the film. *Three Men and a Baby*. It would be great craic!' Dympna was proud of her vintage video cassette collection and insisted we watch one old movie a week on her battered VCR.

'Except we're girls, we've no money and we both have to work.'
I shook my head. 'Not that I have great job prospects now.' There
was a last resort: tell my mother. I didn't need to factor my father
in – he ran out on us years ago.

'Are you going home then?' Dympna slid her tongue over her
teeth, and I knew she was doing the maths. If I left her high and
dry, she wouldn't be able to afford to stay in our flat on her own.

'No way,' I said, pulling a face. 'You can't tell Mammy either.
She's not to know.'

'But . . .'

'I mean it. Swear on your life.'

Dympna crossed her heart with her finger. It was something
we'd done since childhood and we had never broken our vows. I
prayed she wouldn't ask me to fess up about the baby's father. She
would never speak to me again if she knew.

'There's one more option.' Flicking back my hair, I reached for
my battered laptop and opened it up. I brought up the 'Miracle-
Moms' site I'd bookmarked earlier in the week. Guilt consumed
me as I recalled how I'd spent my last €500 on registration costs
instead of rent. But the fees ensured the site's exclusivity; otherwise
all sorts of people would be trying to fob their babies off. Surely it
would be worth it if it helped me out of this mess? At first, it had
seemed crazy. The very thought of giving up my firstborn made me
turn cold. But what choice did I have? My priorities lay firmly with
the cluster of cells growing inside me. More than anything, they
deserved a decent start in life. I'm not saying that money buys you
happiness, but it certainly would have improved my upbringing no
end. No child should have to go to bed cold and hungry, or listen to
their mother cry herself to sleep at night. Besides, Mam had finally
met someone nice. She was settled now, with her own life to lead.

'What do you think?' I said, watching Dympna for a reaction
as I scrolled through the page.

'An adoption site? In America?' She peered at the screen, her red curls shadowing her face. 'Hang on . . . they *buy* your baby?' She pushed my hand aside and clicked on a page. 'Will you look at all these bumps – it's like Tinder for pregnancies.'

'Not buy,' I said sharply, for fear of being talked out of it. 'The couple pay my expenses. If we like each other, they fly me over and put me up until the baby is born.'

'Then pay you a wad of money when you leave the baby there,' Dympna snorted. 'Have you checked them out?'

'The site vets all the couples, so I don't need to worry on that front.'

They vetted participants too. The pinprick on the crease of my inner arm was the result of the private blood test I'd had to take. It not only confirmed my pregnancy, but the potential sex of the baby. Not that I'd wanted to know; it wasn't mine to keep, after all. I straightened my legs, which were fizzing with pins and needles. My size-ten jeans felt tight around my midriff, which was stupid as I was only eight weeks pregnant and hadn't gained a pound.

I gave my friend a warning glance. 'You can't tell a soul. I'll say I've got a new job . . . an internship. That will cover the six months I'm over there. They'll pay me enough to cover my rent here, too.'

'But you've still got to carry the baby. Can you really give it up? What if you don't like the couple? What if the baby's disabled? Would they want it then?'

'Disabled?' My voice rose an octave as I clambered off the bed. 'I thought you'd support me, but all you're doing is making me feel worse! I wish I'd never told you now.'

'Aw, chick, I'm sorry. Come here.' Rising, Dympna dodged the pizza box. 'I'm just looking out for you. Whatever you want, I'll back you all the way.'

I closed my eyes as I succumbed to another hug. My shoulders dropping, I relaxed in her embrace. She smelt of peach-scented body spray and happier times. I made up my mind to protect our friendship.

'Ugh, you've got sauce in your hair,' she grimaced, releasing me from her grip. 'You shouldn't be eating that rubbish any more. I'll make us some scrambled eggs.'

'Thanks,' I murmured, my stomach still tied up in knots.

She gave me a sad smile before walking through the door. I heard her head thunk against the wood as she leaned against it on the other side. She needed time to process things, too. Sitting back on my bed, I opened my laptop and scrolled through the adoption site. The other applicants seemed so glam compared to me. Ex-models and well-educated women with good jobs looking for the best price for their unborn child. Was I strong enough to compete? My life had been turned on its head. I had to try, for the sake of the baby. It deserved the perfect mother – which certainly wasn't me.

CHAPTER TWO
SHERIDAN

Celeb Goss Magazine
By Alex Santana
October 2018
INSECURE SHERIDAN'S BABY ULTIMATUM

Being married to Daniel Watson is every hot-blooded woman's dream, and judging by the couple's Instagram photos, you'd be forgiven for thinking his wife, blonde bombshell Sheridan Sinclair, forty-four, feels the same. But the celebrity couple's relationship isn't as picture-perfect as it seems.

An insider tells _Celeb Goss_ that they are finding things tough: 'Things came to a head between Daniel and Sheridan last month. She's been feeling insecure about her age, and it doesn't help that pretty young women flock around Daniel everywhere they go.' It seems that the New York actress has considered cosmetic surgery. 'She's been having Botox and lip-fillers since she was thirty, but she stepped things up and told Daniel she wanted a facelift. Daniel was totally against it, saying she was beautiful the way she was, but it has caused a rift.'

But fans need not despair just yet. Last week the pair gave separate interviews and reaffirmed their commitment to each other. Speaking on *Good Morning America*, Daniel, thirty-eight, defended the couple's marriage, which was put to the test when he spent eight months filming in his home county of Oxfordshire, England. 'Sheridan and I are as solid as ever, and I hope to take some time out to spend with my family soon.'

Sheridan has been keeping busy in his absence. Since the birth of their only son, Leo, four, her Instagram following has gone through the roof. Her wholesome family photos have attracted millions of followers, nicknamed the 'Sheridanis'. But rumor has it that Sheridan longs for a little girl. When asked if they were going to try for another baby, Daniel said: 'It's not off the cards.'

Sheridan Sinclair first hit television screens at the tender age of six in the long-running TV series *It Takes All Sorts*, and has starred in many Hollywood blockbusters over the years. However, inside sources say that since hitting her forties, offers of work have been drying up. The same cannot be said for her husband, who came to acting later in life and is in high demand. Is it really Sheridan's age that is bothering her, or her husband's flourishing career? Hollywood can't get enough of this hunky Brit. If Sheridan wants to tie him down to family life, it seems she will have a fight on her hands.

'Have you read this?' Sheridan slammed down the magazine on the glossy kitchen counter. 'Is that what people think of me now? That I'm some dried-up old prune trying to keep her claws in her "hunky Brit"?'

Daniel lowered his espresso and picked up the magazine. '*Celeb Goss?* Really? Why do you read this rubbish?'

'That woman . . .' she said, her features grim. '*That* woman has done untold harm to this family. Why aren't you stopping her?'

Daniel returned his gaze to the manuscript he'd been reading seconds before. He was wearing a designer suit and tie, his clothes tailor-made for his broad frame. He was due for an engagement with a producer later that morning. The fact that he was not meeting Sheridan's gaze told her that he was not taking her outburst seriously. 'What do you want me to do, take a hit out on her?' He smiled at the prospect. 'We're not the Mafia. It'll take time for the legal action to go through.'

'Can't they put a gagging order on her or something? We fired her weeks ago.'

'And that's an old quote. A rehash of the story they printed when she blabbed to the press. Relax. It'll settle.' He rose from his chair and smoothed down a loose strand of Sheridan's hair. It was still damp from the shower she'd taken after her morning workout. Her personal trainer had left her feeling energised, ready to face the day.

Daniel's touch had an instant calming effect and as he rested his palm against her cheek, she felt the stress melt away. She rose on the balls of her feet to kiss him, grateful to still feel a spark there.

She wanted to part her silk dressing gown and take him to bed. But his meeting was an important one, and her hair stylist was due to arrive soon. She could wait for now. Isabella, the nanny, was taking Leo to school and Sheridan had scheduled in a few minutes alone with Daniel before he left.

'Have you found a baby yet?' Daniel said, taking half a step back.

'Are you sure it's what you want? It's not too late to back out.'

'You're a great mother. Leo will love having a sibling.'

Sheridan frowned. He had not answered her question. 'If the press finds out . . .' She traced her finger over his chest, imagining alternate futures for them both.

'They won't. We've been stung once. It'll never happen again.' Daniel's voice was deep and filled with conviction.

'I *have* found a potential donor,' she said, a smile rising to her lips. 'Her name is Rosalind Foley. She's from Ireland. I thought it would be nice, given your mom's background.' Daniel's mother was Irish and had passed away just last year. 'If we have a girl, we could name the baby after her. The press would lap it up.'

'That's a lovely thought.' Daniel sat back down, raised his cup for another sip.

'She's living in Dublin, twenty-four years old. She's estranged from her family, so we don't have them to worry about. Nobody knows about the baby apart from her.'

'Sounds promising.'

Sheridan nodded, her smile growing. 'She doesn't drink, smoke or take drugs. A good Irish Catholic girl. But this is what drew me to her straight away. Look.' Lifting her mobile phone from the kitchen counter, Sheridan brought up Roz's profile. Roz was sitting on a park bench and smiling, looking slightly embarrassed as she held her camera aloft. 'Apologies for the selfie,' she said. 'But nobody else knows I'm doing this, and that's how I want it to stay.'

'She looks nice. Why didn't she get a termination?' Daniel asked, his interest aroused. Roz looked remarkably like Sheridan in the early days. Her blue eyes seemed to see right through you, but her most striking feature was her white-blonde hair.

'She's a practising Catholic,' Sheridan continued. 'They don't believe in abortion.'

'If she were a practising Catholic, she wouldn't have got pregnant in the first place,' Daniel grinned, his dimples enough to melt any woman's heart. 'Who's the father?'

Images of a little girl with blonde hair floated in Sheridan's vision. Leo looked just like Daniel. If she had a daughter to focus on, it would put an end to the rumours for good.

'There is no father,' Sheridan said, then raised her hand before Daniel could come back with another quip. 'I mean, it was a one-off. A young army man, so he must be reasonably fit. He doesn't know about the pregnancy.' Sheridan paused for breath as nervous excitement took hold. The palms of her hands felt sweaty and she dried them as she smoothed down her dressing gown. 'What do you think? Should I make contact?'

'Best you do, before someone beats you to it. Hopefully it's a girl.'

They had already discussed the issue. A blood test could determine gender as early as eight weeks into the pregnancy. It would be easy to get Miracle-Moms to send the results directly to them.

'Do you think she'll go for it?' Sheridan said. 'I have a good feeling about this. She's young, healthy, clean-living. Artistic, too.' She scrolled through some of Roz's portraits, which were remarkably lifelike.

'If you tell her what we're offering, she'll bite your hand off.'

'She does say she'd like to travel one day.'

'Well, there you are. If she's carrying a girl, we can bring her over, run a few more tests, check her background. How many weeks is she gone?'

'Eight,' Sheridan replied. 'Which means I could be a mom in just over six months' time.'

Daniel had insisted from the start that she pass the baby off as her own. When you had as much money as they did, it could be arranged in the blink of an eye. Would Roz be happy with such an agreement? It had cost them over $10,000 to register as prospective parents with the adoption website, but it had been worth it to preserve their anonymity, and it had excellent security measures in place. According to the site, their names were Julie and Glenn. Their real details would be revealed much further down the line, when non-disclosure agreements had been signed. Sheridan had made a huge mistake in trusting her former maid, Rachel. It would never happen again. Women would be queuing round the block to have Daniel's baby if their true identities were revealed. That was why she could not use a surrogate. She couldn't bear for another woman to carry his child.

'Let's do it,' she said, beaming at the thought. 'I'll put something together now.'

But as Sheridan turned away, her smile faded, and a tightness grew in her chest. There was much more to all this beneath the surface, but neither of them had said the words aloud. She thought of Roz, a country girl who came across as young and naive. Was she gullible enough to fall for the story that Sheridan was about to spin?

CHAPTER THREE

ROZ

'Yous aren't gonna throw up on me now, are you, girls?'

As I opened the back door of the taxi, I flashed the driver a reassuring smile. 'I've not been drinking.' I followed his gaze to Dympna, whose breath carried the tang of alcopops mingled with cheese and onion crisps. I could have ordered an Uber, no questions asked. But I had my baby to think of and I felt safer in the back of a licensed cab.

'Hop in,' the driver sighed, after I gave him my address. 'But there's an eighty-euro fine if you puke on the back seats.'

'Best we vom on the floor then,' Dympna giggled, her words mercifully muted by Johnny Cash on the car radio, singing a tune about a ring of fire.

I slid into the back seat, pushing a giggling Dympna ahead of me before the driver could change his mind. My tights were laddered where I'd caught them with my nail, and my hair was frizzy from the rain. We looked a right pair. Dympna snorted as she tried to find a home for her seat belt, mumbling something about putting it in the wrong hole.

'Shh,' I warned. 'My head's banging.' The beat of the nightclub speakers still drummed in my ears; the smell of sweat lingered on my skin from my moves on the dancefloor. It was just a headache, though, not the after-effects of alcohol. Our nights out weren't the same now I was the sober one, and I was beginning to feel like Dympna's mother. Still, it was sweet of her to make time for me, now she was all loved up. I kept one eye on the cab fare, aghast to discover what little money I had left in my Hello Kitty purse.

'Sorry, can you drop us off around here?' I leaned forward to ask the taxi driver. 'I've only got five euros left.'

But he was nicer than I gave him credit for, and he took us right to the door. People in Dublin were like that. Some wouldn't give you the time of day, but there were still decent souls around who looked after their own.

I helped my friend up the narrow stairway to our tiny two-bedroom flat. 'Uhhh . . . make the room stop spinning, will you?' Cushions tumbled to the floor as Dympna sprawled herself dramatically across the sofa. 'This is all your fault.'

'My fault?' I queried, pouring a glass of water from the kitchen tap and kicking off my shoes. 'How do you work that one out?'

Our flat comprised of an open living room-cum-kitchen diner, two cramped bedrooms and a bathroom with a leaky shower in which you could not swing a cat.

'I was drinking for two!' Dympna giggled. 'One for me and one for you.'

'Here.' I thrust the water into her hand.

'I don't want water, I want curried chips. Be a love and pop next door . . .'

'I will in my backside! I just spent my last five euros on the cab. Now drink. Then off to bed.' Morning sickness had not hit me too hard, but my sense of smell had taken on superhero proportions. The thought of walking into the greasy caff downstairs made my stomach churn.

'Where's my phone?' Dympna slurped her water. 'I wanna ring Shheamus and tell him how much I luurve him.'

I rolled my eyes. Seamus would hardly appreciate such slurred declarations of love. Normally on our nights out I would be equally hammered and collapse in a giggling heap on the floor. Being the sensible one was no fun at all. I undid my earrings and hair clips, dropping them into an unused ornamental ashtray so they wouldn't get lost.

After finally getting my flatmate to bed, I went to the loo for what felt like the hundredth time that night. Already, the baby was making itself known as pregnancy hormones sent my kidneys into overdrive. A fresh pang of fear struck as I washed my hands in the sink. There was no backing out now. In a few months my stomach would be huge, my pregnancy plain for all to see. The father would guess the baby was his. What sort of life would the poor mite have, being born into such drama? At school, I felt the stigma of coming from what the nuns called a 'broken home'. Single-parent families were accepted now, but I could have done with someone pointing that out to the bold Sister Agatha in the convent school where I spent my teens. I shuddered as the tap water turned cold. The boiler was playing up again.

After warming some milk in the microwave, I took a seat at the wobbly piece of furniture we optimistically referred to as a kitchen table. Beneath one of the legs was a folded-up beer mat – Dympna's idea of DIY. Opening up my laptop, I wondered if I should have heated the milk in a saucepan instead. Calcium was good for the baby, wasn't it? Or had I zapped all the nutrients? I glanced at my watch. It was three in the morning and there was no way I'd get to sleep without checking the adoption site first. I sighed, gently plucking my false eyelashes off and depositing them in the ashtray with my other bits. I'd never felt so torn in all my life. A part of me – the tiniest spark – considered keeping the baby after it was born. I'd muddle through, I told myself. Didn't everyone? But I only needed to look around our flat to know what was best for my child. I was broke, just like my mother had been after Dad walked out on us both. I still remembered the poverty suppers – heels of stale bread drizzled with milk, a sprinkle of sugar on top. Being dressed in second-hand clothes that always smelled of damp. Once, the bullies nicknamed me 'Vinny', after the charity shop St Vincent de Paul, but Dympna put an end to that after giving them all what for.

My eyes danced over the website as I emerged from painful memories of my past. It whispered promises of a better life for my child. One day I would have a family of my own – when I was married and financially secure. I'd push my baby around in a Silver Cross pram and live in a clean, warm house with a fridge stocked full of food. But right now, this was my best opportunity to give this baby what I'd never had.

All that, though, depended on if I could find the right home. I clicked through the site, masking my yawn with the back of my hand. I could feel my attention waning, but the sight of twenty emails in my inbox made me blink my watery eyes in disbelief. Twenty enquiries already! My profile must have finally gone live. Another ding told me three more emails had just landed. Of course. The time difference meant it was evening in the US. Sipping my milk, I peered at some of the responses: promises of a dream home with financial security from desperate couples with so much love to give. I didn't realise I had one hand clasped protectively over my flat stomach until I looked down.

'Don't worry, little bean,' I whispered. 'Only the best for you.'

I meant it. I only wished there was an easier way out of this mess.

CHAPTER FOUR
SHERIDAN

The tune played in Sheridan's head long before she started the recorded TV episode of *It Takes All Sorts*. She hunched in her seat, her fingers tightening around the remote control as she pressed play. *It takes all sorts . . .* The jingle filled the air. *Family comes in all shapes and sizes, life never fails to surprise us, it takes all sorts in our world . . .*

Sheridan sat, her knees pressed tightly together as she stared at the screen. With the curtains closed, her privacy was guaranteed. Nobody came into this room, not even her husband. Her life was a whirlwind of phone calls and appointments and she had dismissed her team of advisors for some much-needed moments of peace. Her viewings were a compulsion, a chance to relive her childhood; her eyes followed the screen as Sherry, her six-year-old self, ran to the Christmas tree. She was wearing her pink dressing gown, her blonde ringlets shining beneath the studio lights. To her viewers, she appeared to have just got out of bed. Sheridan remembered her mother's firm instructions as she raked the comb through her hair that morning. She also recalled the teeth-whitening, the facial scrubs and the drops that made her look dewy-eyed. Her mother's ruthless ambition dictated that the episode entitled 'Jingle Bells and Puppy Tails' was a live show, aired on Christmas Day. 'If we stop making programmes, your fans won't love you any more,' was her mother's stock response whenever she complained of having to work during the holidays.

The episode began with Sherry squealing in delight at the sight of the presents beneath the tree. In reality, most of the gift boxes were empty. Like her, they were perfectly packaged and pleasing to the eye, but it was all a facade. Behind her mother's saccharine smile was an insatiable hunger for more fans, more viewer ratings and more inches of favourable reviews in newspaper columns. Daintily stepping between the gifts, Sherry put four ribboned boxes aside.

'We'll give these to the children in the shelter,' she said, offering Dorothy, her mother, an angelic smile, 'because everyone should have a happy Christmas Day.'

Their support of women's refuges gave them great publicity at that time of year. The charity was carefully chosen by her mother to garner the most approval from their fans.

Sheridan paused the recording as the camera homed in on her six-year-old face. She was good, even then. She had picked up the empty boxes as if they were heavy, her expression filled with sympathy as she spoke of those less fortunate than herself. Now, watching it back, only Sheridan could see the desperation in her eyes as she fought to be the most-loved starlet in the USA.

It wasn't as if she were short of real Christmas presents. Dozens had been sent by fans to the television studios for her to keep. But each time she made a mistake, her mother forfeited one for the shelter, which was why she had to get the live performance just right. She remembered the burning resentment she felt towards the children who stole her presents away.

Pressing play, Sheridan watched as she coveted a tall pink box that vibrated under her hands.

'It's moving!' she squealed, as if she didn't know what it was.

She ripped at the paper, taking in the air holes pressed into the cardboard. Sharp, excited giggling followed as a Labrador puppy bounced out. Well, flopped, really. Her mother had sedated him because he had been making too much noise. Sherry held him close to her chest to disguise the fact that her new pet was spaced out.

'I'm going to call him Bouncer!' she said with genuine delight, as her mother and screen father bent down for a hug.

In reality, the couple couldn't stand each other, but the public was not to know that. Soon her screen friends would join them and a party would take place. They would wish their viewers a merry Christmas, and when the episode ended, her mother would begin planning the episodes ahead. Mother's performances before the camera were brief; it was Sherry who was the star. And just two years after Bouncer's appearance, Sherry's viewing ratings shot up once more. After all, nothing tugs on your heart strings more than the death of a pet. His demise was cruel but, according to her mother, necessary. She said Bouncer was clever – too clever; there was even talk of his own spin-off show. There was no way she would allow Sheridan to be upstaged by a dog. As she cried real tears, Sherry hated her mother for what she did, but she learned a valuable lesson as her popularity grew. Power and wealth were there for the taking, as long as you knew how to play the game. After an award-winning performance at Bouncer's funeral, Sherry's number-one status was restored.

Nowadays Sheridan Sinclair was part of a picture-perfect family; she and Daniel had been voted the most successful celebrity couple of 2019. But others were snapping at their heels and threatening their sponsorship deals. She needed to up their ante. She knew where things were going wrong: their son Leo was the faulty component. He hated having his photo taken, and tugged at the clothes Sheridan dressed him in. He could not sit still for two seconds; he'd pull faces and scratch his head. He was far from a natural in front of the camera. He was not like her.

But a girl . . . Sheridan stared at the TV screen. A girl had the power to delight her audiences. And it wasn't as if she would work her that hard. Things were different now. With social media, they only had to give glimpses, carefully constructed insights into the lives they wanted to portray. She allowed her thoughts to wander. A blonde-haired little girl would secure their position for years to come. And if it didn't work out? She thought of Bouncer. Life was one big stage show . . . and players could be written out.

CHAPTER FIVE
ROZ

I buried my head beneath my pillow and exhaled a low moan. I did not want to get up, but my lie-in had come to an abrupt end with a sharp poke in the back.

'Wake up, you lazy moo. Are you dreaming about Tom Hiddleston again?'

Blinking, I cleared my vision. 'Eww, no. What time is it?'

Dympna's red hair dangled over me, her bacon sandwich making an unwelcome sensory advance. 'It's gone ten. I made you a cuppa. There's toast there, too, if you fancy it.'

I pulled back my new Dunnes Stores duvet, the one with the hearts that I'd saved for a month to buy, and sucked in a breath as Dympna slipped in beside me, her feet freezing as they pressed against mine. It was our weekly ritual. Dympna didn't do hangovers. Each Sunday morning she'd hop into my bed, bringing tea and toast, and we'd dissect the night before. Her afternoons and most evenings were spent with Seamus; I appreciated that she was not one of those fair-weather friends who dumped you the minute they got a new squeeze. She furtively wiped a splodge of ketchup from my duvet. It's a good thing we were besties.

I sat up in bed, rubbing my eyes before gratefully accepting the cup of Lyons tea. Now she had her boyfriend and I was off the booze, there were no regrets about the night before. But I should have known my friend was way ahead of me. Reaching down, she picked up my laptop from our threadbare rug and placed it in front of me on the bed. 'I thought we could go through this instead – see if you've got any replies on that Mammy Mashup site.'

'It's Miracle-Moms, and I thought you didn't approve,' I said, remembering the stack of emails dinging into my inbox the night before.

'I don't, but we're only looking. Go on . . .' She snuggled up beside me with a dangerous twinkle in her eye. 'It'll be fun.'

'Fun' was not the word I would have used, but it was better than some I could think of. 'Well, I suppose we can look at the site,' I said reluctantly. Last night, I'd shut my laptop with a snap, too freaked out to read any more of those responses. 'But I need to pee first.'

After inputting my password, I left her to it while I tiptoed down our ice-cold hall lino to the loo. Outside, the wind howled around our badly fitted windowpanes. Winter was coming early, by the look of things. Five minutes later, we were settled back in bed, our tea topped up from the pot.

Dympna cooed as she took in the site. 'It's very swanky, isn't it? Considering what it's for, like.'

The site was built in a mixture of silver greys and pastel pinks. Miracle-Moms.com was emblazoned across its header, with the tagline *Are you ready for your little miracle?* beneath. I guessed that it was created to appeal to both parties – the header to ease the conscience of the 'donor mom' and the tagline to tempt the wannabe parents into parting with huge wads of cash. The prospect of giving my baby to strangers made me squirm, but I'd still found myself creating a profile on the site. After all, nobody was forcing my hand.

'Here, will you look at this.' Dympna clicked on to the surrogacy page. *Low-cost surrogacy program: only $45,000 – includes three attempts with egg donor and baby birth.*

Beneath it was another headline that made Dympna gasp. *Guaranteed luxury surrogacy option: only $99,999 – unlimited IVF egg collection cycles and embryo transfers. Everything included. We don't stop until your baby is delivered into your arms!*

Shaking her head, Dympna stared in disbelief. 'And here's me on me knees every morning cleaning toilets for nine euros an hour.'

'That's the surrogacy page,' I tutted, turning the laptop back. 'My stuff is on the adoption page.'

But Dympna was not ready to give up just yet. 'Look at the conditions.' She squinted at the screen. Her glasses were in her bedroom, but she was too enthralled to get them now. 'It says here you've not to have smoked, drunk, or used drugs since your pregnancy.'

'Which is why I've given up drinking.' I didn't touch cigarettes or drugs. I sighed, knowing what her next question would be.

'But what about *before* you knew you were pregnant? We were out on the lash just a couple of weeks ago.'

Heat rose to my cheeks. I felt guilty enough about our weekly nights out, but told myself they were history now.

'Have you seen the expenses page?' I asked, in an effort to change the subject, but Dympna's head was tilted to one side as she worked it all out.

'Ah, I get it now,' she said. 'That's why you deleted your Facebook page – getting rid of the evidence.'

'No flies on you,' I smiled, leaning over to sip my tea, which was getting cold.

Dympna did the same before returning her attention to the screen. 'Oh, my giddy aunt . . . you get $27,000 base compensation with a monthly allowance of three grand . . . ' She leaned forward, scrolling down. 'Clothing allowance . . . loss of wages . . . mental health support . . . $250 per counselling session . . . You even get paid to pump breast milk.' A giggle escaped her lips at the prospect. 'Can you imagine it? We could put you on one of those milking machines. Do you get paid per boob?'

'I won't be pumping anything,' I replied, failing to see the humour. 'I'm not a cow.'

'Hmm, Louise Finnegan might disagree. The look on her face when she saw you flirting with her fella!' She was talking about last night. As drunk as she'd been, Dympna's mind was as sharp as a tack.

'*He* was the one flirting with me,' I replied, pulling an expression of mock outrage. The last thing I was interested in was another relationship.

'I know.' She smiled. 'I told her you wouldn't do that to a mate.'

I gave my best friend a watery smile. I was telling the truth about Louise's boyfriend, but she was wrong to have such faith in me. Dympna must never find out who the baby's father was. Which was another reason I had to give her away.

CHAPTER SIX

SHERIDAN

Sheridan's gaze followed her son as he urged his pony to gee up. Leo sat straight in the saddle, his small fingers tightly gripping the reins as he was led around. A soft autumn breeze ruffled his steed's black mane. His name was Rufus, and he was equipped with the imperturbable patience needed for such a role.

'Keep going, honey. Now give me a big smile!' Sheridan called as the pony was led around a second time.

'I've cleared your schedule for today, but I've had to pencil in an appointment with Aaron Schreiber at two on Friday.' The voice was that of Sheridan's personal assistant, Samantha, who followed her everywhere she went. At five feet eleven, she had the body of a model, but combined with a forgettable face. Regardless, she was good at her job and Aaron Schreiber's fashion house would be perfect for Sheridan's new clothing line.

Ignoring her, Sheridan took a picture of Leo, then straightened the peak of her Yankees cap to shield her eyes from the early morning sun. The smell of freshly cut grass wafted from the paddock, making it feel like a spring day. It was hard to believe that such pockets of greenery existed in New York. The stables provided the height of privacy, situated adjacent to an exclusive golf course at the end of a leafy country road. They had changed hands since Sheridan had come here as a child, and had expanded from housing a handful of scruffy horses and ponies to keeping high-quality bloodstock. They now also offered an indoor arena, show-jumping facilities and private hacks along lush green tracks. Such space came at a premium, but the NYC Riding Center had generous backers, and enough exclusive clients to fund its endeavours for years to come.

'Hi, Sam.' Daniel had joined them, his hands deep in his jeans pockets. He was the only one who could get away with shortening her name.

'Hi, Daniel,' Samantha smiled, spots of pink colouring her cheeks. Poising her pen over her journal, she turned her attention back to Sheridan. 'About that appointment. Aaron's leaving for London next Saturday, so this might be the last chance we get.'

'Fine,' Sheridan replied. Samantha's voice felt like a fly buzzing in her ear. 'Schedule it in. As long as you keep today clear.'

Shoving her journal under her arm, Samantha tapped at her phone.

'Why don't you go back with the driver and make the call in the car?' Sheridan interrupted. 'I'll come back with Daniel.'

With a nod of her head, Samantha tottered down the path to the car.

'Thank God she's gone,' Sheridan whispered as Daniel slipped his arm around her waist. 'I told her I was having today off, but she insisted on following me out here.'

'Give her a break,' Daniel said good-naturedly. 'She's only doing her job.' He cast his gaze over Leo, who was calling out to him. 'Hey, Champ! Good job!'

'I'm thinking about buying him a pony,' Sheridan said. 'It might calm him down a bit.' Leo kept his nanny busy. He had so much energy, and sometimes she wondered if he had ADHD; but there was no way she was getting him tested. No son of hers was going to be labelled a problem child.

'Wouldn't it be easier to get a dog?' Daniel's voice broke into her thoughts. 'My beagle was my best friend when I was growing up. Now that's one intelligent pet.'

'I'm not having some hound cocking his leg against my soft furnishings,' Sheridan replied. 'I rode ponies at Leo's age. The fresh air will do him good.'

But Daniel's mind was still in the past. 'His name was Basil,' he said. 'He house-trained easily enough. But when he was mad at me, he'd piss in my shoe.' He laughed under his breath, a deep throaty chuckle. 'I still miss that dog.'

'Please, honey, no dogs,' Sheridan said. The memory of Bouncer was still fresh in her mind after watching last night's episode of *It Takes All Sorts*. 'At least, not until the kids are a little older.'

Kids. The plural of the word evoked a whispered promise of a brighter future. But she knew that if Daniel wanted a beagle, he'd go out and get one. Her husband was an alpha male and she respected him for it. He would never have become so successful if he'd bowed down to everyone who got in his way. Her attention wandered to the teenage girl leading the pony around. There was a spring in her step, an air of excitement as she caught sight of Daniel. But this was an upmarket establishment, where discretion was guaranteed. Perhaps she was a new girl who hadn't been briefed, or maybe just a fan. Sheridan's lips thinned as she followed her gaze. She was a straight female. That was all it took. Sheridan's nails dug into the paddock fence. Couldn't she have a family moment without something like this happening? Her annoyance grew – a hot furnace stoked by the teen's youth and good looks.

Sheridan observed her husband. If Daniel had noticed the young girl's attention, he didn't acknowledge it. He still clung on to the need to live a normal life, but it was growing increasingly hard for him. The more successful he was, the more he became public property. He had gone through years of rejection until he'd starred in his breakthrough movie. They had first met on set. Their love story was leaked as part of the promo, and *Murder Game* was a huge hit.

'Didn't he do well?' the girl said as she approached them, the name 'Tammy' emblazoned on a badge on her chest. She couldn't have been more than seventeen. Her long tanned limbs and strawberry-blonde hair gave her a natural sun-kissed look. With a coy smile, she offered Daniel the lead rein. Sheridan stiffened. It was as if she wasn't even there.

'Want to go around again?' Daniel asked, much to his son's delight.

As Tammy stepped forward to join them, Sheridan called her back. 'Are you new? I haven't seen you here before.'

'I started last week.' Tammy flashed Sheridan a smile. 'If there's anything I can do for you or your husband, just ask. I'm a huge fan . . .'

Sheridan watched her slide her mobile phone from the back pocket of her jeans. She knew what was coming next – the request for a 'sneaky selfie'. She could practically read the words poised on Tammy's lips.

'We don't need your help, now or in the future.' Sheridan's voice was icy cold, cutting the girl dead in her tracks. 'And if you value your job, I suggest you remember that.'

The light of excitement left Tammy's eyes. 'Oh. I'm sorry, I . . .'

Sheridan waved to her son, who squealed in excitement as Daniel encouraged the pony to break into a jog. 'Hold on to the saddle!' she called, lifting her camera and taking another snap.

She paused to give Tammy a withering look, as if to ask what she was still doing there. She was entitled to take such a stance; her family were one of the donors who helped keep this riding school afloat.

'Sorry,' Tammy muttered before turning on her heel. She shoved her phone back into her pocket and gave one last, longing look at Daniel before walking away.

Sheridan sighed as she reviewed the photos she had taken. As usual, Leo was looking the wrong way.

'Everything all right?' Daniel smiled broadly as he rejoined Sheridan after the trot around the track. 'I'd forgotten how much I've missed this. We should come back here one day, just the two of us. Saddle up.' His blue eyes burned with sincerity as he spoke.

Sheridan had encouraged Daniel to ride, a tactic to spend time in his company and open him up to more acting roles. Like everything in life that he set his mind on, he had taken to it effortlessly and was a natural in the saddle. These days he preferred motorbikes to horses, but going for a hack would be a good way for them to spend some quality time together.

'I'd love that.' Sheridan smiled, but her tone harshened as she turned to her son. 'Darling, the pictures are ruined. Why do you have to look so goofy all the time?'

'Steady on, love.' Daniel frowned. 'I thought he looked great up there.'

Sheridan responded with a thin smile before offering the pony a sugar lump. 'See?' She instructed her son. 'You offer it on a flat hand – otherwise he might nibble your fingers off.'

Leo's eyes widened at the knowledge that he was riding a creature who would eat human flesh.

'By accident, of course,' Sheridan added hastily. 'Then he'd just spit them out.'

Daniel's laugh echoed around the corral.

'What?' Sheridan asked, watching him take their son's feet from the stirrups.

'I think it's better if I read the bedtime stories from now on.' He looked around as he slid Leo from the pony. 'Where's the stable hand?'

'She had stuff to do.' Sheridan took the pony's lead rein. 'Why don't you strap Leo into the car? I want a quick word with Wendy. I'll be right back.'

Wendy was the riding school supervisor, and she valued Sheridan's opinions. Tammy would not be bothering them again.

CHAPTER SEVEN
ROZ

The gentle ding-ding of the Luas outside my window signalled that Dublin city was in full Sunday afternoon swing. I didn't need an alarm clock when the tram bell rang with such unfaltering regularity every day. When I first moved from the countryside, it took time to get used to the cacophony of city life. There were the typical sounds of the drunks staggering home from the pub, and the never-ending stream of traffic and hooting horns. Then there were Dublin's signature sounds, such as the seagulls outside our window and the pedestrian crossing which sounded like a game of Space Invaders each time it beeped into life. What did cities in America sound like? I allowed my thoughts to wander as I imagined my baby being brought up there.

'What are you waiting for?' Dympna handed me my laptop, jolting me out of my daydream. 'Roll out the weirdos!'

'Charming,' I replied, budging up on the sofa.

Dympna wasn't going to let it lie. I'd managed to fob her off earlier, but she was right: I was going to have to face the many responses from wannabe parents sooner or later. To think I was worried about competing with the glamorous-looking women on the site. Then it hit me. It was *because* of my background that they chose me, not in spite of it. I may have pushed the 'good Catholic girl' image, but I wanted to appear clean-living in order to attract similar parents for my baby. I could have gone to children's social services, but I'd known adopted kids when I was growing up and they weren't much better off than me.

With a sigh, I opened up the site again, grateful for Dympna's company. 'How am I going to sort through this lot?' I said, clicking through each profile page.

Applicants were capped at a hundred at a time to save baby donors getting overwhelmed. I was meant to reject or accept potential parents to free up applications for more. The idea was to create a shortlist of four or five, talk online and decide who I wanted to meet. I never for a minute thought my list would fill up so quickly.

The minty smell of Dympna's chewing gum invaded my senses as she leaned forward and took it all in. 'Ooh, it's like being Simon Cowell on *The X Factor*. I'll help you wade through it. Anything you don't want from the off?'

I shook my head. They'd already been checked for criminal records and drug use, or as far as they could be. I had already stipulated I wanted a non-smoking home, although vaping was fine as long as it wasn't in the same room. Whatever was best for the baby's health.

'Are you sure you want to do this?' Dympna finally cast joking aside. 'It wouldn't be fair to approve them if you're not.'

It was a fair question, and I took a deep breath. 'I'm sure. I've thought of nothing else since I found out.'

A knot formed between Dympna's brows as she accepted I was serious about the whole thing. 'What about the dad?'

'He doesn't need to know.' The air chilled as I gave her my firm look: the look that told her to leave it at that. She had asked me several times since I dropped the bomb, and I'd finally had enough. The trundle of a lorry outside made our sofa vibrate. Even on Sundays, the city never slept.

Dympna leaned forward and touched my arm. 'I'm just saying.' Her voice was low, as if to say she meant no harm. 'Once you start the ball rolling it's hard to back out. These poor people . . .' She glanced at the screen, demonstrating the empathy I knew and loved. 'They're desperate. It's not right to encourage them unless you're ready to give up your baby.'

Tears welled in my eyes as the reality of the situation hit home. I swallowed the lump in my throat. Picked a dried blob of ketchup from the arm of the sofa. I had to stay strong. 'Most girls in my situation would have had an abortion by now. I only want to do what's right.'

'OK, then . . . If the dad's out of the question then what about us? We could rear it between us . . .'

I shook my head. 'No. Thank you, but no. When you have a baby, it will be with your fella in a nice big house with money to set you on your way. Not with me in squalor without a penny to our name.'

Dympna lowered her head, trying to catch my gaze. 'We could move away. To the country, Tullamore or Athlone. Rent's cheaper there, we could get jobs . . .'

I shook my head, my eyes blurry as I squeezed my tears away. 'It would still be a struggle. I'm not ready to rear a child. Neither are you.'

'So Ferbane is a no?'

Thoughts of my mother only made me more determined to keep on track. 'This way, I find the best home for my baby. It can grow up to be anything it wants. Can you imagine it? Being brought up in a big house, adored by your parents, having all the money you need?'

'Money's not everything.' Dympna shrugged.

'The people who say that are the ones who've never been without it,' I replied.

It was true. Dympna's parents weren't badly off. They had turned her loose to make a living, to see if she could make it on her own. But the 'life lesson' wasn't a permanent one. She was only playing at being a grown-up, and the cleaning job was a stopgap until she decided what she wanted. The thought of her parents' response to my predicament made bile rise in my throat.

'You all right?' Dympna said. 'You're a bit green around the gills.'

I jabbed at the space bar on my laptop as a screensaver of a whale came into view. I was beginning to wish I had never confided in my friend. 'I just want to get this done. It's our only day off work and you'll be out with Seamus soon.' Another thought entered my consciousness. 'You mustn't tell him. Promise. Not a word to anyone.'

Dympna crossed her heart with her finger. 'I swear. If it's what you want, I'm behind you all the way.'

I looked at her earnestly. 'Are you? Really? Because if this gets out, I won't care about anyone else. I'll just need you to be OK with it all.' I wished I could tell her the other half of the story, but I couldn't bear for our friendship to be torn in two.

Throwing her arms around me, she answered with a death-grip hug. She didn't need to say any more. We broke apart, both smiling. It had been tough, persuading her to see things my way, but we had finally broken through. Dympna was the sister I wished I'd had, and I desperately needed her support.

'Let's make a start,' I said, concentrating on the screen.

'Ooh, the power.' Dympna smiled, gleefully scrolling through the list of prospective candidates. Sitting beside me in her sweatshirt and jeans, she was back to her jokey self. Her moods yo-yoed: she was serious one minute and laughing the next.

My plan was to get down to five prospective couples before looking at any more. The weight of responsibility felt enormous. 'This is tricky stuff. Imagine trying to find a home for Diarmuid?' I said, talking about her little brother. 'How would you see these people then?'

'What, devil child?' She laughed. 'I don't hate any of these suckers that much!'

It was easy for her to say. What I would have given for a sibling when I was growing up. Someone who understood what I was going through. Dympna was my best friend, but she didn't know the half of what had gone on. Her parents were young and trendy; they always had her back. Even Seamus, her boyfriend, was being welcomed into the fold. I would love to have known what it was like, growing up as part of a normal household.

I clicked on couple number one. Marcie and Geoff looked decent enough. She was a schoolteacher. He was a Presbyterian minister. Their bio spoke of 'strict family values'. But they were in their late fifties. Did they have the energy to cope with the demands of a newborn child? The site accepted all age groups as long as they could afford the fees.

'Too old and too strict,' I said, narrowing my eyes at the frown lines on Marcie's face. 'She looks like she's sucking a lemon.'

'Agreed. Delete.'

Bubbly-looking blondes Sabrina and Felicity looked more like a pair of models than homely parents.

'How are you with same-sex couples?' Dympna gave me a curious glance. Their faces were pressed up against each other and they both wore cheesy grins.

'They're more than welcome,' I said without hesitation. 'I'm looking for a stable couple who are in love.' I rested a hand on my stomach. 'I'm sure she won't care if her parents are male or female.' And yet as the words left my mouth, I recalled the fire and brimstone sermons I'd sat through as a child and imagined the priest's disapproving glare. But wouldn't a father figure be more likely to do a bunk, just as my own had done? I sighed, wishing everything wasn't so complicated.

'You said she!' Dympna twirled a lock of hair. 'Do you think you're having a girl?'

I shrugged, doing my best to appear nonchalant. 'It's easier to say she. Makes no difference to me.' I kept my eyes on the screen, but in reality, I'd felt like I was expecting a girl all along.

'Do Sabrina and Felicity go to round two?'

I clicked the button in agreement. For now, they were going on my favourites list. They wouldn't be contacted yet – not until I sent a message to confirm I'd like to know more.

'How come these ones don't have a picture?' Dympna scrolled on to a couple named Julie and Glenn. A tiny diamond motif twinkled in the top right-hand corner where their profile picture should have been.

I paused mid-yawn, lowering my outstretched arms from above my head. 'Oh my God, I've got a diamond couple.'

'What's a diamond couple?'

I stared at the screen, excitement stealing my breath. I had to move quickly. This was too good to be true. 'I can't believe it,' I whispered. This was everything I wanted. An opportunity reserved for the very few.

'What? What's it mean?'

'Diamond couples are loaded. They pay twice the amount of everyone else.' A grin spread over my face as the implications sank in. 'They're a stable couple, medically tested and in perfect health. They've been together at least seven or eight years, have more than one home, and a net worth of . . .'

'What?'

'Over a million pounds. They're millionaires. I've got millionaires interested in my child.'

I shifted position, staring at the screen. I wanted to savour this moment just a little longer. Dympna would never understand how it felt for me to come close to arranging something so wonderful for my baby. It was about far more than money. It was the opportunity to give my little one the life I'd never had.

'Why can't we see what they look like?' Dympna asked.

She scratched her hair before tossing it to one side. Her long red curls would look beautiful on a child of her own one day. When her time came, everything would be done by the book. But things were looking up for me as I read Julie and Glenn's profile page.

'They could be celebrities, politicians, anyone in the public eye. Can you imagine it? I can't believe they've contacted me. Look where they're from!'

'New York,' Dympna squealed. 'With properties in LA and Europe.'

Taking a breath, I steeled myself as I tried to find the right words to reply. They were the only diamond couple who had shown interest in me and my baby, and I was not about to blow this. I flexed my fingers before placing them on the keyboard.

> Hello,
> Thank you for your interest. I'd like to talk to you some more, should you wish to progress things further.
> All the best,
> Rosalind

'Best to keep it short and simple,' I said, my heart giving an extra beat as I prepared to press send.

I chewed my bottom lip, telling myself that this was just the first contact. No point in worrying about it. It may not get any further than this. But from what I'd read about the site, the couples who used it meant business. They did not like to wait around. My finger froze mid-air as I debated my next move.

'Oh, for God's sake,' Dympna said, before reaching out and pressing send. 'What?' she said, as I glared at her in disbelief. 'If you don't snap them up, someone else will.'

She was right, but now the ground was beginning to feel like an escalator that was moving a bit too fast. Was I doing the right thing? I could not afford to stand still. This baby was not going to wait.

CHAPTER EIGHT
ROZ

I groaned as I strode down O'Connell Street. The tips of my socks were damp where puddle water had seeped in through my suede boots. My emotions were playing tug of war with me, and I questioned myself with each step I took towards the coffee shop. I was developing a bond with my unborn child already. But how on earth could I keep her, when I couldn't even afford a decent pair of boots? The decision was agonising, and by meeting my mother, I was grasping at straws. There was little point in dreaming of a fairy-tale reconciliation. But what if I told her about the baby? Shouldn't I at least consider the possibility of keeping it, providing I had her support? I thought of my home in Ferbane. Mam's second husband, Tony, had sold his own property and injected the profit into doing the place up. They would surely have enough room for me.

Damp autumn leaves swirled around my feet in their last dance of the season. Their time was almost over. By the end of the day they would be picked up by road-sweepers and turned into mulch. I reflected upon my life, and the need to take control. I felt tender, at the mercy of my hormones. I hadn't spoken to my mother properly in years. I'd tried to visit them last Christmas, but I'd lacked the courage to follow it through. Instead, I'd observed her from my vantage point on the stone bridge over the canal near their home. She was with her new family now, and I felt a pang of jealousy as the three of them pulled into the driveway in their car. They had just bought a Christmas tree, and the lilt of their laughter carried on the air as my stepdad tried to drag it in through the front door. I watched as my mother put her arm around her stepdaughter Jenny's shoulders, chattering as they entered the house. Who was I to invade such a happy scene? Mam deserved peace, not retribution. That day, I turned on my heel and left.

Then she left me a voicemail, asking why I hadn't turned up. I deleted it from my phone. But discovering I was pregnant changed everything. I could not ignore Mam's visit to Dublin, and so here I was. My heart faltered as I caught sight of her in the coffee shop, sitting near the window with her back turned to me. Part of me wanted to run away, but she had come here specifically to see me. My legs carried on, and before I knew it, the bell was dinging over the door to announce my arrival.

The coffee shop was busy, bustling with people seeking respite from the cold. Mam turned to face me, looking as nervous as I was . . . looking like me. Her blonde hair was streaked with natural silver highlights, cut into a shoulder-length choppy style. I looked her up and down; she was only in her fifties but her relationship with alcohol had aged her face. She looked smart in her black shift dress and court shoes. I walked towards her, rigid as she took me in for a hug. It was awkward and horrible, too soon for contact, and I had to force myself to sit down. She quickly recovered, ordering me tea and some Victoria sponge, despite me saying I didn't want food. My stomach felt like a butter churn going at full pelt.

'Thanks for coming,' she said, and through her false cheerfulness I caught a sniff of her favourite scent – Obsession by Calvin

Klein. I knew it was reserved for special occasions. Coming here would have been a big deal for her; she didn't get along with big cities or busy public transport.

'It's not far for me,' I said, feeling like a teenager: my old sullen self, staring at my hands. I caught sight of a piece of broken nail and frowned as I picked it away before it could snag another pair of tights.

'I don't blame you for being angry,' she said, after we'd exhausted our small talk. Her hands were cupped around her mug as if she was clinging to a life raft. 'I've been a terrible mother.'

Finally, I met her gaze, saw the sincerity in her eyes. She meant it, at least for now. But then she always did, in moments of sobriety. The calm before the storm.

'How long have you been sober?' It was the first time I'd openly asked her about her drinking. My words hung in the air like a line of dirty washing, flapping in her face.

'Three years, three months and twenty-one days,' she said immediately. 'Not that I'm counting.'

An awkward laugh followed. I did not join in. Three years was no time at all.

'Things happened in my childhood that I'm still dealing with. But there's a time in your life when you have to stop being a victim,' Mam continued. 'When you take back control.'

I nodded. Who was I to deny her that? I reminded myself that she was trying, but I also recalled her dark side and the sting of her words.

'I fell apart after your father left, turning to drink instead of asking for help. It wasn't your fault. He turned his back on both of us. He wasn't ready for the responsibility.'

I frowned. It was hardly *all* his fault. She was a hard person to live with. I never blamed him for running away. I pursed my lips, kept my silence. I let her have her say.

'I've been wanting to see you for ages, but they told me I had to concentrate on getting well before I took anything else on.'

My spirits sank. There it was, back to me, the burden of her life. I was something she had to be well enough to 'take on'. I pushed the cake to one side. If I had any appetite left, I'd lost it now.

'Things are different now,' she hastily added, seeing my crestfallen face. 'Tony's been my rock, and Jenny . . . she's such a sweet girl.' She paused, sipped her tea to fill the silence. 'I tried to send you an invite to our wedding, but your friend said you'd moved on.'

My friend. I snorted. Dympna and I had been together since childhood and she couldn't even remember her name. 'I got the invite,' I said. 'I didn't want to go.'

I allowed her to express her sorrow. Watched as she visibly ran out of steam. Finally, she sighed and took another sip of tea.

'I've been offered a job in America.' I looked at her thoughtfully as our meeting wound down. 'So you don't need to worry about me.'

It wasn't strictly true. If things didn't work out with the adoption there was no telling where I'd end up. At least now I knew it wouldn't be with her. I would always be her problem child. She was still in recovery. I could not take my baby to her door.

'America? Really?' she said, her face flushed with concern. 'What's the job?'

'It's in an art gallery,' I lied. 'A six-month apprenticeship.'

'But it's so far away.' She cleared her throat, as if knowing her advice was coming a little too late. 'As long as you're sure it's what you want. Can you write to me? Tell me how you're getting on? You always were great at drawing.'

A memory tugged at my consciousness: My mother tearing up a portrait I'd sketched because it made her look old. The sting of her palm as it met my cheek with force, spittle flying from her mouth as she raged. Taking a breath, I reeled myself back to the present day.

'I'm not sure I'll have time. It'll be pretty full-on.' I paused. This was painful for both of us. I needed to bring things to an end. 'Listen, I . . . I've got to go.'

She nodded. I watched her hand stretch across the table as she tried to reach for mine. I gripped my mug tightly. She rested her hand on my wrist.

'I don't blame you for being angry,' she repeated. 'But it's healthier for us both if we can move on.'

'That's what I'm doing,' I replied. 'In a new country, with a new life. You've got your new family, too.'

'But I want you to be part of it.'

I watched, horrified, as her eyes glistened with unshed tears. It was so tempting to stay, but it was too soon for her to take my baby on. I took a deep breath. Patted her hand as I tried to disentangle myself from our meeting. 'It's better this way.'

'Wait,' she said, slipping an envelope from her pocket. 'For later.' Leaning forward, she shoved it into my coat pocket before I could say any more.

I stood, stepping back to allow a woman with a chequered shopping trolley to go past. I looked at my mother as if she was a stranger. I was doing her a favour; she just didn't know it yet.

'I'm glad we were able to clear the air. Take care of yourself.' I squeezed her shoulder. Tore my gaze away.

'But . . . Roz . . . Don't go.' Clumsily, she rose from her chair. I could not watch. I couldn't . . . My movements jerky, I stumbled out of the coffee shop and did not look back.

CHAPTER NINE
SHERIDAN

'Gone, has she? It's about time she left.' Sheridan pulled a face. The journalist from *Esquire* magazine had commandeered her husband since they'd returned from the riding school. It was meant to be their day off, but that woman had monopolised Daniel for almost an hour. Not that Sheridan had been twiddling her thumbs. She had spent the time on the phone to her head of public relations, who had managed to bag her a cover shoot with *Vogue*. But Daniel didn't need to know that; she hadn't finished guilt-tripping him yet. 'It was embarrassing,' she continued. 'I'm surprised she didn't leave a puddle behind her, the way she was drooling over you.'

'Really? I can't say I noticed.' Daniel joined her on the sofa, his legs spread wide.

Sheridan shot him a disbelieving glare. The piece was good promo for his forthcoming spy movie, but she hated it when journalists came to their home. She had grown used to women fawning all over Daniel, but behaving in such a way right under her nose left a bitter taste in her mouth – especially when they were as attractive as the young woman from *Esquire*.

'Alexa, close the curtains.'

The swish of her blinds signalled that the electronic device was doing as instructed. Sensing the dimness of the room, high-tech lights filled the space with a warm orange glow. The late morning was fresh and sunny, but a stress headache was forming a band around Sheridan's recently Botoxed forehead and she needed some kinder light. She picked up her laptop and kicked off her designer shoes. Her calves were aching from wearing heels, but she would not be dwarfed by that flirt from the magazine.

'Any nibbles from the site?' Daniel asked, swinging her bare feet on to his lap in preparation for a foot rub.

Sheridan admired his attempt at changing the subject. She didn't mind; the hunt for a child was the most exciting thing going on in her life right now. A lifetime of photoshoots and interviews paled in comparison. She opened her laptop, groaning in satisfaction as Daniel gently kneaded the soles of her feet with his thumbs. He had the magic touch, and she was only too happy to succumb to it.

'I was waiting for that journalist to leave before I checked,' she said, feeling the stress ebb away. 'You can't be too careful.'

They had already taken the utmost care with security. They owned their own internet servers, and Daniel used burner phones, changing them every month. There were only a few people in his life he needed to contact – his agent and immediate family – and they all had his email address. Privacy was everything. The journalists granted entry to their home visited designated areas only. All press and promo happened strictly under their own terms. Leo featured only in the publicity shots that Sheridan took herself. They were released at a premium, strengthening the brand she was working so hard to build. These days, she monitored her social media profiles more than she read scripts. Fifty-nine million Twitter followers. The arrival of another child would easily bring that up to sixty. She imagined the sponsorship deals, smiling as Daniel kissed the tips of her manicured toes. She must have been a saint in a former life, to deserve such a devoted husband. And now one more child to seal their success. Was her wish really going to come true?

'Yes!' She bounced on the sofa as the notification on her computer came into view. 'She's replied.'

'Cool,' Daniel grinned. 'What's she said?'

'Only to ask if we'd like to progress.'

'You still want her?'

Sheridan curled up next to him, tingles of excitement chasing her headache away. 'More than anything.' She turned the laptop to face them both. 'She's perfect. I have such a good feeling about this.'

'Mother knows best,' Daniel said, giving her a squeeze before rising to his feet. 'I'm going to take a bath. Keep me in the loop.'

'Your script's in the drawer next to your side of the bed,' Sheridan replied, unable to tear her eyes from the screen. Their bathroom was his sanctuary, and more like a hotel spa. With a monsoon shower, ambient lighting and Bluetooth speakers built into the ceiling, it was no wonder Daniel spent over an hour in there most days. Lying in the freestanding tub, he would use the time alone to memorise his lines.

Sheridan checked her watch. Leo was on a play date. She would have dropped him off herself, but she couldn't go very far without paparazzi cameras being thrust in her face, along with the usual questions about where her husband was. It was all about Daniel these days. She touched her face, as if her wrinkles were scars. Botox could only hold them back for so long, and she couldn't bear to end up looking like a shop-window dummy, like some of her friends. It was time for her to accept that her best days as an actress were behind her. Her heart throbbed with longing to be needed. She had precious minutes to compose a response to Rosalind. There would be lots of prospective couples after her, given that 99 per cent of the women who used the site were from the US. She didn't need to check with Daniel. He was happy for her to reply on his behalf.

> Dear Rosalind
> Thank you for getting back to us both. We are thrilled you would like to progress things further. Apologies we have been unable to reveal our identities just yet . . .

She paused, her fingers hovering over the keyboard.

> But if you'd like to talk over the phone, I can call at a time which is convenient to you.
> I think you should know that we already have a little boy. He has started school and would love a sibling. Unfortunately, I'm unable to have further children. My husband and I are very happily married, and we can provide a wonderful safe, secure home for our new baby. We would like our donor to come to New York to live with us until the baby is born. Full costs would be met, as well as a generous living income and the expenses listed on the Miracle-Moms site. We will always be truly indebted for such a generous gift and will do everything in our power to make the birthing experience as pleasant as possible, particularly for a first-time mom. Our donor would be welcome to stay with us after the birth for as long as she needs to.
> I hope this all sounds acceptable to you and I wait for your response.
> Warmest regards.

She leaned back from the keyboard, rereading her words. She could make this work. She had to. Yet a small, creeping voice whispered from a distant place. A place she could not escape. Rosalind sounded like a nice girl. Naive. Alone. It was the reason she had chosen her. She was a vessel, nothing more than an object that fitted a set of criteria and had the right set of genes. On the plus side, she was young, pretty, artistic. But how would she react when she discovered the true nature of Sheridan's plans? Her lips thinned in a cold hard line. It would be too late by then.

CHAPTER TEN

ROZ

There were times when the realisation of my pregnancy hit me with the force of a steam train. I didn't want kids – at least, not yet. Yet there I was, a cliché. The result of a drunken night with the worst possible person. I tried to pinpoint what had stopped me from getting the morning-after pill. Was it my moral compass? Fear of God's judgement and the fires of hell? Or was it a spark of love for the bunch of cells growing inside me? It was all of the above and more. Love is a dangerous emotion. It can lead to bad judgements and a lifetime of regret. I couldn't spend my life resenting this baby – like my mother had resented me.

I researched why some couples choose a pregnant donor rather than go down the surrogacy route. There were blogs by infertile women whose lives were dominated by chemicals: hormone injections, followed by egg harvests and transfers, granted them short periods of hope. But each month, they were plunged into depression as their attempts at pregnancy failed. Many could not bear the thought of another woman carrying their husband's child. Adoption seemed their only hope. It was hard not to feel some sympathy for these parents, so desperate for a child. Could I kid myself into believing that I was doing some good? Or would the guilt of handing over my baby haunt me for the rest of my days? Not that I was complacent. I was only a couple of months gone. There was nothing to say this pregnancy would even go to full term. But I wanted it to. Despite my conflicting emotions, I wanted my little bean to live.

I sat back on my bed, staring at the ceiling, my hands resting over the waistband of my jeans. It felt good to mull over the thoughts and emotions swirling around in my head. Things were moving quickly, and I still couldn't believe a diamond couple were interested in me. Well, interested in my baby; but we came as a package for now.

I turned to my computer and brought back up their message, my nerves tingling with anticipation. She wanted a phone call already. Normally, donors shortlisted a few couples, spoke to them online, got a feel for what they wanted and then made contact by phone. I hadn't messaged anyone else, but instinctively I knew that talking to this woman was the right thing to do. It wasn't just her wealth that attracted me. It was the way her words hung tantalisingly in the air. *Safe, secure and stable.* Plus, a happy marriage and a big brother to look out for my baby. What more could I want?

The television chattered in the living room as some reality TV show played. Dympna was curled up on the sofa with Seamus. They were going to visit her parents soon for an early supper. Her brother was home from the army and they were having a party afterwards to celebrate. As for me, reheated fish fingers would do; they'd invited me along, but there was no way I could go now. I fantasised about standing on their lavish dining room table. Their shocked faces as I announced I was pregnant and that someone in the room was the father of my child. It would be like something out of *Fair City*, Dympna's favourite TV soap. Of course, it would never happen. But I had a vivid imagination and could not help playing the scene in my mind. These thoughts made me all the more certain that I was making the right decision in allowing my baby to live elsewhere. I typed in my response on the Miracle-Moms site.

> Hi Julie,
> It would be lovely to chat. I'm available now if you are?
>> And please, call me Roz :-)

I couldn't stay up too late, I had to be out the door by seven in the morning. The hotel had asked me to work out my month's notice, which would keep me going financially for a couple more weeks, at least. I nibbled on my bottom lip before deleting the last line and inputting my full name. Nobody called me Rosalind, but perhaps it was too early for informalities. It felt unnerving, not knowing who I was talking to. It could be anyone. But it was doubtful I'd recognise her by her voice. I was about to get up when another message flashed up on the screen. I was surprised, because my profile had been hidden from potential new candidates. I clicked on my inbox. It was Julie. Had she been sitting by her computer, waiting for me to respond? What time was it over there?

> Hi Rosalind,
> Yes, I can call now if you like. I'm not working today so I'm flexible.
>> Speak soon
>> Julie

Springing from my bed, I paced the room, feeling panicky. She wanted to call me, and I looked a right state in my faded jeans. I wasn't even wearing any make-up! I picked up a hair bobble from the carpeted floor. Winding my hair into a bun, it was only when I looked in the mirror that I asked myself what on earth I was doing. It was a phone call, not Skype or FaceTime. She wouldn't actually see me in my grotty little flat. It was just as well. I took a breath in an effort to slow the beat of my heart, which felt like a bongo drum. Opening my drawer, I plucked out the 'do not disturb' sign I'd stolen from Jurys hotel. It was a signal to Dympna not to burst in at full volume, as she usually did. One advantage of her recent weight gain was that she was no longer able to fit into any of my clothes, so there would be no wardrobe emergencies before she slipped away to her parents for the evening. After putting the sign on the door handle, I closed the door. Hands trembling, my fingers clacked on my crumb-speckled keyboard as I replied to Julie that now was fine. I took another soothing breath and told myself to calm down. It was just a phone call. Nothing was set in stone.

Yet I could not avoid the feeling that something monumental was underway. I had always wanted to broaden my horizons. Excitement bubbled inside. As well as doing something wonderful for my baby, this could change my life for the better, too.

I jumped as my mobile phone rang. That was quick! Closing down my computer, I pulled my duvet up to my waist, keeping the chill at bay.

'Hello?' I said, trying not to sound too countrified down the phone.

'Oh, hi, is that Rosalind? It's . . . Julie. From the Miracle-Moms site.'

I pursed my lips. She sounded so American! So New York! My cheeks flushed as I held the phone tightly in my hand. It was as if I was scared the opportunity would slip away.

'Hi. Yes, it is. Please call me Roz,' I replied, forgetting my earlier decision to keep things formal.

'Nice to speak to you, Roz. I hope I haven't disturbed you.' I could hear the smile in her voice, and it made me smile too.

'No, not at all. It's great to hear from you, too.' I chewed my inner lip, unsure what to say. 'I'm sorry . . .' I exhaled the breath I was holding. 'This is all new to me and I'm a bit nervous.'

'Me too,' she chuckled. 'But it's better to chat in person than by email, don't you think? I'm sorry I haven't given you my real name just yet. I hope you understand.'

'Sure, no worries. And I won't breathe a word. Not that I have anyone to tell.' I coloured at the lie as I heard the front door of our flat slam; Dympna and Seamus had just left. But as far as Julie was concerned, I was estranged from my family and living on my own. She was not the only one with a lot to lose if this got out. The line fell quiet and I sensed she was gearing up to something.

'It's just that . . . ' She paused, her accent strong but crisp down the line. 'Well . . . we hope to raise the baby as our own. Would that be a problem for you?'

My mouth dropped open at her directness and I felt a pang of gratitude that we weren't on Skype. She wasn't just talking about adoption. They wanted to pass the baby off as their own. That's why there was so much onus on secrecy, why nobody else could know. Would she wear a pretend bump? Keep me hidden from the world?

'Of course, we'd keep a medical record of the donor's background in case of future health issues. We would tell the child when the time was right, but nobody else would know, and it's unlikely they would seek you out.'

'That suits me fine,' I replied. 'I'd rather not have future contact. I don't want him or her getting confused.'

'I'm so pleased to hear it.' Her relief was audible. We were on the same page. 'If things work out, we would need you to live with us before you show. We have a basement luxury apartment so you would have complete privacy. We have a full medical team, and it would be a home birth.'

'Home birth?' I echoed, my eyes widening as I imagined myself lying on a beanbag in some New York flat.

'Don't sound so scared,' she laughed. 'You'd have access to all the drugs you need, as well as one of New York's best ob-gyns. If there were any complications, you'd be whisked away for a hospital birth.' She paused. 'I'm just getting the deal-breakers out of the way before we progress.'

I nodded into the phone, my mouth dry. I was gagging for a cup of tea, but didn't want to move in case Dympna hadn't really left.

'That all sounds OK,' I said.

'What about you? Any must-haves?'

I smiled as I imagined relaying the conditions of six months' supply of Häagen-Dazs and a subscription to Netflix.

'I'd like to go to church at some point,' I said, which was a great fat lie. But I had told them I was a practising Catholic and I needed to follow it through. 'But mostly . . . a secure and happy home for the baby.'

'Of course. And financially, we're as secure as you can get. Our child would have a private education, the best healthcare money can buy and entry into one of the top universities in America.'

'I thought that was down to results.' I switched the phone and rubbed my right earlobe, which was red and sore from pressing my mobile hard against it.

'Honey, this baby *will* have great results, but a huge donation pretty much guarantees the best spot in class.' Her breath ruffled the line. 'Anyway, listen to me, running away with myself. The most important thing is love. Our baby will have a childhood, too. Our son is an absolute delight. We're pretty inspirational parents. We've worked hard to make our dreams come true.'

I thought about my life in comparison. I couldn't even keep down a cleaning job. I cast an eye over the many pictures I'd drawn that were Blu-tacked to my wall. Not exactly gallery material. This baby would hardly be inspired by me.

I snapped out of my gloom. I was being thrown a lifeline. I needed to grab it with both hands. 'What's the next step?' My stomach grumbled, reminding me that my fish finger sandwich was overdue.

'Oh.' Julie inhaled sharply. 'You want to progress things? That's awesome. Me too!'

The next round meant telling all other applicants I was no longer available and arranging a meeting with the couple in person, where we could talk things through. There would also be further documents, Q&A, health screening on both sides. All organised by Miracle-Moms.

'I can't wait to find out who you really are,' I said. But there was an underlying current of concern. What if they were politicians I hated, or people with chaotic social lives? I needed to put a face to the names.

'Of course. And if all goes well with the next round, we'll get the non-disclosure agreement signed. You've already completed the blood tests, so technically we could be flying you to New York in a couple of weeks.'

My mouth fell open for the second time. Me? Fly to New York?

'But my job . . . I'm not sure if I can get time off at such short notice.'

It was a lie. I only had a couple of weeks left to work. But it was all beginning to feel real now, and I needed more time to think.

'We'll compensate you. You won't be out of pocket. My PA will take care of the visa. As long as you don't have a criminal record, it won't be a problem at all.'

It was all moving so fast and felt so surreal. I had to force myself to reply. 'OK, then. I'll have the records released to your doctor as soon as you send me through the details.'

'Don't worry, the agency will take care of that.' Julie spoke with authority. 'Just check the consent box and they'll do the rest. Once you're happy with everything, we'll arrange to meet. If you have any questions in the meantime, just drop us a line.'

I hunched my shoulders as a stiff breeze crept in through the cracked windowpane. Opportunities like these did not present themselves to people like me. I strung together a few polite words, thanking her before we both ended the call.

Dropping my phone on to the bed, I hugged my knees to my chest. Just like that, a piece on the chessboard had been moved. The game was on. There was no going back from this. Tears welled in my eyes.

'How about that,' I mumbled to my baby. 'I've only gone and done it, little bean. We're going to New York.'

CHAPTER ELEVEN
SHERIDAN

Sitting with her head bowed, Sheridan picked at the label on her bottle of beer. She had not been out in public without her entourage for four years and she felt vulnerable on her own. In this bar, with sawdust on the floor and country music playing on the jukebox, she was confident she would go unrecognised. She was dressed in keeping with her surroundings, wearing cowboy boots and low-slung jeans, and a padded jacket bulked out her thin frame. Her long blonde hair was in a French plait, tucked beneath her peaked hat. She sipped her beer. Pulled a face. There were some celebrities who enjoyed going incognito, but it was not for her. Daniel would be horrified if he knew she was there on her own. Not that she was totally alone. She watched the door from her viewpoint as her old acquaintance strode in. He extended his hand, his skin rough from physical labour, his face weathered from working outdoors. Looking at him now, with his sandy moustache and unkempt hair, it was hard to believe that Mike had once lived in her world.

'How's it going, buddy?' she said, patting his back as he leaned in for a hug. He reeked of cigarettes and chewing gum, and his leather jacket smelt like horse hide. 'Sit,' she said, in response to his incoherent murmurs. 'I got you a drink.'

Sliding on to a stool next to her, Mike raised the bottle of Budweiser to his lips. The years had not been kind to him since he'd stopped working on *It Takes All Sorts*. While Sheridan's career had flourished, Mike had been unable to deal with the pressures of being so famous so young. Failure after inevitable failure had led him down the slippery path of alcohol and drug abuse. It was five years since he'd been released from prison after serving time for assault and theft. Since then, Sheridan had given him a lifeline, buying him medical insurance and providing a yearly wage. The money had been earned. He had made contacts while inside, and in times of trouble, Mike was her go-to man.

'How you doing?' he said, his eyes roving over her form. 'I read about you in the papers. Family life suits you.' Sheridan was about to respond when he leaned in, his voice soft and low. 'Tell me it was worthwhile. I still think about her, you know . . . I still see her face.' His features were haunted by the memory of an incident Sheridan could not bring herself to discuss.

'I didn't ask you here to talk about her,' she said, quickly glancing around to ensure they weren't being overheard. 'I need another favour.'

Mike shook his head, a bitter smile twisting his chapped lips. 'Not gonna happen, Sherry baby. I'm sorting my life out. I'm not interested.'

Sheridan flinched at the use of the nickname he'd resurrected from her past. 'Are you forgetting who's been funding your lifestyle these past few years? That money won't last forever. You know that, don't you?'

Mike shrugged, tipping the bottle of Budweiser to his lips. 'I figured as much. Which is why I've got a job. I'm in construction now, learning the ropes. Hope to work myself up the ladder someday.'

Sheridan sighed. It was so long since she'd had social interaction with ordinary people; now she realised she had gone about this all wrong. Mike was doubting her. She could see his trust ebbing away.

'Sorry, I'm nervous,' she said, reaching for his hand and clasping it beneath her own. She watched his frown fade, his shoulders drop. At the bar, an old drunk drawled a Tammy Wynette song about standing by your man. What would Daniel say if he could see her now?

Sheridan threw Mike a roguish smile, tilting her face to one side. But it wasn't her. It was one of the many personas she had played over the years. 'C'mon, you remember me, you know what I'm like.' She concealed her disgust as Mike rubbed his thumb along the back of her hand. It felt like sandpaper against her smooth skin. 'We've got history,' she continued. 'That's why I always come to you first. You're my protector. You keep me safe.'

'Do you mean it?' Crossing his legs, Mike regarded her with mild suspicion. 'Or are you just yanking my chain?'

Sheridan knew she was leading him on, but she could not back out now. 'I always thought we'd end up together,' she said wistfully. 'Who knows, maybe in another dimension . . .' She allowed the words to linger. There was a lifetime of longing on his face. She had him exactly where she wanted him. Now it was time to seal the deal.

But Mike broke their contact, finishing off his beer. 'I meant what I said. I can't do that again.'

'I know, honey,' Sheridan quickly replied. 'I'm not asking you to. I just need you to shut someone up for a little while.' She pushed her beer towards him. 'Here, have mine.'

'Is it Rachel?' Mike wrapped his hand around the bottle as Sheridan responded with a nod. 'I had a feeling that that's what this was about. She's always had it coming.'

Sheridan fought to contain her smile. She knew there was no love lost between them. Sheridan, Rachel and Mike had acted together side by side for years on *It Takes All Sorts*. Sheridan's popularity had grown as a teenager when she and Mike shared their first on-screen kiss. It was her first kiss in real life, too. From the ages of six to sixteen years, every milestone in Sheridan's life had been choreographed for the screen. She spent so long on the show that by the end of it, she didn't know who she was any more. Then, five years ago, Rachel had approached her. As with Mike's, Rachel's career had failed to bloom. Like a fool, Sheridan had taken her into her home, giving her a well-paid housekeeping job. She had to admit, she had taken a little satisfaction in getting Rachel to carry out menial tasks.

'I should have taken you in, not her,' Sheridan said, as thoughts of Rachel tied her up in knots. 'But Daniel gets jealous. He would have felt the spark between us. I couldn't take the risk.'

'Really?' Mike said, his eyes alight. 'You feel it too? It's still there, isn't it?'

Sheridan resisted the urge to laugh out loud. As if.

Her heart began to beat double-time as she progressed to her next move. She had to do this. He was the only person she trusted not to go to the police; by doing so, he would be implicating himself. Later, she could be asking much more of him. She leaned forward and swallowed back her revulsion before pressing her lips upon his. He may have been her first kiss, but like now, it had all been for show. As if cameras were rolling before them, she injected meaning into the contact, as if he were her long-lost love. She knew by his response that their stolen kiss meant so much more to him.

Slowly, they parted. 'I'll always care for you, Mike. I wanted to show you how much.'

'I . . . I've got a place not far from here.' He shifted in his seat, his face flushed.

Sheridan shook her head. 'You know I can't do that. I love Daniel. You and me . . . we're like two pieces of a jigsaw puzzle that don't fit together any more.'

Slowly, Mike's tongue traced his lips, as if he could still taste their lingering kiss. He smiled. 'What can I do for you?'

Sheridan returned his smile. This time it was genuine, because Rachel would get what was coming to her. 'She's been blabbing to *Celeb Goss* magazine. I want you to arrange a little accident, something to shut her up.'

Mike stiffened as the drunk at the bar wobbled past them on his way to the toilets, humming out of key. Satisfied he was out of earshot, Mike leaned closer, his words hushed but sharp. 'I won't kill her. I can't stand the bitch, but please . . . not that.'

'I'm not asking you to.' Sheridan's eyebrows shot up at the mention of murder. Why did people always think the worst of her? 'Just lay her up for a few weeks. There's a hundred grand in it for you. That should keep you going for a while.'

'Make it two. Come on, Sherry, you can afford it – it's a drop in the ocean to you.'

Sheridan pursed her lips. 'It's still a drop I have to explain to my auditors when they do my accounts. A hundred k can be explained away as a gift to an old friend, but not two. I'll keep up your health insurance. It'll give you peace of mind.'

'Yeah, but . . .'

Sheridan checked her watch. She was growing bored now, and she needed to get back. 'Listen,' she said, cutting him off. 'I'm offering you a lot of money to teach that poisonous bitch a lesson. If you're not interested in helping me, then . . .'

'Of course I'll help. You're my Sherry baby.' Mike's grey eyes held a depth of emotion. 'I've seen all your movies a dozen times or more.' He paused. 'You had a tough time with your mom growing up. I know that things haven't always been easy for you.' Sheridan's mother both wrote and produced the award-winning show. Even when they were off air, she was constantly pushing her daughter for a better performance. 'People talk as if reality shows are a new thing, but we'd been doing it for years,' he added as an afterthought.

Sheridan squeezed his hand in thanks. 'Good. I'll leave you to it. Don't get caught.' She rose from her stool.

Mike stretched his long limbs as he stood before her. 'Do you have to go so soon? It would be nice if we could spend time together. Talk about the old days.'

'I'm sorry, honey, but I've got to get back. Daniel will be wondering where I've gone.' Now she had got what she wanted, Sheridan couldn't wait to escape Mike's company.

'We did the right thing, didn't we?' Mike asked, his face haunted with past memories.

'What's done is done,' Sheridan replied. 'Put it out of your mind. You've been to prison. You know I'd never survive it.' Sheridan felt no guilt for what she was asking him to do. She was doing this for her family. She had no regrets.

'Bloody hell!' Daniel stared at his newspaper open-mouthed.

'Don't swear in front of Leo,' Sheridan said, before signalling to the nanny. 'Isabella, clean his face, will you? It's almost time for school.' She turned to her child, who was sitting between them at the kitchen table, evidence of his peanut butter and jelly sandwich sticking to his face. It was hardly the breakfast of champions, but he refused to eat anything else.

Sheridan was less than happy. Having dismissed Samantha, her PA, to wait in the living room, she expected some family time with Daniel and Leo. It was not often the three of them got to sit down for breakfast together. If Daniel wasn't glued to a manuscript, he was on the phone to his agent. Why couldn't he give them his undivided attention for twenty minutes in the day?

'Time for bluddy school!' Leo giggled, his blue eyes twinkling with delight. He had his father's dimples, pressed firmly into his chubby cheeks. He was intelligent enough to recognise one of Daddy's bad words and was happy to repeat it when it popped up.

'See?' Sheridan snapped at her husband. 'I told you he had a foul mouth. I've got you to thank for that.'

She turned her attention back to a clean-faced Leo and straightened his tie. She adored his school uniform. It made him look like a miniaturised little man. But she hardly wanted such vulgar language completing the image; the prestigious Saint James Christian school demanded more of its pupils. It was the number-one elementary school in New York, with an overall average grade of A+. At $48,000 a term, Sheridan expected nothing less. Education was important to her, particularly as she'd been home-schooled herself. If the press knew about her fake university degrees, they would have a field day.

She gazed into her son's eyes. 'Now listen, darling, Daddy said a bad word. You mustn't say that to anyone, do you hear me? You're a *good* boy.'

Leo slid down from the kitchen chair, his face sullen from the reprimand. 'I love you, Mommy,' he recited.

'That's nice, darling,' Sheridan said, patting him on the back. It was Leo's immediate response whenever he was in trouble, which seemed to be all the time. 'Now give Daddy a kiss goodbye.'

'Sorry, mate,' Daniel said to his son before giving him a squeeze and ruffling his hair. Isabella gave Sheridan a look to say she would comb it before they left. So much was said without words in this household. Sheridan liked it that way.

Checking they had gone, Daniel slid the newspaper across the table. 'This is what I was reading.'

Sheridan scanned the headlines, taking care to keep her expression fixed. The story was about Rachel, who had been involved in a hit-and-run. Mike had stayed true to his word and wasted no time. '*IT TAKES ALL SORTS* STAR IN INTENSIVE CARE.' Sheridan's lips moved soundlessly as she read the article. 'Huh,' she said eventually. 'I can't say I'm sorry.'

'That's what I'm worried about,' Daniel replied, clearing his throat. 'You didn't have anything to do with it, did you?'

Sheridan blurted an exaggerated laugh. 'Please! It's a hit-and-run. They happen all the time. You don't seriously think I was behind the wheel, do you?'

But Mike was. You did this. She could have died. The words formed in her mind like an unwanted invader.

She brought her attention back to the article, unable to look her husband in the eye. Even if Mike was caught, he would never rat on her. Not after that lingering kiss. She sipped her coffee, ridding herself of the memory of his taste.

Daniel pushed his plate of half-eaten scrambled eggs away. 'You can hardly blame me for asking. The last time we spoke about her you wanted to take out a hit man.'

'No, it was *you* who used the words hit man, and you were joking, if I recall . . .' Sheridan paused, fixing him with her best surprised gaze. 'Oh, honey, you didn't, did you? When I said shut her up, I didn't mean . . .'

Daniel frowned as she turned the tables on him. 'Of course not! What do you take me for?'

'The same thing you took me for ten seconds ago,' Sheridan said, prodding herself in the chest. 'So try not to look so insulted.

Either way, she won't be blabbing to the gossip mags any time soon.' She imagined Rachel attached to monitors, a tube shoved down her gossiping throat. 'Serves her right.'

Sheridan made a mental note to pay Mike when things died down. Perhaps she should give him the amount in full; let him blow himself away with coke and booze. Then again, she might need his services a little longer. She scanned the list of Rachel's injuries, biting back her smile. That was what happened to people who crossed her. Perhaps she should send her a 'get well soon' gift, in case the police came sniffing around later on. She would give one of her winning performances, expressing how sorry she was. Hell, she might even visit her in hospital, just for kicks.

'You're not going to see her,' Daniel told her, ignoring the persistent ring of his mobile phone.

'How did you . . ?' Sheridan's voice melted away. Her husband's ability to read her mind was uncanny sometimes.

'I know you. If you go there you won't be able to resist gloating. They've got CCTV everywhere these days. Best to maintain a dignified silence.'

I wouldn't be able to resist pushing a pillow on her face, more like, Sheridan thought, smiling sweetly at her husband. 'Of course,' she said. 'I'll send something over to wish her a speedy recovery.'

CHAPTER TWELVE
ROZ
NOVEMBER 2018

I thumbed through the pregnancy book Dympna had left next to my bed. She knew what she was doing. She hoped I'd change my mind. In the privacy of my bedroom, I could not resist the urge to look up how much my baby had grown. I scanned the page as it described the eleventh week of pregnancy.

'You're smaller than my pinky finger, little bean,' I said, glancing down at my stomach. 'You've got tiny fingers and toes, and . . .' I smiled as I read. 'You're the size of a lime. Your heart is beating twice as hard as mine.'

I felt a warm glow as I saw myself as a safe incubator for my child. But that was as far as it went. As a mother, I wouldn't have a clue. Growing up, Dympna was my measurement of normality. When we were kids, I studied her like a curious magpie discovering a piece of jewellery for the first time. I remember being in awe of her insights and the little things she took for granted every day. 'These earmuffs tickle my ears,' she'd complain. 'And how can I make a proper snowball with these gloves?' I'd shove my hands deep into my pockets, the tips of my fingers numb. My bare legs felt frozen in the winter because the school wouldn't let us wear trousers and my mother couldn't afford to buy me tights. It was only when Dympna was older that she realised how insensitive she had been.

In the mornings, I would get myself ready for school. A piece of rough string tethered the front door key, which I'd post through the letterbox when I left. When I came home, my dinner would be on the table, cold and congealed on my plate. My mother would be sprawled on the sofa, her movements slow as hurtful words lazily rolled off her tongue. I pushed away the memory and slid the pregnancy book into the suitcase on my bed.

A rap at my bedroom door made me stiffen. I guessed Dympna was mad, because unless the 'do not disturb' sign was hanging, she'd have burst in by now.

'Come in,' I said, throwing an armful of clothes on to the bed next to my open suitcase. It was two weeks since my first contact with Julie, and things had progressed at a rapid pace.

Dympna's face was flushed, her red hair tied up in a nest on her head. She had come straight from work, still wearing the hotel tabard she should have changed out of before she left.

'What's going on?' she demanded, taking one look at my suit-case before pinning me with a gaze.

'What?' I feigned innocence.

Dympna's anger had a short shelf-life and it didn't take long for her to run out of steam. I caught a whiff of her sweat laced with the high-strength lemon cleaner we used to clean the en suites in the hotel. She must have left in a serious rage if she hadn't changed and showered yet; I could imagine her stomping all the way over here. I felt glad to know that she cared. Growing up, I'd mistaken my mother's depression for indifference, but I knew better now. I folded my best pyjamas and sleep socks and tucked them into my case.

'Orla said you gave in your notice. What's that all about?' she quizzed.

I sighed, unable to meet her gaze. Dympna had a right to know, but lately I was feeling the heat of her judgement. As for Seamus . . . I could barely look him in the eye. I reached for my stretchy tracksuit bottoms and placed them in the case.

'I was made redundant, but I didn't want to worry you until I'd sorted something out. Cutbacks. They're keeping it hush-hush.' In truth, it was my lack of commitment that had led to me getting the sack.

'So you're selling your baby because you can't afford the rent?' Dympna glared at my suitcase, as if seeing it for the first time. 'And what's this? Running out on me, are you?'

My jaw tightened. I had been through a lot of soul-searching and was in no mood for a row. 'If you let me get a word in edgeways, I'll tell you. Julie's brought forward the meet-up to this weekend. I'm packing for New York.' I was doing this for the baby. But I was doing it for Dympna, too.

She rested her hands on her hips, oblivious to my thoughts. 'Except she's not Julie, is she? You're meeting up with a stranger in a strange country. And as for throwing in your job . . .'

Patience exhausted, I threaded my hands through my hair. 'For feck's sake. Last in, first out and all that. It's only a cleaning job.'

It was easy for Dympna. She only took the position as an act of rebellion against her parents because they were pressurising her to join the Gardaí. It was only meant to be temporary, a means to pay the rent until something better came along. But life wasn't so easy for me. Why couldn't she see that?

Dympna flapped her arms theatrically. 'I see. I suppose I'm not good enough for you either, now you're off to your fancy New York friends. Is that why you've been avoiding me?'

I sighed. She could be such a drama queen when she didn't get her own way. 'Please, Dympna, I don't need this right now.'

On autopilot, I folded my clothes. Jumpers, cardigans, dresses; I had no clue what the weather would be like in New York, or what I should wear. Normally I'd consult Dympna, but she was right; I *had* been keeping my distance. Up until now, I'd appreciated her nurturing nature.

We weren't getting anywhere bickering like this, but Dympna was not content to let the subject lie. 'How are you going to manage if it doesn't work out?'

'I'm getting expenses. More than we earn in a month – and that's only for one weekend. Besides, I have to meet them. How else will I know if they're the right fit?'

'I know, but . . .' The wind taken from her sails, she plopped on to the bed. 'I can't believe you're going through with it. Everything's moving so fast and I'm worried about you travelling on your own.' She picked at a loose thread hanging from her blue tabard.

Her crumpled face reflected her own insecurities and I felt my heart melt. 'Hey . . .' I squeezed her shoulder. 'I know you don't like flying, but there's nothing to be scared of. I'll be fine.'

Dympna was right about one thing. Things *had* happened quickly. But the baby would be here in six months and preparations had to be made. If Julie and Glenn were not suitable as a couple, I would have to start all over again. I folded up a hoodie and placed it in the suitcase. 'Julie said she'd help me to meet other prospective parents if it doesn't work out with them. Isn't that nice?'

But my friend narrowed her eyes, far from comforted by my words. 'Wait. She's offered to help you meet other couples to adopt the baby *they* want while you're staying under *their* roof? Why would they do that?'

'Jeez, you sound just like your da. They're being nice, that's all. They just want to help.'

Dympna shook her head. 'Strangers don't help you. Not unless they're getting something in return. That, or they've no intention of letting you go.'

I rolled my eyes. Rising from the bed, Dympna left me to my own devices without saying another word.

'Culchie,' I muttered, stung by her departure. 'Anyone would think I was going to the moon.'

But thirty seconds later she returned with a mobile phone in her hand.

'I got you this,' she said. 'There's twenty euros' worth of credit loaded and it can make international calls.' The model was basic, a small round bullet-shaped phone. In her other hand was a charger. She pressed both into my hands. 'Keep it as a backup. Call me if you need me any time, day or night. I'll get Dad on to it if I have to. I don't like you going over there without knowing your address.'

Her concern wrapped itself around me like a warm hug, but I was too stubborn to back down just yet. 'This is mad. You've been watching too many cop programmes on TV.'

'Please. Keep it hidden.' She tightened her hands over mine as I took the phone. 'They picked you because you're a loner. You've got to ask yourself why.'

'I've got you.' My words were quiet and low.

'Yes, but *they* don't know that. I saw your profile. Why did you tell them you had nobody at home?'

I shrugged, placing the phone next to my suitcase to be packed. 'Because it's easier that way.'

Dympna tilted her head to one side. 'Is it a one-way or a return ticket?'

'One-way . . .' I watched as her eyes grew wide. 'But only because I might want to meet some other couples while I'm there. They're booking my return flight when I'm good and ready. I'll be staying at the Grand Hyatt Hotel. Don't tell anyone. Please.'

Dympna's features relaxed a little. 'You're not staying with them? Well, I suppose that's something.'

'They thought I'd be nervous about staying with strangers. We're going to meet up a couple of times and we'll be chatting on the phone. It's all above board. I'll be back before you know it.'

'Then promise me you'll hide the phone.'

I crossed my heart. It wouldn't do any harm to stash it away with my things. Not that I would need it, but it would put her mind at rest.

'And don't forget the code word.'

'Seriously?' I chuckled at the mention of the word we'd been using since primary school. The word 'pickle' meant 'rescue me'. If I was ever trapped at a party in a boring conversation, I only had to text or say that one word and Dympna would be ready with an excuse to help me leave.

I couldn't stay annoyed at Dympna. She was only watching my back. In truth, I was a little scared myself. She had raised some very important questions. Why the need for all this secrecy? They were going against site protocol and should have divulged their identity by now. I was as scared as I was excited about such a big journey. But who would be meeting me on the other side?

CHAPTER THIRTEEN
ROZ

'I don't want you to go.' Dympna stood in the doorway, her backpack slung over her shoulder. 'I have a bad feeling about this. Like, a really bad feeling that's giving me stomach ache.'

She was on the pre-dawn cleaning shift and was running late, but her feet seemed rooted to the floor.

'It's probably wind.' I smiled weakly, my suitcase by my side. 'Besides, the taxi will be here any minute. I'm hardly going to change my mind now, am I?'

'Why do you have to be so stubborn?' Dympna sniffed, wiping away an errant tear.

'And why are you so controlling?' I retorted, my voice breaking.

'Well, shoot me for caring,' was her instant reply. 'You'd better come back, Roz Foley. And don't take any shite over there. Any trouble and you call me, you hear?'

I nodded before being enveloped in a bone-crushing hug. It marked the end of our conversation; she turned and walked out the door.

I checked my compact mirror, groaning at my tear-stained reflection as I dabbed away the mascara smudges beneath my eyes.

I cast one last, lingering gaze around the room. Seagulls screeched outside the kitchen window, fighting in mid-flight. I shook my head, wondering what state the place would be in when I came back. As for me . . . how would I be when I returned, no longer carrying the baby that was constantly in my thoughts? The prospect weighed heavy on my mind as I felt the monumental change ahead. Would I be able to give my firstborn away? But some mistakes were impossible to get past. Had Dympna known the truth, she would have pushed me out the door.

I found myself redoing my make-up in Dublin airport. There was no way I was turning up in New York looking like a panda. Dympna had said they should take me as I was; it was my baby they were buying, not me. Her comments were barbed, a reflection of her concerns. I spent my last few euros on make-up in the duty-free counter just the same. I must be crazy, flying to America with hardly any money to my name. But I had checked with the hotel. My room was booked and paid for, including any meals I ordered while I was there. I'd explained to Julie that I felt bad about being unable to contribute, but she'd made it very clear that I had nothing to worry about.

'As if I'd let you spend a dime,' she'd said, 'when you're good enough to travel all this way.'

It was true. Couples were meant to travel to their donors for the first meeting. But because of work and other restrictions, they'd asked me to go to them. Besides, if we decided to go ahead, a generous deposit would be hitting my bank account. I looked around the airport, trying to figure the screens out. I'd been told to pack light; just enough for a long weekend. Wheeling my hand luggage, I joined the line at the British Airways check-in desk.

'You didn't need to queue.' The young girl behind the counter smiled. 'You're booked into first class. Why don't you pop into the first-class lounge, and you'll be called when the plane is ready to board?'

I stared at the ticket as she handed it back. 'Are you sure?' First-class flights to America did not come cheap. 'I mean . . .' I cleared my throat as I prepared to lie. 'My prospective employers bought me the ticket. I didn't expect to be first class.'

'Lucky you,' the girl said with a hint of envy in her voice. 'They're obviously very keen.'

I took a deep breath, following her directions to the lounge. Sitting with a coffee and pastry, I pushed aside my worries and reflected how lucky I'd been to find my mystery couple. *How generous. They must really want me. May as well enjoy it*, I thought. Perhaps it was time to let down my guard. It was a once-in-a-lifetime trip, after all.

The eight-hour flight passed much quicker than I expected, and my nerves dissipated after a few hours on board. I felt like royalty, but swapped the glasses of fizz that were offered for orange juice instead. Amidst all the excitement I could not lose sight of the fact that this trip was for the baby, not me. At least I'd arrive in New York with a clear head. My morning sickness was abating, and I was too excited to think about it very much. I knew so little about the arrangements that lay ahead; only that someone was meeting me when I got off the plane. What a lovely change, to be staying in a hotel rather than cleaning it. *At the end of the day*, I told myself, *if they abandon me in New York I'll go to the Irish embassy for help.* And if I really got desperate – and I mean *really* – I had just enough money on my high-interest credit card to afford a one-way flight home.

Two in-flight movies and a relaxing snooze later, I awoke to discover we were shortly touching down. My heart skipped a beat as I stared out of the window, my eyes on the landscape below. My fingers tightened around my armrests, my stomach somersaulting as the airplane came to ground with the slightest of bumps. I prayed for a successful conclusion. I had not come all this way to back out now.

I searched the sea of faces as I made my way through the airport, coming to a standstill as I glimpsed a man holding up a card with my name on it. I was sweating like a pig, but there was no time for a freshen-up now. Was this one half of my mystery couple, or a driver they had sent? My legs felt weak. Who would have thought that I would be in JFK airport, meeting strangers whose names I didn't even know? A wave of dizziness came over me as I eyed up the police officers armed with guns. The fact I was in a country where firearms were freely available was not lost on me. Straightening my step, I told myself to be strong. I was constantly in awe of the police, but given I had never put a foot wrong my whole life, I couldn't explain why.

'Rosalind, I presume?' the suited man said, holding his hand out towards me. He was broad, tanned and wearing sunglasses. He looked like a driver, so I presumed he was.

I shook his hand, then realised he was reaching for my luggage instead. 'Sorry,' I said, a flush rising to my face. My trouser suit may have seemed like a good idea in Ireland, but it was sticking to my skin now. I had heard someone say that New York was unseasonably warm for the time of year, although it was probably my nervousness making me sweat. 'Nice to meet you,' I said to the man before me. 'And please, call me Roz.'

'Welcome to New York, Roz. I'm your driver, Carl.' He led the way to the car park. 'Have you been to New York before?'

'I've never been outside Ireland,' I said, realising how lame that sounded.

'Boy, you are in for a treat.' Carl opened the back door of a sleek black limo and I slid inside.

I was grateful for the air-conditioned car. It was my first time in a limo, apart from a tacky pink one I went in once during a hen party. But it was nothing like this. This was luxury. I sat in the back and slid on my seat belt, taking care around my stomach.

'Help yourself to drinks,' Carl said, before putting the car into gear.

I cracked the lid off some chilled mineral water and gratefully knocked it back. Before long, New York's breathtaking skyline appeared ahead. Seeing the outline of the city's iconic buildings made me inhale a sudden breath.

'Wow,' I said, feeling like I was entering a movie set. My journey was fast, with lots of swerving and sudden beeping of horns. My driver took no prisoners and was far more daring than the taxi cabs I took in Dublin. After a few minutes the conversation between us dried up. I sat back and enjoyed the view.

'Here we go,' he said, pulling into the entrance of the Grand Hyatt.

'Sorry,' I replied, remembering an article I'd read about etiquette in the US. 'I haven't been able to get any dollars out yet. I don't have a tip.' I had hoped to get to a cash machine in the airport, but I hadn't had the chance.

'Don't you worry about that, it's all taken care of. You have a good day.'

I took the suitcase from him and watched him turn back towards the car. 'But what do I do now?'

'I'm sorry?' He turned to face me, a little bemused.

'Well, um . . . the people I'm supposed to meet . . . when will they be in touch?'

'I'm just paid to bring you here safe and sound.' He paused, flipped off his cap and smoothed back his hair. 'Why don't you check in – you can freshen up while you wait to hear from them.'

It was obvious. Something I should have thought of myself. 'Thanks, will do.'

I hated the feeling of aloneness, and I stood there, watching him leave. But I could not act like a child forever. I had to stand on my own two feet. I was an adult now. Hell, I was almost a mother. I thanked the porters as I was shown inside the hotel. A sense of self-assurance settled over me as I took the escalator to reception. *Fake it till you make it*, I told myself, striding towards the front desk.

It was only just gone noon, but early check-in had been paid for. It seemed like Julie and Glenn had thought of everything. I pocketed my key card and entered the lift.

'You're not in Dublin any more, Roz,' I muttered to myself, grateful for some time alone to catch my breath. But the speed at which the lift raised itself to the thirtieth floor took me by surprise. I grinned. This was certainly not Jurys hotel.

I was there in a matter of seconds, and in my hotel room. My smile grew as I entered the suite with the city view. Despite my tiredness, I was tingling with excitement. I turned my attention to a gigantic fruit basket with a welcome note inside.

> Dear Rosalind
> Welcome to New York! I expect you are tired from your journey, so please take this time to settle in. We will send someone to meet you this afternoon at two-thirty. We look forward to meeting you.
> Best wishes
> Julie x

Two and a half hours would buy me enough time to snooze and shower. Perfect. But what did they mean when they said they would send someone? Why was everything so cloak and dagger? I plucked a grape from the fruit basket and popped it in my mouth. Walking over to the window, I watched the iconic yellow New York taxi cabs drive up and down the streets. I could see the Pershing Square bridge from my window, and watched, fascinated, as tides of people walked beneath. Kicking off my shoes, I turned on the television and lay back on the bed. Had I known what lay ahead of me, I would not have been so easily drawn into sleep.

CHAPTER FOURTEEN
SHERIDAN

'I should have chosen the other cushions,' Sheridan said, furiously plumping and punching the ones laid on the sofa. 'And what about the drapes? It's too dark in here. This place is more like a hotel than a home.'

'Throw some Lego about if it makes you feel better,' Daniel said, standing in the doorway.

Sheridan pursed her lips. He had caught her talking to herself. She only did that when she was in panic mode. 'Do you think I should?' Her head swivelled left and right. 'Where's Leo's toy box gone? I swear the nanny has a secret portal where she stashes all his stuff.' Her long blonde hair was knotted in a sleek ponytail, her wrap dress a gift from her favourite designer's autumn collection. She had struck up a friendship with him after wearing his clothes to one of her premieres, which in turn sky-rocketed his career. That was five years ago. These days, the only premieres she attended were Daniel's.

'You're panicking,' he said, closing the double doors as he entered. 'She's from a small town in Ireland. She'll be more focused on us as parents than the colour of our curtains.'

'You're right. But first impressions count.' Sheridan patted her hair. Smoothed down her dress. 'What if she doesn't like us?'

Daniel wrapped his arms around her in a bear hug before murmuring into her hair, 'There'll be hundreds more expectant mothers happy to take her place.'

'But not ones that we like this much.' Making space between them, she rested her hands on his chest. He remained unruffled, which had an instant calming effect. Often, a hug was all it took to bring her to ground.

'We're doing the right thing, aren't we? I mean, after what happened before . . .' The rest of her sentence was left unspoken. She could not voice her thoughts aloud. 'Don't mind me. I'm nervous, nothing more.' She gazed into his eyes. 'I'm so lucky to have you in my life. And not a day goes by that I—'

Her words were interrupted by the ring of the phone in the hall. They didn't need to answer. The home help would screen the call.

'Just remember,' Daniel said, 'we're doing Roz a favour. She'll be desperate to find a home for the baby before she starts to show.'

'You're right.' The words were said on the exhale of a sigh. Sheridan picked up the remote control and activated their artificial open fire. 'Pine cone' mode instigated sound effects that crackled and hissed, and the comforting smell of burning moss and pine filtered into the room. Another piece of high-tech equipment she'd had installed. She normally reserved it for the holidays, but today it felt like Christmas had come early. Her excitement unnerved her. She could not contemplate the fallout if things with Roz didn't work out.

'Are you really going to help her find other couples?' Daniel said. 'I couldn't believe she took you up on that.' He had read their conversation history, and it seemed the offer had taken him by surprise.

Sheridan offered up a wicked grin. Her hand danced along the fireplace, a twinkle in her eye. 'I was throwing her a bone to gain her trust. I'm not going to follow through.'

'Risky.' Daniel raised an eyebrow.

'Not really,' Sheridan smiled. 'I have some couples lined up. The sort who will make her come running back to us.'

Three knocks on the door signalled it was Anna. Sheridan responded, and the door cracked open a few inches.

'Sorry to interrupt.' Anna spoke in Spanish, but Sheridan easily interpreted the words. Anna's gaze remained on the floor. 'Your assistant George called. He's on his way to pick up your guest.'

Anna was stocky and middle-aged with a solid, lived-in face. Her long dark hair was twisted into a bun and secured with a clip. Like the rest of the housekeeping staff, her uniform was plain but functional, consisting of a knee-length black dress, black tights and flat shoes. As well as helping the nanny care for Leo, she ran the household. Her granddaughter, Juanita, had recently been employed part-time, too. A timid, meek young woman, she would be perfect for catering to Roz's needs. Anna and her granddaughter were trusted, as much as Sheridan could trust anyone. With Sheridan sponsoring Juanita's education, Anna had good reason to keep her employer on side.

After delivering her message, she softly closed the door with a barely audible click. Sheridan valued her peace, and Leo was napping upstairs; it didn't take a lot to wake him during the day.

'I take it you have an angle?' Daniel said, returning his attention to his wife.

Sheridan flashed a row of perfect white teeth. 'Roz is no gold-digger, but she does have issues around money, and equates wealth with a happy home. If we can find out a little bit more about her past and play on her insecurities, it will reinforce the idea that she's doing the right thing.'

'You really are used to getting your own way, aren't you?'

'Oh, come on, don't give me that look. If I sat back and let life come to me, I wouldn't be with you now.' She slipped out her phone and brought up the Friend Finder app. 'George is at the hotel.'

'Are you seriously tracking his movements?' Daniel took a seat.

It had been a long time since they'd had a proper chat. These days, he was always rushing off somewhere, and he seemed surprised to discover just how tightly Sheridan was holding the reins. She liked George; they both did, but she could not afford any more slip-ups.

'Of course,' she said, as if it were the most normal thing in the world. 'I keep track of all our staff. They turn it off when they're not working but when they're on duty I need to know where they are.'

'But no cameras.' Daniel's voice was firm. The prospect of internal CCTV was something they had argued about in the past.

'No cameras,' Sheridan confirmed.

'What do you think they're getting up to?' Daniel checked his watch before slouching back on the chair. It was agreed that Sheridan would meet Roz alone at first, so as not to overwhelm her.

'While they're on my payroll, every movement is accounted for.' Sheridan gave Daniel a look that relayed it was non-negotiable.

He watched as she pulled back the curtains, allowing an extra inch of light into the room. Despite all her neurosis and complications, Sheridan knew he loved her. Or perhaps because of them. Life was never dull, and no two days in her company were the same. She just hoped that this baby would be worth the gamble: the ultimate self-promotion tool. Their social media followers loved their happy family image. There was power in their brand, and her perfume and clothing lines would ensure her continued success. It was just as well, given the menial acting parts she was being offered these days. Younger, more inexperienced actresses were stepping into leading lady roles that she could easily play. Sheridan knew she was not the easiest person to work with. Several producers had complained that she was too high-maintenance, and said they would not hire her again. If only she could be more like Daniel, who was more amenable when producers came knocking on his door. He lived by one rule: that the people you pissed off on the way up in this industry met you on the way down. They could either give you a foot back up that ladder or kick it from beneath your feet.

Sheridan knew that Daniel could never go back to his old life in England. Working as an actor was all-consuming, but the buzz was like nothing else on earth. He craved the excitement of not knowing what was around the corner, and of taking over his character's role. It was like living several lives at once, and being able to do things he would never get away with in the real world. He was an assassin, a spy, a villain and a dad. He had met all his heroes, people he was proud to call his friends. Daniel Watson and Sheridan Sinclair were deemed Hollywood's most powerful showbiz couple. Were they rocking the boat by asking for more? How would the introduction of Roz affect their family dynamics? Sheridan had a personality that did not gel with everyone. Strong and unpredictable, how would she get along with this young woman from Ireland who had never even travelled on a plane?

CHAPTER FIFTEEN
ROZ

I twisted my silver Claddagh ring as I sat on the edge of my bed. At least my afternoon shower had left me feeling fresh again. My rumbling stomach reminded me it had been hours since I'd eaten, but I had too many butterflies floating around to think about food now. My thoughts wandered to Dympna. Perhaps it was intuition, but I felt a tug, a calling to home. I stared at the telephone on the bedside table. What time was it in Dublin? Weren't they five hours ahead? But a call home would surely show up on an itemised bill. I should have been honest about having a friend. How would I get by without speaking to Dympna? Why had I lied in the first place? I bit down on my lip harder than intended, wincing as I felt the pinch. *The mobile*, I thought, pain clarifying my thoughts. I could have used my own phone, but that would give an open invitation for Dympna to call me back. It would be better to call from the mobile she'd given me. Or, better still, send a text.

Retrieving the phone from the folds of my suitcase, I mentally prepared my text. Relief flooded my system as I switched it on to see no missed calls. My thumbs worked quickly as I tapped in the words *Landed safely. Flew first class, limo brought me to hotel! No need to worry, all is well. Meeting the couple soon. Hope all is good with you XX.*

I checked my watch. I had an hour to kill. A short walk around the block couldn't do any harm. I smiled to myself. I had only just landed in America and already I was using their terms. After whizzing down to the ground floor in the lift, I was soon breathing in the smell of the city streets. It was a far cry from Dublin, which carried the tang of the River Liffey on a warm day. New York City assaulted my senses, bombarding me with a cacophony of sounds and smells. There was no standing still as crowds of people walked shoulder to shoulder to a backdrop of beeping taxi horns. I inhaled the scent of street vendors, of popcorn and hotdogs mingled with car exhaust fumes. I became part of the tide of people, my horizons expanding with each step I took. Following the signs, I headed towards Times Square. I still couldn't believe how warm it was for November and I was glad I had changed out of my sweaty clothes.

'Can you spare me twenty dollars so I can get a job?' The request came from a skinny, toothless man, but his words made me stop in my tracks. He must have only been in his thirties, but it looked like life had hit him hard.

'How can twenty dollars get you a job?' I asked, with genuine curiosity. I had managed to get to the cash machine in the hotel foyer, but I had so little money and every note was precious to me.

The man scratched his unshaven face, buying himself a few extra seconds to come up with a believable response. Grinning, he lifted his chequered shirt. I followed his gaze to his midriff, and saw that his weather-worn jeans were held up by a plastic bag tied around the loops.

'I can't get a job with my pants hanging off. Twenty dollars will buy me a belt.'

I snorted a laugh. At least the beggars in Ireland were content with a couple of euros. In New York, they aimed high.

'I don't have a job either, so that makes two of us,' I replied. I unpeeled two dollars from the small fold of notes in my pocket and pressed them into his palm.

'Good luck,' the guy said with a gap-toothed smile. 'You're a long way from home.'

Indeed I was, and it became more evident with every step I took into Times Square. The buildings were high above my head as giant ads and neon signs fought for my attention. It felt closed in but marvellously impressive at the same time. Ireland was changing, but progress was slow, and New York felt like a different planet by comparison. I tried to train myself not to jump every time a taxi beeped its horn, and to watch for the flashing lights telling me how many seconds I had to cross the road. Doubling back, I strolled through Bryant Park, taking comfort in the seasonal gardens. The vibe was more relaxed here and I watched couples playing with children, people sitting at reading stations and others playing chess. How different this was to my upbringing in Ireland. A world away from my life. What was in store next?

I had just got back to the room when a sharp knock on the door made my heart jump up into my throat. I had counted the hours to meeting my mystery couple, but now I felt glued to the spot. It had to be the PA. Inhaling a deep breath, I forced myself to open the door.

'It's about time, dear. I was beginning to think you weren't in. You're Roz, I presume?' A short Asian man bustled inside, his eyes dancing around the room. His black hair was gelled into a small wave over his forehead, and he wore his navy suit with a slim purple tie. He had a face made for smiling, but his eyes were determined, lacking any real warmth.

'Yes . . . Sorry,' I said. Already, he was telling me off and I didn't even know his name. 'Are you the PA?'

'Goodness, don't look so scared!' he said. 'Yes, I'm George, not the big bad wolf.' He held out his hand.

I gripped it with terrified enthusiasm.

'Nice firm handshake,' he smiled, shaking his fingers as I let go. 'Now, are you sure you're OK? Because you look like you're about to faint.' He looked me up and down, his eyes resting on my stomach, which was still relatively flat.

'Sorry,' I said again. Why was I apologising? 'It's my first time in America and I'm a bit overwhelmed. I don't know where I'm going or what I'm meant to do.'

'Ah.' He looked at me knowingly. 'It explains why you're wearing *that*.'

My smile faded. I had changed into my jeans – white ones, which I'd complemented with a flowery blouse. From the look on George's face, anyone would think I was wearing a bin bag.

'Have you got anything else to wear?' He made his way to my wardrobe. 'I'm presuming you'd like to impress this couple.'

'I . . . I was told to pack light,' I stuttered, watching him throw back my hangers and sort through my things. There wasn't a lot there, so it didn't take long. He tutted at my paltry offering. 'Are there no designer stores in Ireland? Or maybe we should go for a subtler look.'

'We have plenty of designer outlets,' I retorted, feeling my cheeks burn. 'I just can't afford to shop in them. And I don't see the point in pretending to be something I'm not.' My annoyance was evident in my voice. I'd promised myself a long time ago that I would not be treated like a second-class citizen again.

George raised his perfectly formed eyebrows as he glanced my way. 'Ooh, sassy, I like it. How about . . .' He pushed a hanger aside. 'This.'

The white knee-length dress was relatively new, and I was keeping it for a special occasion. It was linen with tiny flowers above the seams, and still a good fit.

'If you think it's best,' I said haughtily.

'I do, darling. I'm just trying to help, and we do have a little time to kill. Now, take off that make-up so I can redo your face. It's too vampy for my liking. Utterly gorgeous, but first impressions count.' He tilted his head to one side. 'You need to be more of a girl next door.'

Sitting me at my dresser, he proceeded to rifle his way through my make-up bag. There was no point in arguing, and he seemed to know his way around a make-up brush. I was relieved I'd invested in a new palette, rather than bringing my grubby cosmetics from home.

'Is this all you have?' he said, picking up the packet of Boots make-up remover wipes. 'Darling, you must cleanse, tone, moisturise with Clarins at the very least. You may have perfect skin now, but it won't always be that way.'

I mumbled something about my baggage allowance as I wiped the foundation off my face. I wanted to dislike him, but I found myself warming to his brutal honesty. Besides, he was right; I *had* overdone it, and red lipstick was probably not the best choice when I had been coming across as holier than thou up until now.

'Have you just straightened your hair?' he said, after applying a gentler coating of make-up to my face.

'Um . . . yes, I . . .'

He plucked my hair straighteners from my bag and plugged them in to the hotel travel plug. 'Mind if I soften it with a little wave?'

He would be undoing all my hard work, but again, I agreed.

My hair and make-up complete, I heard George chuckle as I went into the bathroom to dress. Dympna used to call me a prude, but I valued my privacy. Besides, I had known George for all of twenty minutes.

I surveyed my face in the mirror. He had done a good job. When I emerged from the bathroom, he had found a pair of white sandals in the back of the wardrobe and instructed me to slip them on.

'Better,' he said, tapping his chin. 'Do you have any decent sunglasses?'

'Only ones I bought in Penny's for five euros,' I replied. I hadn't thought I'd need them at this time of year. I was beginning to feel like I was playing the starring role in an episode of *Pretty Woman*. But I had to admit, when it came to makeovers, George knew his stuff. I could see how nice it would be, having him around.

He checked his watch, which glinted gold on his wrist. 'There's a Sunglass Hut not far from here. I'll buy you a pair.'

I opened my mouth to protest, but George raised his hands in the air. 'We've got to give you a *little* bit of class, darling, and you won't be financially embarrassed for long, not if this works out. You've landed on your feet here.'

'I'm not in it for the money,' I said, pocketing my key card as I prepared to leave.

'And I'm not here to judge.' He picked up some blusher and gave my cheeks the once-over. 'Nice,' he said, stepping back to admire his work. 'You have beautiful cheekbones, but it's best to keep the look as natural as possible. We don't want the lady of the house feeling threatened, now, do we?'

'Threatened? By me?' I burst into laughter. 'You're codding.' George frowned ever so slightly, and I realised he wasn't familiar with the term. I cleared my throat. 'I mean, you're joking, right? I'm no threat to anyone.'

'And that sort of naiveté will knock them dead.' He checked his watch again. 'C'mon, we can't keep them waiting. We've got lots to do.'

I wrung my fingers, feeling rooted to the spot. 'Can you tell me who they are? Please. I'm so nervous, not knowing who I'm going to meet. Can you at least give me a clue?'

George pursed his lips, looking left and right, even though we were alone in the room. 'They're a Hollywood couple, actor and actress. Very famous.'

My mouth formed in an O at this news. For some reason I'd got it into my head that they were politicians, pop stars or presenters in the public eye.

George fiddled with his phone before meeting my gaze. 'They're outrageously wealthy and very handsome,' he continued. 'Your baby will want for nothing if this comes good. Everything hangs on you, so don't blow it.' He took in my expression and gave me a sympathetic smile. 'It's fine to be nervous, just . . .' He sighed. 'Don't interrupt when they talk to you. Keep your eyes off the man of the house. Be polite, gracious, and keep that good firm handshake. I have a feeling they're going to like you. And that blonde hair of yours . . . it's going to blow them away.'

'My hair?' I ran my fingers through the tips of my blonde waves. 'Why?'

'You'll see soon enough. Now, come along, we've got sunglasses to buy and an attorney to meet.'

'Attorney?' I echoed his words. 'I thought we were meeting the couple.'

'You've got a confidentiality agreement to sign first. I'll explain on the way.'

My heart was beating like a drum. I had not agreed to anything officially, so what did they want me to sign? And what did George mean about keeping my eyes off the man of the house?

CHAPTER SIXTEEN
DYMPNA

Dympna stared out of the rain-speckled window, feeling as if one of her limbs had been cut off. The fact she had not parted on the best of terms with Roz had left a sour taste in her mouth. One of her earliest memories was sitting next to her in the school playground and peering into her lunchbox to discover the odd things wrapped in there. The box was an old biscuit tin, battered from use. Dympna had watched Roz peel the crumpled tin foil to discover a small rubber ball. Next to it was a half-packet of dry crackers. There was no drink. Dympna hadn't understood. Was it some kind of joke? The last mystery package contained a hard-boiled egg with a purple tinge.

'Mammy gets mixed up,' Roz said sorrowfully as she pocketed the ball. 'She's not well.'

'That's OK,' Dympna had replied.

Her daddy used to tell her stories about kids who had it tough at home. Despite her early age, she'd understood Roz's predicament and hadn't said another word. Opening her lunchbox, she split her own lunch in half. Sandwiches, juice, strawberries, cheese squares and carrot sticks – she'd had enough for a picnic for two.

Dympna used to envy her friend's freedom. Roz went to bed whenever she wanted and chose what time to get up. Looking back now, she could see that her friend had got the short end of the stick. It was easy to see where Roz's anxieties stemmed from, but would things have been any better if she'd been taken into care? Dympna picked at the paint-chipped window and barely heard Seamus enter the room. Her concerns must have been laid bare on her face, because he asked what was wrong.

'It's Roz,' she said, reluctant to break her promise. 'She might be in trouble and I don't know what to do.'

Seamus followed her over to the sofa. He looked smart in his shirt and tie, having finished late at work. Dympna had met him through his father's estate agent business when she was looking for a place to rent. She'd immediately been taken in by his dark wavy hair and warm hazel eyes.

'What sort of trouble?' Seamus said, his face scrunching into a frown. Three years older than her, he was a man in Dympna's eyes. She admired his ambition. There wasn't a day that passed when he didn't say something to encourage her to aim a little higher herself. She trusted him, which was why she needed his advice.

'I can't say. I promised Roz I'd keep it a secret.' She sighed, gathering up a pile of magazines to clear a space on the sofa for them. 'It's hard, though. She made a decision I don't agree with and now I'm worried about how she's getting on.'

'Is this to do with the job abroad?' Seamus threaded his fingers together as he sat down. 'I thought that all happened a bit fast.'

Dympna picked at a loose thread in the knee of her jeans. 'There's no job.' That much she could say. She had agreed not to mention the pregnancy, so her promise was still technically intact. She wished she'd inserted a clause in case of extreme worry.

Seamus began cracking his knuckles, and she gave him an elbow to the ribs. She hated it when he did that.

'So . . . she's not gone to America for a job?' he said, but his words were stilted, as if he was reluctant to hear her response.

Dympna let it go. She had a tendency to read too deeply into things. 'She's gone away to sort something out. Something she couldn't fix over here.' She pursed her lips. She was close to the imaginary line that should not be crossed. 'I can't say any more than that.' But Seamus was clever. If he figured it out on his own it was hardly her fault.

'And it's nothing to do with work?' Seamus said, staring ahead at the television, even though it was turned off.

'No, it's not.' A sense of betrayal crept in. She could almost feel Roz's disapproving glare. She inhaled deeply, catching the scent of Seamus's aftershave. It was spiced musk, sexy and inviting. She wished she could forget about Roz and drag Seamus off to bed.

'So how did she afford the flights?'

Dympna sighed. She did not trust herself to answer.

'Someone paid for her to fly abroad?' he said.

She nodded, feeling like she was in a game of charades.

'So, she's gone to sort out her problem,' Seamus continued. 'Is it to do with her mother?'

'No,' Dympna replied, 'and she can't know about this.'

Silence fell between them. Outside, car horns beeped and late-night shoppers chattered below their flat window, but Dympna barely heard them. She was too wrapped up with Seamus, willing him to guess correctly so she didn't have to deal with this on her own. She toyed with the ends of her hair as she stared, unblinking, at his face. She could almost hear his thoughts ticking over in his brain.

'Is she pregnant?' he said quietly. 'Has she gone for an abortion?'

The practice was illegal in Ireland, although most women in this predicament went to the UK. Seamus's first presumption was right but the second was wrong, so Dympna shrugged in response.

'I've said too much. Besides, she's gone. There's nothing I can do except wait to hear from her.'

Seamus nodded, giving her knee a squeeze. 'When she comes home, will everything be back to normal and the problem sorted out?'

'Yes.' Dympna exhaled a low breath. 'That's what she said.'

Seamus turned to her, finally meeting her gaze. 'Look, from what you've told me about Roz, she's taken some hard knocks and come out the other side.' He checked for Dympna's understanding. 'She's strong. And I'm not saying she always makes the right decisions . . .' His words floated away as he paused, deep in thought. 'But things have a habit of working out in the end. Just be there for her when she comes back. And keep your promise. Don't let on I know anything. Friendships like yours are hard to come by.'

'Thanks,' Dympna said, as Seamus leaned forward and picked up the TV remote control from the coffee table.

Their conversation was over. He had imparted his advice and he didn't want to know any more. He threw an arm over her shoulder and she relaxed into his embrace. But the air was thick between them, filled with a sense of words left unsaid. Dympna told herself Seamus did not want to come between her and Roz by giving bad advice. That was why he had changed the subject so quickly; nothing else. But still, unease lingered. She could not escape the niggling feeling that there was more to his response than that.

CHAPTER SEVENTEEN
ROZ

George did not just buy me designer sunglasses; he insisted on purchasing a pair of shoes too.

'You can pay me back from the money they're paying you,' he said confidently, referring to the couple whose identity I had yet to learn.

'But what if they don't like me? What happens then?'

I slipped my feet into the new kitten heels. George failed to hide his disdain as he deposited my grotty old sandals in a bin.

'The lady of the house takes no prisoners,' he said, giving me a knowing look. 'If you don't click, then you'll be flying back to Ireland before your pretty little feet touch the ground.'

Weaving through shoppers, I trotted after him as he signalled to a shiny black sedan across the road. 'But she said she'd help me interview new couples if it doesn't work out with them.' My voice jiggled as I tottered behind him.

As George turned, he saw my crestfallen expression and gave my arm a squeeze. 'Darling, you're living in cloud cuckoo land if you think she's got time to interview couples with you.' He guided me to the kerb. 'Let's focus on the best-case scenario. You're going to knock her socks off, as long as you abide by her rules.' I noticed he referred strongly to the woman of the house and guessed that she was the main decision-maker. He pointed to the Mercedes he had signalled earlier, which was now pulling up next to the kerb. 'Hop in.'

I peered through the tinted windows, Dympna's previous warnings to be cautious echoing in my head.

'It's OK, we're not the Mafia.' George held the door open as I paused. 'Remember I told you about the lawyer's office? They've drawn up an NDA for you to sign. Non-disclosure agreement,' he explained in response to my blank expression. 'It's just a precaution, so you won't kiss and tell. Now, hurry up.' He nodded towards the car. 'He can't park here all day.'

'Aren't you coming too?' My knees felt suddenly weak.

George rolled his eyes. 'For Pete's sake, are all Irish people this suspicious? How about I get in first?'

I slid in beside him, inhaling the scent of soft leather – that lovely new-car smell.

'I'm not going to tell anyone.' I clicked my seat belt into place. 'And it works both ways. I don't want anyone to know about . . .' I eyed the back of the driver's head. 'My predicament, either.' The car pulled away, and I gripped the armrest as if I were on a rollercoaster ride. In a way, I was. This was the adventure of my life.

George pressed a button on the side of the door and a glass barrier rose from behind the driver, keeping our conversation private.

'They're just protecting their family,' he said. 'But remember: if you break the confidentiality agreement, they'll make an example of you, just like they did with the last member of staff.'

'What? Do you mean someone else had a baby for them?'

'Keep up, dippy. I said member of staff. You're not a member of staff, are you?' George met my gaze and I saw amusement in his eyes. 'It was their housekeeper, Rachel. She got the sack after selling her story to some gossip magazine. Turns out she'd been blabbing to them for years – she was their inside source. Aren't you lucky, arriving in the wake of that shit-storm?'

'I take it she didn't say very nice things?' I looked out of the window at the streets I had not yet visited, at the buildings passing in a blur.

'They were burned. Badly. Hence the new and improved agreement we all have to sign.' He turned to me, his face growing serious as the driver pulled up to the kerb. 'We're here. Now, Roz, this is a deal-breaker. You can walk away, and we can have you on a flight home tonight. You can tell your friends that you had a really weird weekend with some gay guy who did your make-up and gave you fashion advice. But you'd be blowing the chance of the best start in life for this little one.' He nodded towards my tummy and his voice grew quiet. Sincere.

My breathing fell in line with his as I drank in his words. This was serious. My last chance to back out.

'There's nothing to be scared of,' he continued. 'It's just an agreement saying that you can't talk about them or tell anyone who they are. It's customary. We're well paid for our loyalty and that is all they ask of you.'

'Along with the baby, of course,' I smiled.

'No, they're not asking you for your baby. You're asking them to give your baby a home. They're being gracious enough to compensate you for the next six months of your life.' He paused as his mobile phone beeped with a text notification. 'Don't lose sight of that, Roz. They are giving you the biggest gift of all. Hell, I wish they'd adopt me. What I'd give for a life like that!'

I nodded. He was right. It was just so much to take in.

'Be humble. They will love you for it. But darling, if this is all too much for you, and I can see how it would be, do yourself a favour and back out now. The people you're about to meet will be beyond your wildest dreams. But an experience like this . . . it's not for everyone.'

I almost laughed. I mean, who were they? His admiration for them was obvious, but he was talking about them as if they were gods. I wanted to tell him not to patronise me, but took his earlier advice to be humble instead. To tell the truth, I was grateful for his presence, and a bit of hand-holding never did any harm. I took a deep breath and unclicked my seat belt.

'I'm in.'

◆ ◆ ◆

Twenty minutes later I had signed the documents and was leaving the way I came.

'All done?' George said, sliding his phone into his breast pocket as he met me in the corridor of the lawyer's office. I followed him outside, in no doubt that the lawyer had already confirmed to him that I had signed. Regardless, I nodded, offering him a wide smile.

'Well, in that case we have some very important people to meet.'

'Who?' I said, unable to wait a second longer.

'Hmm . . .' His eyes twinkled as he enjoyed drawing out the suspense. 'Can you handle it, though? You might be better off sitting down.'

'Just tell me!' I shrieked, grabbing him by the arm.

Beaming, he put me out of my misery, drawing me close as he uttered the words. 'It's Daniel Watson and Sheridan Sinclair.'

I barely remember getting back into the waiting car as George's words began to sink in. 'You're joking.' I shook my head in disbelief. 'Who are they really?'

George pursed his lips, a habit I was beginning to recognise. He was trying but failing to contain his smile. 'I told you they were special, didn't I?' He looked me up and down. 'Best you compose yourself, though. You're catching flies.'

I snapped my mouth shut. Daniel Watson and Sheridan Sinclair? It couldn't be. This was all one big joke. George was pulling my leg. There was no way I was making myself look any bigger a fool than I already had today. But the confidentiality agreements, the lawyers – it all seemed possible.

'I had a feeling you'd find this hard to swallow. Here, cast your peepers over this.' George thrust his phone under my nose. I glared at a series of photographs on the screen. It was George, his arm around Sheridan Sinclair. They looked pally. Comfortable with each other. In another photo he sat in a booth drinking coffee with Sheridan and her husband Daniel. His arm was held aloft as he took the selfie, trying to squeeze them all in. 'These are my personal photos. I try to stay out of the public eye.'

'How do you manage that?' I had read of some celebrity PAs who had become famous in their own right, with a huge number of followers on social media, too.

'Samantha Lockwood takes care of public engagements. Sheridan has a dozen or so people on her team.'

His face soured as he said Samantha's name and I guessed there was no love lost between them.

'But I'm the only one in her inner circle,' he said proudly, twirling his finger in a circular motion. 'And I'm a member of the NYCA.'

'NYCA?' I said blankly.

'New York Celebrity Assistants,' he said proudly. 'It's an elite association for assistants to celebs such as Oprah, James Patterson and so on. We all look out for each other. They help me resource anything from mink eyelashes to diamond-studded boots.'

'Mink eyelashes?' I said in surprise as a whole new world opened up to me.

'Check this out,' George continued. Flicking through his collection of pictures, he came to a video. The three of them – George, Daniel and Sheridan – were dressed up to the nines. It looked as if they were at some kind of award ceremony and George seemed a little the worse for wear. 'Who's the best PA in the world?' he was saying, his words slurred.

'My Georgie-Worgie,' Sheridan replied, leaning into the camera phone until she kissed the screen. The clip came to an abrupt end.

'That's where she dropped my phone,' he said. 'I don't normally go to ceremonies – Sheridan prefers me to be incognito.' He swiped away the images and pocketed his phone. 'So how do you feel about meeting them both? Daniel's hot property, isn't he?'

'They're amazing,' I said, barely able to string together a coherent sentence.

Daniel Watson and Sheridan Sinclair. I knew they were married because they were such a famous couple, although I hadn't heard about her in a while. Daniel, on the other hand, seemed to be everywhere these days. He was so damn gorgeous, and I'd watched most of his movies; not that I would be telling George that. It was his characters I fell in love with, and the roles he played: British tough guy with a soft heart. Kind but protective, tough but caring. My ideal man. I knew it wasn't real and I didn't want it to be, but now, knowing I was going to meet him in the flesh, I felt like I was made of jelly.

'Oh!' George's exclamation made me jump. 'There's one more thing. I almost forgot.' He thrust an empty hand towards me. 'I'm going to need your phone.'

'My phone? Why?' I reached into my jacket pocket and handed him my mobile.

'In case you're tempted to share all this on social media.' He raised his eyebrows. 'Is that a problem? You'll get it back when you leave.'

'Um . . . no,' I replied, feeling like I had given a little piece of myself away.

'Good. Now. Are you ready to meet them?' George pressed the button to lower the glass between us and the driver.

'No . . .' I shook my head. 'I mean, yes . . . Oh God.' I took a deep breath. What would Dympna say? No wonder there was so much secrecy. This celebrity couple wanted to raise my child and pass it off as their own. How would I feel afterwards, seeing them splashed all over the media? I realised George was staring at me. *Say something!* I screamed at myself. 'I grew up watching Sheridan on TV. I'm a huge fan of *It Takes All Sorts*.' I drew my hands to my face, the warmth of my fingertips reassuring me that I was wide awake.

George nodded in approval. 'Me too. We'll get to them in about ten minutes. That'll give you time to digest it. Unless you've changed your mind? You know, if you're worried about anything, you can confide in me. I won't breathe a word.'

'No, I'm fine.' My reply was immediate. 'If my friends could see me now . . .' I shook my head in disbelief. I was about to say *if Dympna could see me now*, but something stopped me. I swallowed back my words as I caught the guarded look on George's face.

'Your friends? You said you didn't have any close friends.'

Quickly, I composed myself. 'I don't. I meant my old school buddies. I lost touch with them years ago.' I dabbed my eyes with a tissue from a box in the car. 'Sorry. I'm being weird. Just give me a minute.'

But George was stony-faced. Had he been testing me? I took a calming breath. His loyalties lay with Sheridan and there was a lot at stake. I must not let down my guard again.

CHAPTER EIGHTEEN
SHERIDAN

Sheridan slipped into the library. Daniel rarely came in here; it was her own private space. She felt guilty keeping a secret from him, but she knew he would not approve. She sat on the leather sofa, listening to the latest voice recording on her phone. George had been reluctant to go along with things, but she had persuaded him that it was for the best.

'What if things don't work out with the baby?' she'd said. 'How are we going to feel six months down the line if everything goes wrong?'

Besides, it wasn't as if he was wearing a wire. All he had to do was turn on the voice recorder app on his phone, pop it in his breast pocket and leave it running in the background. So far, she had listened to three recordings. Now Roz was on her way over and this was the last one.

The brief had been simple. *Be friendly; take her under your wing. Make her feel like she can trust you.* She had even given him carte blanche to provide some gossip, although the comment about Roz making her feel threatened was pushing it a bit. And as for telling her she could change her mind and walk away . . . Sheridan's expression darkened. Was George trying to get a message to her? Trying to warn her that she might not be safe? She paused the recording, then replayed his words. No, she was being silly. George was her trusted friend. Besides: he owed her. After everything she'd done for his family . . . His mother would not be alive had Sheridan not funded her medical care. That's the way it was with her staff. They were all indebted to her. George was simply doing his job.

Roz had opened up a little about her family while getting her hair done. Estranged from her mother, with no father to speak of, it seemed she really was alone in the world. Best of all, when Daniel was mentioned, Roz had spun the conversation around to Sheridan. A lifelong fan of her work. Her words injected Sheridan with a warm glow. Perhaps she should have felt bad, spying like this, but it was the only way to know for sure. So far, Roz was passing each test laid before her and after some reassurance from George, had signed the agreement without complaint.

If only she had taken such care before. Sheridan tried to dismiss the thought, but it clung – a rotten, festering memory that would not go away. This was meant to be a new start, a chance to begin again. She had made a pact with Daniel to accept their mistakes and move on. But memories of Kelly came just the same. Leo might look like Daniel, but she could still see Kelly in his eyes. Sheridan ground her back teeth. Why must her life be marred by the past?

It had taken time to persuade Daniel to go down this route, but this time she would get it right. If there were any other traitors lurking in the corridors of their home, they would have known by now. She opened her laptop. It couldn't hurt to put some safeguards in place. Roz was ridiculously trusting and hadn't complained when George had asked her to give up her phone; Sheridan could not afford for anyone to track it to their New York address through GPS. She tapped her keyboard, bringing up the Miracle-Moms site.

Her conversations with Roz had been enlightening, and they had discussed everything from Roz's first pet to her mother's maiden name. It had not taken Sheridan long to work out her password for the site. From her username of Julie, Sheridan sent a message to Roz, pulling out of their deal.

'I'm sorry to lay this on you at such short notice,' she typed as Julie. 'But I can't progress. I'm pregnant. It's been a wonderful shock for us both.'

Logging out, she typed in Roz's username and replied to the conversation as Roz. 'Oh. Congratulations. That's wonderful news. Don't worry about me. I've got other couples to talk to. Can I still use the hotel room?'

Sheridan checked the time on her computer screen before quickly logging back in as Julie. 'Of course, that goes without saying! And please, have your meals and room service with my compliments, too. I'm sorry, but I won't be able to help you interview the couples, as I prefer to keep my identity private. I hope you understand.'

Fingers clacking on the keyboard, Sheridan logged back in as Roz. A sheen of sweat broke out on her forehead. She was running out of time, but it needed to be done.

'No worries,' she typed, recalling some of the Irish terms Daniel's mother used to use in an effort to sound like Roz. 'Thanks a million for the hotel room. I'll be grand. Congrats again on your baby. It'll be lucky to have you as a mom.'

Sheridan paused, reading over their conversation. She knew the Miracle-Moms site might be able to access deleted files, but thanks to her anti-spyware program, they would not trace her computer IP address. She pressed a button and a message flashed on to the screen. *Are you sure you want to delete your account?* Sheridan paused before pressing enter. There. It was done. There was no turning back now.

Sheridan rose, wishing she could quieten her negative thoughts. She looked down at her hands, noticing the slight tremble that had returned. A glimpse of a memory broke free: of when her fingers were laced with blood.

Ten, nine, eight. She closed her eyes, counting backwards in her mind. *Seven, six, five* . . . She took a slow breath, just as she had done a thousand times before. *Four, three, two, one* . . . She opened her eyes and turned to the apartment window to see her driver pulling up to the kerb on the street below. They were here. Sheridan fixed a smile. It was time to greet her guests.

CHAPTER NINETEEN
ROZ

'Are you ready?'

George turned to me as the car pulled up. The corners of his eyes crinkled but there was tension behind his smile. I used to think that celebrities had no real worries in life. I was slowly discovering that fame brought its own set of problems. It must be hard, not knowing who to trust.

'I'm fine,' I smiled. 'Can't wait to meet them.'

I was sitting on my hands, desperate to keep my nerves at bay. I had a habit of picking my nails and could do without George's disapproving glare. I'd used the journey to pull myself together, projecting an appearance of normality. Of someone in control. But inside, the steady beat of my heart was pounding in my chest. I was about to meet two of the highest-paid celebrities in the world. And while some people might not be fazed by the rich and famous, to me it was a huge deal. *Just enjoy it*, I told myself. And I would. Sitting forward, I waited to get out of the car.

After checking his phone, George leaned forward and hissed into my ear. 'You're being watched. Let the driver open the door and keep your knees together when you get out.'

His words were delivered like bullets, his breath cold on my skin. I stiffened. I was being watched? By whom? But I had little time to register my surprise as a blast of fresh air whooshed through the open car door. I exited with as much grace as I could muster, resisting the urge to look up as we headed towards the building. Was there really someone watching me? How did George know?

He took my elbow, ushering me up the steps. The entrance was grand, flanked by security and with a reception worthy of a five-star hotel. After being cleared by a couple of uniformed security guards, I followed George as he strode down a corridor on the ground floor. Every surface sparkled and the faint smell of fresh linen hung on the air. It was not an overpowering smell, like the air fresheners we used at home, but a delicate scent, lightly carried. I cleared my throat, feeling as if I'd swallowed a cup of sand. I couldn't remember when I'd last had a drink. I checked my watch. It was five-thirty on the dot.

A sturdy-looking Spanish lady answered the door. She was wearing a maid's uniform and a slight scowl on her face. The entrance hall was impressive – wide enough to drive a car through.

'Thank you,' I said, taking in the decor as I was shown in.

'You're not expected to speak to them,' George rasped.

His demeanour had changed since we got inside; his back was rigid, his fingers clenching and unclenching. It seemed I was not the only one who was anxious. But he was friends with Sheridan, so what had he to be nervous about?

'Now, George, don't chide her for having manners.' A woman's voice echoed from the hallway and I turned to see Sheridan Sinclair.

She looked so glamorous compared to me, in her heels and wrap dress. It was then that I realised what George had meant about my hair. As I gazed upon her blonde locks I saw the likeness. Hers was neatly tied up while mine was loose, trailing down my back.

Holding out my hand, I offered the firm grip George had approved of. But where was Daniel?

I kept my gaze firmly on Sheridan's face. I had read the recent press reports. I knew how hard it had been, living in her husband's shadow. But she had been nominated for an Oscar. She deserved to be recognised in her own right.

'I'm Roz,' I said, stating the obvious. 'It's so good to meet you.'

But Sheridan ignored my hand and took me in a light embrace. She smelt amazing, like an exotic flower garden in a faraway land. She was as beautiful in real life as she was on screen. Her lips were full, no doubt from the fillers she was rumoured to receive, and wrinkles were few and far between. I realised I was staring, and a flush rose to my cheeks.

'Sorry,' I said. 'I can't believe it's you.'

No explanation was needed. Everyone knew who Sheridan was. Many had grown up with her, watching her blossom from child star to adult actress. Even now, the reruns of *It Takes All Sorts* were streaming on Netflix. I'd watched them so many times, crying when her dog Bouncer died and melting at her first on-screen kiss. There was very little of Sheridan's life that was not public knowledge, although lately, the press that had once loved her had turned bitter and cruel.

'Daniel will be joining us later,' she said. 'I thought it best if we have a chat first. Have you had something to eat?'

'No, I was a bit queasy,' I said, still in awe of her presence. It was all so much to take in.

'You must eat, no matter how bad you feel,' she said, touching my arm. Her expression was stern, which took me aback. Her grip relaxed. 'For the baby. It's never too early to eat well.'

I gave her a tight smile, taking it as a good sign that she cared so much. It was a novelty. Apart from Dympna, who was a junk food queen, nobody ever cared what I ate. I followed Sheridan like a lamb looking for its mother, taking in the artwork on the walls as we went through to a dining room. I was fed an omelette with wholegrain bread, and a shot of vegetable juice that tasted so foul I almost spat it out. A bowl of fruit salad cleansed my palette and I sipped a glass of mineral water as Sheridan spoke. We chatted a little about my journey before turning our attention to the reason I was there.

'You must have so many questions,' Sheridan said, 'but there's something I want to address first.' She leaned forward, not waiting for my response. I was all ears. 'There have been some unsavoury articles about me in a certain gossip magazine.' She sighed, meeting my gaze. 'They could write about my happy marriage, my relationship with my beautiful son. But happy stories don't sell. And their source has an axe to grind.'

'I don't believe what I read in the press. I know most of it's not true . . .'

'I'd be happier if I could explain,' Sheridan interrupted. 'Their source is an ex-employee of mine. I fired her after I found her out.'

'I see,' I said, crossing my legs beneath my chair. The truth felt awkward. It was none of my business and I felt like I was intruding.

'I know it's early days, but I want us to get off to a good start. You didn't know who we were when you accepted us online. Now you know, have you had any second thoughts?'

'No,' I said, exhaling a sudden breath. 'Sorry, I'm nervous. Only last week I was watching you on Netflix and now you're sitting in front of me.'

Sheridan flashed a row of perfect teeth in a dazzling smile. 'Oh, honey, it's OK, I'm flesh and blood like everyone else. But we can't let the grass grow under our feet. If we're not the right couple for you then we can't afford to waste time.' Her words reminded me that my trip here was no jolly. This was business. She wanted an answer. Sheridan was not one to delay. 'What can you tell me about the father?'

This was a subject we had already discussed, and I gave her my stock response. 'He's my age, good-looking, healthy – he's in the army. He doesn't know about the baby and that's the way I want it to stay.'

'And are you sure you won't regret it? Is there any chance of you getting together in the future? How would you feel then?'

I shook my head vehemently. 'It was a one-off. I was at a low point in my life – I'd lost my job, I didn't have much money and I didn't know where to turn. He offered me a bit of comfort. But I don't sleep around. In fact, he's only the second fella I've ever slept with. Just my luck, eh?' But I don't think Sheridan got my humour, as it failed to raise a smile. I rubbed my right heel against the front of my other leg. The shoes George had bought me were pinching like hell.

'You don't need to justify your sexual history, honey. I'm only interested in the father and the chances of you regretting this.'

'He's got a girlfriend,' I blurted, realising how bad it made me look. 'I didn't know at the time. He doesn't come home very often. I knew after it happened that I'd made a huge mistake.' I had been about to say that he was my best friend's brother, but then I remembered I wasn't meant to have any current friends. Sheridan's shoulders dropped half an inch as she relaxed. I'd given her the answer she wanted to hear.

But it was all a lie. If it were Dympna's brother, I might have coped. I hated lying about such an important thing, but the truth was too ugly to bear.

Sheridan seemed unconcerned. 'Come with me,' she said, beckoning towards the doorway. 'Let me show you around.'

The ground floor consisted of a vast kitchen, with gadgets I didn't even know had been invented yet. Every surface was smooth and shiny, the antithesis of my flat back home. The air was crisp and clean, thanks to built-in purifiers; the water was purified, too, the showers infused with vitamin C. I walked with her up the winding staircase, a leather-clad handrail guiding my way.

'Stop,' she said, as I turned left. 'That's Daniel's wing.'

'Sorry,' I said, understanding the need for privacy.

'You weren't to know.' She smiled. 'It's where he keeps all his Bond memorabilia. Very few people are allowed anywhere near it. Come, let me show you Leo's room.'

'Wow,' I whispered as I walked inside.

'This room was designed by Louis Spencer. I like to keep the decor gender-neutral.'

I didn't know the name, but looked suitably impressed. The room was actually a suite, almost as big as my flat. In the corner was a teepee, and light oak floorboards complemented the natural room colouring. Cheerful yellow cushions and curtains added a pop of colour.

'I love it,' I said, wondering what was in store for child number two. There was no television in the room, but I saw a shelf full of books. I imagined my baby playing with art supplies. Would it be creative, like me?

'Roz?'

I snapped out of my daydream. Sheridan was calling my name. I followed her on to the landing, and she pointed to a closed door.

'That's our bedroom,' she said, walking past without further explanation, and moving on. 'This will be the baby's, after she has left our room. I like to keep them beside my bed for at least the first six months.'

It was music to my ears. I would have been the same, listening for every little sniffle. Listening to the baby breathe. As she opened the door, I was hit by a waft of fresh paint.

'Oh,' I said, taken aback by the stark white walls.

'It's just an undercoat,' Sheridan said. 'It's waiting to be decorated. Waiting for that special touch.' She turned to face me, her eyes moist. 'Louis has so many amazing ideas.' She glanced around the empty room. 'I wanted to work with the donor mom when it comes to picking colours and design. Combine our energies into choosing the decor, so the baby can feel our love.' She chuckled. 'You probably think I'm silly, but—'

'It's a lovely idea,' I interrupted, feeling my emotions swell.

Sheridan looked to my tummy where I had rested my hands, and then back to me. She was smiling, her words softly spoken. This was another side to her. A softer side.

'Then what do you think?' she said. 'Will you do it? Have your baby for me? I know you haven't met Daniel yet, but he's a sweetheart. He'll love you as much as I do.'

The contracts were already signed, but I guessed Sheridan wanted me to voice my approval aloud, now I knew who they were.

'I'd love to,' I said, without a second thought.

'Excellent!' She joined her hands, her middle fingers pressed against her lips, as if giving a silent prayer of thanks. Taking a sharp breath, she took my arm and turned back towards the stairs. 'Come with me,' she said. 'I can't wait to show you your room.'

'My room?' I said, following her down the stairs.

'You've got the whole basement floor to yourself. It's gorgeous.' She checked her phone as it beeped with a text. 'Good. George has collected your things from the hotel and brought them to your room.'

I was speechless as I followed her down. George had been in my hotel room, touching my things? This was a woman who was clearly used to getting what she wanted. How did she know I was going to say yes? But then I remembered what George had said about my feet not touching the ground. Had I said no, my bags would be packed, and I'd be on my way home.

CHAPTER TWENTY
ROZ

I looked around what would be my home for the next six months. It was a relief to be alone for a few minutes. With Sheridan upstairs, I had just enough time to gather my thoughts. The space was completely open plan. As my footsteps echoed on the wooden floor, I noticed that each of the living areas was cleverly defined with furniture. The space seemed vast compared to my little flat back home. I walked towards the sleeping area, which was yards away from the lift. It was dominated by a king-size bed, its black metal headboard dramatic in contrast to the white-painted brick walls. I imagined myself lying there, switching on the bedside lamp to read a book. The black and white theme continued throughout the room, with a glossy black wardrobe big enough to house a year's worth of clothes.

This is nuts, I thought, leaving the bedroom area and walking halfway across the room. The living space was marked out with a three-piece leather suite, which faced an oversized television. On the coffee table was a remote control, and a floor lamp provided cosy lighting should the spotlights be switched off overhead. A deep rug softened the wooden floor, and I slipped off my shoes, enjoying its plushness beneath my toes as I explored the nearby bookcase. I paused for breath. Was all this really for me? I walked to the beautifully tiled bathroom that housed both a shower and bath. The decor consisted of a functional white cupboard and glittering black tiles on the wall. After a quick pit-stop, I washed my hands before exploring the nearby dining space, which consisted of a small round table and two chairs. I noted the sink and mini fridge against the wall, but there was nothing to cook with. Was this because my meals would be eaten upstairs?

They really have thought of everything, I mused, glancing at the treadmill in the other corner. The room was bathed in artificial light, given that the basement didn't have windows. It felt odd that there was only a lift to take me upstairs. I looked around, noticing that I could see it from almost any angle of the room. My gaze rested on a locked door near the lift on the far wall. Were there stairs behind it? It seemed at odds with fire safety protocols. And as for Wi-Fi? It seemed there wasn't any. I wondered how I was going to manage without my phone and laptop for the next few months. I snooped around the bedroom furniture, noting that none of it was new. Who had slept here before me? I pulled open the drawer of the locker next to my bed and was surprised to find an old copy of *Celeb Goss* magazine. It had been folded open at page twenty-one. I scanned the story, my heart faltering as I realised I was standing in the very apartment the article was about.

Celeb Goss Magazine
August 2013
A BABY TO SAVE CELEBRITY MARRIAGE?
By Alex Santana

Rumors are rife after Hollywood starlet Sheridan Smith was recently pictured in Downtown Manhattan browsing in the baby section of one of our favorite designer haunts. Earlier in the week she was pictured at a charity event, her hand resting on her stomach as she chatted with friends. Is there a baby on the way? A source close to the couple said that the actress has threatened to walk away from her marriage to hunky Brit Daniel Watson unless he starts putting his family first. Will a baby give their marriage a much-needed boost?

Daniel has been hot property since appearing on the scene in Hollywood blockbuster *Murder Game*. The same cannot be said for his Oscar-nominated wife. A friend of the couple said, 'Since offers of work started drying up, Sheridan has become obsessed with extending their family.' But not everything is rosy in the garden for Daniel. 'He is growing increasingly frustrated with the amount of media attention, which curbs his freedom. He loved riding his motorbike to let off steam. But now everywhere he goes, paparazzi are in tow. Everybody wants a piece of him. It's hard to keep such a free spirit hemmed in.' Sheridan must be scared that he will revert to his old wild lifestyle. But will a baby be enough to tame him for good?

Sheridan is certainly doing her best to hang on to her man. She's recently purchased a four-bedroom apartment in Midtown Manhattan. 'The NYC pad would be an ideal place for them to raise a child. Daniel is committed to several film projects in the area. It would enable Sheridan to keep a close eye on him to ensure he stays on the right path. They would have the best of both worlds – work and family on their doorstep. A native of New York, Sheridan has lots of friends in the area, too.'

She certainly won't be short on space to entertain them. The $19.5 million home comes with herringbone floors, a white marble fireplace and a leather-wrapped handrail on the stairs. Circadian rhythm lighting is featured throughout, as well as a home-made juice bar and vitamin-C infused showers in the bathrooms. But that's not all. An elevator carries its occupants to a basement floor equipped with its own doctor's surgery for those ultra-private health appointments. Who needs to go to hospital when you can bring the best of medical care to you? There is also a gaming station, gym and lavish bedroom housed in the basement below. Could this be a man-cave for Daniel? What's in store for our favorite celebrity couple? Only time will tell. Our source is optimistic. 'Everyone has their fingers crossed that they will be announcing some happy news soon.'

I placed the magazine back in the drawer. Who on earth had put it there? Perhaps this had been used as a guest room, and it had been left behind by the previous occupants. There was so much to contend with. I was still getting my head around the fact that Sheridan expected me to stay with them until the baby was born. I liked her, having seen a whole other side to her from the one presented on screen. She was brave to have opened up about her employee's betrayal, and her plans for the baby's room warmed me from the inside out. But still, tiny alarm bells rang in the periphery. George was far from relaxed in her company. He seemed permanently on guard. And as for the housekeeper . . . she could barely look her in the eye. Surely the rumours about Sheridan's marriage being in trouble were a lie?

Sheridan had presence – a Hollywood starlet, she lit up the room when she walked in. When she'd shown me around the basement flat, I could hear the passion in her voice, the need for another child in her life. My baby – I caught my thoughts – no, *her baby* would want for nothing. And as for Daniel . . . my legs felt weak at the prospect of meeting him. I knew he would be a fantastic father, so charismatic and kind. I had read about his love for his son and how Sheridan had tamed his wild side.

I thought of Dympna, with her trendy parents: her father a detective in the police, her mother flying around organising events. She was lucky to have a family that stayed together no matter what.

At least I'd have enough money to start again. I could go to college, get a part-time job and still be able to pay my rent. I could make something of myself.

I unzipped my case, too preoccupied with my thoughts to remember the mobile phone I had packed away. Then it hit me, and my breath quickened as I searched the secret compartment to see if it was still there. If George had found it, there would be questions. Its presence could ruin everything. Tugging at the zip, I slid my hand to the back of the suitcase, sighing in relief as I felt the phone's outline. Above me, a door creaked shut, followed by a man's voice, deep and smooth. My heart flipped. It was Daniel.

Keep it together, I told myself. Sheridan would not want me mooning over her husband. I made a vow to appear immune to his charms. What would Dympna say? *Pretend he's your brother.* I heard her advice as if it were real. *Show Sheridan you're no threat.* I rolled my eyes. Who was I kidding? How the hell would I be a threat to someone like Sheridan? I chuckled to myself as I unpacked. Some days my thoughts felt like the most ridiculous things on earth. A whirring noise caught my attention. It was the lift. I froze. Who was coming down to see me?

It was Anna, the housekeeper.

She beckoned. '¡Ven acá!'

Given her expression, you'd be forgiven for thinking we were both facing the firing squad.

'I don't speak Spanish,' I said, although it didn't take a genius to work out that she wanted me to go upstairs.

'*Vamos,*' she chided, as I took my time.

My legs felt like lead as I followed her into the lift. It was controlled by a card that was pressed against a panel before the buttons could be activated from within. An added security measure, necessary for the rich and famous, but Sheridan had yet to provide me with a card so I could activate the lift myself. I inhaled a deep breath, feeling my panic rise. It was ridiculous, but I was scared. Daniel was up there, and he was waiting to meet me. *Breathe*, I thought, as Anna pressed the button to close the lift doors. They slid shut with an ominous thunk. But as the lift rose, the food I had eaten threatened to make an appearance. Throwing up all over Daniel would hardly make a very good impression. Briefly, I closed my eyes and forced my limbs to relax. I would not meet Daniel Watson looking like a rabbit caught in headlights. This was a business deal, and I needed to be heard.

I followed Anna into the kitchen, where Sheridan was drinking a glass of water at the breakfast bar. It was only seven in the evening, but my head felt all over the place as it fought against jet lag. Daniel was next to Sheridan, looking drop-dead gorgeous in a crisp white shirt that defined his chiselled chest. He had a few wrinkles that didn't show in the promo pictures, but they only added to his charm. I tore my eyes away, only meeting his eyes when I was introduced.

'Daniel, meet Roz Foley,' Sheridan said, her gaze intense as she scrutinised my face.

'Good to meet you,' Daniel said. 'And all the way from Ireland, too.'

I extended my hand, swallowing the lump in my throat as he took it in a firm grip. I kept my gaze steady, smiling but not falling over myself.

'Hi, nice to meet you,' I said politely, before glancing at Sheridan. 'Thanks for getting my things brought over. The room is amazing.'

I hoped I was not being rude, providing such a brief response, but I knew the importance of keeping Sheridan the priority in this situation. First impressions counted, and everything felt like a test.

I watched as Daniel exchanged a glance with Sheridan, his eyebrows raised. He seemed surprised by the fact that I was unpacking already.

'If it's too soon . . .' I glanced at Daniel, willing my heart to slow down. 'I can go back to the hotel tonight, leave you to talk things over. I don't want to be in the way.'

'Honey, you're not in the way. We want you here,' Sheridan said. 'It's Daniel's fault for not answering his phone when I called to let him know.'

'Sorry,' he replied. I wasn't sure who he was talking to as he looked at us both. 'I didn't mean to make you uncomfortable. You're hardly getting in the way downstairs, now, are you? Can I get you anything? A coffee?'

'Caffeine is bad for the baby.' Sheridan's reply was instant. 'Anna will get you some kale juice.'

As Sheridan reached for her laptop, Daniel gave me a conspiratorial grin. 'Got you on the kale juice already? I'm surprised you're not running for the hills.'

'Nonsense. You like it, don't you,' Sheridan said. It was not a question.

'I'll get used to it,' I said, barely able to hide my disdain for the stuff.

'Good,' Sheridan replied, pointing to her laptop screen. 'Because I've got the contract from the Miracle-Moms site.'

'Exciting,' I said, well aware that this was the final step. I was already familiar with the agreement, as it was drawn up by the website's attorneys. At least this time I'd been able to read it thoroughly before I signed. It was drawn up and verified by independent attorneys and, unlike the confidentiality agreement, I understood what it meant. I would have no claim over the baby once it was born. It felt strange that such a binding document could be signed digitally, and I tried not to hesitate as Sheridan handed me her iPad and digital pen. With Anna acting as our witness, I wondered if it was even legal. Surely they needed someone independent to verify things? But then these were unusual circumstances, and I had little time to dwell on it; Sheridan monitored my every move. Taking a deep breath, I signed away the rights to my unborn child. It was a sombre moment, broken by the shrill sound of Sheridan's voice.

'Excellent!'

She whisked the iPad away from me before calling a dark-haired young woman into the room. She was of slight build, with long sleek hair tied up in a ponytail. She couldn't have been much older than me.

'This is Juanita,' Sheridan said, and I watched the woman flinch as Sheridan laid her palm on the flat of her back. 'She's your personal maid. She'll be looking after you for the next few months.'

Sheridan uttered a few words in Spanish and, bowing her head, Juanita forced a smile.

I felt like a lemon, wondering if I should shake her hand. 'Um . . . nice to meet you.'

'She doesn't speak English.' Sheridan paused to dismiss her. 'She'll be cleaning your room, doing your washing, bringing you your meals. You won't need to lift a finger while you're here.'

I watched over Sheridan's shoulder as Juanita walked away. But as she opened the door to leave, she gave me an imploring look, her lips thinned as she delivered a sharp shake of the head. Her eyes were dark and full of knowing. As Sheridan turned to follow my gaze, Juanita quickly slid through the door.

'Everything OK?'

'Yes . . . It's just that . . .' I paused as I tried to come up with a response. 'I feel a bit funny about having staff. I'm happy to clean up after myself.'

A flutter of laughter left Sheridan's lips. 'Honey, they're not slaves. They're very well paid. Here.' Sheridan produced a schedule and waved it under my nose. 'Read it in your spare time.'

My face fell as I flicked through the paperwork. The next few months were planned with regimental precision from early in the morning until late at night. I was to be awoken at seven in the morning, six days a week. My meals were planned without my input, nutritionally sound, to meet the baby's needs. I skim-read the programme, realising that I was supposed to spend most of my time in my room. A room that was beautiful, but windowless and closed off from the world. I was a free spirit, a creative soul; I would go stir-crazy if I had to spend the next six months inside.

'I was wondering . . .' I said, not wanting to sound ungrateful. 'Can I do some sightseeing? I don't mind going on my own.' Six months seemed like such a long time to be hidden away. I wondered if I could get some time off to return to Ireland in between.

'And, um . . . how long am I here for? I mean, you mentioned me being here for my pregnancy. Now we've met, can I come back when I start to show?'

'I thought I'd made it clear.' Sheridan's smile thinned. 'You don't leave until the baby is born.' By the sound of her voice, it was not up for negotiation.

'Of course,' I said. 'As long as you're sure.'

'I'll arrange some sightseeing. George can go with you. Show you Times Square.'

'I've seen it.' I smiled at the memory. 'I walked down there when I was waiting for him.'

Sheridan stiffened. 'You went out on your own to Times Square?'

'I . . . I didn't think it would do any harm,' I said, looking from her to Daniel, who was closely watching his wife. The atmosphere changed as I was met with hostile silence. All the earlier positivity was sucked out of the room.

Daniel touched her arm. 'It was the middle of the day. There's nothing to worry about.'

But Sheridan seemed oblivious to his words. She took a step towards me, her features strained. 'Anything could have happened. What were you thinking?'

I couldn't believe my ears. I had barely signed the contracts and she was telling me off.

'I only went for a walk,' I said in a quiet voice. 'I wasn't gone long.'

'Against my strict instructions.' Sheridan prodded the air with her finger. 'Who paid for you to fly over here? Did you think you were on some sort of vacation? Anything could have happened to you.'

Stepping between us, Daniel squeezed his wife's arm. 'But she's OK, isn't she? She wasn't to know.' He turned to face me, taking me

125

by the elbow as he steered me away. 'Why don't I see you to your room? You must be worn out.'

'I'm sorry if I did anything wrong,' I said, my words trailing behind me. 'I didn't know . . .'

'It's OK, don't worry,' Daniel said, ushering me into the lift. 'I'll have Anna bring you some food. Why don't you take some time out and relax?'

But relaxing was the last thing I'd be doing. I had seen another side to Sheridan, and I didn't like it one bit.

CHAPTER
TWENTY-ONE
ROZ

'I have a surprise for you,' Sheridan said, jingling a bunch of keys in her hand.

I was watching TV in my basement flat, grateful for this connection with the outside world. I had not heard the lift until she stepped out of it, her heels clicking on the varnished wooden floor.

'But you've already done so much for me,' I said, turning from the sofa as she approached.

I did not like surprises. I was in the grip of culture shock, having come from Dublin to New York, and so far I was wholly out of my depth. After consuming Sheridan's schedule, I realised that my time in her household would be a solitary one. Then there was her earlier disapproval of me sightseeing on my own. I needed to hear a friendly voice, which was why I had risked making a call on Dympna's phone. But it was almost impossible to get a signal, and whenever I did, it never lasted long enough for the phone to ring more than once.

'Come along,' Sheridan said. 'Aren't you curious to find out what's behind this locked door?'

That was an understatement. Switching off the television, I followed her.

Sheridan was beaming now, as if her earlier chastisement had not happened at all. 'Isn't it exciting?'

'Yeah,' I said flatly, watching as she unlocked the door.

Behind it was a narrow corridor with strip lighting overhead. I glanced at a door at the far end.

'That's private,' Sheridan said, in the same tone of voice she'd used earlier when I'd turned left on the stairs. I followed as she plucked a key from the bunch and opened another door. It creaked as she led me into a sterile space.

The hairs prickled on the back of my neck at the sight of what looked like a doctor's examination room. But there was no new paint smell, just the stringent tang of cleaning fluid on the surfaces. I cast a glance over the paint peeling from the walls and the ceiling yellowing with age. I took in the tiled floor, the medical equipment. The room was clean, but definitely not new.

I wondered who used the desk in the corner, complete with leather swivel chair. This was no study. On the wall was a medicine cabinet with a key in the lock. A computer and some folders took up space alongside a filing cabinet. What was in there?

'I don't understand,' I said, unanswered questions springing into my mind.

Sheridan walked towards an examination table, patting the blue tissue running down its length.

'Haven't you worked it out? It's time for your three-month scan. Come on, hop up.'

Her smile was off-kilter. The kind of smile that told me to hurry up before it cracked. I clasped my hands tightly together. I wasn't prepared for this.

'But . . . who's going to do the scan?'

My question was answered as a short, bald man shuffled in from the corridor. Where had he come from? Was there another entrance to this room? He grabbed a lab coat from the back of the door and slid his arms inside. He must have been in his mid-seventies, and he barely acknowledged me. So much for New York's best ob-gyn. His full attention was on Sheridan, and I caught the look of undisguised admiration on his face. It was not just Daniel who had members of the opposite sex falling at his feet. Sheridan had many male and female admirers, and it appeared that the doctor was one of them.

'This is Dr Blumberg,' Sheridan said, not waiting for him to acknowledge me. 'C'mon now, hurry up,' she ordered for the second time, patting the examining table with a perfectly manicured hand.

I stiffened. They may have been using me as an incubator, but I still got embarrassed at the thought of stripping off in front of strangers.

'Don't be shy,' Sheridan said. 'You only need to roll your top up over your stomach.'

I did as instructed. Dr Blumberg leaned over me, his breath smelling of garlic and mints. Glancing over the doctor's shoulder, I squirmed as I noticed Daniel walk in. His hands deep in his trouser pockets, he acknowledged me with a smile and a gentle nod of the head.

I sucked a breath between my teeth as freezing cold gel was applied to my stomach.

'You must be dying to see the baby. I know I am.' Sheridan flashed me a smile.

I couldn't believe that she was talking to me. Seeing the baby would be so hard, given I was about to give it up. She was a mother; she had given birth. Why didn't she understand that?

As if reading my thoughts, Daniel spoke. 'Roz is bound to be apprehensive in the circumstances.' He looked pointedly at Sheridan. 'But it will be good to know the baby is healthy and well.'

I made a concentrated effort to keep my expression impassive, but my thoughts were whipped away as a *thump thump thump* echoed in the room. It was fast; much faster than mine.

'It's your baby's heartbeat,' the doctor said – not to me, but to Sheridan as he turned up the volume on the machine. 'Nice and strong.' He had yet to look at me, which I found odd. Daniel stepped forward, staring expectantly at the screen.

My heart skipped a beat as I followed his gaze. What if something was wrong with my baby? What would happen to us both then? I had not even considered this until now. From the corner of my eye I saw Sheridan take Daniel's hand. I felt a pang of longing. This was meant to be a momentous occasion, but I was in a room full of strangers. Just me and my little bean. Daniel hovered over me, his closeness making the blood race a little faster through my veins.

'What's that?' Sheridan pointed to the screen. The doctor slid the probe back and forth on my stomach until it picked up a grainy grey image on the screen. A few clicks later and he was describing the chambers of the heart, showing fingers and toes. *Hello, little one*, I thought, the image blurring as I blinked back the tears. My breath was shallow as I took it all in. I could not let them see how emotional I was over this baby. The doctor explained each body part, making measurements and giving comforting nods of the head.

'Baby is perfectly healthy, as far as I can tell.'

I exhaled a sigh of relief.

'And it's a little girl?' Sheridan said.

'It seems that way.'

'Wait, what?' I said, returning my gaze to the screen.

'The eight-week blood tests said you were carrying a little girl, but it's nice to have it confirmed,' Sheridan said. She was glowing now, her eyes dewy as she stared at the screen.

A mixture of hot anger and amazement welled up inside me. A girl. I had been right all along. Sheridan had known the sex of my baby for weeks. I closed my eyes, tried to get a handle on my emotions. I knew I was being irrational, but it suddenly felt wrong that she had found out before me. I felt like getting off the examination table and telling her the show was over. But why? I'd known what I was getting into, after all. I lay back, staring at the ceiling, as Dr Blumberg finished the scan. I was carrying a little girl . . . and in a few short months' time I would be going home to Ireland and leaving her behind.

CHAPTER
TWENTY-TWO
SHERIDAN

'Where do you draw the line?' Daniel asked, sitting at the head of the marble dinner table.

A magnificent spread was laid before them as they entertained their friends. Adam Weiss had co-starred with him in his latest movie and they were both rumoured to have been shortlisted for an Academy Award. That had led to a celebratory dinner. It was not often they were able to get together like this. 'It pays to keep the competition close,' Daniel had once said, which led Sheridan to believe they were not as friendly as they seemed.

Adam was three years younger than Daniel, blessed with natural talent as well as effortless good looks. His mother was African-American, his New Yorker father a Democrat working in Washington. Monica was different from his previous girlfriends, although her Boston accent was more JFK than Wahlberg.

Sheridan focused on her guests, pushing all concerns about Roz to the back of her mind; while preparing for dinner, she had surfed online, due to a niggling seed of doubt. The internet search had thrown up something that surprised her, but she would wait until the morning to confront the young woman in her care.

The dinner conversation was animated as Daniel discussed the price of fame.

'Even the places that were too cool to recognise celebrities are off the cards now. You know, the type of places where they'd go out of their way *not* to recognise you.' Daniel laid his dessert spoon on his plate. 'I almost punched someone after he shoved his camera right at Leo the other day. It was Melrose. You know the guy? A nasty piece of work.'

Adam nodded in sympathy. 'He sells his stuff to *Celeb Goss*.'

'And then there's the selfie brigade,' Sheridan added, keen to sway their conversation from the magazine she loathed. 'They think it's their God-given right to shove their phones in your face. Half the time they don't even know who you are, only that they vaguely recognise you from somewhere.' She sipped her soda water, giving Monica a wry smile. 'One asked me who I was *after* she took the photo. I said I was Jennifer Aniston.'

'But then there's the genuine fans who appreciate you,' Daniel said. 'Man, I hate to let them down because without them, I wouldn't be here. You need your followers to champion your work.'

'You find it hard, not living a normal life. But who's to say what's normal and what's not?' Monica said, observing their conversation with interest. Her thick black hair was stiff with hairspray, her false lashes framing her piercing green eyes.

'The problem is . . . my world is growing smaller and the walls are getting higher,' Daniel added. 'The number of people I trust is smaller and smaller every day. I know we sound ungrateful . . .' He looked at Monica. 'If I was in your shoes, I'd be thinking, "What an arrogant prick." I hope you won't judge us too harshly.'

'I don't,' Monica said. 'But there are lotsa worse-off folks in the world. You gotta protect yourself from negativity and count your blessings. Life is all about perception.'

'How can you be happy when people keep letting you down?' Sheridan asked. She loved Monica's choice of words. It was all 'gotta', 'havta', 'lotsa' and 'howareya'. A refreshing change from most of her friends, whose accents had been driven away by elocution lessons.

'You gotta choice,' Monica replied, toying with her chunky gold necklace. 'Choose what to focus on and live your life in line with your beliefs.'

'Blinkered, you mean?' Sheridan said, a prickle of annoyance creeping in. Monica was a therapist; she couldn't fully comprehend celebrity life.

'Don't knock it till you try it,' Adam said, looking at Monica with undisguised admiration. 'Mon's optimism has really rubbed off on me.'

'Sounds like you're doing well. Sadly, Daniel is stuck with my pessimistic nature.' Sheridan forgot her irritation as her lips twitched with satisfaction. 'But I won't bring the party down, because I have some good news to share.'

'I know what this is . . .' Adam said, his mouth jerking upwards in a smile. 'You've made the shortlist for James Bond. I was turned down for the part today.'

Sheridan shared a glance with Daniel. He and Adam had run a tight race, but it seemed that Daniel had beaten him once again. She was about to say that that was not the news she meant when Daniel slapped Adam on the back.

'What can I say, mate, you either have it or you don't.' He laughed. 'Seriously, though . . . nothing's been confirmed. It's all rumours and speculation, so who knows?'

'No matter. I've never been a huge fan of the franchise,' Alex said, in an obvious attempt to save face. 'There have been some real stinkers over the years.'

'There are no bad Bond movies, just some that are better than others,' Daniel replied. 'In fact . . .'

'If you don't mind,' Sheridan interrupted. 'Perhaps you'll allow me to share our *real* news?' She plucked a black and white picture from her purse.

'Is that what I think it is?' Adam said, his eyes growing wide.

'Yes, it's a sonogram – the first picture of our little girl.' Sheridan beamed.

'Wow,' Monica said, her expression relaying her surprise. 'That's . . . Wow. I wasn't expecting this.'

'You haven't been reading the tabloids then?' Sheridan replied. 'They've been talking about us trying for the last six months.'

'Yeah . . . of course.' Monica chuckled. 'It's just that . . . you mentioned having health issues after Leo.' She inhaled a deep breath. 'Sorry,' she apologised again. 'I'm thrilled for you both.'

Tears pricked Sheridan's eyes as she leaned forward and squeezed Monica's hand. It was good to have a friend who wasn't afraid to express real emotion. 'So sweet of you to worry about me, honey.' She rose from her chair to hug her. 'I've been given the all-clear. As long as I don't overdo things, I'll be fine.'

'Then I wanna hear all about it,' Monica replied, her chin on Sheridan's shoulder. She parted to kiss Daniel on the cheek. 'I'm made up for you both.'

'Come, I'll show you my plans for the nursery.' Sheridan led Monica into the hall.

'A boy and a girl.' Adam turned to Daniel as he raised his glass in a toast. 'Congratulations! You really have it all.' Their cheers rang in Sheridan's ears as she led her friend towards the room that was waiting to be decorated. She inwardly glowed from the warmth of their well wishes, her thoughts with Roz on the floor below. Prior to dinner, she had done some online snooping about their Irish guest. All was not what it seemed with her, but Sheridan was in too deep to back out of their agreement now.

CHAPTER
TWENTY-THREE
DYMPNA

Dympna jumped from beneath her covers. It was winter dark outside, yet a shrill ring had drilled into her brain. She glared accusingly at her alarm clock. Was it time for work already? She hated getting up in the dark, but the red numerals flashing told her it was 3.30 a.m. Tapping her fingers against her touch lamp, she tried to get her bearings, then realised it was her mobile creating the disturbance. There could only be one person ringing at this hour of the night. What time was it in America? She fumbled for her phone and accepted the call.

'Hello?' she said, hoping it wasn't bad news.

'Hi, sorry, did I wake you?'

The sound of Roz's voice made Dympna smile in relief.

'What time is it over there?' Roz continued, her words barely audible.

Dympna frowned. Why was she whispering?

'It doesn't matter,' Dympna replied, not wanting to put her off.

She was surprised she'd been able to get to sleep. Her imagination had been on overdrive. Roz had only been gone for one day, but she had spent the whole time wondering how she was getting on. She leaned against her headboard, feeling better for having heard from her friend.

Dympna's ability to assume the worse had been gifted from her father, helped by the horror stories he used to recount about his police work. Time after time, her mother had warned him not to be so graphic at the dinner table, but his eyes would be alight as he regaled them with stories of the people he had put behind bars. Dympna grew accustomed to it over the years, but it had left her with her father's cynicism which, according to him, was a good thing.

'I haven't got long,' Roz said. 'I just wanted to let you know that I'm OK. I'm staying at the couple's place now. It's amazing – I have a ground-floor luxury basement to myself.'

'Who are they?' Dympna said, wide awake now. An icy breeze crept in through a gap in the bedroom window and she pulled her duvet up to her chest. Her flat was far from luxurious, but at least she was safe.

'I signed a confidentiality agreement. If I tell you, they'll have my guts for garters. They're just protecting themselves,' Roz added hastily. 'They're lovely people. You'd be blown away if you knew who they were.'

'Did you get it checked by a solicitor?' Dympna said. 'You should never sign anything without getting it checked first.'

'There was no time, but I read it over and it's fine.'

No time indeed, Dympna thought. 'They shouldn't pressure you into signing something until it's been checked out.' But she knew her words were falling on deaf ears, and besides, it was too late now. All she could do was fish for further information. She gripped the phone tightly but tried to sound relaxed. 'Tell me about it. What's it like there?' A continuous bad feeling in her gut told her that Roz's predicament was something worth worrying about.

Roz sounded hesitant. 'I wish you could see it. They're taking such good care of me. I just wanted to let you know I'm OK.' She paused, took a breath. 'I don't know if I'll be able to ring you again, so don't worry if you don't hear anything.'

Dympna's jaw tightened. 'Now you listen to me, Roz Foley. You *will* ring me again, at least once a month, to let me know that you're OK. Even if it's just a text. You hear me? Because if I don't hear back, I'll get the guards on to you, I swear to God . . .'

'All right, all right, I promise.' Roz chuckled. 'Although I doubt the Gardaí would find me in the heart of New York.'

'Why the secrecy?' Dympna replied, pulling her duvet further up.

'Because they want to pass the baby off as their own. Honestly, nobody is holding me prisoner. I can come and go as I like.'

'So why are you whispering?'

'You know why. I don't want them to think I'm blabbing already. Besides, I had to give George my phone. They're dead against personal calls.'

'George?' Dympna frowned. 'Who's George?' She listened as Roz swore under her breath.

'Um . . . he's nobody. Forget I said that. Please, Dympna, don't ruin this for me.'

'All right, all right, I won't ask about him again. Listen, Roz, I need to ask you something . . .' Dympna prepared to say the words she had rehearsed. 'It's about the father . . .'

'Sorry, I've got to go, someone's coming. Take care, hun, love you.'

Dammit, Dympna thought, blurting out a quick response. 'You too. Make sure you ring me, text, anything.'

'Will do. Stop worrying. Bye.'

Dympna pushed her hair back from her face. Slouching in her bed, a rising storm of emotions made her turn cold. Things had changed since Roz had told her about the pregnancy. Seamus had been acting odd ever since finding out, too. She had broken a bond by speaking to him about it, but Roz's secrecy had planted a seed of suspicion that had bloomed into something dark and ugly. Up until lately, they had shared everything, as true friends did. She thought back to when she and Seamus had last rowed. He had been distracted and moody from the moment they hooked up that night, but had refused to tell her what was wrong. It was three and a half months ago, the date etched into her diary along with her outpouring of annoyance as she wondered what the hell had got into him. Even then, she wrote that Seamus was wrestling with something that he didn't want her to know about. Something he was ashamed of.

Was he the father of Roz's baby?

Dympna looked around her room, cloaked in shadows cast from the street lights outside. The flat was so quiet now that Roz had left. She did not want to believe that her best friend could commit the ultimate betrayal. 'Water finds its own level,' her mother sometimes said. Was it inevitable that the two people you loved the most would be drawn to each other, too?

She snuggled beneath her duvet, tears pricking her eyes. Was she seeing things that weren't there? But she hadn't imagined the awkwardness between Seamus and Roz. It was only when Roz had announced her pregnancy that everything had fallen into place. Dympna pictured the baby, a little miniature Seamus running around the flat. This wasn't how it was supposed to be. She snuffled, tears drizzling down the side of her face as she lay on her side. She was reading a lot into something that she knew very little about, but fear had taken root inside her. She could not bear to lose both her boyfriend and her best friend.

CHAPTER
TWENTY-FOUR
ROZ

I lay back on the sofa, listening to the celebrations taking place on the floor above. Sheridan had already informed me that she was breaking the news to her closest friends and cautioned me not to venture up. As if. The warning had been redundant, as she had yet to give me a lift pass. I could barely believe that not only were Daniel Watson and Sheridan Sinclair upstairs, but now, so was Adam Weiss. I had yet to step out of the sense of surreality that had cloaked me since my arrival.

At least I'd found time to give Dympna a quick ring. I hadn't told her there was darkness to my arrival, an edge to Sheridan's behaviour that made me feel afraid.

I looked again at the schedule Sheridan had given me. My day was broken up into three blocks. Morning consisted of medication, meditation and something called birth affirmations. After that came pregnancy stretches and drinking copious amounts of water. Then it was time for my breakfast of kale juice, muesli and fresh fruit. The afternoon schedule was much the same: a twenty-minute walk on the treadmill was followed by a lunch of 'pregnancy super-food'. My downtime consisted of reading and researching natural births. Even my 'afternoon nap' was timed. My evenings consisted of more supplements, pregnancy yoga, then birth affirmations as part of what Sheridan called her 'body and mind' routine. My spirits plummeted. Every day, every hour was accounted for.

I scanned the rest of the sheet to see what was termed 'morale boosters'. They consisted of time watching TV or a creative pursuit. But there was nothing in the schedule about going outside. Did she plan on keeping me hidden away for the next six months? My apartment was luxurious, but without windows I had no sense of time. I could be anywhere in the world. I turned the page, blurting a laugh.

'She's not serious . . .' I said aloud, scanning Dr Blumberg's appointments for weight and body measurements, spit and urine samples and once-a-month blood tests. But most mortifying of all was that I had to chart my bodily functions – how often I used the toilet, and what for. What bearing did these have on my baby? Was this some kind of joke? What gave her the right to say what time I woke and what time I went to bed? I curled up on the sofa. It was gone 11 p.m. and the day had taken its toll. I picked up the television remote control and was surprised to find a Netflix account already set up in my name.

I was drawn to one of Sheridan's early movies. In *The Greatest Gift* she played the role of a pregnant teenager who gave her baby to her sister in England when it was born. It was an old, obscure film, one I had not seen before. I covered my legs with a blanket off the sofa and soon became immersed. But there was something familiar about the scene as it played out, and it set my nerves on edge. I watched, gripped, as they walked down the corridor of the stately home.

'I've started the nursery,' the sister said, as she opened the bedroom door. 'It's just an undercoat. It's waiting for that special touch.' She turned to face Sheridan, her eyes moist. 'I have so many ideas.' She glanced around the empty room. 'But I want to work with you to pick out colours and design. Combine our energies into choosing the decor, so the baby can feel our love.' She chuckled. 'You probably think I'm silly, but . . .'

My mouth dropped open. Those were the same lines that Sheridan had used on me. Picking up the remote, I replayed the scene, over and over again. How much of her life was real and how much was made up?

'Sorry, I didn't mean to wake you,' Daniel said, as he took in my startled expression.

'What?' I said, shaking off sleep. 'I must have dozed off.'

I looked over his shoulder. He was down here on his own. What would Sheridan think? I was glad of his company, just the same. Human contact was more important than I realised.

'I brought you this.'

Daniel handed me a bowl of the most glorious-looking chocolate cake. He leaned forward as I took it and I caught the smell of whiskey on his breath. The top buttons of his shirt were open, revealing a tanned chest. I scooted up on the sofa, but he sat in the chair across from me and I relaxed, taking a spoonful of what tasted like heaven in my mouth.

'Are you OK?' he said, seeming genuinely concerned. 'Is it all a bit much?'

'A little,' I said honestly. 'But I don't want to sound ungrateful. This is an amazing opportunity and I . . .'

He raised a hand, interrupting my flow. 'No need to explain. It only feels like yesterday that I was struggling to find work. Now I can barely step outside the door without being papped.'

I nodded. Listening at the air vent, I'd heard most of their earlier conversation as they discussed the pressures of fame.

'I'm glad the baby is healthy,' I said. 'It's just strange, you know?' I licked the chocolate from my lips. 'I never thought I'd be sitting here talking to you. Only a couple of weeks ago I was stuffing my face with popcorn, watching you in the cinema . . .' I stopped myself. I had almost said 'with my best friend'. It was easy to let down my guard with Daniel, but he and Sheridan came as a pair.

'Ah, so you *have* heard of me,' he grinned. 'You played it so cool when we first met, I wasn't sure.'

I smiled as a blush fought to rise to my face – an instant reaction to being in his company.

'I've spoken to Sheridan,' he continued. 'Told her to take your feelings into consideration. We'll keep the scans to a minimum. She's just excited, that's all.'

'I'd be worried if she wasn't,' I said, twiddling the fringes of the blanket beside me on the sofa.

'If you ever need to talk, I'm here . . . Well, most of the time. My mum was Irish. Your accent – it reminds me of her.'

I wanted to ask him about her, but I was scared Sheridan would discover us cosily chatting about my hometown.

'That's nice,' I said, 'and I'm sure I'll settle in soon. It's amazing here.' My eyes fell on the schedule, but it was too soon to complain about Sheridan's plans.

Daniel seemed to sense my concerns. 'Don't worry about your schedule too much. Sheridan will get George to show you the sights. It'll take your mind off the baby for a while.' He checked his watch before rising. Taking the woollen blanket, he wrapped it gently around my shoulders before extending his hand for the empty bowl. I gave him a guilty smile. I had wolfed it down without thinking.

'Getting rid of the evidence?'

'Exactly,' Daniel replied. 'Best you get to sleep. She'll be down to check on you before she goes to bed.' He winked before turning away.

I fought a yawn. Watched as the lift was called to the upper floor. Was it Sheridan? What if she caught us together? I felt a sudden spike of fear. But Daniel wasn't taking the lift. Pulling a set of keys from his trouser pocket, he slotted one into the locked door. After giving me one last glance, he slipped away into the corridor. But before I could make out any more, the door had closed.

Seconds later, the lift door opened. It was Sheridan. The motion reminded me of a cuckoo clock I once owned. When it chimed, a little man disappeared through one door while a woman came out of another.

'Didn't you read the schedule?' Sheridan said, her eyes dancing around the room. 'It's well past your bedtime.'

She handed me a glass of some purple-looking liquid and I downed it in one go. It tasted like beetroot and had a bitter edge, but I was too tired to argue about the juices she insisted I drink. I slipped between the covers, wondering what she would say if she knew her husband had been in my room just seconds before. The way he'd winked at me was almost conspiratorial. I began to grow woozy, my eyelids like leaden shutters as I struggled to stay awake.

'I forgot to brush my teeth,' I murmured, although my words came out like gobbledygook.

'Shhh,' Sheridan said. 'Go to sleep. It's good for the baby.' She pulled up my covers as my eyes began to close. It felt strangely comforting to receive such tenderness from a woman who I was growing increasingly intimidated by. Even if I wanted to, I could not stay awake. Sheridan's perfume lingered as she leaned over my midriff. 'Goodnight, little starlet,' she whispered, and I realised she wasn't talking to me. But there was no sound of footsteps as I waited for her to leave the room.

I blinked, feeling disorientated. The room lights had been dimmed. How much time had passed? And how had Sheridan slipped away without making a sound? I squinted to make out a form on a chair at the end of my bed.

'Sheridan?' I said, my heart faltering as I leaned up on my elbows.

Sheridan had not left. She was sitting in the darkness, watching me sleep.

CHAPTER TWENTY-FIVE
SHERIDAN

Sheridan had gone to great lengths to find a sedative that would not harm the baby. Mike assured her the diphenhydramine powder was nothing more than an antihistamine laced with something extra to give it a little kick. It was bad enough coping with Leo's disruptive behaviour; she could hardly have her new arrival born with a birth defect. It was quite easy to disguise the powder in the juice and to be fair, she had tested it on herself first. The headaches it produced were her markers, and soon she had got the concoction down to a dull throb.

She balanced the shot glass in her hand as she walked into the lift and pressed the button to close the door. Her initial impression of Roz was good. But how much of that was an act? Regardless, Roz would bend to her will soon enough.

The lift doors opened before her, and Sheridan stepped out. With long strides, she made her way to the sofa, taking in every inch of the open-plan living space. The bed had been sat on but not slept in, and Roz's empty suitcase gaped open on the floor.

She advanced towards Roz, feeling a frisson of annoyance as she caught sight of the paperwork on the rug. 'Didn't you read the schedule? It's well past your bedtime.'

Roz stared, half-asleep. Jet lag must have kicked in. She accepted the drink thrust into her hand and knocked it back. She licked her lips, running her tongue over the beetroot-coloured stain left behind.

'Sorry . . .' she said, half-frowning as she seemed to wonder what she was apologising for. She looked dazed – was it from tiredness, or fear? The blanket that had been wrapped around her shoulders fell to the floor as she stood.

Sheridan thought of Daniel, and his caring nature. Had he been down here? She inhaled deeply through her nostrils. Was that alcohol she could smell hanging in the air? No. It must be the juice. He was upstairs, wasn't he?

'Come along, sleepy-head,' Sheridan said, echoing the words of her mother from what felt like a lifetime ago. 'You have a full day tomorrow. Best you get to bed.'

Meekly, Roz followed, slipping between the sheets. Humming softly, Sheridan pulled the duvet up to Roz's shoulder and tucked her in. The drug worked quickly, and Roz mumbled a string of incoherent words as she fought to stay awake.

'Shh, go to sleep. It's good for the baby.'

She ran her hand over Roz's hair. It was flaxen with natural highlights, just like hers. She pictured her little girl, imagining how she would look in plaits. The ribbons and bows would knock her Instagram followers dead.

As Roz softly snored, Sheridan dimmed the lights and slid into the wingback chair at the end of the bed. She observed their new purchase. Getting her here had been one of the hardest parts, and that was over with. No matter what happened from now on, the baby was hers. It would be the best investment they had ever made.

Sheridan's thoughts strayed to Leo, asleep upstairs. At least, she presumed he was. Her nanny took care of that side of things. She knew she should feel bad, but guilt failed to materialise. She'd heard about maternal feelings, that sudden rush of love, but it had never happened to her. Perhaps it was because she'd gone back to work once the initial shine of Leo's arrival had worn off. Or perhaps it was because she resented him. Each day she spent less and less time in his presence, and he became like a demanding puppy rather than her son. She thought about a scene in a movie she loved, in which one member of the family died just as a new one was brought to life. It was so very poignant, it almost brought a tear to her eye. That was a feat in itself. If it weren't for Daniel, she wouldn't miss Leo at all . . . Thoughts bobbed to the surface in the dark waters of her mind. He was an innocent child. Yet . . . She tried to imagine life without him. Just her, Daniel and their perfect little girl.

She watched Roz toss and turn, flinging an arm out to the side. She smiled, shook her head. Sometimes her own thoughts frightened even her.

What was Roz dreaming about? Daniel was probably asleep now, too. She did not realise that Roz was awake until the young woman sat up and stared at her in surprise.

'Sheridan?' she said, blinking in the dim light.

Sheridan rose, smoothed her duvet as she encouraged her to lie back down. Everything was under control. There would be no mistakes this time.

Sheridan walked towards the lift, her eyes flicking to the door-way that led to the secret room. To think, she was entertaining her friends just hours ago on the floor above. If they knew what was down here . . . She imagined their horrified faces if they were to discover the truth. People thought they knew her. They hadn't got a clue.

CHAPTER TWENTY-SIX
ROZ

The next morning, Sheridan wasted no time in introducing me to my new routine.

'I've cleared my schedule for the next six months, so I'll be working from home.' Her lips curled in a smile as she spoke.

I, on the other hand, wasn't sure how to feel about that. I stretched out on the yoga mat she had unrolled near the end of my bed. My living space smelt of oil burners, and the heady scent of frankincense tickled my nose. As we sat with our legs crossed in meditation, she told me to empty my mind, but all I could think about was the night before. Was she really watching me as I slept? If so, that was as creepy as hell.

Thirty minutes later, I worked on my pregnancy stretches and surmised it had probably been a dream. My head throbbed as I bent over into what Sheridan called a downward dog. Her body was lean and toned, her Lycra clinging to her like a second skin. I envied her flexibility as she changed positions with ease.

Dympna would have laughed her head off if she'd heard me chanting the birth affirmations Sheridan insisted I repeat: 'I am healthy and strong . . . Baby is perfect in every way . . . I am open and accepting . . . Baby is strong, healthy and beautiful . . .'

I noticed that Sheridan didn't ask me to say 'my baby', as was often the case with such chants. Each sentence was incorporated into a breathing pattern that gave me the giggles, but one disapproving look from Sheridan was enough to sober me up. Finally, she left me to go upstairs to check that Anna had prepared breakfast as instructed. I had barely five minutes alone before Juanita arrived to tidy my room. I had made the bed before her arrival. We were only a couple of hours into my schedule and already it felt so intense. I needed to draw, to walk the streets for inspiration. To explore.

Standing under the shower, I felt the last of my headache ebb away. Perhaps Sheridan was right, and the stretches and meditation had done me good. She only wanted what was best for me, after all.

'Tell me about yourself. I want to know everything about you,' Sheridan said as I took a seat beside her at their expansive kitchen table. It was made of marble, just like the kitchen counter, and was far superior to what I'd seen in kitchen showrooms at home. Dympna and I used to visit them, dream about the houses we would one day own. But I could never have imagined myself enveloped in such luxury as this. Every facet of this home screamed money, and felt so at odds with what I was used to in Dublin.

'My life's not very exciting,' I said, tucking into my breakfast of muesli with fresh fruit. The smell of Sheridan's freshly made coffee teased my senses, and I realised that I had yet to see her eat.

I looked around the room, which was as shiny as a new pin. All of this, just for the three of them. *Four.* I corrected my thoughts. Soon my baby would have a lifestyle others could only fantasise about. Sheridan's presence felt like a dream and I was sure I would wake up any moment with Dympna shoving a mug of tea under my nose. It was inconceivable to think that I had started off by subscribing to a website and ended up in the home of Daniel Watson and Sheridan Sinclair. The only way I could cope with it was to place all my focus on my unborn child. Not an hour of the day passed when she wasn't in my thoughts.

'I grew up in a sleepy town in Ireland,' I said eventually. 'My dad ran out on us when I was very young.' I swallowed my muesli, which now tasted like sand in my mouth. I hated talking about my past, but I did not want Sheridan to think I had something to hide. 'We were dirt-poor. I didn't know it back then, but my mother had issues with alcohol. She struggled with basic things and I was left on my own a lot while she went to work. It was tough.'

'You poor thing,' Sheridan said, her eyes flicking to the clock on the wall.

I responded with a watery smile. We were poles apart. How could she possibly understand? I shovelled in another mouthful of cereal.

'I wasn't short of money.' Sheridan picked up the reins. 'But my childhood was far from normal. I was earning a wage at the age of six. My mom was wildly ambitious. My dad had early-onset Alzheimer's. He died when I was eighteen.'

'I'm sorry to hear that. I thought your dad was the man in the show,' I said, after clearing my bowl. Regardless, my childhood self would have swapped places with her in a heartbeat. I would have lived my life in a shop window display if it had meant I had somewhere warm and secure to grow up, with food on the table and a clean bed at night.

'It's a common misconception,' Sheridan replied. 'Work featured in my life from a very early age, so sometimes even I got confused. I was educated from home and I didn't have time to make friends or develop relationships naturally. My friends were made on set; they auditioned for the part. It came as a shock when I hit my teens and the show ended. My real dad died and, well, Mom lost interest after that. I had to make my way in the real world by myself.'

I tried to imagine what it was like for Sheridan, going from everything to nothing at such a young age. 'I can't imagine it was easy working in the movie industry, especially with everything you hear about the "me too" movement.'

Sheridan arched an eyebrow. 'I could tell you a story or two. But I don't want to dwell on negativity, not when we have so much to look forward to. Tell me about the night you conceived. I want to hear how my baby was made.'

I baulked. How her baby was made? That question was even more intrusive than the one about my childhood. From what I was learning about Sheridan, she had no inner filter when it came to other people. Was it down to her upbringing, or did she see me as someone she had hired, just like the staff who cooked and cleaned for her? I looked around the kitchen for Juanita. She'd seemed to vacate the room the moment we stepped in. There was no sign of Anna or Leo, either. He must have gone to school.

'I don't like to talk about it,' I said, feeling the heat of Sheridan's gaze. 'Do you mind?'

Sheridan sipped her coffee, then gracefully placed the cup back on the gold-rimmed saucer. It was most likely designer, like everything else in this place. I thought of our chipped crockery in Ireland, of the ashtray I put my trinkets into. I'd barely arrived in New York and was already feeling the tug of home.

'You weren't in love?' Sheridan interrupted my thoughts, not one to let the subject lie.

I shook my head. 'Does it make a difference?'

She passed me the kale juice I had yet to drink. 'Of course not. If it did, I'd have asked before we signed the contracts.' She flashed me a smile. 'I'm enjoying getting to know you. I can't remember the last time I had a proper girly chat.'

I sighed. She was being so nice to me; I had to give her something. 'The day I got pregnant, hooking up was the last thing on my mind. But I was upset, lonely. He offered to take care of me. It was nice to feel protected.' My words were heavy with the burden of my secret. 'I'd always had a crush on him, but never acted on it. That night . . . it felt right.'

'I know what you mean.' Sheridan's kohl-lined eyes twinkled as she absorbed my words. 'Daniel and I tried for over a year to get pregnant with Leo. We were both under a lot of pressure at work. I'd all but given up. Then one night we got really drunk and it happened. The one time we didn't think about it was when I took.'

'Tell me about it,' I laughed. 'If it wasn't for Mr Jameson I wouldn't be here today.'

'Jameson?' Sheridan tilted her head to one side.

'Irish whiskey,' I chuckled. 'I don't normally drink it but we . . .' My words were cut short as I caught the expression on Sheridan's face. *Shit.*

'You were drunk when you conceived my baby?' Her words were low and thunderous, her expression icy cold. I stiffened. I had to come clean. Sheridan could see right through me and lying would only make things worse. Besides, how come it was OK for her and not for me? Slowly, I nodded.

'It's not as if I planned it. As you said yourself . . . these things happen.'

'Juice.' She pushed the kale juice into my hands, making it slop over the side. 'Drink your juice.'

'What?' I frowned, looking at the glass. The room fell silent, the air between us was thick with tension. I knocked the drink back, downing it in one. My stomach rolled, more with nerves than anything else. I wiped my fingers with a napkin. 'I'm sorry, I . . .'

But Sheridan seemed in no mood for my apologies. Her body was rigid, each word delivered with the simmering fury that bubbled underneath. 'What if you've damaged the baby? Have you thought of that? What else have you lied about?'

'Nothing, honestly. I stopped drinking the second I found out I was pregnant.' But my words were digging me into a deeper hole. It was weeks before I did a test. I could feel the blood draining from my cheeks.

Sheridan glared at me, her nostrils flaring as she inhaled. I was so shocked I could barely move. Only a couple of minutes ago we were chatting like old friends. I had never seen anyone in such a state of quiet fury, not even my mother.

She broke her gaze to glare at her watch before standing up. 'Get up. Breakfast is over.'

Her words were abrupt, her movements jerky. I remained in my seat, my mind racing as I tried to figure out what to do.

'I said get up!'

In one swift movement she wrapped my ponytail around her fist and yanked hard.

'Ow!' I screamed. 'You're hurting me!'

I tried to wriggle from her grasp, but she was a lot stronger than she looked. I had no choice but to follow as she marched me towards the lift.

'Please, Sheridan, I'm sorry – let me explain!'

But she was beyond reason, summoning the lift with her spare hand as I tried to loosen her grip.

'Go to your room!' Her words echoed in the hall. 'Go to your room and think about what you've done!'

The roots of my hair burned as they were plucked from my scalp. As she marched me into the lift, the doors began to close and she turned to walk away. I gasped as I lost my balance, falling on to my backside. Flashes of light pierced my vision as I hit my head against the handrail on the way down.

'Roz!' Sheridan cried after me, her voice imbued with instant regret. 'Are you OK?' Her voice echoed as the doors shut and the lift made its way down. *What the hell?* I was pregnant. She could have knocked me out cold.

With heavy legs I staggered to my feet as the lift reached the basement floor. Despite my head being woozy, self-preservation had kicked in, and I was not risking Sheridan coming down. *What happened back there?* I thought, as I wedged the doors open with a chair, a temporary measure to make the lift stay put. Wobbling to the en suite, I wet a towel under the cold tap and gently pressed it against the growing bump on my head. What had Sheridan said? *Go to your room and think about what you've done.* Was that how she had lived her early years? Groaning, I rubbed the back of my head. Right now, more than anything, I needed to speak to my friend.

I held my breath as I heard Sheridan's high heels click rapidly along the floor above. A sense of dread rose inside me. What if she came down the stairs? It wasn't as if I could lock the bathroom door. Sheridan had removed the key. What if I needed to protect myself?

I walked out into the open living space. There used to be a gym here, but all the weights had been removed. There was nothing I could use to defend myself. I stared at the door that led to the corridor, my anxiety growing as I waited for Sheridan to come down. Was I overreacting? Surely she meant me no harm. But still, the door remained closed.

What was she doing? Was she still furious or had she sent for help? A small voice piped up inside me: *You have only yourself to blame.* Sheridan had made it clear from the beginning: no smoking and no booze.

I ran over the events in my mind. It was just a bit of hair-pulling, wasn't it? It wasn't her fault I'd fallen. But I was pregnant. My hands went to my stomach. It was my job to protect the baby growing inside me. I would talk to Daniel, make things clear. If Sheridan laid another finger on me, I was out of here.

CHAPTER TWENTY-SEVEN
ROZ

I awoke with a start as fingers dug into my shoulder. It was Daniel, shaking me awake. I blinked to clear my vision. I must have fallen asleep. A sharp pain in the back of my head made me wince.

'Roz, are you OK?' Daniel asked, his handsome face creased with worry.

Why is he asking me? Why doesn't he ask his precious wife? I thought, scooting up on the sofa.

'What?' I said, trying to piece things together. I vaguely remembered getting the phone from my suitcase, then pacing the floor when I couldn't get a signal. I had wanted to let Dympna know where I was, in case things escalated even more. But had I put the phone back? If Sheridan found it there would be hell to pay. *Think, Roz, think.* My brain felt as if it had been replaced with cotton wool.

Taking a bottle of water from the mini fridge, Daniel strode across the room and offered it to me. 'Here, take a sip. Sheridan said you fell over in the lift.'

'Thanks.' I exhaled a relieved breath as I remembered shoving the mobile beneath the sofa cushion when I lay down to rest.

'What time is it?' I unscrewed the lid from the glass bottle of spring water.

'It's just gone two. Are you OK?' he repeated, sitting across from me. 'Sheridan said you were upset.'

'*I* was upset?' My eyes widened. 'She grabbed me by my ponytail and threw me into the lift. I . . .' Tears sprang to my eyes. 'I want to go home.'

'Hey, now,' Daniel said, his voice warm. 'Sounds like one big misunderstanding. Sheridan would never hurt you.' He extended his hand and I took the tissue he offered, watching him warily. 'I told her that you're young. And she has to take your hormones into account. You're bound to feel a little erratic with everything going on. I remember when I first came over from England . . .'

'Me? Erratic?' I interrupted. I was beginning to sound like a parrot, continuously repeating his words. I rubbed the bump on the back of my head. I certainly hadn't imagined that. 'What did she say happened?'

'Just that you were having a lovely morning, but then you had an argument over the kale juice. You knocked over the glass before stomping into the lift. Some of it must have been on your sneakers, and that's when you slipped and fell.' He held up his hands. 'I hold no judgements. I hate that stuff too. But you can't go off in a huff like that. And blocking the lift door open . . . it's not on. I had to access the stairs to check that you were OK.'

'I didn't block the lift . . .' I said, my back rigid as I sat up. Yet when I peered over, I could see that a chair had wedged the doors permanently open. 'I . . . I don't remember doing that.'

'It's no wonder – you've had a nasty bump on the head. Here, let me look.'

I sat in disbelief as Daniel moved closer, his words rebounding in my mind. Sheridan couldn't have told him about my drinking, and I wasn't keen on bringing it up myself. Perhaps it was a deal-breaker for Daniel, too. Now my memory of this morning's events was one big blur. The dull throb of a headache returned. I swallowed, my mouth dry. I was painfully aware of Daniel's proximity as he gently probed my scalp. His suit looked expensive, his cologne infiltrating my senses. Had he come back from work for this? The warmth of his hand sent tingles through me as he smoothed down my hair.

'It's just a bump,' he said, oblivious to my reaction. 'But we'd like the doc to check you out just the same. You OK with that?'

'OK,' I nodded glumly, needing reassurance myself.

'Good.' He pushed back his shirt sleeve and checked his watch. 'I've got to get back to work. Sheridan is desperate to sort things out. Will it be OK to leave you two together until the doctor gets here?'

I stiffened, and he crouched to meet my eyeline. I saw genuine concern in his eyes. 'Look. I know it takes two to tango. Sheridan can be bossy, but she'd never hurt you. One thing about her . . . she's always in control.'

He extended his hand to help me to my feet and I could not ignore the gesture. I watched him remove the chair before slipping on my shoes and following him into the lift. My soft spot for Daniel was probably clouding my judgement, but this was Daniel Watson, the man everybody loved. I so wanted to trust him.

Had I put the chair in the lift doorway? I could barely remember taking Dympna's phone out of my suitcase, so it was possible. Butterflies fluttered in my stomach as Daniel smiled. I told myself to get a grip. Thinking with my heart instead of my head was what had got me pregnant in the first place. Being abandoned by my father at such an early age had affected me more than I thought.

Daniel was beginning to feel like the safe harbour I needed. I watched as he pressed his security tag against the panel and pressed the button for the ground floor. As we moved upwards, I told myself that as long as he was around, I would be OK.

I held my breath as the lift doors opened. Sheridan was waiting for me in the hall.

CHAPTER TWENTY-EIGHT
SHERIDAN

Sheridan stood in the hall, arms tightly folded as she waited for the elevator doors to part. This morning's confrontation had back-fired – she'd never intended Roz to fall over like that. She wasn't thrilled about sedating her again so soon, but the girl had demonstrated a tiny spark of defiance that needed to be stamped out.

Yesterday's internet search had been fruitful. After looking up HEAT nightclub in Dublin, she had found Roz's image online. Sheridan wasn't doing anything underhand. Roz had listed it in her bio as a place she sometimes went to. It was a silly mistake, given the picture Sheridan had found of her. Bleary-eyed, the young woman was pictured raising a glass to the camera. But what was in it? Sheridan had itched to know. The date beneath left her in no doubt that Roz was in the early stages of pregnancy at the time. The image portrayed was far from the persona of the sweet Catholic girl that Roz had conned her with. Sheridan could not let it rest. She had to know for sure if Roz had been drinking on the night she conceived.

She could have confronted her last night, but she used the opportunity to test her this morning instead. Sheridan's lips thinned as she recalled their argument. It soon became apparent that if she wanted, she could extract any information from the young woman in her care. But could she make her believe that she was to blame for what happened?

Her question was answered the moment Roz stepped out of the lift. Her gaze low, she looked like a remorseful puppy after it has peed on the floor. *Good*, she thought. A sedative-induced sleep followed by reassurance from caring, trustworthy Daniel had left a whole ton of self-doubt lingering in the air. Sheridan made a mental note to tell Juanita to check Roz's dirty laundry for spots of blood. She would have to keep a close eye on her, now the trust between them was gone.

'Roz, honey, you gave me a terrible fright,' Sheridan said, placing her hands on her shoulders. 'Are you all right? How's your head? I've called Dr Blumberg – he'll be here in twenty minutes or so.' Her words were rapid, a panicked mother fretting over her child. Whatever she felt about Roz, Sheridan would never put the baby at risk.

Daniel left them to it as Sheridan led Roz into the living room.

'Sit.' Sheridan patted the sofa cushion next to her. Just like the rest of the house, the reception room was furnished in a simple yet elegant style. Vast windows were filtered by white net curtains, which acted as a precaution against the paparazzi's powerful zoom lenses. Usually, at this time of day, she would be going through her schedule with Samantha, her PA. George would be here too, keeping her up to speed with the latest celebrity trends. It was challenging, juggling the needs of her career with keeping Roz underground. Today an early morning appointment with her hair stylist had been followed by a Skype with her agent in LA. Privacy was everything, and Sheridan had fought to keep them all at bay.

'Have you had any bleeding?' Sheridan said. 'Any pains?'

'No,' Roz replied, with a gloomy shake of the head.

'I almost died when you fell over in the elevator. Then when I couldn't recall it . . . I thought you'd collapsed in there.'

'I'm sorry,' Roz blurted, her fingers tightly clasped together on her lap. 'I shouldn't have blocked the doors.'

'No, you shouldn't have,' Sheridan said, but there was disappointment, not animosity, in her voice. 'I would never have brought you over here if I'd known it would turn out like this.'

She had set the scene for full reconciliation mode. Vases of wild flowers filled the air with the sweet smell of meadow honey, and in the fireplace, artificial flames danced.

'But you pulled my hair,' Roz said, finally meeting her gaze. 'I've got a bump on my head. It really hurts.'

Sheridan lifted the sleeve of her blouse. 'So does the bruise on my arm, but we don't want Daniel knowing about that.' Roz's face paled as Sheridan displayed the bruise she had given herself the night before.

'How did that happen?'

Sheridan tilted her head to one side, mirroring Roz's movements. 'You did it. Don't you remember?'

Roz closed her arms across her chest, as if warding off her negative words. 'No . . . I don't remember doing that.'

'It started off as a silly argument. You knocked over your glass of juice . . .'

'I . . . I don't know.' Roz frowned. 'I remember getting juice on my fingers and using a napkin to wipe it off.'

'Yes, that's right. That's when you threatened to leave. I followed you to the elevator, begging you to come back. I know I shouldn't have but I . . .'

'What?'

'I reached out to grab you but got your ponytail instead.' Sheridan turned to Roz, well-practised angst expressed on her face. 'You spun around and hit me on the arm. But some of the juice must have been on the soles of your shoes because you fell back into the elevator.'

The fall had not been part of Sheridan's plans. Sometimes, she didn't know her own strength. She remembered jabbing the elevator button, distraught when she couldn't call it from the basement floor. Roz was the vessel for her baby. She could not afford for anything to go wrong now. She watched as Roz rubbed the back of her head, confusion creasing her features.

'I remember banging my head against the handrail. I heard you calling me when the doors closed.'

'I was in shock. I tried to call the elevator, but I figured you must have jammed the doors on the basement floor. I was so worried about the baby that I rang Daniel straight away.'

Roz twirled the silver Claddagh ring on her right hand. 'Why didn't you come down the stairs?'

'I couldn't find the keys to the basement,' Sheridan replied. 'Daniel carries a set for safe keeping.'

'I don't know what to say.' Roz sighed as if the weight of the world was on her shoulders. 'I'm sorry if I hurt you. That's not me at all.'

Sheridan felt the atmosphere change between them. Roz was falling for every word.

'I'm sure it's not,' she replied. 'Let's draw a line under it all.' She took Roz's hands in her own. 'I'm worried about you passing out.' She paused. Was she pushing her too far? Daniel insisted on no CCTV in the house, but if Roz agreed . . .

Before she knew it, the words had left her mouth. 'If it makes you feel better, I could install a monitor in your room . . .'

'No. Please,' Roz replied. 'I'd rather you didn't. I'll be fine.'

The doorbell signalled an end to their conversation and Sheridan let go of her hands. 'That must be the doctor. Anna will see him in. Are we good?'

'Yes,' Roz nodded. 'Of course.'

But Sheridan detected a hint of wariness. She didn't mind. Roz was her property and she would learn to comply.

CHAPTER
TWENTY-NINE
ROZ
JANUARY 2019

I absorbed week twenty of the pregnancy diary Dympna had gifted me, reading the words back to my unborn baby.

'You're the size of a banana now,' I said, the thought bringing a smile to my face. 'Not so much of a little bean any more, are you?' I flicked to the measurements on the page. 'You're six and a half inches from your little bottom to the tip of your head.'

I carried on reading as the book recommended the classes I should be taking at this stage. The thought of childbirth classes hadn't entered my brain. I was still dealing with the post-Christmas anticlimax and not seeing Dympna over the festive season.

It had been a miserable event compared to previous years. I had spent the day eating dinner for one in the basement as Sheridan entertained friends on the floor above. Sheridan and Daniel had bought me a present, and I enjoyed putting my new art supplies to good use. But lately all my sketches were of my little bean. Tucked away beneath my mattress, the pictures ranged from how I envisioned my daughter as a baby, right up until her wedding day. But it was not Sheridan pictured standing by her side – it was me. I'd talk to my bump as I drew, imagining an alternate universe for us both. One where lack of money wouldn't separate us. Where we could live our best lives. Some were spotted with my tears; others crumpled in a fit of frustration. But they were all hidden away.

I dared not draw Sheridan in case I offended her, and if I sketched Daniel, Sheridan could get the wrong idea and think I had a crush on him. So I opted for creating a few self-portraits to justify my allowed free time. But the mirrors in my room were plastic, so my sketches looked more like a Pablo Picasso than my own work.

Not that it mattered today. All my concerns were focused on the latest magazine I'd discovered nestled inside my pillowcase, placed there while I'd been in the bath last night. There could be no doubt that this issue of *Celeb Goss* had been left for me to find. Like magic, the previous magazine that had been in my bedside table had disappeared. I'd panicked until I found the other edition in my pillow. Its main story was about Sheridan. Was someone trying to warn me? Someone who had a lot to lose themselves?

Celeb Goss Magazine
SHERIDAN'S BABY JOY
By Alex Santana
July 2014

Last week, fans of celebrity couple Sheridan and Daniel were thrilled to hear the news of the birth of their baby boy. In the run-up to Leo's birth, Sheridan was seen looking pale and drawn, sparking concerns for her health. This week, she was spotted leaving her therapist's in New York. All traces of her baby bump have disappeared, and she appeared painfully thin. 'Motherhood has taken its toll on Sheridan,' our source says. 'A week before the baby's birth, she dismissed her staff, apart from one. This was a time when she should have been accepting help from others, not sending them away.'

Rumor has it that Sheridan's mother, Dorothy, has yet to see the new arrival. 'Things have always been tense between Sheridan and her mom, and Sheridan isn't accepting visitors at this time.'

It's hardly surprising that Sheridan is not seeking parental advice from her mother, given how badly things ended between them. For years, the public were glued to *It Takes All Sorts*, this part-drama, part-reality show. But the series ended after allegations of abuse were made. Things turned ugly and Sheridan, then eighteen, was later awarded $20 million in a landmark case regarding her mother's abuse and neglect. Allegations of non-payment, child cruelty, a lack of education, and overwork were made.

Here at *Celeb Goss*, we hope that Sheridan's new addition will heal the rift that still exists. But could growing up in such a dysfunctional bubble be partly why she is struggling with her new baby today? Surely at times like these, every woman needs her mother to provide guidance and support. So why is Dorothy nowhere to be seen? Last week, Daniel's mother made the trip from the UK to the States to meet her first grandchild. 'Seventy-year-old Lesley was completely smitten by the newborn,' our source says. 'However, New York was all a bit much for her, and she stayed for just a few days.' With his mom having returned home, and his wife seemingly unwell, how is Daniel coping with juggling work and fatherhood?

We hope our favorite celebrity couple get back on their feet soon.

Beneath the veneer of the reporter's concern, I could sense the spite. My frown deepened as I shoved the magazine into my pillowcase. I had put off calling Dympna for fear of upsetting her, but now, more than ever, I needed advice. Easing myself off the bed, I searched the wardrobe for my suitcase, which was stored at the back. My thoughts were racing as I found the phone and quickly switched it on. Shouldn't I wait and give Sheridan a chance? I gripped the phone between my fingers. If nothing else, I could tell Dympna where I was, and if she persuaded me to go home . . . well, perhaps it wouldn't be such a bad thing after all.

My mouth grew dry as I dialled her number. What was I going to say? But after five rings, I was greeted with her answer phone.

I took a deep breath. 'Hi, Dympna, it's me . . . Roz.' It felt strange uttering her name aloud. It was eight weeks since I'd called. 'Listen, sorry for not ringing sooner. I miss you all like hell. I, um . . .' I paused to gather my thoughts. 'I need your advice. I'm fine and everything but . . .' *Oh God*, I thought, *I can't just blurt out that I'm being kept prisoner*. 'I thought I should give you my address. It's just that . . . I've not been able to come and go as I like. In fact, I've not been able to leave at all.' I sighed, imagining her reaction. 'Anyway, no need to call the cavalry. They've not hurt me or anything, but I'd really like your advice. I've got to go but I'll ring you again in an hour. We can talk about it then. I'm staying in

New York, with Sheridan Sinclair. Crazy, right?' I forced a chuckle before realising something was wrong. I pulled the phone away from my ear and stared at the blank screen. 'No,' I whispered. The battery was dead. How much of my message went through before it was cut off? Returning to the suitcase, I rifled through its folds. My spirits plummeted as I curled my fingers around the three-pin plug. What was I thinking? It wouldn't fit a US plug socket. What part, if any, of my message would Dympna receive? I checked my watch as the lift activated from above. Shoving the phone back into the suitcase, I prepared to go upstairs. Sheridan must never know about the call.

Easing into the chair at the kitchen table, I rubbed my stomach as the baby did the fandango under my skin. My mood was low, but I tried not to let it show.

'Is she kicking?' Sheridan asked, invading my personal space. As always, she didn't ask before lifting my sweatshirt and placing her hand on my bump.

'Yes,' I said awkwardly as she leant over me. 'She's lively this morning.'

Sheridan's hair was styled back from her face and she had changed into a designer dress. I felt like a slob in comparison, wearing my tracksuit bottoms now that I had outgrown my jeans. I was torn, because part of me still wanted to go home. There was no denying that Sheridan was head over heels in love with my baby. The trouble was, so was I. I told myself I was being selfish, that she was the perfect mother for my child. But still, I felt a prisoner in my surroundings, and a sense of foreboding remained.

'I can feel her.' Sheridan smiled, her eyes alight as she bent to speak to my bump. 'Hello darling, this is your mommy.' Both her hands were on my stomach now. I turned my head to escape the citrus smell of her perfume, which would have been pleasant in any situation but this.

A small gasp escaped her lips as she was rewarded with another kick. 'What does it feel like?' she asked in wonderment, her hands warm on my skin.

I looked at her quizzically. 'The same way it felt when you were expecting Leo?'

'Of course,' she said, her smile wavering. 'I meant, what does it feel like for you?' Her hands cupped over my belly button as I failed to respond. 'I wish Daniel was here for this.'

Heat rose to my cheeks as I imagined Daniel's hands on my stomach. We had grown friendly over the last few weeks, although he seemed more interested in me than the baby I was carrying. I had come to treasure his secret visits, but lately he was working all hours and I hardly saw him at all.

As she left to answer her phone, Sheridan's comment about the baby kicking burned in my mind. Had she been pregnant with Leo at all? And why was she so possessive of my bump? Her obsession with health checks and schedules was relentless, and I hated the creepy adjoining surgery I had to attend for Dr Blumberg's weekly blood and urine tests. Sheridan worked hard to keep me apart from Leo, and I caught a glimpse of the little boy only once. He was adorable, and with Daniel as his father it was easy to see where he got his looks from. The question was, did he carry Sheridan's genes? I lacked the courage to ask her. After all, what did it have to do with me? I understood the risk involved in her keeping me in her home. Every day she was surrounded by people, and it wouldn't do to have Leo telling tales. I sat quietly eating my muesli as I mulled everything over. My problem was that I had far too much time to think. I masked the aftertaste of my kale juice with some chopped strawberries from a bowl. Everything tasted so much better now I had given up junk food.

'Don't forget to take your supplements,' Sheridan said as she returned, punctuating her words with a sigh. 'I wish you'd taken folic acid during the first three months of your pregnancy.'

I had apologised a thousand times, yet she kept bringing it up.

'That's all right,' I said, in an effort to please her. 'I'm Irish. I've eaten lots of cabbage to make up for it.'

My words evoked a smile.

I thanked Juanita as she took my bowl, but no response came. Not a word of English had passed between us over the last few weeks – and it wasn't for a lack of effort on my part. Surely she could understand the basics, like 'hello' and 'thank you'? Each time I spoke, her eyes flicked to Sheridan, and I wondered if Sheridan had issued the order not to speak.

George was here already, his presence filling the room.

'Good morning, Buttercup,' he said, bending to give me a side hug.

'Morning. Nice threads,' I replied, referring to his mustard-coloured suit.

'Thanks!' he said proudly. 'I bought it in a charity auction. It's the same suit Ryan Reynolds wore to the screening of *Deadpool*.'

'You should have seen it when he got it – the arms and legs were out to there,' Sheridan laughed, extending her hands.

I could see what she meant. Ryan Reynolds was a heartthrob of mine, and over six foot two.

'Nothing a good tailor couldn't fix,' George sniffed, quickly changing the subject to complain about the weather.

It was good to speak to someone other than Sheridan, and George always seemed to lighten her mood. After talking to her about her schedule, George turned back to me. 'Looking forward to our little trip out?'

'What trip?' Weeks had passed and I couldn't remember the last time I'd been allowed out in the fresh air.

'Forgotten already? I told you I had a treat in store,' Sheridan said, flashing me a smile. 'My baby has hit the twenty-week mark today – it's something to celebrate.'

My brow furrowed. I had no recollection of such a conversation. Since becoming pregnant, my memory had suffered. I could be fine for days, and then out of the blue I'd wake up with a throbbing headache and little recollection of the night before. Sheridan said it was my body's way of telling me to slow down, but I was not convinced. I consoled myself that the blood tests would pick up any underlying health issues.

'I've asked George to take you sightseeing,' Sheridan continued. 'I'm meeting Monica for lunch and you deserve a rest from the schedule for today.'

I could only imagine what her friend Monica looked like, as every time visitors arrived, I was banished to the basement. Thoughts of getting outside instantly lifted my mood. I was already anticipating filling my lungs with crisp fresh winter air.

'I'd love that. Thank you,' I said, beaming at them both.

Sheridan expressed her sorrow at not being able to come, but to be honest, I was glad. I was still unsure how I felt about her. The hair-pulling incident had left me with a sense of unease. I'd been getting flashbacks, and the incident had not been as she described.

This was my opportunity to get George alone and get his take on things. Someone was leaving magazines in my room. I knew it wasn't Sheridan, because they were back issues of *Celeb Goss*. The only other people with access were Juanita or Daniel, and I couldn't see it being either of them. I recalled the last time

George and I were alone together, when I was getting out of the car. His walls had come down for a brief moment, and I remembered his grip tightening around my arm, his words urgent as he whispered that we were being watched. Behind his jokes and banter I sensed another side. Someone whose actions were measured. Someone on their guard. One thing I knew for sure: there was a lot more to this set-up than Sheridan was letting on.

CHAPTER THIRTY

ROZ

By lunchtime, George and I were in a restaurant in Downtown Manhattan. I liked the Hollywood-type setting and took in the pictures of celebrity visitors lining the walls. But today each seat was filled with tourists, their faces alight with wonder as they chatted about their itinerary. I was glad to be wearing the Sketchers that Sheridan had gifted me. The weather was gloomy, in keeping with our visit to the 9/11 Memorial, which made me forget my own worries for a while. George told me of his own experiences of the tragedy, and it was interesting to focus on something different. He took me to Macy's, and I gladly endured the bracing winds as we took a quick boat ride around the Statue of Liberty. I felt like such a tourist, and wished I could have taken pictures of each trip.

The restaurant was pleasantly warm, and I wiggled my toes as the heat returned to my feet. I observed George check his phone for the hundredth time that day. The closer I watched, the more guarded he became.

I was desperate to talk about what had happened with Sheridan in the lift, but equally scared that my gossiping would get back to her. I missed my phone. I even missed my mam. Pregnancy had opened my eyes, highlighting the importance of the mother/ daughter relationship. I picked at my French toast and caramelised bananas, trying to work out a way to separate George from his screen. Feeling the heat of his gaze, I looked up.

He lowered his phone, placing it face down on the table. He had already finished his club sandwich, and all that remained were crumbs on his plate. 'What's wrong? Aren't you having a good time?'

There was no point in asking him outright just yet, if my suspicions were correct. 'It's been amazing, thanks. Just my bladder playing up. Do you know where the toilets are?'

George craned his neck behind him towards the far corner. But instead of following his gaze, I reached out, snatched his phone and switched it off.

'Hey! What are you doing?' he said, scrambling to grab it back.

'Sshh.' I nodded towards the other diners as I held the phone tightly to my chest. 'You don't want to make a scene now, do you?'

Grumbling under his breath, George sat back down. 'Hand it over,' he spat.

'Not until you tell me what's going on. Is Sheridan recording us?'

'Don't be stupid,' he answered, but the fear in his eyes told me I had hit the nail on the head. 'Now give it back. I need to turn it on.'

I shook my head. If Sheridan wasn't tracking us, why was he so desperate to get it back? 'Please, George. I've got nobody. I need your help.'

'You don't understand.' He stretched out his hand. 'There's a lot riding on this. I could lose more than my job.'

So not only was Sheridan keeping tabs on us, she had something on George. I sighed and handed the device back. Yet his fingers hovered over the on button.

'What do you need to know?' George asked. 'Make it quick.'

I pushed my plate away and leaned over in his direction, keeping my voice low. 'A few weeks ago, Sheridan pulled my hair, and I fell over and banged my head. Is she a violent person?'

'What? You must have done something to upset her. What did you say?'

'She found out that I was drunk when I conceived.' I was horrified to feel tears rising to my eyes as each anxious word left my lips. 'I want to go home, but she's insisting I stay. I . . . I don't think I have any choice.'

George sighed, deep and heavy. 'Are there any other secrets you've kept from her?'

I shook my head. I had lied about the baby's father, but even Dympna could not extract that from me. A gale of laughter rose from a family in the corner and my frown grew as I folded my arms tightly across my chest.

'I warned you that you were arriving in the middle of a shitstorm. A member of staff let her down and she can't stand being lied to. Just be on your best behaviour and do everything she asks.'

'Then there's the magazine articles . . .' I checked for a flicker of recognition in George's face, but there was none.

'What articles?'

I waited for a waitress to pass before continuing. 'In *Celeb Goss*. They said Sheridan's marriage is in trouble. That all's not as it seems.'

'Are you crazy? Don't mention that rag around Sheridan – they've had it in for her since day one.' The whites of George's eyes grew as he drove his message home.

'I know, but it's the baby . . . I worry how she'll be with her.'

'Have you ever heard Sheridan raise her voice to Leo?'

I shook my head. I hadn't heard Sheridan shout at Leo because she never spent any time with him.

George fiddled with his phone. 'Sheridan's protecting her interests. You can't blame her for that.'

My pulse quickened. 'What if I don't give her my baby, what then?'

George leaned forward, his words harsh and low. 'I like you, Roz, but I don't owe you anything and I'm not putting my neck on the line for you.'

But I was not ready to let the subject drop. 'Am I in danger? Is that what you're saying?'

George swore under his breath. 'Nobody crosses Sheridan Sinclair. Give her what she wants and you'll be fine.'

'But you said she had something on you . . . Maybe we could help each other.'

'Will you give it a rest!' George's face flushed. 'In a few months you'll be back home, with a big wad of cash in your account. It's not so easy for me. I can't just walk away.'

My frown deepened as I watched him turn on the phone and bring the app back to life. He pressed a finger against his mouth, a gesture of warning. I was right. She was recording our conversations, and I wasn't the only one with something to lose.

CHAPTER THIRTY-ONE
DYMPNA

'I need to talk to you.' Dympna cornered her father, John, in the hallway of her family home.

'Sure thing, princess. What's the problem?'

Dympna hooked her thumbs into her jean pockets. She loved her father but hated asking him for help. Since when had their relationship become so strained? If she had to pin it down, she would say it was in her teens, when she'd stopped being his little girl. She knew he would drop everything to come to her aid.

'Not here,' she said. 'Somewhere private.' Her mother was in the kitchen of their four-bedroom home, most likely listening in to every word they said. It wasn't that she was particularly nosy; just that she knew Dympna would not ask for help unless there was something drastically wrong.

Her father's features were unreadable as he rubbed his unshaven chin. Years of being in the police had helped him develop a perfect poker face.

'Fancy coming for a drive?' he asked, fishing his car keys from his pocket. 'I have a quick call-on to make. We can chat in the car.'

Dympna recognised the term. A 'call-on' was an enquiry with regard to a police case. It was meant to be his day off work, but he never truly switched off. 'I'd rather we went for a coffee first. Can you do your call-on after that?' She needed his undivided attention. This could not wait.

'Sure,' he said, opening the door. Dympna dipped her head as she ducked under his arm and escaped into the fresh air.

The coffee shop was warm and not particularly busy thanks to the post-Christmas lull. Dympna knew this was one of the places where her father spoke with informants. She could imagine him sitting at the back with a good view of who was coming in through the door. Her dad had all sorts of contacts in the underworld, mixing with people her mother called the undesirables of society. But someone had to keep them in line. Given the number of commendations he received, he seemed to do a good job. Police life had always interested Dympna, but her fear of failure was all-consuming, and she was too scared to follow in her father's footsteps in case she did not match up. She was short, overweight and with a terrible head for figures. She knew she could do better than her cleaning job, but she couldn't bear to embarrass her dad. One day her brother would join the Gardaí and make them all proud.

Safely ensconced in the booth with their coffees, Dympna rested her notebook and phone on the table. Taking a few precious seconds, she orchestrated her words so she'd sound like an adult and not some upset kid who had lost her favourite toy. She knew what she was about to say could be construed as far-fetched, and she hoped her father would not laugh in her face.

'Are you in trouble?' John said, reading her worried expression. 'Is that what it is?'

'No, of course not. It's Roz,' Dympna replied. 'She's gone to America and told everyone it's a work placement, but it's not.' Dympna stared at her mug, sliding her fingers through the handle and taking comfort from its warmth. 'I'm scared she's in trouble over there.' Her eyes flickered to her father's. His gaze was firmly on her. 'I want you to use your contacts to find out if she's OK.'

'Really?' John chuckled, shaking his head. 'You want to involve the police because you miss your friend?'

'Please, Dad, it's serious. I'm worried about her.'

'I see,' he said, giving nothing away. 'And what's the real reason she's over there?'

'You can't tell anyone. She's sworn me to secrecy.' Dympna flushed as she recalled telling Seamus, who had refused to discuss it ever since.

'Is she breaking the law?'

'No.'

'Then you have my word. What's she up to?'

'She's selling her baby.' Dympna blurted the words. She hated to break their promise, but this could be a life-threatening situation – in which case, all bets were off.

Her father's eyebrows shot up. All traces of his smile had disappeared. A long torturous silence passed between them. Dympna shifted in her chair. His unreadable expression was useful when dealing with criminals, but Roz was not a criminal; she was her best friend. Her stomach knotted at the thought of her being so trapped and alone.

'She got pregnant from a one-night stand,' Dympna said, her words tinged with shock and disbelief. Was it *really* a one-night stand with a stranger, or had Roz left because she couldn't face up to what she had done? Dympna pulled the sleeves of her woollen jumper up to her fingers – something she had done since she was a little girl. A small part of her wondered about the identity of the baby's father. She wanted Roz to be safe, but she wanted the truth, too. 'She left me a voicemail. I'm really worried . . .'

'Wait a minute, let me get this straight.' Dympna's father gesticulated with his hands. 'Not only is Roz pregnant, but she's gone to America to sell the baby. To whom? Where's she staying? What do you know?'

Dympna's shoulders dropped as she exhaled a long, heavy breath. Not enough. She didn't know anywhere near enough. She told her father about the website, how they had laughed as they picked prospective couples as if it were some kind of joke. Why hadn't Dympna taken things more seriously? Was it because deep down she wanted the baby out of her sight? She wanted to replay the message but had to get things into context first.

'The adoptive parents are a diamond couple, which basically means they're millionaires,' she explained. 'Once Roz saw that, her head was turned. She's always had a hang-up about money because of the tough time she had growing up.' The words seemed tragic as they left Dympna's lips. 'She rang me when she got there, but only because I gave her a mobile phone and told her to hide it from them.'

'She had to hide it? Why? Surely she has a right to call?'

Dympna shook her head. 'She lied on her profile. Said she had no family and no friends. Now do you see? They took her on because nobody would miss her when she was gone.' Dympna opened her slim black notebook to a bookmarked page. 'She first rang me from the hotel.'

She handed the notebook to her father, and his eyes moved from left to right as he read through scribbled details of her call. 'It was in the centre of New York. She said she had a view of a bridge with writing on, and a road underneath. Then there was this mention of someone named George who confiscated her phone. He took her to the couple's house and I've barely heard from her since.'

She met her father's gaze, realising she had taken on the role of police officer in this conversation. If it weren't for the awful circumstances, she would enjoy having to think on her feet. She explained about the confidentiality agreement and how Roz had not checked it out first. 'She was set to make a lot of money, but it makes me wonder if they intended paying her at all. I mean, why the one-way flight? And why were they so cagey about who they were?'

Dympna realised she was expressing her thoughts aloud. Thoughts that had plagued her for months. Activating her voicemail, she played the message on speakerphone. If this didn't persuade her father, nothing would. Roz's voice haunted the air between them, and she watched as he scrutinised the call.

'Hi, Dympna, it's me . . . Roz. Listen, sorry for not ringing sooner. I miss you all like hell. I, um . . . I need your advice. I'm fine and everything but . . . I thought I should give you my address. It's just that . . . I've not been able to come and go as I like. In fact, I've not been able to leave at all.' Roz's words came in stops and starts, followed by an inhalation of breath before the message came to an abrupt end.

'She was about to give me her address.' Dympna said. 'She could be hurt. I've tried ringing her back, but the phone line is dead.'

'Well, let's not get carried away here,' John replied. 'She sounds worried, but not scared. She said she's unharmed. But the fact she wants to give you her address means that something is potentially wrong. My biggest cause for concern is that she's not able to come and go.' He met Dympna's gaze. 'You're right to be concerned. Let's get the ball rolling and see what we turn up.'

'Thanks,' Dympna said, relieved her dad was taking her seriously. It was good to share the burden at last.

Her father was deep in thought, already planning ahead. 'I'll look into the legitimacy of this Miracle-Moms site first. The fact that she signed an official agreement suggests that they planned to follow this through.'

'Roz told me it would blow my mind if I knew who the couple were.' Dympna slipped on her glasses before flicking through the pages of her notebook to a list. 'I've narrowed it to about fifty people who would blow me away, and if it's a celebrity couple then there are a lot less.'

'Very good,' her father said, looking suitably impressed. 'Did she sound scared the last time you spoke?'

'That was two months ago.' Dympna licked the froth from her lips after a sip of her cappuccino. 'She said she was fine, but she was whispering, and she didn't text or ring on Christmas Day. Please, Dad. She's in trouble. I can feel it in my bones.'

'OK,' John replied. 'What about the baby's father? Did she say who he was?'

Dympna shook her head. She was too upset to relay her suspicions. She didn't know if there was a future for her and Seamus any more. 'The da didn't come into it because they want to raise the baby as their own. I told her she should stay in Ireland and . . .'

'Wait,' her father interrupted. 'They want to pass the baby off as theirs?'

Dympna nodded.

'Then go through your list of people and find any celebrities who've announced a pregnancy over the last few weeks. Their baby should be due around the same time as Roz's. That should narrow it down.'

'Oh, yeah . . . why didn't I think of that?' Dympna's pulse quickened at the prospect of finding her friend.

'Remember – all we have is a concern for her welfare. Without a crime, there's not a lot we can do. I'll enquire with the New York police, but I can't see them giving me much time.'

'It's worth trying to get the hotel CCTV – that is, if it's not taped over.' Dympna's knowledge of closed-circuit television had been picked up from her dad.

'Hmm . . . But these hotels make their living off discretion. In the unlikely event that they have it, they're not going to hand it over just like that.' John paused to gulp his coffee. 'I need time to think about this, come up with a plan. Listen.' He scratched the back of his head. 'Best we keep this to ourselves for now.'

Dympna nodded emphatically, a red spiral curl falling into her face.

The coffee shop was almost empty now, and one of the waitresses began to sweep the floor. 'I can't see this place lasting much longer . . . Shame,' Dympna's father mumbled under his breath. He pocketed the notebook. 'I'll hold on to this for now. If you hear from Roz again, let me know.'

'What should I say if she rings? They might be listening in.' Dympna had imagined all sorts of awful scenarios since Roz's call.

'Ask if she's in danger. If she says yes, then it will give us more leverage to work with.' He raised a cautionary finger. 'No exaggerating, though. If these people are as powerful as you say, then we have to tread carefully.' He checked his watch before rising from his seat.

Dympna's legs felt weak with relief. To think she'd been worried about her father's reaction. A swell of pride rose. He was there when she needed him. Now it was up to her to be there for Roz.

CHAPTER THIRTY-TWO

SHERIDAN

Sheridan rested her menu on the crisp white table linen. She ate for sustenance, not for pleasure, but Raffaele's was one of the few places in New York where the food made her mouth water. There was a simplicity to it that appealed to her, a wholesomeness she could not find elsewhere. The low clunk of double doors signalled meals making an arrival, and the aroma of creamy pasta dishes roamed tantalisingly in the air. She would order her favourite: Parmesan-crusted chicken finished with a Chardonnay butter sauce, accompanied by whipped potatoes and steamed broccoli. She glanced around, taking in the recent refurb as she relaxed into the Italian leather seat. Chandelier after chandelier sparkled like diamonds overhead, and exquisite glass pillars contained myriad tropical fish darting this way and that. They were the restaurant's talking point, deflecting from the absence of windows, which protected the identity of the diners within. Privacy was everything, hence the distance between tables and the background music that softened the chatter in the room.

Sheridan's eyes flicked to her Cartier watch. If Monica didn't arrive soon, she would start without her. Sheridan could not be away from home for very long because she needed to keep an eye on Roz. She surveyed her fellow diners, allowing the soft piano music to wash over her. The restaurant was one of New York's top establishments, and there, amongst her own people, she felt truly at home. Their money was so tangible you could smell it. In her social circle, you were a nobody if you didn't own your own private jet.

People like Monica were merely visitors, pressing their noses against the windowpanes of their world. Monica was sweet, but she avoided publicity, which suited Sheridan just fine. Like Daniel, Adam was on his way up, and the last thing Sheridan needed was another power couple threatening to take their thrones. She took a sip of her virgin martini. The usual people were in town; a mixture of agents, celebrities, supermodels and pop stars contributed to the low chatter in the room. The people here had egos so large they needed their own zip code. But not Daniel; not yet. He'd given up everything to establish their brand: cigarettes, booze, playing around. But he did not react well to having his freedom curbed. A shiver ran down Sheridan's spine as her old fears came into play. The odds were not in her favour, which was why she had to work twice as hard to keep their union solid. Dipping her hand into her bag, she slid out her mobile phone and checked on George's location through the Friend Finder app. A separate notification came through as George sent the latest recording of his conversations with Roz. She would listen to them later, checking for any gaps between recordings so every minute was accounted for.

As she lowered her phone, her gaze fell on Felicity Grey. Twenty years Sheridan's senior, she was a fading actress well beyond her prime. Inhaling a sudden breath, Sheridan took in her ragged features. What surgeon had butchered her this time? Her lips were bulbous; the skin on her face tugged so tightly it appeared painful to the touch. Twin black lines represented her eyebrows, setting her face in cartoonish shock. Not that the obscenely young actor across from her seemed to mind. Sheridan recognised him as a clinger-on. Rumour had it he was willing to sleep his way to the top. He made an adequate replacement for Felicity's movie producer husband, given he had left her for a much younger model, too. Sheridan sighed. Would that be her in twenty years' time? Or would she end up like her mother, penniless and alone? Cold dread spread like ice water through her veins.

'Sorry, traffic was hell.' Monica's Boston accent infiltrated her thoughts. Slightly breathless, she paused to air-kiss Sheridan's cheeks. Sheridan mentally assessed her wardrobe, a low-cut Saint Laurent print blouse with a knee-length black skirt.

Monica briefly acknowledged the maître d' as he pulled out her chair. 'Howareya?'

It was the typical Bostonian greeting, a mixture of eastern New England dialect delivered in her own unique style.

'Fine.' Sheridan wasted no time in ordering Monica a drink.

'I'm impressed you got a table. Adam called yesterday – they said they had nuthin' until next week.'

Sheridan forced back a smug smile. Tables were allocated on a tier system and she never had to wait. 'I can't stay long, I'm afraid – I've got a new member of staff I need to keep an eye on.' It was a lie, a cover in case Monica should ever see Roz at the house.

'Really? What's she like?' Monica paused. 'I say she, but I shouldn't presume.'

'She's inexperienced, but Daniel loves her. He only hired her because she's Irish.' She smiled at Monica's quizzical expression. 'His mom's Irish. You must be the only person on the planet who doesn't know that.'

Magazine articles contained everything from the colour of his eyes to his favourite flavour chewing gum. In the early days, Daniel used to chat to interviewers as if they were his friends. He was more guarded now, but his early indiscretions still did the rounds. Sheridan had learned from her childhood to only tell people what you wanted them to believe.

In the end, she went for a salad; no dressing, no oil. Felicity Grey's presence was enough to curb her appetite. *The ghost of her future self?* She picked at her iceberg lettuce while Monica devoured her pasta dish.

'How's Adam?' Sheridan asked, nodding towards the diamond on Monica's pinky finger. 'Is that a precursor to an engagement ring?'

'Not much chance of that,' Monica replied, her hand before her mouth as she chewed the last of her food. She rested her cutlery on her plate. 'To be honest, I'm worried . . .' She dabbed the napkin against her lips. 'But you knew Adam before me . . . I shouldn't be bringing this to your door.'

Now she had Sheridan's attention. If developments were under-way, she needed to know. She reached across the table, squeezed Monica's hand. 'Hey, you're my friend. Now tell me . . . what's wrong?'

Monica chewed on her bottom lip, her conflicted emotions creasing the corners of her eyes. 'I promised not to say anythin'.'

'I won't say a word. Is it work? Has he been offered a part?' It was not unusual for actors to be separated from their loved ones for months when they filmed on location abroad.

'It's his agent,' Monica replied with a sigh.

Sheridan knew TJ Greene, the renowned agent to the stars; he was Daniel's agent, too. She could see him in her mind's eye: his over-tanned skin, too-white teeth and crocodile smile. Sheridan had sought out a female agent because she refused to deal with TJ, that misogynistic pig. She waited for Monica to continue, refusing the waiter's offer of dessert. The restaurant had grown quieter, and she felt a little better now that Felicity Grey had left.

'He wants to pair Adam with a supermodel. You know, the Swedish one that won Miss World?'

'Klara Johansson?' Sheridan replied.

Monica nodded. 'He's already coming up with a double name for them both. The Kladams, or something stupid like that. He said it's all for show . . .' Her chin wobbled as she fought a battle to hold everything in place. 'But birds of a featha flock togetha. What chance have I got against someone like her?'

Monica enumerated all the reasons why she was not in the same league as Klara Johansson. Sheridan had to agree. A few photos of Adam and the beautiful Klara kissing on a white sandy beach would be beneficial to them both. Monica was sweet, but she would not advance Adam's career. That was exactly why Sheridan couldn't allow them to break up.

'This is typical of TJ,' Sheridan replied, with genuine annoyance in her voice. 'I'll talk to Daniel. We won't let this happen. Don't you worry about it.' Talk to him she would. She could not allow Adam's profile to grow bigger than theirs.

'Thanks, sweetie.' Monica swirled her wine before knocking it back. 'Put your money away. Lunch is on me.'

Sheridan rested her purse on the table. Monica was no freeloader, and she was right; it *was* her turn to get the check.

'You won't be seeing as much of me from now on,' Sheridan said. 'I'm going to be working from home.'

'You've got a new script? What's it for?'

Sheridan shook her head. 'No, I'm too busy with my sponsorship deals. I'll be working on my social media profile, and I'm planning on writing a book.' Another lie. Sheridan would be too occupied watching Roz to write.

'Good for you,' Monica replied. 'Fiction or non-fiction?'

'An autobiography. *Celeb Goss* has made enough money off my back all these years. I may as well put the record straight.' As the words rolled off her tongue, Sheridan realised it might not be a bad idea.

'Is Santana still bitching about you two? Honestly, it makes me so mad. You and Daniel have the strongest marriage I know.' Monica rested her elbows on the table, her considerable cleavage peeping through the gap in her blouse.

'Ugh.' Sheridan grimaced. 'Santana is the author of my pain. But he doesn't care about the truth, only what sells.'

'So how do you guys do it? Seriously, I'm impressed. Love, I suppose.'

'Love can only take you so far,' Sheridan said truthfully. 'Having a history together helps, and knowing each other's secrets inside out.'

'Ooh, your deepest darkest fantasies . . . Next thing, you'll be tellin' me you have a red room.'

Sheridan laughed. 'I wouldn't go that far, but there's nothing wrong with being adventurous, taking risks. In this business, you don't keep your man by playing it safe.' Sheridan paused to sip the last of her drink. 'Sorry, that's a bit old-fashioned. Even I cringed at that.'

'On the contrary, I'm all ears. I'm dying to know more.'

'Another time, maybe.' Sheridan checked her watch. She needed to get back. She had an hour before Roz returned from her little excursion. Just enough time to go through her things. 'Duty calls. I'm afraid I have to go.'

After saying her goodbyes, Sheridan made a quick call to summon her chauffeur-driven car. When it came to secrets, Monica didn't know the half of it. Having Roz under their roof would bond Daniel to Sheridan for life.

CHAPTER THIRTY-THREE

ROZ

I jabbed the button to lower the car window, groaning as it refused to budge. Neither George nor I had the energy for fake cheeriness, and our earlier snatched conversation played heavily on my mind. I sat pressed against the car door, half-tempted to pull the handle and escape on to the streets of New York. I didn't want to return to Sheridan because I didn't trust her any more. The memory of our first argument replayed in a loop in my head. Why had she said I'd bruised her arm when I hadn't laid a finger on her? She seemed confident that I would accept her version of events. It wasn't as if she'd known my memory would play me up. Unless . . . Sheridan said I hadn't drunk my juice that morning, that I had knocked over the glass. Yet as my memory returned, I clearly recalled being forced to swallow every drop. It seemed odd, her barking at me to drink it right after she'd discovered that I'd lied. I chewed on my thumbnail, ignoring George's tuts of disgust. I didn't care about his approval any more. He was too caught up in his own worries to help me. Sheridan had said *she* was drunk the night she conceived Leo. Was it a ruse to get me to confess? If so, how had she known I'd been drinking that night? It was not as if she could ask anyone . . . I wracked my brain, ticking off a mental checklist. I had deleted Facebook so I couldn't be tagged. I wasn't on Twitter, and Dympna's settings were set to private because of her dad's job in the police.

I looked out of the tinted car window, staring but not seeing as I lost myself in thought. It was crazy; she couldn't have known I was drunk, not unless she'd visited the nightclub in person and talked to the staff. I was paranoid, my imagination galloping away with me. Then it hit me. When I'd first filled in my online bio, it had asked about my social life. Not wanting to appear too much of a nun, I'd listed HEAT nightclub in Dublin as one of my old haunts. HEAT took photos, stamped with a time and date. Their photographer had a soft spot for me, and often snapped pictures for their Facebook page. My stomach lurched as the realisation hit home.

'Are you all right?' George said. 'You're very pale.'

'I'm Irish,' I replied, trying to sound upbeat. 'It goes with the territory.'

If Sheridan was devious enough to record our conversations, then she was easily capable of looking up HEAT online. How could I have been so stupid? I recalled the cold expression on her face as I'd crumpled in a heap in the lift. I needed to find a way to call Dympna and tell her my exact location. I didn't feel safe in New York any more.

◆ ◆ ◆

I forced a smile on to my face as we entered the kitchen, George filling Sheridan in on our trip.

'I had a great time. We packed loads into one afternoon,' I added. 'My calves are killing me from all that walking. I might go for a lie down, if that's OK.' It was the first time I had volunteered to go to my basement, but I was desperate to speak to Dympna. I thought about the hotel travel plug I'd used for my hair straighteners. Had George packed it by any chance? Could it be shoved in one of my drawers?

'Did you have a nice time with your friend?' I asked, as Sheridan stood before me.

'It was fine, thank you. I didn't stay long.' Sheridan handed me a sheet of paper. 'Your updated schedule. It covers trimester two.'

'Thanks,' I said, despite the fact that I hated Sheridan's stupid schedules with a passion. Getting out of the apartment for a few hours had reminded me how nice it was not to be committed to a timetable.

I turned to George. 'Thanks for everything, Mr G.' I meant it. He had probably imparted far more than he had meant to with me. He could have said nothing, or worse still, told Sheridan that I'd switched off his phone.

'Ooh, Mr G, I like it,' George replied, his gaze flicking from me to Sheridan. Despite his smile, he seemed on his guard and did not take his eyes off her for very long.

'Leo's due home any second,' Sheridan said, giving me the hint to go to my room.

Wearily, I made my way to the lift. I knew Anna would activate the pass to allow me down. But as I turned the corner in the hallway, I froze in my tracks. Anna was at the front door, trying to stop a visitor from coming in. I recognised the thick Boston accent from Sheridan's dinner party. It was Monica, and she barged past Anna as she allowed herself inside.

Swearing under my breath, I jabbed at the lift button, but it wouldn't work without a pass. Besides, it was too late. She had already seen me.

'Hello there, who are you?' she said, giving me the once-over. She was curvy with big hair, and a couple of inches smaller than me. She was also in my face. Instinctively, my hands fell to my bump. 'I . . . I . . .' I stuttered, wishing the lift would swallow me up.

The sound of Sheridan's footsteps made me fold my arms tightly in a knot.

'Maria,' Sheridan said, her voice as taut as a violin string. 'I was looking for you. Can you get Leo's clothes ready? He's got a play date scheduled in an hour.'

My eyes darted from left to right and I realised she was talking to me.

'Yeah . . . sure,' I said, jabbing the lift button again.

Sheridan glared, her annoyance evident. 'You're not an invalid, are you? Take the stairs.'

Spinning on my heel, I left them both to it, the echoes of Monica's voice in my ears: 'You left your purse behind. I thought I'd drop it in. It's a killa finding pahking around here . . .'

I stopped around the corner and realised I was trembling. Why didn't Sheridan tell her who I really was? I knew she was passing my baby off as her own, but couldn't she have confided in her friend? I took a deep, soothing breath. Told myself to get a grip. I walked into the kitchen, waiting for Sheridan to return.

'What's going on?' George paled as I returned. I was about to explain when I heard the front door close.

'I . . .' My words were cut short as Sheridan marched in, her arms swinging by her side.

'Why were you standing there like a gormless idiot?' She jabbed the air with her finger. 'I had to tell her you were a member of staff.'

'I'm sorry. I . . . I didn't know what to do.'

'What if she saw your bump?' She narrowed her eyes. 'She didn't, did she? Because that's a whole can of worms you don't want to open.'

I remembered laying my hands on my stomach. Had Monica seen? I couldn't honestly say. My top was baggy, and I wasn't big.

I shook my head. 'We only spoke for a second. I don't think she saw.'

'As for pressing the elevator button for the basement floor . . .' She prodded the side of my forehead, her finger like a woodpecker burrowing into my brain. 'Think, girl, think! If I issue my staff a command, they bow their heads instead of replying, "Yeah, sure."'

I bristled at her attempt at copying my Irish accent. If it were anyone else, I would have given them a mouthful and slapped their hand away. It was hardly my fault that she'd left her purse at the restaurant and that Anna had let Monica in. Yet I was the one taking the blame.

'I'll go to my room.' I shuffled out to the corridor, exchanging one last look with George as she dismissed me with a wave. He appeared uncomfortable throughout our exchange, but remained silent just the same.

I stepped inside my basement room, trying not to cry. This wasn't the family I had envisioned for my child. After kicking off my trainers, I pulled on a thick pair of socks and padded over to the air vent above. Craning my neck, I strained to hear George mention a bad signal and Sheridan saying it was fine, as she hadn't been listening anyway. She had to be referring to when I turned off his phone. Why did she need to listen? What did she think we were going to do?

Quick footsteps above me were accompanied by a door slamming shut. Leo was home from school. I returned my attention to my surroundings, my senses on high alert. Something was different. It was more than the usual housekeeping. Things had been moved.

I cast my eye over the bulging bookshelf. Sheridan had added to it in my absence. Had she been through my things? Being seen by Monica would only make Sheridan tighten the reins on me even more. Her employees acted like robots whenever she was around. Was that how she expected me to behave, too? I thought of George, and the act he put on in her company. I thought of the servants too scared to meet my eye. Everybody except Daniel was walking on eggshells. George had seemed unsurprised when I told him that Sheridan had pulled my hair. Had he seen her do this sort of thing before? I glanced around the ceiling. Had she fitted cameras in this room? Microphones?

I opened the double wardrobe. I was grasping at straws. If George had unpacked a travel plug I would have seen it by now. The thought dissipated as I noticed something was wrong. Gone were my blouses, dresses and jeans. Row upon row of grey shapeless maternity dresses hung in their place. I pulled open the drawer underneath. Next to my sweatshirts were belly-hugging grey knickers and regimented-looking maternity bras. I checked the crumpled label on a maternity dress. Was this even new?

It was bad enough that I had to give my clothes to Juanita to wash. But for Sheridan to come in here and remove my underwear . . . it was beyond belief. This was the real reason for my sightseeing trip. She must have come back from lunch early to snoop through my things.

My heart faltered. *My phone. What if Sheridan found my phone?* I had broken the rules by having it in my room.

I pushed aside the hangers, searching for my suitcase at the back and feverishly pulling it out.

'No,' I whispered aloud.

The phone had gone.

CHAPTER
THIRTY-FOUR
SHERIDAN

'Are you looking for this?' Sheridan held up the mobile phone as she stood a few feet away from Roz.

'Oh!' Roz exclaimed, almost jumping out of her skin. Littered at her feet were items of underwear next to the open suitcase on the floor.

Taking the clothes had been an act of punishment and Sheridan observed her with the morbid curiosity of a cat playing with a mouse.

'You lied,' she said, 'for a second time. There will be consequences.'

But it seemed this little mouse had had enough of being pushed around.

'Give me back my phone,' Roz spat, her apparent nervousness giving way to anger. 'You had no right to touch my stuff.'

Sheridan had anticipated her annoyance. After all, you can only bend a branch so far until it snaps. She had learned that with Kelly. She would not make the same mistake again.

'Here, have it. It's fully charged. Unlike you, I own a travel plug.' She threw the phone towards her and it skittered across the wooden floor. She watched with some satisfaction as Roz frantically tried to turn it on.

'You've taken out the SIM.'

'Of course.' Sheridan folded her arms. 'I presume Dympna was the girl pictured with you in the nightclub – the one with the red hair?'

Roz stared, her eyes flicking from her phone to Sheridan. 'I . . . I don't know what you're talking about.' But her face relayed a different story.

'I have to admit – you reeled me in with that good-girl act.' Sheridan's face hardened. 'Who else knows you're here?'

'Nobody. I've stuck to my side of the agreement. But you'll know that because you've read my texts.'

Sheridan delivered a wry smile. Roz was getting to know her well.

'What have you done with my passport? And my clothes . . .' A sob rose in Roz's throat. 'I've had enough. I want to go home.'

'I locked your passport away for safe keeping,' Sheridan replied, unmoved by her outburst.

'I'm going.' Roz slipped back on her shoes. 'With or without my passport. You owe me money. I'll go to the Irish embassy if you don't pay up.'

'Honey, until you give me my baby, you're not getting a dime.'

'She's not your baby, she's mine!' Roz screamed.

A sharp laugh escaped Sheridan's lips. 'Oh, you poor deluded thing. You really think you can be a mother to your child?' Shaking her head, she observed Roz with disdain. 'You're a loser. A pitiful nobody without a penny to your name.'

Tears brimmed in Roz's eyes as her words hit home.

'Your mother's an alcoholic. Your father doesn't want to know you . . .'

'Don't . . .' Roz clutched her belly, as if to shield the baby from her tirade. But Sheridan continued, each word as sharp as a knife.

'You had a job cleaning hotel rooms and you couldn't even keep that. You're talentless – your pictures are mediocre at best. Face it, Roz, this is as good as it gets. I wouldn't trust you with a hamster.'

'You . . .' Roz faltered. 'You can't stop me. I'm going home.'

Sheridan's eyes locked on to Roz. Sliding her hand into her pocket, she carefully palmed the item within. She had guessed Roz could react badly and there was no way she was letting her leave. But the last thing she wanted was a physical altercation with the pregnant woman in her care.

Sheridan tilted her head, giving an ice-cold smile. 'You came from such humble beginnings, yet you demand so much. What more do you want?'

'My freedom,' Roz sniffled, edging towards the lift. 'I can't stand it down here. You've got to let me out.'

Sheridan side-stepped in front of her. 'And risk you bumping into Leo? I don't think so. What if he tells his schoolfriends?'

'Then, please, let me stay somewhere nearby. You don't need to keep me here.'

'But I do. You said yourself, you've no intention of giving me the baby.' Sheridan's eyes were like flints as she glared. 'Don't you realise? You've signed your rights away. She's mine.'

'I'm going and you can't stop me,' Roz said, trying to dodge around her.

Sliding the syringe from her pocket, Sheridan blocked her path. 'It's just a sedative. It won't hurt the baby.'

'Ow!' Roz cried, bending over in pain as Sheridan approached.

'What is it? What's wrong?' Sheridan watched with horror as Roz struggled to breathe. She hadn't even touched her yet.

'It's the baby,' Roz gasped. 'I've been getting pains all day. I think something's wrong . . .'

'No. It's too early.' Pocketing the syringe, Sheridan leaned forward, lowering to one knee. 'Where does it hurt?'

But Sheridan's question was answered by a sharp elbow to the face. Blinding white pain accompanied starbursts in her vision as she fell back on the floor. A howl escaped her lips as she fought to stem the blood spurting from her nose. She barely felt Roz rummage in her pocket as she snatched the elevator pass.

Crawling to her feet, Sheridan raised her head to see Roz run to the elevator. The bitch had been lying. There was nothing wrong with her. Panic gripped Sheridan's being like a thousand icy shards. If the police came here, found what they had hidden . . . There was more to this than Roz. She would end up in jail.

'You bitch!' Sheridan screamed, her voice thick with rage as she slowly got to her feet.

Roz slammed the pass against the security panel before jabbing at the elevator button. 'Come on, come on . . .' she repeated, staring back at Sheridan.

Blood drizzled through Sheridan's fingers as she clasped her nose. 'I'll kill you, I'll fucking kill you for this!' she said, her voice thick with congestion. She was dizzy, disorientated, no longer in control. Roz was taking her baby. She had to get to her before she stepped inside the elevator. But Roz had hit her with the force of a steam train. Her mouth filled with the taste of iron and she paused to spit out blood. Like an extra in a zombie movie, she shuffled towards her captive.

'Stop!' she screamed, as Roz slipped through the open doors.

Sheridan clawed to keep them open, her fingers wrapping around each edge as they almost slid closed.

'Get away from me!' Roz screamed, recoiling against the wall.

Slowly, Sheridan prised the doors open, a dark smile growing on her face.

CHAPTER THIRTY-FIVE

ROZ

Fear sharpened my senses as Sheridan's threats rang in my ears. I would have preferred to face an oncoming car than contemplate what she had in store for me. She had finally lost it. The queen of control had had enough.

Sheridan's bloodied fingers stained the lift doors as she prised them apart, her face shoved into the widening gap. I jabbed the lift button to press the doors closed, but Sheridan's rage powered her strength and there was no stopping her. But she had been wrong. She was my baby, not hers, and that was worth fighting for. I lunged forward, biting down on Sheridan's hand. Howling in pain, she relinquished her grasp. The lift doors shut with a clunk.

I pressed my palms flat against the cool metal wall and exhaled a lungful of air. But I couldn't relax as the lift travelled upwards. Sheridan was gunning for me; she would be racing up the stairs. I braced myself, planned my escape through the front door. I wouldn't stop at security. I would see myself clear of the building. I did not trust anyone around her. There were bound to be police on the street. My legs trembled with a spike of adrenalin and I clenched my hands into fists. I was getting through that door and nobody was stopping me.

As the lift doors rolled open, it was not Sheridan standing before me, but Daniel. He looked behind me into the lift, taking me to one side as I stepped out.

'I heard screaming. Where's Sheridan?'

'Let me past,' I said, as he tightened his grip on my arm. 'Please. Sheridan's lost it. She wants to kill me!' I could see the front door ahead of me, so tantalisingly close. But Daniel's broad frame was in my path. I flinched as he rested both hands on my arms. 'Hey, don't be silly. Sheridan would never hurt you.'

'No . . .' I said, trying to wriggle out of his grasp. 'You don't understand. She's been drugging me. It's not safe . . . You've got to let me go.'

'Roz, calm down. This isn't doing you or the baby any good.' He pressed me against the wall, trapping me in his grip. My heart pounded with the need to escape. I looked deep into his eyes, desperate to get my message across.

'Why aren't you listening? Sheridan . . .' I caught his gaze and swivelled my head around. Daniel wasn't listening because Sheridan was coming. That's why he was holding me still. Then it hit me: the realisation that they were in this together. Daniel may have liked me, but he would take his wife's side every time.

'No!' I screamed, pummelling his chest with my fists. But it was no use. Daniel was too strong. 'Help!' I shouted, praying someone would hear. 'Please, help me, someone, help!' But all I could see was Sheridan's bloodied face as she approached, a syringe in her hand. 'Hold her still!' she spat through gritted teeth.

Daniel took in her smashed-up face, paling at the sight. 'What happened down there?' He glared at the needle. 'And what's that for?'

'It's just a sedative. Hold her still before she hurts my baby.'

It was an order, not a request, and to my horror, Daniel complied. Extending my arm, he exposed the flesh on my wrist.

'It's OK,' he said, his breath coming quickly. 'I'll stay with you. We'll sort this out.'

The sedative worked quickly, draining the strength from my legs. I began to crumple, but Daniel's strong arms encompassed me. My eyelids felt like lead shutters, forcing themselves closed. Everything grew dark as Daniel's words became faraway. I felt him gently scoop me up in his arms. I heard the disbelief in his words. 'For God's sake, Sheridan . . . What have you done?'

CHAPTER THIRTY-SIX

ROZ

I blinked, feeling as if I was rising from an underwater sleep. My eyes were gritty, but I couldn't rub them clean. I met resistance as I tried to move my hands. I was bound, soft bandages tying each of my wrists to the pillars of my bed.

Tugging at my bindings, I panicked with a need to feel my stomach to check my baby was OK. Sensing a presence in the room, I lifted my head from my pillow to see Daniel standing at the end of my bed.

'Daniel . . .' I panted, a shot of pain driving like a nail into my head. I winced. It was the after-effects of the drugs, which I'd felt so many times before. But this dose had been serious. It hadn't just made me sleepy. It had knocked me out stone cold. What had she given me? I drew in a sharp breath between my teeth as I pleaded to be freed. 'Please. Let me go.'

'I'm sorry, Roz, but it's for your own good.' His voice was remorseful.

'You drugged me,' I croaked, my throat scratchy and sore. 'You had no right.'

'You were out of control. How is Sheridan going to explain her injuries? You could have broken her nose.'

'My baby,' I said. 'Is she all right?'

Daniel frowned. It was the first time he'd heard me call the baby mine, and he picked up on it instantly. 'We scanned you when you were unconscious. The baby's fine.'

He spoke as if it were the most normal thing in the world, but the thought of Sheridan touching me when I was at my most vulnerable made my skin crawl.

'This is kidnapping – you know that, don't you?' I reined in my temper. It would not help to antagonise my kidnappers. My baby and I were completely at their mercy. 'Please. I won't tell anyone. Please let me go.' I lowered my head and gazed at the ceiling, my head pounding.

'Don't be silly,' Daniel said. 'We're just looking after you. It's either this or Sheridan has you sectioned. She said you threatened to kill yourself.'

'What? No . . . no, I didn't . . .' But my words lacked conviction as I searched the corridors of my mind. I could barely remember what had gone on. 'Promise me.' I blinked away my tears. 'Don't let her drug me again. We both know it's not good for the baby. It can't be.'

Taking a tissue from his pocket, Daniel leaned forward and dabbed my face. 'Sweetheart, you really hurt her. You should see the state of her nose.'

'It was self-defence!' I cried, tugging my wrists once more. My baby moved inside me. I could feel the ripple of a limb beneath my skin. 'Daniel, listen to me. You must know what she's like. This is wrong. Please. I won't tell anyone. Just let me go.'

Daniel knew it was wrong. I could see it behind his eyes.

'She's been recording our conversations. Everybody's terrified of her. Please, Daniel . . .' I watched his expression soften as my words sank in. 'I'm scared. The drugs . . . they're not good for the baby. You know what happened when she pulled my hair.'

Slowly, he undid my bandages, untying me from the bed. 'I'm not saying I believe you, but I can't condone keeping you like this.' He paused as he loosened the bandages of my right hand. 'You've got to tell her that you're sorry. Beg for forgiveness if you have to. It's the only way this will work.'

I opened my mouth to protest and he raised his hand, silencing me. 'I know what you're saying, but it's best all round if you apologise. She's just worried about you. What if you hurt yourself? Or the baby? We have a responsibility to keep you both safe.'

'And what happened to the last person you were meant to keep safe?' I asked, rubbing my wrists.

Daniel's back was to me as he placed the bandages at the end of the bed. I watched as he stiffened, his movements coming to a halt.

'What do you mean?' he replied, turning round.

I ran my hands over my stomach. It was obvious from Sheridan's attitude that she had never given birth. Her question about my baby kicking was still firmly in my mind. 'Sheridan used a donor for Leo, didn't she?'

'Has someone been gossiping?' Daniel's voice sharpened.

'No,' I replied. 'But it's obvious in the way she acts. She doesn't understand how pregnancy feels.' The mattress springs bounced as I shuffled up in my bed.

'Your imagination is running away with you,' Daniel said. I took it as a warning and held my tongue as his annoyance grew. 'Punching her in the face. That was a new low. Don't ever do that again.'

It was an elbow to the face, not a punch, and only done so I could get away, but I doubted my explanation would gain me any sympathy now. From what I could see, Daniel had no intention of letting me go. Just like with Leo, he and Sheridan would gloss over a truth that was decaying and rotting underneath. Who was Leo's mother? What had they done with her? I burst into tears. It was the only tool left in my armoury.

'I'm sorry,' I sniffled. 'I really wanted it to work out.'

Handing me my box of tissues, Daniel sat on the side of my bed. My hair fell over my face, but I could feel him watching me intensely. Silence fell between us. My sobs subsided, and I wondered where Sheridan was. I threaded my tissue through my fingers, hoping that Daniel's thoughts were kind.

'I'm sorry, too,' Daniel said, and for a while, he seemed lost in thought.

I said nothing, but my heart was pounding as he began to stroke my hair. I could hear his breathing now, feel the warmth of his skin. 'You're not bad, you're just misunderstood . . .' His hand reached my face and he thumbed away the last of my tears. He was my captor, yet I was grateful for his touch. After months of being on my own, I needed someone to save me. Someone to be on my side. I knew a part of him was wavering, and I ached with the need to be comforted. Perhaps it had all become too much for both of us. At first, the kiss was tentative, and I was too shocked to draw back. Is this what I needed to do to keep him on side? Slowly, I responded, winding my fingers around the back of his neck. Above us, footsteps grew louder. Daniel broke away. I could barely look him in the eye.

'Sorry,' he said, clearing his throat. But the fire was still behind his eyes. 'I shouldn't have done that.'

'I won't say anything.' My voice was low, my breathing out of sync as I recovered from his kiss. I shifted awkwardly in the bed. How far was I willing to go to keep his allegiance? What did he even see in me? And what would Sheridan do with me if she ever found out?

CHAPTER THIRTY-SEVEN

Celeb Goss Magazine
By Alex Santana
January 2015

SHOCK DEATH OF DOROTHY SINCLAIR

Dorothy Sinclair, the producer of hit show *It Takes All Sorts*, has been found dead in her Chicago apartment. Her body was found last Thursday morning when her neighbor, Beryl Witherspoon, became concerned after not hearing from her friend in over a week. 'At first I thought she had gone to visit her daughter, Sheridan. She was desperate to make up with her, especially since she had the baby. Leo was all Dorothy would talk about, even though they had never met. She tried to get in touch, but Sheridan had changed her phone number.' When asked about the rift between mother and daughter, Beryl said: 'Dorothy was thrilled when she read about the pregnancy. She said her daughter must have had treatment because she was infertile, as far as

Dorothy was aware. She tried to contact her through her agent, but her letters were returned.' When asked if Sheridan ever visited her mother, Beryl replied, 'She came to see her once, years ago. Dorothy even gave her a key. It's a sorry state of affairs when your own daughter won't acknowledge you. After all Dorothy did for her, to die alone in squalor like this, it's so sad.' Reports state that the one-bedroom apartment was in a shocking state. Her bedroom was filled with hundreds of newspapers featuring clippings of Sheridan's success, along with dozens of VCR tapes, DVDs, posters, and memorabilia of the show. Press cuttings were pinned to the wall from as early as the 1970s. Police have ruled that Dorothy's death was accidental, but Beryl is not so sure. 'The police said she tripped over a pile of newspapers and fell down the stairs. But I've been there plenty of times. She may have been a hoarder, but she was ever so careful getting around, and she never kept anything near the stairs.' There's another reason why Beryl believes in foul play. 'The night before the accident, I heard shouting coming from Dorothy's apartment. It was a man's voice, I'm sure of it. I should have called in to check on her. The police said it was her television that made the noise that night.' Beryl has spoken to the police and they appear unconcerned. 'I saw a van in the area earlier that day. The man driving it had a mustache and wore a cowboy hat. I know everyone in this area. He looked like he was up to no good.' But the police's apathy could be due to the number of calls Beryl makes. 'I call them every time I see anyone suspicious – sometimes every day.' Police state there was no evidence of a forced entry at Dorothy's address.

CHAPTER
THIRTY-EIGHT
ROZ
MARCH 2019

'You're the size of an aubergine now,' I said to my baby as I read aloud. 'You can blink, see light, and you're a whole thirty-seven centimetres long.' At twenty-eight weeks, my pregnancy was advancing, and I was finding it difficult to sleep at night. I closed the pregnancy diary as bittersweet memories of Dympna invaded my thoughts. I wished I could call her. She couldn't have received the message that I left eight weeks ago. Had she known my address, someone would have called to check up on me by now. Dympna had tried to warn me. She'd been right. I glared at the air-conditioning unit, wishing I could rip it out of the walls that imprisoned me here. Sheridan had turned it up: her punishment for my refusing to follow her schedule. I knew by now how the game went. Behave and I received privileges. Misbehave and punishment ensued.

Call it my hormones or my inbred streak of stubbornness, but I could not simper and smile for her today. The bitch. The thought of her bringing up my baby made me feel physically sick. I only saw Sheridan at my scans and health checks, and that suited me just fine. She never spoke to me. These days, she sent Juanita to monitor my schedule. The girl would stand before me, her brown eyes as big as saucers as she pleaded with me to comply. But not a word of English would pass her lips. Back issues of *Celeb Goss* were still coming and going, with snippets of gossip about Sheridan's past life. It didn't surprise me that her relationship with her mother had been fraught. But was there more to it than that? There was no forced entry at the address where Dorothy died, yet the same article mentioned Sheridan being given a key.

Was Juanita issuing the warnings? If so, she was staying tight-lipped. I wondered what she was thinking on the days she watched me do my pregnancy stretches and repeat the stupid chants that Sheridan had made up. Daniel had kept his distance since we'd shared our first kiss, but I knew he was busy at work. For days after I hurt Sheridan's nose, I had screamed for release. I even tried refusing to eat, but I could not deprive my baby for very long.

I never received the security pass to activate the lift that Sheridan had promised when I arrived. I dreamt about breaking through the locked door of my room and running out of the apartment to freedom. But all my efforts to escape were exhausted, and my tummy seemed to grow bigger each day.

Groaning, I rose from the sofa and waddled the short distance to my wardrobe. It held plastic hangers on one long rail, which was screwed tight to the inside. Beneath, two fat drawers housed my underwear. There were no belts, no ties, and even the cords in my hoodies had been removed. It had taken me a little time to figure out why I had no scissors, no cutlery, and why the mirrors were made of plastic. Solitary confinement did not suit everyone. It seems Sheridan had taken precautions in case I tried to top myself.

This wasn't a recent development. My room had been suicide-proof from the moment I arrived.

I ran my fingers over the hangers, stopping at my coat. I was grateful that at least Sheridan had left this behind. I remembered when I'd worn it to see my mother in the coffee shop in Dublin and how upset she had been when I left. Tears edged my eyelids as I recalled her need to put things on an even keel. I slid it from the hanger and shrugged it on. It gaped open over my stomach. There was no way it would button up now. But still, it felt nice to wear something from Ireland. I lifted the collar to my nose and inhaled. It was still there, a faint flowery trace of the perfume I used to wear. Sheridan had taken away all my toiletries, replacing them with some organic stuff that smelt like mud. The make-up I'd bought in Dublin airport had also disappeared.

It must have killed her to see my glowing skin, my fuller breasts, the shine on my hair. In an ideal world, women looked out for each other, harbouring empathy for issues our male counterparts could never experience or understand. Sadly, both Sheridan and I were lacking when it came to sisterhood. The identity of my baby's father only served to prove how selfish I could be at times. I pulled the coat around me, as it offered some protection from the cold. I returned to the sofa, closing my eyes as I tried to imagine myself back in the coffee shop in Dublin. What would I say now, if I were sitting across from my mother? I could feel the strength of the bond between my baby and me. Was it like that for my mother, too? Shoving my hands into my pockets, my eyes snapped open as my fingers rested on a pointed edge. There was something behind the lining. What? I frowned as I delved my hand further, through the torn lining and into the innards of my coat. My heart fluttered as I pulled out the hidden treasure. I stared at the dove-grey envelope. It was the letter Mammy had given me, the one she had hastily shoved into my pocket and I had not had the heart to open. I clutched it to my chest and sighed.

It was a blessing that Sheridan had not found it. I imagined her delving into my pockets, not realising the lining had given way. Slowly, I tore the envelope open. Could I bear to read the words, for fear of what they might say? But I remembered the look on her face as I left. The love I couldn't see before. My baby kicked, reminding me that I was almost a mother. That I had made my fair share of mistakes.

'Do you want to hear from your granny?' I said softly, as I talked to my little bean. Taking a deep breath, I pulled out the notepaper, smoothed it back and read the words aloud.

> Dear Roz,
> If you're reading this letter then our meeting didn't go as hoped. I only have myself to blame, but I'm not going to give up just yet. Believe it or not, I've changed. When you hit rock bottom, the only way is up.
> I'm not going to say it was easy. I have a lot of issues from my childhood which I'm still working through. But the best things in life are worth fighting for, and you're always in my thoughts when times get tough. The truth is, I was an alcoholic. I tried to keep it from you, but I imagine you've worked it out by now. Alcohol helped blur the edges of past problems that I wasn't able to cope with. You see, my mother didn't protect me either. I only thank God that unlike me, you were able to keep yourself safe. I hope you can forgive me. It's taken me a long time to forgive myself. I want, no, I *need* to change.

Sweetheart, I wouldn't blame you if you grew up thinking that I didn't care. But you couldn't be further from the truth. I was so proud of you, but too ashamed of myself to bring you into town or pick you up from school. I couldn't stand for your friends to see what a failure your mother was. When you drew those pictures of me – I couldn't bear the face of the cruel, bitter woman staring back from the page.

I still have issues. I struggle with crowds and I hate being the centre of attention. I shy away from people I don't know. All these years, I thought you were better off without me. But Tony encouraged me to get back in touch. I was terrified you wouldn't see me, and who could blame you? But the bond between mother and daughter is not so easily broken, is it?

They say mothers and daughters are closest when daughters become mothers themselves. I dream about having a grandchild. I can even see it in my mind's eye. I hope I'll get to share the wonder of it all with you one day.

I love you, Roz. I always have. I'm sorry for hurting you in the past.

With all my love,

Mam xxx

I rested the letter on my lap, taking a deep breath to ease the quiver in my hand. Tears blurred my vision and my breath jerked in a sudden sob. I knew of the bond she spoke of. And as for her wanting grandchildren . . . what a fool I had been. I had an inkling of her past issues. There was a rift in her family because of something her uncle had done to her when she was young. Granny's funeral had been a tense gathering, and we did not stay for long. At last, I understood. I wanted to tell her that even if she fell, she was still moving forward, and I would be there to help her up. But all I could do was wrap my hands around my bump and cry for the opportunities I had missed. I might never see my mother again.

CHAPTER THIRTY-NINE

DYMPNA

Dympna wrinkled her nose at the smell of burnt offerings hanging in the air. Her mother was not the best of cooks, but her brother had wolfed down her rubbery lasagne just the same. When they were young, the only way of knowing supper was ready was if the fire alarm was going off in the hall. It had been nice to catch up with her brother; she'd even helped him with his homework. She had matured a lot since leaving home. But now she had more important things on her mind – getting her father alone, for one.

Outside an icy gale was blowing, testing every windowpane in the house, but the radiators pumped heat into her parents' kitchen and their house was tropically warm.

'What are you two up to?' Dympna's mother, Ann, regarded them with a measure of suspicion. Up until recently, Dympna had rarely spent five minutes with her father. Now the two of them were as thick as thieves.

Dympna sat ensconced at the kitchen table, having just made them both a cup of tea. 'Nothing,' she replied, undoing the zip of her hoodie. Since living in her flat, she had become unaccustomed to the heat. 'Want one?' She raised the teapot in the air. It still sported the home-made rainbow tea cosy Dympna had knitted when she was in school.

'I'd prefer an explanation.' Folding her arms, Ann leaned against the fridge and stared at them. Everybody said that Dympna was the spit of her mother. They had the same wild red hair, the same dogged determination and the same healthy cynicism at times.

'Dympna's thinking about joining the guards,' John chipped in. 'She's been coming to me for advice.'

Dympna raised her eyebrow. How easily the lie had slipped off her father's tongue. She would have to up her game if she wanted to keep Roz's predicament from her mother.

Ann's face lit up with delight. 'Ah sure that's grand. You'll make a great *ban garda*. Aren't I always saying . . .'

'They don't call them that any more. It's just *garda*,' Dympna said, referring to her mother's term for female police.

'What does it matter?' Ann said, reaching for a bottle of wine from the fridge. 'It'll be enough to wipe the smile off that old biddy next door.' She poured herself a glass of white, looking more than a little smug. The jingle of a television ad filtered from the TV in the living room, momentarily distracting her.

Dympna sighed. 'Don't go telling everyone. There's all sorts of exams to pass, and they might not even be taking on . . .'

'They're taking on.' Her father paused to sip his tea. 'If not now, soon. You won't have long to wait.'

Dympna had enjoyed spending time with her father and was genuinely coming around to the idea of joining the police. But she had Roz to think of first. Everything else could wait. Her phone flashed with another missed call from Seamus. She couldn't bring herself to speak to him right now.

'I'll leave you to it.' Ann raised her glass in a salute. '*Fair City* is starting – they've got the wedding tonight. Something's bound to go wrong!'

Dympna returned her smile. It was nice to have both her parents under the same roof for a change. If her mother wasn't off event-planning, her father was usually at work. She waited for the audible click of the living room door before she leaned in towards him. 'I've not been able to find any pregnant celebrities on my list. Have you had any joy?'

He nodded, sliding a folded piece of paper from the pocket of his jeans. 'It took a while, but I managed to get some information from the Miracle-Moms site.'

'That's great,' Dympna said, feeling a spark of hope. 'Did they tell you who the mystery couple were?'

John shook his head. 'I don't have the justification nor the jurisdiction for that.' He slid the paper across the plastic table cloth her mother had just wiped down. 'The couple used fake names when talking to Roz. Here's a printout of the last messages between them.'

Dympna hungrily scanned the page, her concern growing as she read:

Julie: I'm sorry to lay this on you at such short notice, but I can't progress. I'm pregnant. It's been a wonderful shock for us both.

Roz: Oh. Congratulations. That's wonderful news. Don't worry about me. I've got some other couples to talk to. Can I still use the hotel room?

Julie: Of course, that goes without saying! And please, have your meals and room service with my compliments too. Look after yourself while you're over here. I'm sorry, but I won't be able to help you interview the couples as I'd prefer to keep my identity private. I hope you understand.

Roz: No worries. Thanks a million for the hotel room. I'll be grand. Congrats again on your baby. It'll be lucky to have you as a mom.

'Hang on a minute . . .' Dympna jabbed at the printed page. 'This isn't right.'

'That's what I thought,' John replied. 'They were deleted from the main folder, although they were able to recover them easily enough.'

Dympna reread the messages, hearing Roz's voice in her mind. But the voice in the emails was wrong.

'Roz didn't write that,' Dympna said, a sick feeling rising in her throat. She knew that Roz was in danger. Now it was written in black and white.

'It's the use of the word "mom", isn't it? Very American. But the other words – "grand" and "thanks a million" . . . Whoever wrote this is trying to sound like Roz.'

She gazed at her father. 'Will the NYPD investigate this?'

'They'll say it was a slip of the tongue. That Roz has been talking to this Julie so long that she's repeating her words.'

'But that's not true,' Dympna said. 'When Roz left Dublin, she was a hundred per cent sure she was meeting this couple. Remember I told you that she rang me when she got there? She said she was with them.'

'Darlin', I'm not disagreeing with you, but people have been known to lie.' He reclaimed the piece of paper, tucking it back into his pocket. 'Whoever this Julie is, she's deleted her account on Miracle-Moms.'

'But the site checks them out. Roz told me. They do a full background search.'

'Yes, and that was two months ago. It's their policy to shred their users' details the second they close their account. Even if I got a court order, they wouldn't have a lot to give me.'

Outside, the rain slammed against the window, followed by an ominous howl of wind.

Dympna's glance fell on the wall clock as the seconds counted down. What was Roz doing now? Was she even alive? 'We need to go public with this,' she said, breaking the silence. 'We should tell Mam, and Roz's mam, too.'

'Aye, I suppose we owe her that,' John said gloomily, running his fingers through his hair. 'Why don't you go back to your flat while I have a chat with your mam.'

◆ ◆ ◆

Dympna hated breaking her vow of confidentiality to Roz, but there was no doubt there was something underhand going on.

Battling the wintry weather, she boarded the bus for home. She pressed her phone to her ear, listening to a voicemail that Seamus had left. He sounded low, a world away from his usual cheery self as he asked her to call him back.

Shoving her phone back into her pocket, Dympna reflected on how much things had changed in the last few months. As scary as it was, there was a side of her that enjoyed being pushed out of her comfort zone. She remembered the look on her mother's face when she said she was joining the police, felt a tingle of excitement at the prospect of applying for the role. Perhaps this was the shove she'd needed all along. She stared out of the dirt-streaked window. Deep down, she knew that if she found Roz, she would also discover the answer to the question playing on her mind – who was the father of her baby? And by the sound of Seamus's voice, he already knew.

CHAPTER FORTY

ROZ

I closed my eyes and inhaled the cool night air. It felt so good to be outside. Each breath revitalised my senses and I savoured every precious moment on the rooftop bench. Sheridan was away, at a business meeting with her agent in LA. Daniel had brought me up here via a private lift that came straight to the roof. I absorbed the smells and sounds of New York. Silence was a stranger to its streets. In the distance, a police siren wailed, and I was brought back to ground.

'The depth of your religious conviction . . . It's inspiring,' Daniel said. 'I wouldn't for a second want you to give it up.'

He was responding to my request to go to church the next day. Getting a straight answer from him was tougher than I'd expected. He had changed since Sheridan had injected me, and had apologised for the situation I found myself in. Yet he was at the mercy of his wife's decisions – for now. Slowly, I was gaining his trust, making him see things my way. We had shared several stolen kisses since he'd untied my bandages from the bed. And tonight, my compliance had been rewarded with a breath of fresh air.

I realised he was staring at me, and a flush rose to my face.

'You look so like Sheridan when she first started out.' His hand crept to mine and our fingers intertwined. 'Don't tell her, but I had a crush on her when I was a teenager. I used to watch her in *It Takes All Sorts*.'

I smiled in response. It felt strange that he was talking about his wife while holding my hand. 'I don't think I look that much like her,' I said awkwardly.

'But you do. The beauty is that you don't realise it. She used to be like that. Wholesome. The girl next door. At least, her character was . . .' His voice trailed away as he stared at the skyline, lost in thought.

I had my own priorities to worry about. What would I do when Daniel got fed up of hand-holding and wanted more? Being on the roof was a breakthrough, but did it lead me any closer to escape? Daniel had insisted I wear one of his hoodies and tuck my hair underneath my top. My eyes had roamed the hallways for CCTV cameras, but there were none to be found. It was why I was persistent in my request to go to church.

'I'm not asking for confessions,' I said, steering the conversation back to the topic in hand. 'I just want to sit and pray. George can chaperone me. I won't break into conversation with someone mid-prayer.'

Daniel tightened his grip on my hand. His presence was intoxicating. I reminded myself that he was also my kidnapper, and I could not grow too attached. But he was the person who snuck chocolate bars into my room, persuaded Sheridan to go easy on me. And tonight, he had taken me out after I had been stuck inside for weeks. Each time we spoke, I chipped away at his loyalty to Sheridan. But time was not on my side. Weeks were passing at a frightening rate. I did not want to contemplate my future after the baby was born.

I tuned in to Daniel's narrative.

'Honey, I know this has been hard for you,' he said. 'You think I haven't noticed you getting attached to this baby? You think I haven't seen you rub your stomach or heard you talking to your bump?' A beat passed between us. 'But there are compromises to be made. I know we've not handled this well, but trust me when I say your baby couldn't be in safer hands.'

'I know . . .' I lied. 'I just want to do the right thing. But I don't know what that is any more.' I bowed my head, one hand over my bump as I tried to communicate to my baby. I would do whatever it took to get us both out of here.

Releasing my hand, Daniel rested his arm around my shoulders. 'I'll speak to George. We'll get you to church.' He squeezed my shoulder. Another secret to share.

'Thank you,' I said as he rose. I took his outstretched hand, slowly rising from the bench. His hugs were gentle now, and he ended our time outside with a soft kiss.

'Feeling better?' he said, stroking my cheek.

'Yes.'

The word was a whisper, because I was fighting back my tears. I did not want to go back to my basement room, but I had to keep up the charade. If Daniel thought I believed him, then I would have no reason to run. A soft breeze played with a loose strand of my hair and I savoured the final seconds of night air.

Back in my basement flat, the hairs prickled on the back of my neck as I realised my nightdress had been moved. Slowly, I unfolded the garment, slipping out a piece of paper tucked beneath the crease. Someone had been in my room. But who? Old newspaper headlines delivered a warning as I unfolded the page. This message was different. It wasn't *Celeb Goss* magazine; it was a photocopy of a news story from several years ago. Swallowing the lump in my throat, I read on.

CAROLINA WOMAN MISSING
By Peter Barker

Police are appealing for help in finding twenty-one-year-old Kelly Blunt, who has been missing from her home in South Carolina since 14th September this year. Her family and police are asking for the public's help in finding her. Kelly gave up her waitressing job and traveled to New York in the hope of becoming an actress after communicating with an alleged celebrity couple in a chat room online. She told her mother she was going to live with them while they helped establish her acting career. It has been six months since her daughter was last in touch.

'I'm crushed,' her mother said, speaking from her trailer park where she lives with her five children. 'Some days it feels like I can barely breathe. Kelly was a kind girl who saw the good in everyone. She would never go this long without calling to see how we are.'

Kelly's bank account has not been used since her arrival in New York, where the trail has gone cold. She told colleagues that she was meeting industry insiders who would help her get started in her acting career.

'She was very trusting,' colleague Bobbi-May said. 'We warned her that going on her own was a bad idea, but she was excited to meet whoever was waiting for her. When we asked, she said it was "top secret," and that she would be staying in New York for ten months of coaching before moving to Hollywood.'

Kelly Jade Blunt has long white-blonde hair, is five foot five inches tall and weighs around 120 pounds, according to police reports. She was last seen wearing a canary-yellow sweater, black trousers, and pink Converse sneakers. She had a black holdall with a minimal amount of clothing, despite the proposed length of her stay.

This was different to previous communications, but one thing was clear: another message had been left for me. But who had placed it in my room? And when? I checked the date, counting on my fingers. Kelly had left home ten months before Leo was born. He would have been conceived around October. Were Sheridan and Daniel the secret couple she had spoken about? I imagined Kelly living in a trailer park full to the brim with siblings. No room, but plenty of time to daydream. A life different from mine in so many ways, yet the same. Was she driven to desperate measures, too? In the photo she was a pretty girl with long blonde hair. The same shade as Leo's. The same blue eyes. I had gazed into Daniel's long enough to see a likeness there, too.

But if Kelly had agreed to meet them, she could not have been pregnant at that point. Had she acted as a surrogate? Did Sheridan promise to train her in return for hiring out her womb? I played the scenario out in my mind. Kelly with Daniel in this room . . . maybe even in this bed. Sheridan had taken a risk, if this was the case. Kelly had met the couple in a chat room, not a private site. She had not been bound by a confidentiality agreement before she left. Had Sheridan learned from her mistakes this time around? Where was Kelly now? I folded back the paper, then noticed another clipping that must have been tucked into the first. This clip was smaller, and I opened it tentatively, filled with a rising sense of dread. The headlines were enough to make my world come to a standstill.

FOUR-YEAR ANNIVERSARY OF CAROLINA WAITRESS DISAPPEARANCE

The mother of a Carolina waitress who went missing four years ago has pleaded with the public to end her suffering and help reveal if her daughter is dead or alive. Kelly Blunt, then aged twenty-one, gave up her job and traveled to New York to pursue her dream of becoming an actress. She told family and friends she planned to stay with a couple that she met through a chat room online. She has not been seen since. Numerous friends, family, and work colleagues have been interviewed regarding her disappearance, but no further ground has been made. 'It's like she disappeared into thin air,' her mother said. 'I need to bring my baby home.'

Carolina State police investigators are appealing to the public for help. 'Someone knows where Kelly is. We ask that they come forward, using our anonymous helpline if necessary.'

I read the rest of the story. Kelly had never been found.

CHAPTER FORTY-ONE
ROZ

I raced around grabbing my clothes, barely able to believe that my request had been granted. Not only had Daniel agreed to my visit to a church, but we were also bypassing Sheridan's schedule and going today. This could be my last opportunity to get a message to the outside world. A thousand thoughts ran through my mind. Why was I panicking? I had planned for this.

I shoved my foot through the thick woollen tights that Sheridan insisted I wear. I had told Daniel that I would hardly interrupt someone mid-prayer, but that was exactly what I was going to do. I would scream the church down if I had to. I was not leaving until I got help. I could imagine the church filled with people, a hundred pairs of eyes on me. Would they think I was a crazy woman? What if George dragged me out? I slipped my grey smock dress over my head. Now I had grown, it fitted quite nicely over my bump. I thought of the homeless people I had encountered in New York. Of how people stepped over them as they lay on the pavement, ignoring their pleas for help. Would they ignore me, too? I needed a back-up, just in case my plan didn't work. I checked my watch, my stomach doing somersaults. I had five minutes.

Pulling open my dresser drawer, I rooted through my art supplies. Ripping off a sheet of sketch paper, I gripped the pencil, writing as quickly as I could.

My name is Roz Foley. I am being held captive. I shook my head. Where? I didn't even know the address. *By Sheridan Sinclair – basement apartment. Please send help.*

Oh, God, I thought. *This is so stupid! Imagine finding this note. Would I take it seriously? Of course not.* I needed someone to back up what I was saying. Someone to explain. I scribbled Dympna's phone number on the bottom, along with the Irish country code. At least if the police spoke to her, she could verify my situation. Dympna would defend me with her last breath – she would make people believe.

I swore as the lift whirred into life. Someone was on their way down. Closing the drawer, I folded up the notepaper, my panic increasing as each second passed. Where should I hide it? My shoe? My pocket? As the lift doors dinged open, I quickly shoved it down my bra. There was a thud as the sketchbook fell to the floor. In one swift movement, I kicked it under the bed, grabbing a hairbrush at the same time. My hands were clammy as I held the brush, trying to appear casual as I dragged it over my blonde hair.

I breathed a sigh of relief as George approached, wearing a bomber jacket and jeans. At least it wasn't Sheridan. It was the first time I'd seen him dressed casually. Was it so he could blend in? Judging by his expression, he was worried, too.

'Here, my little Irish shamrock.' He thrust a bag in my direction. 'Stick some bobby pins in your hair and put that on. Honestly, if this goes tits up, there'll be hell to pay.'

I peeped into the bag and found a long mahogany wig.

'Sit.' George issued instructions as he helped me put it on. It was a far cry from the makeover he'd given me when I first arrived in New York. Just as before, I watched him via the mirror of the dressing table. His expression was guarded as he tugged the wig into place. For the hundredth time, I wished I could read his mind. Did Sheridan know about our trip to the church?

◆ ◆ ◆

St Patrick's Cathedral was stunning, the biggest Gothic cathedral in New York. George had filled me in on it on the way over and my mouth fell open as we approached. It was a world away from the church I attended in Ireland, which was on a much smaller scale.

'Don't try anything,' he said as he led me to the building, his arm tightly interlinked with mine. 'There's security all over the place. Say one word and you'll be carted off to the funny farm.'

Really? I set my jaw, held my cool. He was calling my bluff. George didn't care about me; if he did, he would have reported Sheridan to the police. I had no doubt that she had him over a barrel. I had to put myself first.

But when I entered the church, my plan fell apart. It was empty. We were the only ones inside. Like a child, I fell into quiet awe. Jewels of light flooded the stained-glass windows, with giant marble pillars adding a sense of opulence.

'What time is mass?' I whispered to George, pausing to genuflect before taking a seat in the back aisle.

He answered my question with an incredulous look. 'There's no mass. You've got five minutes to say your prayers and then we're heading back.'

There was no point in arguing, and I slid on to my knees in the pew. I thought of Dympna, and the masses we attended in our local church as children. How we had warbled in the choir as schoolgirls, the teacher telling me to mouth the words. I wondered if God was watching me, and I closed my eyes in a silent prayer. I took comfort in my surroundings. For all my mother's failings, she'd insisted that I keep up the weekly ritual of attending church. I was happy to comply, because it gave me an excuse to spend an extra hour with my friend. Without Dympna, the weekends would have been very gloomy, and she was grateful for the opportunity to sit away from her family, who sat at the front.

Not that her father could always attend. His job dictated that he was usually elsewhere. I remembered looking at him as if he were some kind of superhero, and in comparison to my father, he was. Dympna's dad not only looked after his family, he made the streets safer for them too. I loved her stories of the things he got up to, and although I knew she embellished them, it was obvious that she took great delight in it all, too.

I reined in my thoughts. I was here for a reason. Not just to pray, but to ask for help. But how? My anxieties rose as I tried to orchestrate a way. My time in the basement had left me unfit and out of shape. With the size of my expanding midriff, running would not get me very far. My glance fell to the prayer book, my thoughts on the note nestled in my bra. Why hadn't I put it up my sleeve or in my pocket?

I sniffled, holding my hand to my nose. 'Have you got a tissue?'

George pulled a face before searching his pockets. In the seconds his gaze was drawn away, I delved down my top for the note. Hiding it in the palm of my hand, I took the tissue and gracefully blew my nose. George checked his watch, making it obvious he would prefer to be anywhere but here.

'Just a couple of prayers,' I whispered softly, picking up the prayer book. It felt like fate that it had been left behind, and I slowly read through the words. The double doors behind us clunked as members of the public entered the church. Holding my breath, I deposited the note between the pages of the prayer book, willing it into the hands of someone who would help.

CHAPTER
FORTY-TWO
ROZ

The traffic moved slowly in New York today, and our driver kept his hand on the horn. Then I saw them. Two police officers, leaning against their parked car. My heart skipped a beat. What would happen if I jumped out right here and screamed for help? My hand crept to the car door handle. The chances of my note being taken seriously were slim to zero. I leaned forward, under George's scrutiny, pretending I was staring at the traffic ahead. Homesickness felt like a physical ache in my chest. I could not stand another second of this. But as I jerked on the door handle, George turned to me. The expression on his face made me afraid. He had a deadness behind his eyes. Not hate. Not fear. Just a part of him that had died. What the hell had Sheridan done to him?

'It's locked,' he said, in a tone that matched his expression, and I sat back, folding my arms so tightly that I was hugging myself.

With a start, the car moved forward, weaving in and out of the traffic ahead. I watched the police disappear, hope fading with each passing second. I never thought I would get sick of this view. Of the luxury travel and accommodation that I'd once craved. What I would give to be sitting in the coffee shop with my mother, or to be on the receiving end of one of Dympna's bone-crushing hugs. Tears welled in my eyes as I thought of the note nestled in the prayer book. George had barely uttered a word to me since leaving the church. I wiped away my tears, catching his gaze. He knew Sheridan was keeping me against my will. How could he sit there and let it happen? If it was him planting the magazines, it was not enough.

'Best you go straight to your room,' George said, as we entered Sheridan's home. Since when did he start telling me what to do? A sense of unease rose. Was he trying to get me out of the way?

'But my schedule . . .' I said, the words dying in my throat as I caught his glare. Eyes narrowed, he signalled at me to do as he asked. I felt there was a message there. Something unsaid, but a warning just the same.

I took the lift down to the basement and sat in my room. Tugging the wig from my head, I unclipped the bobby pins that had held it in place. Was I in trouble? Had something happened, or was it nothing to do with me? My stomach growled. Lunchtime had passed and there was no sign of my food. I went to the air vent and strained to listen to a muffled conversation between Daniel and George. The pipes were knocking as the heating system kicked into life, and I could barely make out their words. Was Sheridan back yet? Their voices were low, and I knew instinctively that they were talking about me.

CHAPTER
FORTY-THREE
SHERIDAN

From the moment she walked into her apartment, Sheridan knew that something was wrong. Roz's presence had instigated drama after drama; but she had to admit, a little piece of her enjoyed breaking the spirit of the young woman in her care. No longer was she fretting over her fading acting career. *She* was the one in control. Even their fight had released a surge of adrenalin she had not felt in a long time. Dormant feelings had been awoken in the bedroom, too. Sex between her and Daniel had always been good, but lately it was like nothing on earth. He was a sucker for a damsel in distress and she would take advantage of the primal instinct Roz had awoken in him.

Roz could bear the stretchmarks and sickness, and the pain of childbirth to come. Sheridan would keep her perfect figure and pass the little girl off as her own. That baby was hers – *all* hers, and Roz was nothing more than a rented womb. Her meeting in LA had been a success. She had taken Samantha, and together they had worked out her schedule for the next month. Delegating as much as she could, she put her absence down to her advancing pregnancy but promised she would be back at the helm soon. Her agent had lined her up with a plethora of deals for when the baby was born. Wearing the fake bump had been cumbersome, and deflecting people's grubby hands away was a task in itself.

She did not imagine in the short time she was gone that she would have so much to face upon her return. Walking along the hall, she cast her eyes over the glossy tiles, checking every surface was spotlessly clean. She paused at the lift doors. The memory of her fight with Roz still lingered: her blood dripping down the surface of the lift doors as she prised them open. The taste of metal in her mouth. It was a long time since anyone had hurt her like that.

First came the phone call. A message from Daniel telling her that he had allowed Roz to go to church. Sheridan was furious, but by the time she had picked up the message, Roz had already left. It was utterly frustrating. Daniel did things his way, then let her know as an afterthought.

As Anna opened the lounge doors, Sheridan raised an eyebrow at the sight of George standing with his back to the fireplace. He was dressed like a street hoodlum, his face stony, his hands clasped behind his back. He looked as if he were about to face the firing squad.

'It's OK,' Daniel said as he took in Sheridan's worried expression. 'Roz is home safe and well. Juanita's preparing her lunch now.'

'Nice to see you, too.' Sheridan frowned, waiting for the 'but'.

Wearing an apologetic smile, Daniel kissed her on the cheek. The musky aroma of his aftershave still made her stomach flip.

'I've missed you,' he murmured, his breath warm on her face. 'How was your trip?'

'Good,' she said, drawing away. He was not off the hook yet.

Sighing, she wished she could kick off the heels that were making the balls of her feet ache. Briefly closing her eyes, she inhaled the delicate scent of burning logs. So that's why Daniel wanted to meet in the living room. She had once told him it was one of the few places in the house where she felt truly relaxed. Things must be bad.

Her thoughts returned to Roz, her frown deepening a notch. 'Where is she? Down below?'

'Yes.' Taking a seat in the leather wing chair, Daniel spread his legs wide. George, on the other hand, had yet to move an inch. 'Nobody saw her at church,' Daniel continued. 'It all went as planned. Oh, and Monica called. She sounded upset.'

Sheridan rolled her eyes. Monica would have to wait. She turned to George. 'If everything's all right with Roz, why do you look like you're about to faint?'

'I'm sorry,' George said, his gaze creeping to Daniel. 'I didn't want to go.'

'Baby, it's not George's fault,' Daniel interrupted. 'There was never anything to worry about.' He relaxed back into the chair, his eyes chasing the dance and sway of the imitation flames in the fireplace. His beard had grown, making him appear mature, relaxed, in control. Sheridan wanted to shake him. After all her hard work in LA! He couldn't even see what he had done wrong.

'Why don't you get to the point so I can decide for myself?' she said.

Sheridan watched as George revealed the prayer book he had been holding in his hands. Stiffly, he approached, his mouth a thin white line of regret.

'I found this in the church.' Opening the book, he produced a folded scrap of paper inside. 'I saw Roz slip it in when she was saying her prayers.'

Snapping the note from his outstretched fingers, Sheridan raced over the words.

My name is Roz Foley. I am being held captive. By Sheridan Sinclair – basement apartment. Please send help. The note ended with a phone number next to the name Dympna.

'I don't believe this.' Sheridan's mouth fell open at the prospect of the damage it could have caused. 'What the hell . . . is she up to?' Her words were staggered, disbelieving. 'After everything we've done . . .'

'She doesn't know I found it,' George replied, his knuckles white as he clasped the prayer book. 'I thought you might like to deal with it yourself. Or if you prefer, we could say nothing – keep up the pretence that we're friends.'

Sheridan turned to her husband, waving the piece of paper before his face. 'Now do you see? She's been scheming against us all this time.' She shook her head in disbelief as Daniel said nothing in return. 'I'm over in LA, working my buns off to get us sponsorship deals, when all the while you're playing the good guy. How could you let her wander around New York? She's pregnant with my child!' Sheridan's voice raised an octave. 'What would it do to us if this got out? Our careers would be over. Don't you get how serious this is?'

But when it came to Roz, Daniel was not one to apologise. 'I sent George to keep an eye on her and that's exactly what he did. What do you want me to do?'

'That's a discussion for later.' Sliding the note into her dress pocket, Sheridan turned to George. Her voice lowered, she was back in control. 'Do you know what's *really* bothering me about all this? How quickly Roz got spooked. Anyone would think there was someone whispering poison in her ear.' Stepping towards him, she nailed him with her gaze. In the background rose the crack and hiss of artificial flames. 'You wouldn't happen to know anything about that, would you?'

'What? Me? Of course not. I'd never gossip about you.'

'You say that, but Roz has been jumpy from day one. Why do you think that is? Do you know something I don't? Does she?'

George inhaled a breath to speak, paused, then swallowed his words.

'Spit it out,' Sheridan replied. 'Don't hold back.'

'Well . . .' George continued. 'She wants to go home. She thinks you're keeping her prisoner. That's why she's so scared.'

'Prisoner indeed,' Sheridan snorted. 'We're making sure she sticks to the terms of the agreement, which was that she would stay here until the baby's born. I've been photographed in public with a bump. I've struck deals. She can't leave now.'

George's Adam's apple bobbed as he swallowed. 'I think she's worried about what will happen to her once the baby is born.' He stood like an errant schoolboy, staring at the floor.

A dark chuckle left Sheridan's lips. 'And what do *you* think will happen to her, George?' she said, approaching him. 'What do you think I'm going to do? Gobble her up? Like we're in some kind of fairy tale?' She was enjoying playing with him. 'How's your mother these days?'

'Not good. They've put her on new medication but the cancer's spreading.'

'Such a shame,' Sheridan tutted, sounding anything but sympathetic. 'But she's comfortable, yes? In that nice private ward, being waited on hand and foot?'

'Yes, very.' George cleared his throat.

'Do you remember what it was like before, when you couldn't afford the medication? How you had to clean up after her? You wouldn't want to go back to that again, now would you?'

George responded with a tight shake of the head.

Sheridan ran a manicured nail over the back of his shoulders. 'She's so lucky, having a son like you . . . unlike my mother. She wasn't lucky at all.' Her words hanging in the air, she monitored his expression for a spark of defiance. But there was only fear. *Good*. Satisfied, she turned on her heel.

'Where are you going?' Daniel called after her, delivering a warning glare. His annoyance at her game-playing was evident. It did not faze Sheridan. He shouldn't have gone against her wishes in the first place.

'To get Roz, of course. Stay where you are. It's time we had this out with her.'

CHAPTER FORTY-FOUR

ROZ

By the time lunch arrived, my appetite had vanished. Something was going on upstairs. Sheridan was home. The thought of her discovering my note was enough to chill the blood in my veins. What if somebody had gone to her instead of the police? But surely she wasn't that easily contactable? I checked behind Juanita's shoulder as she approached me with a tray of food. Her face was gaunt, her eyes full of knowing, the air thick with unspoken words. She must understand a little English, surely?

'Juanita, please . . . *por favor* . . . I know you understand.' I touched her wrist as she laid the tray on the small circular table, wishing I could remember more of the language I had once tried to learn. Surely she could see I was being kept against my will? I could rush her, push her out of the way and get as far as the lift. But she was broad and strong and I had the baby to think of. Neither did I want to be sedated again. I was stuck down here like a rat in a cage waiting to be experimented on.

But Juanita was acting as if I did not exist at all; she just slipped her hand away. The tray held my supplements, a plate of tuna sandwiches, a protein yoghurt and a glass of juice. I would pour that down the toilet later on. I'd rather drink bottled water than chance it. Frustration burned as I tried to communicate in broken Spanish.

'*Soy* . . . um . . . *soy irlanda* . . .' I muttered. 'What's the word for help?' They didn't teach that in language class. '*Mi casa irlanda . . . estoy triste, muy mal* . . .' I groaned. This was no use. I was throwing random Spanish words together. 'Please,' I said, my words falling on deaf ears. 'Go to the Irish embassy. Tell them my name is Roz Foley. I'm being kept prisoner.' I spoke to her back as she turned to walk away. Tears gathered in the corner of my eyes. I stood, cumbersome as I followed her to the lift. 'Kelly . . . she was here before me, wasn't she? What happened to her?' I paused for a reply, but no words were returned.

'Please,' I said. 'You won't get into trouble. I'll help you. Keep you safe.'

I wanted to scream. It was as if I was trapped behind glass and she could not hear a word I said. In reality, there was little I could do if Juanita was an illegal alien or if Sheridan had something else on her. We both knew that as soon as I was free, I would disappear back to Ireland. I sensed she was a good person, but ill-equipped to deal with me. I thought about George and the hold Sheridan had over him. The woman was not stupid. She manipulated everyone. Sheridan knew I would no longer hand over my baby willingly and she had no intention of letting me go. As Juanita walked away, she was taking any hope I had of escaping with her.

I balled my fists, stamping my feet like a five-year-old who has just been told she can't go to the playground.

'If you won't listen to me then I'll scream until you do!'

It was stupid. A last resort. But what else could I do? I inhaled a lungful of air, but the scream was silenced as Juanita properly met my gaze for the first time. Shaking her head, she pressed her finger to her lips.

'Shhh,' she said. Taking a step backwards, she stepped into the lift, mouthing the word, 'No.' The doors closed, and all I could see was her face.

I stood like a statue, grateful for that one second of contact. She could understand English –well, a little bit, anyway. I watched as the lift rumbled up on its runners. The old Roz would have screamed the house down until Juanita said more. But that small gesture was made to silence me and instantly I complied. I was cage-bound. Weeks in captivity had turned me into someone I no longer recognised.

I dragged my feet back to the table, picking up the sandwich and placing it back on the plate. Was this progress? Would Juanita say more the next time? Robotically, I took my supplements, transferred the food from the tray to the table to eat. I moved the plastic spoon along with the folded napkin, blinking to clear my vision as I saw what was nestled beneath. A knife. She had left me a weapon. I stared at it, knowing I should hide it before Sheridan came down. But my body would not move. A part of me was too scared to pick it up in case Sheridan had installed CCTV. But surely whoever left it would know if that was the case? It was small, the kind for peeling potatoes. But if I used it, someone could seriously get hurt. My breath quickened as I imagined the consequences. What if the knife were turned back on me? On my baby? Was I willing to take that risk?

Upstairs, the murmur of conversation came to an end and Sheridan's heels clicked against the tiled floor. She was coming for me. I had to hide the knife. But where? I thought of the one place they were likely to keep me bound. My bed. But there was no time. My hand hovered over the cutlery. Could I really do this? I could not risk Sheridan knowing I had help on the outside. For now, my baby was keeping me alive. Juanita would be in more danger than me. Holding the knife pointed down, I strode to my bed and put the knife under my pillow – where I could reach it if need be.

I held my breath as the lift began its journey down. Pursing my lips, I made it back to the kitchen table, as if my small interaction with Juanita had never happened at all. But a spark of hope had lit inside me. I had an ally. I picked at my sandwich, forcing down a mouthful of tuna and mayo.

'We've got a friend,' I whispered to my baby in relief. But how far was she willing to go to help me? The magazines, the weapon – they were equipping me with what I needed, but I was still on my own.

CHAPTER
FORTY-FIVE
ROZ

'Come up.' Sheridan beckoned me to join her in the lift. But my feet were rooted to the spot. Everything felt out of kilter. She was dressed for business, her lips showing the after-effect of recent fillers.

'Oh, you're back.'

I tried to act surprised as I joined her, offering her a half-smile. In the confines of the lift I felt the low thunder of her anger from deep within. I stood there, my stomach churning as I remembered our altercation: me sinking my teeth into her hand to make her release the lift doors. The taste of her blood on my tongue. Was that why she'd stopped asking me about the baby? I could feel her hatred for me growing with every day that passed. She led me into the living room, and my internal warning bells rang as I saw Daniel and George sitting there. Anna closed the door firmly behind us as she left.

'What's going on?' I said, trying to muster some bravado.

Turning towards the marble fireplace, Sheridan picked up a prayer book and threw it at my feet. I jumped at the sudden act of violence, emitting a terrified squeak. Dread washed over me as I realised I had been betrayed. George must have seen me slip the note into the book and picked it up as we left the church. How could he? He knew what Sheridan was like: the danger he had placed me in. As Sheridan read out the note, my shame grew.

'Why?' Sheridan said. 'After everything we've done for you?'

'I'm sorry, I . . . I just wanted to let my friend know where I was.'

'I trusted you.' Daniel's voice was steady, but his expression was one of hurt. 'Anyone would think you were being held hostage. If you wanted to leave, you only had to ask.'

My mouth dropped open. I could barely believe what I was hearing. My gaze fell on George. Surely he knew this was not true?

'I . . . I thought . . .'

'We had an agreement,' Sheridan said. 'You leave after the baby is born. If you were unhappy you should have said so. But to do this . . . to betray our trust. Why?'

'I want to go home,' I said, confused. Why were they acting as if I were here of my own free will? 'I've asked, so many times. But you won't let me go.'

'Because I'm scared of what you might do to yourself . . . to my baby.'

Sheridan stepped forward, and I flinched as her hand fell to my growing stomach, resting on the outline of my belly button which was evident through the grey material of my maternity dress. She was in movie mode now, no doubt playing some character from a past role. It was all for Daniel's benefit, to cast me in the worst possible light.

'Have you written any other notes?'

I shook my head. I wanted to dig a hole and bury myself in it. The note made things a hundred times worse. Only Daniel's presence was stopping Sheridan from flipping her lid. Her face had healed from our last bust-up, but the memory still remained.

'*Quid pro quo*. Do you know what that means, Roz?' she said in the sweetest voice.

I nodded, recalling an old Hannibal Lecter movie I had once watched.

'You scratch my back and I'll scratch yours?' I replied, unable to word it more eloquently than that.

'That's right,' she said, her hand rising to smooth back my hair. My skin crawled beneath her touch and the look in her eye told me she was getting a perverse kick from my reaction. I didn't dare step back. There was something about Daniel's expression as he watched us both. Something I didn't like. My gaze flickered to George, and immediately, he looked away. A reluctant voyeur.

I could smell Sheridan's skin. What I once perceived as exotic now made me feel sick. She continued to speak, her words like silk as she invaded my personal space. Daniel watched as she finger-combed my hair. I felt invaded. Used. I wanted to spit in her face. But from what I'd read, Sheridan was dangerous, and I was in no position to retaliate now.

'Simply put, it means "something for something",' she continued. 'You understand that, don't you? It's what our relationship has been based on these last few weeks. You play by the rules and you enjoy the fruits of my labour. You break my trust and I . . .' I winced as she pulled on a knot in my hair.

'I repay you in kind.' Shaking her fingers, she allowed the blonde strands to fall to the floor. 'So tell me. What am I to do with you now?'

CHAPTER
FORTY-SIX
ROZ
APRIL 2019

'What's a Chinese cabbage?' I said, reading about pregnancy week thirty-two in my book. 'Is it smaller than an Irish cabbage, do you think? Whatever it is, you're about the same size.' I was talking out loud again; these days I was doing it more and more. Sitting in silence was getting me down. 'It says here that you've got fingernails and toenails, and it's normal for me to be short of breath. That's a relief, hey?' My chin wobbled as I sat alone, deep in a pit of anxiety and loneliness.

I chewed on my nails, which were now reduced to stumps. Weeks of isolation had frayed my nerves and left me on edge. I thought about my life in Ireland, of the myriad communications I took for granted every day. Of Ronnie, the postie, who always seemed to catch me on my way out of the flat. Of Maggie, the seventy-year-old who begged on the street for money to help towards her electric bill. I missed our chats in the morning as I handed her a euro or two. Then there were the cleaning ladies at work. Half of them spoke a language I did not understand, but we still managed to have a laugh. I missed Dympna's wild stories, and the voicemails my mother used to leave. So much human connection, all before twelve o'clock in the day. I had taken it for granted and now I was totally alone.

Now my life was a network of sounds. The pipes woke me up each morning as the apartment heating kicked in. Then there were Anna's heavy footsteps as she drew the mop and hoover across the floors above. Next came Leo's high-pitched squeak as the nanny picked him up for school. Then came the voices of Sheridan, Daniel and George. But there was no joy up there. No music, no dancing, no parties and no TV. Monica had not returned since she'd seen me in the hall, and Juanita had not been down since George told Sheridan about the note. I spent hours trying to work out if her absence was linked to the knife I'd nestled beneath my pillow. Had she got cold feet and confessed to leaving it, or was Sheridan being intentionally cruel? Perhaps she saw Juanita as a privilege that she had now taken away.

I rummaged in my wardrobe, trying to find something clean to wear. My dressing gown was grubby, the socks on my feet stale. I was reduced to washing my underwear in the bathroom sink with hand soap and drying it across the back of the chair. Occasionally, I'd hear Sheridan bark something in Spanish, but I guessed Anna, not Juanita, was on the receiving end of it. Even Daniel had stopped visiting me. Work was claiming his attention; I knew that from the conversations he'd had with Sheridan upstairs. I hated myself for missing him, and home seemed a million miles away.

I spent hours talking to my baby, but in reality, I was rambling to myself. Her kicks were getting stronger now, and at least I was still getting fed. Once a fortnight, Anna escorted me to Dr Blumberg's surgery for blood tests and a check-up. There was no point in pleading with him; my words fell on deaf ears. Even the door of the surgery was locked until my visit was complete. Sometimes Sheridan would stand over me. Other days, she would wait until I was gone. I'd hear her voice carry through the corridor outside the surgery as I was returned to my room. It was always about her baby: her health, her dietary needs and any changes that needed to be made. Once a day, Anna placed a tray of enough food to last me twenty-four hours on the floor outside the lift: one hot meal at lunchtime, with a cold supper and breakfast provided for the next day. So much for my schedule. Everything had gone out the window in the last few weeks. I never thought I would come to miss our Pilates sessions, or even those stupid chants. It was as if Sheridan still wanted my baby, but I was a shiny toy and my novelty value had worn off.

Days and nights merged together. Without windows, it was hard to tell what time it was. I couldn't even draw anymore, now Sheridan had removed my art supplies. I wanted to scream, to thrash about, to kick up the biggest fuss, but if Sheridan heard me, she would realise that I could hear her, too. I could not bear for her to block up the air vent – my only link to the outside world.

Sheridan spent hardly any time with Leo, and when she did, she was always telling him off. I'd hear her shrill voice telling him to look at the camera in a certain way, calling him stupid when he failed to comply. Things were worse for everyone when Daniel was away.

I sat at the table in the basement, biting into a protein bar that tasted like sand.

Sheridan's voice came through the air vent. She was having a heated phone conversation, by the sound of things. Slowly and carefully I clambered on to the chair, and listened intently to her words.

'I need another favour . . . I wouldn't ask unless it was important.' A pause as somebody spoke on the other end of the line.

'Daniel's on location in Washington. He won't be back for
another week.'

So that's why he hadn't visited me. But if it wasn't Daniel on
the phone, who was Sheridan talking to? I knew it wasn't George,
because he had only just called; from the gist of their conversation,
he had cancelled coming over because his mother had taken a turn
for the worse. Sheridan had spoken to him with a lot more sympathy than she did to whoever was on the phone now. I listened,
cocking my head to pick up her words.

'I need you to come here. I have a job for you . . .' Another
pause. 'Yes, here, to my apartment. It's time-sensitive. It won't wait.'

I gripped the chair as it wobbled. What job? What was she up
to now? A sinking feeling made it hard to swallow. Was she talking
about me?

'I need it done before Daniel gets back.'

My hand rose to my mouth as I emitted a squeak of fear. She'd
had enough. She was getting rid of me. What else could it be?

'You won't get into trouble if you keep it to yourself . . .' Her
words were sharp, as they always were when she was met with a
barrier of any kind. 'I've been good to you, Mike . . .'

Mike. Where had I heard that name before?

I listened as Sheridan's words softened, as she suddenly changed
tack. 'You and I, we go back a long way. You were my first kiss. You
don't forget stuff like that.'

My mouth fell open behind my hand. Was she trying to seduce
him? Then I remembered: *It Takes All Sorts*. Sheridan's first kiss was
with a boy named Mike.

Oh, my God, I thought, was that the case in real life, too? To
think she'd lived such precious moments choreographed for the

viewing pleasure of others . . . No wonder she had such a warped mindset.

'Thanks,' she said to Mike on the phone. 'I knew you wouldn't let me down.' Another pause. 'You'll need a shovel . . . I don't know, put it in a bag or something . . . Call me when you arrive. I'll get you in through the back.'

Fear encompassed me as my fate was decided. I could not believe my ears. They were planning to kill me. What else would they need a shovel for? But we were in the middle of New York. My rational brain assessed the situation. What about my baby? It made no sense.

I could not catch the end of their conversation as Sheridan walked into another room. All I could hear was the clicking of her heels and the sound of my own heartbeat. This was it. Sheridan had had enough. She was getting rid of me.

CHAPTER
FORTY-SEVEN
DYMPNA

'Why aren't you answering your phone? I was worried.'

Sitting on her bed, Dympna blinked at Seamus as if he were a stranger. She was so wrapped up in her investigation that she had not heard him let himself in. He was dressed in a navy suit as he was on his way home from work. A newspaper was under his arm, a set of spare keys in his hand.

Dympna scratched her head. 'What time is it?' She turned her cheek as he leaned in for a kiss, aware of her stale breath.

'It's half seven. Didn't you go to work today?' Seamus's eyes trailed over her walls at the clippings she had pinned overnight.

'Nah,' Dympna replied. 'I called in sick.'

'That's the third time this month. You'll get the chop if you keep this up.'

As Dympna straightened her legs, a plethora of printed papers fell on to the floor. 'I'm quitting soon anyway. Dad's helping me with the rent until Roz gets back.'

But the look on Seamus's face told her he did not approve. 'You look knackered. Did you get any sleep last night?'

'Sleep is overrated.' Dympna suppressed a yawn. 'I'll catch a few z's tonight.'

Picking up a sweatshirt from the floor, she pulled it over her head. It was official. She had become a slob. Soon Seamus would be wondering what he saw in her at all. Not that it mattered all that much these days – she was still trying to figure out if he was the father of Roz's child.

'Are you staying over?' she said, grabbing a hairbrush from the dresser table and raking it through her hair.

'If you want,' Seamus said, turning up the heating dial on the wall. 'Fiona's opening up in the morning, so I should be OK.'

Dympna pulled a face at the mention of his assistant's name. She had seen how Seamus's skinny new assistant looked at him in admiration and glared down her nose at her.

Once a cheater, always a cheater. The words floated into her consciousness, making her stomach churn. Ironically, it was Roz who had said it to her, in what seemed a lifetime ago. She followed Seamus into the kitchen. He was sniffing a carton of milk, having already put the kettle on.

'Do you not think . . . ?' he faltered, spooning coffee into mugs for them both.

'What?'

'Don't bite my head off, but do you not think you're getting a bit obsessed?'

Dympna sighed. She could hardly disagree. Over the last few weeks, all she'd been able to think of was finding Roz. It was as if there were invisible distress signals coming from her best friend. To an outsider looking in, she must seem like the hoarders you see on TV. Notebooks stuffed full of hastily written theories were piled up on her bedside cabinet. Printed papers of information were pinned to her bedroom wall, along with a map of New York. If that wasn't bad enough, celebrity mugshots were pinned beneath, as if they were suspects rather than A-listers. Her room was beginning to resemble something from the set of a crime-fiction drama on TV. She had investigated celebrity after celebrity and narrowed it down to the most likely couples. She then accumulated everything printed about them online and in gossip magazines. When she had fully explored that avenue, she hunted for other missing women, too. After all, Roz had mentioned that this was not their first child. What if they had done it before?

One of the saddest cases she'd heard of was of a blonde-haired young woman named Kelly Blunt, who had gone missing after contacting a couple in a chat room. Dympna had found out about Kelly after randomly searching the terms 'missing girl, celebrity couple' online. Her likeness to Roz made Dympna's senses tingle, so much so that she made contact with Kelly's mother in Carolina. It wasn't difficult to find her as she had set up a Facebook page in her daughter's honour. Introducing herself as the daughter of a detective inspector in Ireland, Dympna explained that she was worried about her friend, who might have fallen into the hands of a celebrity couple, too.

She wanted to explain everything to Seamus, but she didn't know where to start. 'All this,' she said, waving her hands over the notepapers gathering on the kitchen table. 'It's made me feel useful for the first time in years.'

'I get that.' Seamus handed her a mug of coffee. 'I've always said you were wasted as a cleaner. But Roz . . . you know what she's like. She must be, what, eight months pregnant now? Give her another month and she'll be blasting back in here like nothing's happened.'

Dympna rolled her eyes. If he believed that, he didn't know her at all. 'It's been months since she left that voicemail. I've heard nothing from her since.' Taking a sip of her coffee, she brought Seamus up to speed on her investigation. 'I think we should fly over there. I'm going to put it to Dad tonight. The cops will take us more seriously if we turn up in person.'

Seamus looked unimpressed as she came to the tail end of her findings.

'You don't want me to find her, do you?' Dympna placed her mug on the counter.

Taking it to the sink, Seamus washed their crockery in silence. It was his way of deflecting her question.

'Are you listening? I said . . .'

'I heard you,' Seamus replied, his back turned to her. 'You're blowing this all out of proportion. Roz will come home when she's ready.'

'Are you sure that's all it is? Because things haven't been right between us for a while.' Dympna's heart thundered with ferocity. 'Did you get her up the duff?'

Stony-faced, Seamus turned around. 'As if I'd do that to you. I can't believe it even crossed your mind.' Throwing the tea towel in her direction, he headed towards the door. 'I know where I'm not wanted. I'm going home.'

'But we need to talk.' Dympna stood, wringing the gingham towel in her hands.

The door slammed, making her wince as Seamus left without saying another word.

Dympna scraped her hair back into a ponytail as she glanced around her cluttered flat. Even the air smelt unclean. She would clean up the place, make it nice again. Do an online shop and get some food in for the next day. Then she would cook Seamus a meal and bottom this out once and for all. She turned to check her laptop as an email pinged in. All at once the chores were forgotten and she was embroiled in the case again. Kelly's mother had replied to her email. She seemed glad to hear from her, desperate for someone to delve further into her daughter's case. Dympna absorbed her words, feeling her pain.

> She was so excited about leaving, because the couple she was meeting were really well known. Celebrities, she said, high up in the acting world. The police said they were probably scammers, but I don't reckon so. Kelly spoke to the woman on Skype. She saw her face. I'm as sure as I can be of that.

Dympna pored over her words. Dad had warned her about going down blind alleys and the perils of wasting time on dead-end leads. But it was the last line of the email that made the hairs on the back of her neck stand to attention.

> She was really taken by that couple, although she only spoke to the woman to begin with. Kelly said they'd blow my mind if I knew who they were.

CHAPTER FORTY-EIGHT
SHERIDAN

It was happening again, Sheridan could feel it: the spiralling descent into oblivion she had clawed her way out of before. Roz was beginning to feel more like an unwanted pet every day. With Daniel gone, it was easier to pretend Roz wasn't there at all. Sheridan had enjoyed playing with her in the beginning, but a show of power is only fun with an audience. Daniel was her safety net. With him, she knew how far she could take things. Without him, she could not trust herself with Roz alone. Why did he have to go away now, of all times? She loved the baby with all her heart, but Daniel had been right. It was all too much for her.

Lately, all she could see was Kelly's face. Sleep deprivation brought waking nightmares as the young woman haunted her thoughts. It didn't help that Leo was looking more like her every day. It had gotten to the stage where she could barely look him in the eye. It wasn't his fault, which was why she had to put an end to this while Daniel was away. She picked up her phone. Inviting Mike to her home felt like a betrayal; Daniel would not be happy to have him under their roof. The phone rang only once before Mike picked up.

'I need another favour . . . I wouldn't ask unless it was important.' There was an edge to Sheridan's voice as formalities were dispensed with.

'Hey, Sherry baby, are you all alone? I take it that's why you're ringing me from home.'

Shit, Sheridan thought. He must have saved the number on his phone. She was distracted, unfocused, and had broken the rules by not using a burner phone. 'Daniel's on location in Washington. He won't be back for another week.'

She paced the floor, trying to straighten her thoughts. 'I need you to come here. I have a job for you . . .' A pause fell. 'It's time-sensitive. It won't wait.' Her muscles tensed. The thought of having Mike in her home made her skin crawl. It was an invasion of privacy afforded to the very few, and after their last meeting, she could guess the thoughts running through his mind.

'I take it you're after more than my company,' Mike said. 'When do you want me?'

She could almost hear the smile playing on his lips. She was grinding her back teeth so hard her jaw began to hurt. 'Tonight. I need it done before Daniel gets back.'

She listened as he drew on the cigarette he was smoking, exhaled a long breath. 'That's short notice, baby. How much trouble is this going to get me in?'

'It won't get you into trouble if you keep it to yourself. I've been good to you, Mike . . .'

'Yeah, and from what I remember, I've paid that debt in full. Or have you forgotten about your mom?'

Sheridan flinched. His words were a loaded gun.

'Why do you keep coming back to me?' Mike continued. 'Surely someone else can do your dirty work.'

Sheridan pursed her lips as a swear word skimmed her tongue. It wasn't as if he'd had to do a lot. Just let himself into her mother's house and set the scene. A quick push down the stairs in exchange for a wad of money and a lifetime of health insurance. But she kept her thoughts to herself. *You'll catch more flies with honey than vinegar* . . . Ironically, it was one of her mother's sayings that popped into her mind. She thought her mother's death would put an end to the memories of her. She was wrong. Sheridan fixed her smile and softened her words as she resumed playing her part.

The air conditioning came on automatically, making Sheridan spin around at the sudden whirring sound. She had sent the staff home, apart from the nanny, who was upstairs giving Leo a bath and knew better than to eavesdrop on Sheridan. One bad reference from her and the girl would never work in New York again.

She returned her attention to Mike, the words rolling off her tongue like scripted lines. 'You and I, we go back a long way. You were my first kiss. You don't forget stuff like that.'

She paced the tiled floor, waiting for his response. Wondering if she'd said enough. She would have to handle this carefully – reel him in, but not too much. Mike was strong, with enough muscle to overpower her if his frustrations got the better of him. She knew he could kill; that much was proven. But what if he turned the tables on her? Her gun . . . it was nestled in her bedroom cabinet upstairs. Perhaps she should wear it when Mike came around. It was small but provided lethal force.

'All right,' Mike finally replied, oblivious to Sheridan's darkening thoughts. 'I'll come around. Text me your address.'

Sheridan changed the phone to her other hand, wiping her sweaty palm on the back of her dress. She'd better wear jeans. A baggy sweatshirt so he didn't get any ideas.

'Thanks,' she said, her mind racing ahead. 'I knew you wouldn't let me down.'

'Do I need to bring anything? I'm presuming you'll fill me in when I get there?'

Sheridan nodded into the phone, her mind on the occupant of the basement below. She had been there too long. It was time for her to go. Mike would find a burial place. Mike would sort it all out. But how far would she have to go to persuade him? She pushed the thought away. Took a calming breath. Told herself to stay in control. 'You'll need a shovel . . .'

'A shovel?' Mike interrupted. 'How am I meant to hide that?'

'I don't know, put it in a bag or something . . . Call me when you arrive. I'll get you in through the back.' She stood firm, kept her voice light. If she sounded scared, he'd never come.

'Now I'm interested,' Mike replied. 'Husband's away, you're sneaking me in. If it wasn't for the shovel, I'd think you were seducing me. How am I going to get in without being seen?'

Sheridan forced a flirty laugh. 'Let me take care of that. There's a private entrance to this building. I'll meet you when you call.'

Her hands shook as she placed the phone back on the receiver. In that moment in time, she'd had a frightening moment of clarity. How far was she willing to go to get what she wanted? And was it worth it? She thought of Roz, below her. She was overdue a scan, but today Sheridan had dismissed Dr Blumberg, unable to face seeing her again. The key to the secret room burned in her pocket. She could not bring herself to walk down that corridor, let alone open the door. Because it wasn't just Roz down there.

It was Kelly, too.

CHAPTER
FORTY-NINE
ROZ

I lay on the bed, the sheets damp beneath my body. I had washed them but couldn't get them dry. My room smelt like a laundromat, set in permanent dim light; three of the spotlights had blown. Even Anna had looked at me with sympathy when she delivered my latest meal. Not enough to help, though. I had thrown my dirty laundry into the lift and it was still there when she returned the next day. I told her about Sheridan's plans and how she was preparing to bury me. As usual, Anna's visits were brief, my words falling on deaf ears.

I reached beneath my pillow, my fingers winding around the handle of the knife. It was time to gather my courage, dry my tears. I could be in for the fight of my life. I listened to heavy footsteps as Mike arrived on the floor above. Soft murmurs were exchanged. Fear permeated my being and I was too scared to eavesdrop on the exchange.

If only I had listened to Dympna when she warned me that I was making a mistake. Tears welled in my eyes as I thought of my friend so many miles away. How different my life would have been if I had taken her advice. Guilt sucked me in like quicksand, dragging me down until I could barely breathe. Was it the lure of New York that first drew me in? Or the empty promises that were made? I wiped away my tears with the back of my hand, telling myself to get a grip. How could I have predicted how this was going to turn out?

'It's OK, little bean,' I whispered to my unborn child. 'I'll keep you safe.'

I tried to stay calm in case my baby sensed my fear. There was movement as she pressed against my ribcage. The thought of her entry into the world was making me sick with nerves. It was not the prospect of giving birth that worried me; it was what would happen the second she was born.

A door slammed on the floor above and a muffled argument ensued. I knew it was about me. My basement accommodation may have been luxurious, but it was not soundproof. Slowly, I crept around the apartment and fetched a chair. As I dragged it to the air vent, its legs scraped the wooden floor. I bent my knees as I stepped up on to it, trying to hold it still. It was risky, but it was the best place to hear what was going on above. I held my breath as I listened for key words. They thought I couldn't hear them, but I knew what they were capable of. Air conditioning blasted from the ceiling, and I snuffled through my congestion. It was too dry, too cold, and goose bumps rose on my skin. The argument descended into soft murmurs. A decision had been made.

I waited for the whirr of the lift, but no movement came.

Groaning, I climbed down from the chair. Then I heard it: soft steps. Quiet voices as a lock was turned with a key. I grabbed my knife, scurrying over to the door that was always closed. They were out there, in the corridor. Sheridan was telling Mike not to wake me. My fingers tightened around the knife. I was shaking, my breath trembling on my lips as adrenalin coursed through my veins.

'She's in there,' I heard Sheridan say; yet they walked past my door.

'I remember when she went missing,' Mike replied. 'I can't believe she was here all this time.'

What? My frown deepened as I pressed my ear against the door. Their voices trailed away. I thought Mike was here to kill me, but had I heard wrong? My back aching, I grabbed a blanket and took a seat on the nearest chair. I needed to be on my guard. I needed to be ready for anything.

CHAPTER FIFTY
ROZ

Footsteps echoed above my head. What now? My breathing was shallow as I strained to hear every sound. Straightening my aching body, I rose from the chair. I had been sitting there for what felt like hours, but now it was apparent that Sheridan and Mike had gone back upstairs. I flexed my puffy ankles. My limbs had finally stopped trembling from the flow of adrenalin in my veins. I ground my fist into my lower back. I had more pressing things on my mind than my pregnancy discomforts. Upstairs had turned eerily quiet. Where were Sheridan and Mike now? I grabbed the plaid blanket I had wrapped around myself and threw it back on the bed. The lift was being called. This was it.

My lower back sent another dart of pain through me as I waddled over to my wardrobe. It provided good cover, and I pressed my body against the side. A bead of sweat broke out on my forehead. It was now or never for me and my baby. The lift was coming, those dreaded mechanisms locking into place as it brought its occupant down.

I raised my hand above my head, ready to slice down with the knife. My heartbeat pounded like thunder in my ears. I could smell my own fear as perspiration laced my skin. Even if I stabbed my captor, I still had to make it upstairs and escape.

But the person who exited the lift was not Sheridan. It was Daniel, and I was flooded with relief. I watched him approach my bed, my gaze falling to his hand. He was holding something . . . a Hershey's bar. That was when I knew I could not stab him in the back. Such actions were only seen in movies. I was not strong enough. Confusion streaked his face as he pulled back the covers to see a pillow underneath. For a second, his expression changed to one of panic, and he strained to see in the dim light.

'Roz?' he said, trying to switch on my bedside light. But Sheridan had had the bulb removed. I stepped out of the shadows and he inhaled a sharp breath as the knife glinted in my hand.

'Roz?' he repeated as he slowly approached. 'What are you doing?'

His hands were held up in surrender; he looked tired but worried. I took in his tousled hair, his sweatshirt and jeans. He must have travelled through the night. But where were Sheridan and Mike?

'Stay where you are,' I said, holding up the blade.

Raising his palms in a gesture of assurance, Daniel forced a smile, but he could not hide the concern behind his eyes. 'Come on, no need for that. I know you won't hurt me.' His voice was low and comforting, with another empty promise ready to roll off his tongue.

'You left me,' I said, the knife trembling in my hand. 'You left me for dead.'

'Oh, Roz . . . I'm sorry. Hasn't Sheridan been looking after you?' He looked from left to right, taking in my laundry, the unkempt room.

'Nobody's spoken to me since you went. I've had one meal a day dropped on to the floor. Prisoners on death row are treated better than this.'

Daniel exhaled a low breath. Ran his fingers through his hair. 'Christ. I'm sorry. She said she was looking after you.'

'And you believed her?' My voice cracked. 'You know she hates me!'

'I'm sorry. You're right. But please . . . put down the knife.' Another step forward. He held up his hand. 'C'mon . . . you don't want to hurt me. Whatever's wrong . . . I'll make it right.'

He was right. I couldn't hurt him. But I wasn't threatening to. I turned my knife to my stomach.

'Take one step towards me and I'll do it,' I said. 'I'll kill my baby, then myself. Then at least we'll be together.'

'No.' Daniel paled at the sound of this horrific threat. 'You don't mean it.'

'I'm a Catholic, Daniel. I believe in heaven.'

Daniel retorted instantly, 'Not if you take your own life.'

But I was ready with an answer of my own. 'Unchristened babies go to limbo, the same place as people who commit suicide. I'd rather spend eternity with my baby than another minute down here.'

It worked. Daniel froze as uncertainty twisted his features. He was not in an action movie. Without his lines, he didn't know what to do.

'I'm sorry,' I said to the baby. 'But it's better this way.' The words tumbled from my mouth and I wondered if I really had been driven to this. Was I cracking up or playing a part, joining in with Sheridan and Daniel's games? It felt good to take back some control.

'Wait!' Daniel fumbled in his pocket. 'Here, take my keys.'

I watched with astonishment as he threw them in my direction. They skidded against the wooden floor, sliding towards me with a jingle of promise. 'Turn right at the top of the stairwell. Follow the exit sign.'

'Where's Mike?' I asked, working out my chances of escape. But I was met with a blank expression. 'He was here before you turned up.'

'Mike?' A shadow crossed Daniel's face. 'You're wrong. Mike wasn't here.'

I had hit a nerve, and I was ready to capitalise on it. 'He was. I heard Sheridan talking to him. She said she couldn't forget their first kiss. Then she snuck him in through the back entrance, but a little while later, you came in.' I cursed my inability to hear everything that had gone on. What had happened between Mike being here and Daniel turning up? 'Stay where you are,' I instructed, as I approached the door. 'I mean it . . . Follow me and I'll end it.'

'Roz, if you want to go, then leave. You're not a prisoner. I won't follow you.' Crestfallen, Daniel sat on the bed.

My knees weak, I breathed a sigh of relief. I turned the key in the lock of the thick wooden door. All I could think of was finally being safe. Of going home.

Relief flooded my system as I slipped through the open door, and it closed behind me with a satisfying click. I could almost taste freedom, feel the sun on my skin. But I had to negotiate my way out of the building first.

In the dim light of the corridor I remembered Daniel's words. The stairs were to the left. The surgery straight ahead. A locked door was on the right. I thought about Kelly. About what Sheridan had said. What if she was still alive? I could not leave her the way others had left me. I looked from left to right, the door to freedom so tempting, so close. But still, I turned around. If I didn't help now, this could haunt me forever.

I crept towards the door and shoved the second key in. The click seemed like the loudest thing on earth as the lock slid back. I swallowed, my mouth dry. I gripped the knife in my other hand. Where were Sheridan and Mike?

Tentatively I opened the door, whispering a croaky, 'Hello?' It creaked in response, releasing a musty stench. I covered my nose and mouth with my free hand. The room was cast in darkness: the blackness of a windowless space. Was that excrement I could smell? What if Kelly was alive, being held captive, just like me? I grasped the wall for the light switch, listening for every sound. Flooded with light, the room revealed its contents. I struggled to draw breath. My knife fell to the floor.

CHAPTER FIFTY-ONE

ROZ

'You should have run when you had the chance.'

The voice was Sheridan's, but it barely registered with me. I was on my knees; the strength had left my legs. It felt as if I were in a tunnel, and the rest of the world seemed so very far away. I couldn't believe what I was seeing. But I was aware of the implications. I'd heard a strange noise while sitting in the other room – a repetitive chuck, chuck sound. I'd blamed the building. Presumed it was the pipes. But there was something about it that didn't quite fit. Only now could I comprehend what it was. A spade hitting soil. Locked in horror, my gaze was on the ripped-up floorboards and what lay beneath.

I had come here to find Kelly, only to be faced with a gaping hole in the centre of the room. I'd forced my feet to move, one in front of the other, as I crept closer for a look. How I wished I hadn't. Believing the grave was meant for me was easier than facing this. I'd found Kelly all right, but it was way too late to save her. My stomach lurched, and I gagged and spat as I threw up into the dirt.

Sheridan was standing behind me now. Yet I could not avert my eyes from the remains of the body curled up in the ground. Long strands of white blonde hair peeped out from the dirt: the same colour as mine. A scrap of grey material poked through, like that of the maternity dress I wore. My dresses weren't new. They had once belonged to her. My stomach lurched for a second time as I realised that I was wearing a dead woman's clothes.

I saw the tips of Sheridan's Converse trainers from the corner of my eyes as she stood over me. I returned my gaze to the grave and made out the remains of a hand. The sight of brittle skin and bones made me dry-retch once more. It was as if Kelly was reaching out to me. Waiting for help which would never come. My tears flowed through my fingers as I buried my face in my hands.

'Please don't hurt me,' I begged, both for me and my baby. 'I'll do whatever you want.' They were monsters. But it was pointless trying to fight them, because they would always win.

'Shhh now . . . it's OK,' Sheridan said, even though we both knew it was not.

I had been so close to freedom. But the ground crumbled beneath my feet as I came face to face with the aftermath of Sheridan and Daniel's acts.

As Sheridan faced me, I could not meet her eye. 'C'mon,' she said with authority. 'Back to your room.'

I dragged myself to my feet. 'It's Kelly, isn't it?' I wiped my tears with my sleeve, short sharp bursts of anguish stealing my breath.

'How . . . how do you know about her?' She seemed astonished by my knowledge but didn't deny it.

My gaze returned to the hole in the ground. 'Am I . . . ?' I could barely utter the words. 'Am I next?' I looked around the room. This was a place of death. I smelt the decay, felt the absence of hope. I rested my hand on my chest, which had grown tight as I clawed for breath. 'Please. I won't tell anyone . . . Let . . . let me go.'

'I won't tell you again.' Sheridan's words were cold, her eyes dark. 'Back in your room.'

I touched the wall to steady myself, my eyes on the object in her hand. There was no arguing. No fighting and no running away. Sheridan was holding a gun.

CHAPTER
FIFTY-TWO
SHERIDAN

Sheridan held the gun with confidence as she prodded it into Roz's back. She enjoyed the feel of the cold metal in her hand. The safety catch was on; she didn't want to shoot. She would never hurt her baby, for a start. She'd had her doubts about Roz, but now Daniel was home, all would be well. She flicked her head to one side. This place gave her the creeps.

'Move!'

With the gun to her back, Roz had no choice but to comply. At least Sheridan could stop pretending. Everything was out in the open now. Their little triangle would have no boundaries as their secrets were slowly revealed. She was looking forward to filling Roz in. Roz's eyes flicked to the knife on the ground where it had fallen from her grip.

'Go ahead . . . pick it up . . .' Sheridan said sarcastically. 'If you want a bullet in your brain. Daniel might fall for your suicidal bullshit, but I won't.'

Roz looked longingly at the knife one last time before the last spark of defiance left her eyes. After months in captivity and escaping to find this . . . Sheridan had finally broken her.

Sheridan paused to pick the knife up from the floor.

'Where did you get it?'

'My food tray. Someone must have left it there by mistake.'

'There are no mistakes when it comes to looking after you,' Sheridan sniffed. 'Still, I'll get to the bottom of it. Now, get moving, it stinks in here.'

In the short journey from Kelly's grave to her basement accommodation, Roz seemed to fall into shock. Her shoulders hunched, she hugged her stomach, shuffling to her room as if she were on her way to the gallows. Life had given up on her, and now she was doing the same in return. With Daniel's keys safely in her pocket, Sheridan returned Roz to the room. Now it was time for her to experience the other side of the Sheridani coin.

Daniel tutted as they entered, his features creased in concern. 'Sheridan said you weren't well, but I didn't think it was as bad as this.'

Sheridan watched, the gun tucked into the waistband of her jeans.

'I'll have Anna bring you a nice hot chocolate. She can strip your bed while she's here, wash your things.' Daniel smoothed down Roz's hair. 'We'll fire up Netflix. How about that?'

Sheridan rolled her eyes. He was trying too hard. Why must he pander to her?

Roz's teeth began to chatter, her face chalky-white.

Daniel looked to the young woman for a response. 'Roz?'

'Yes,' she said quietly. 'I'd like that.'

'Good girl.' Daniel wrapped a blanket around her shoulders, gently guiding her to the sofa. 'Anna will be with you soon.'

He smiled as he left her, but the smile dropped from his face the second he joined Sheridan in the lift. 'What the hell were you up to? I told you to leave Kelly be!' His words were harsh, his eyes narrowed.

Sheridan pressed her body against the wall of the lift. She hated it when he was like this.

'You've been taking too many chances,' she replied, feeling small in her sneakers. 'I was scared Roz would escape, that they would pin Kelly's death on us.'

'So you got your old boyfriend around here the minute my back was turned.' Daniel's anger was rising now, and they both ignored the lift as it dinged. Aware of her gun in the waistband of her jeans, Sheridan hung her head. 'I'm sorry,' she said, knowing how much Daniel hated Mike. 'I couldn't see any other way out.'

'How did you get him to agree?' Daniel was standing over her now, his body rigid, his fists clenched. He punched the button to close the doors of the lift as they began to part.

Sheridan swallowed. How could she tell him that they had kissed? That Mike's hands had roamed her body as she whispered promises of so much more. She had worn the gun for a reason but lacked the courage that was so readily available when it came to her female counterparts. Mike understood about Kelly. He was willing to help.

'He . . . he said he'd get rid of the body – for a price. We couldn't keep her down there forever.'

She waited for the fallout. Up until now, she had welcomed Daniel's possessiveness; she saw it as a sign of love. But she had bent over backwards to accommodate him. Why couldn't he do the same for her?

'What's the price?' Daniel's words were spoken through gritted teeth.

When Sheridan failed to answer, he pressed his fingers into her jaw. She gasped at the sudden contact. Daniel so seldom lost his temper, but when he did, he was capable of anything.

'I paid him off!' she cried, her skin burning beneath his touch. 'A hundred grand.'

'Liar!' Daniel's eyes bored through hers. 'I know he's got a thing for you. What else did you do?' His fingers squeezed tighter with each word, and Sheridan cried out to be freed.

'We kissed!' Sheridan flinched beneath his touch. 'Nothing more.' She rubbed her jaw as he released it. 'I did this for us. If you hadn't let Roz go to church . . .' Her gaze roamed the lift walls, which felt like they were closing in.

'This is my fault, then, is it?' He spoke in a low growl, pressing her into the corner. 'My fault that you brought that scumbag into *my* home and kissed him while I was away.'

'I'm sorry,' Sheridan said, panic cutting her breath short. 'It meant nothing.'

Daniel's nostrils flared as his temper grew. 'Do you want to be down there with her? In the mud and shit, with maggots digging holes in your pretty face?' He touched her cheek, his movements rough against her skin. His fingers fell to her mouth and he forced her lips open. 'Say *No, Daniel, I should have cleared it with you first.*'

Sheridan glared at him in disbelief. He couldn't be serious . . . She baulked as he squeezed her lips. 'No, Daniel.' Her words were distorted as Daniel squeezed hard. 'I should have cleared it with you.'

'Damn right you should have.' He pushed her back against the wall. 'You don't make a single move without asking me first, do you hear me?'

Sheridan nodded, blinking back her tears in an effort to regain control.

'Where are you going?' she called after him as he strode out of the lift.

'To my room. Some of us have work to do.'

'What about Roz?'

'What *about* Roz?' He spun on his heel, making Sheridan step back. 'You heard what I said. Clean up that shit-hole downstairs and make her some hot chocolate. And if you ever neglect my property again, there'll be hell to pay.' Grabbing her by the waist, he pulled her towards him. But it was not to touch her; it was to remove her gun. 'You'll get this back when you can be trusted. Get washed. You reek of him.'

CHAPTER
FIFTY-THREE
SHERIDAN

Sheridan lay on Leo's bed, trying not to pull away as he wound his fingers around her neck. She wasn't made of stone. Seeing the remains of Kelly's body had brought back the old feelings of guilt and regret. She smoothed down Leo's errant hair, staring into the depths of his deep blue eyes. It was hardly his fault the camera didn't like him. You either had it or you didn't. She only hoped his new sister would be able to pull things back.

'Why don't you go back to sleep?' she said, swallowing back the tears that threatened to overflow. He had been awoken by a nightmare, but he would soon forget all about it. She wished she could escape hers as easily. Daniel was the only person in the world who could reduce her to tears. Such outbursts were thankfully rare – as long as she kept things on an even keel. But tonight, she had overstepped the mark by having Mike in their home.

'That's lovely,' she said, as Leo pointed at a crayon scribble on the wall.

'It's a dog. Daddy's getting me one.' His cheeks dimpled as he beamed. 'We're calling him Jake.'

Sheridan sighed. Daddy did whatever he damn well pleased.

◆ ◆ ◆

After spending half an hour grilling Juanita, Sheridan gave her the sack. The girl had pleaded innocence, but somebody had leaked information to Roz. Checking on her baby donor was Sheridan's next unenviable task. A sense of vulnerability crept in as she ventured below. Daniel had locked her gun in the cabinet and entrusted the keys to George. Sheridan's face soured at the memory. It was as if she were a child. Her lips were still tender from where Daniel's fingers had dug in. Sometimes he didn't know his own strength.

She would beg Daniel to allow Mike in so he could finish what he started and dispose of Kelly for good. It was pure luck that she had managed to sneak Mike out just as Daniel came home.

It wasn't just Mike that Daniel was angry about. Moving Kelly's corpse had triggered something in him. The months following her death were the toughest of their marriage. Sheridan's fingers touched her throat. The marks might have gone, but the memory remained. She recalled when her mother-in-law had come to visit, not long after Leo was born. Daniel had broken down, admitted every horrible twist and turn that had led to Kelly's demise. For a long time, Sheridan had expected his mother to turn them both in; but she had taken their secret to the grave.

Sheridan fixed her face as the lift doors opened. She would make it up to Daniel. She would start by being honest with Roz. With a few words of Spanish, Sheridan dismissed Anna from the room.

Roz was sitting on the sofa where they had left her, hunched and staring into space. Sheridan glanced at her freshly made bed. The floor had been mopped, the room tidied, the light bulbs replaced. On the table was a plastic vase filled with fresh flowers, along with an array of food: chocolate muffins from their local bakery, sandwiches and a jug of juice. Yet not a bite had been taken from any of it. She cast an eye over Roz, who was now chewing what was left of her nails. She looked like a terrified creature, and somewhere deep within, Sheridan felt sympathy.

'Roz,' she said flatly. 'Why haven't you eaten?'

But Roz did not reply. Her face was haunted, her eyes puffy and red-rimmed.

'You know how this goes,' Sheridan continued. 'Stick with the programme and you get benefits. I'm willing to overlook what happened earlier because it's obvious you're not well. But we need to get you scanned. I can't call the doctor in and have you looking like this.'

'What's the point?' Roz sniffed, her voice thick with congestion. She must have been crying all this time. 'I'll never see my baby. You want rid of me.'

Sheridan sighed as she took a seat. 'You think you've got it all worked out. But you couldn't be further from the truth. Why do you think we brought you here?'

Roz delivered a one-shouldered shrug. 'To take my baby, the same way you took Kelly's. But now you don't want either of us.'

Sheridan snorted. 'What happened with Kelly was an accident.'

She paused, the memory returning like a bullet from nowhere. She had never seen anyone lose so much blood. Her hands were covered in it. Towels were not enough. Even after Leo was born, it had dripped down the bed and on to the floor in a sea of red. She recalled Kelly's grey-blue lips. The life leaving her body as Leo cried from his bassinet.

Sheridan took a deep breath. 'She died in childbirth. But that won't happen to you. We have a doctor now. You don't need to worry on that front.'

But the fact that Roz had guessed the body was Kelly's aroused a prickle of irritation. Now that Sheridan had fired Juanita, there should be no more leaks. Sheridan watched Roz staring, zombie-like, into the distance. The girl was in shock and of no use to Daniel like this.

'Remember the first time you asked to leave here? What did I tell you?'

Roz stared at her, her mouth tightly clamped shut.

'I said we weren't just buying the baby, that we were buying you, too.' Sheridan crossed her legs, never taking her eyes from Roz's face. 'That's why you can relax . . . We've no intention of hurting you.'

'But you're not letting me go, either.' The words were mono-tone, punctuated with a snuffle.

Sheridan didn't deny it. How could she? 'There are plenty of women who'd be thrilled to spend time with my husband.'

Her statement went unanswered, and Sheridan rose to plate up some of the food on the table. She picked up a chocolate muffin and coupled it with a plastic tumbler of orange juice.

'Eat,' she said, handing Sheridan the plastic plate. 'For the baby.'

She watched as Roz opened the paper wrapping, pulled chunks of muffin away with her fingers and popped them in her mouth.

Regret hung heavy in the air. The two women sat together in silence. How had it come to this?

Sheridan's thoughts floated back to when she first met Daniel, and how she had set her sights on him. But once things had pro-gressed between them, he'd warned her that he would break her heart. She remembered his mother's prophecy long before they tied the knot. 'He's just like his father,' she said, but the words were not meant as a compliment. 'The more you drag him into domesticity, the more he lashes out. He's a free spirit. You'll never tie him down.'

She knew that Daniel *wanted* to be monogamous, but he was a pressure cooker. Too much work and no play made him blow his top. He'd told her he was scared he would hurt her, that it would all become too much. But then came the night when they'd shared their fantasies, and everything had changed. She remembered the rain pattering on the window of her LA apartment as they lay naked together in bed. Cradling his whiskey, Daniel had spoken in soft tones.

'Have you read *The Collector* by John Fowles?' His words were fuelled by alcohol, which opened up parts of him inaccessible to anyone else. 'That's as close to my fantasy as you can get.'

Sheridan nodded, grateful for his trust. 'You fantasise about abducting someone? Keeping them locked away?'

'It's not real, Sheridan – I wouldn't be telling you if it was.' That much was true. She'd had to get him very drunk for him to speak like this. 'But, yes . . .' he'd continued, throwing an arm around her shoulder. 'It's not about sex, and it's certainly not about love . . .' He paused, his face far away. 'It's about control. Bending the will of another until they're totally dependent on you, to the point that if you open the door they won't run away.'

'Like Stockholm syndrome?' Sheridan's pulse quickened at the thought. That's what she liked about Daniel. His dangerous side. The people she had grown up with were on screen, written in to be picture-perfect and candy-cane sweet.

'More like a dirty little secret.' Daniel paused to sip his whiskey. 'The satisfaction of knowing I've got this whole other world going on that people know nothing about. It's dangerous, a break from the mundane, you know?'

And mundane was the last thing Sheridan needed. It would be the death of their marriage, for starters. It would collapse her life like a deck of cards.

Over time she'd begun to justify it. It was no different from Daniel playing a leading movie role. A fantasy world, with no outside attachments. She learned to recognise the signs of his growing unease. Knew when it was time to intervene. As publicity became fierce, he began to feel hemmed in. No longer could he ride his motorbikes or go out in public alone. Work was all-consuming, as was the pressure to present a clean image to the world. He needed an outlet. Which is where Kelly came in. She was a pretty girl, with light blonde hair. Exactly Daniel's type.

At first, it was a game. Something to bring Sheridan and Daniel closer. Their own private secret that nobody else knew about. Sheridan even found herself enjoying it – until it all became too real.

'What about her?' she'd say, browsing online escort sites.

'Too slutty,' Daniel would reply. 'She has to be wholesome, innocent. Think girl next door.'

Sheridan should have heeded her internal warning bells and passed it off as a bit of fun. But as more women chased her successful husband, the greater the risk that he would stray. A cheating husband would jeopardise everything they had built.

Kelly was perfect. Young and naive, she was a wannabe actress who was desperate to leave home. Sheridan had been chatting to her for two weeks online when she told Daniel what she had done.

'Are you nuts?' he'd said, running his fingers through his hair. 'If she calls the cops . . .'

'She won't,' Sheridan replied. 'I've offered to take her in, help her get her foot in the door.'

'You're crazy,' Daniel said, but she could see from his expression that his interest was aroused. 'Nobody is that stupid, and I don't want some redneck hillbilly . . .'

Sheridan clicked on the monitor and brought up the pictures of Kelly's profile that she had saved. They were enough to silence Daniel's protests.

'I met her through a mentor chatroom,' Sheridan said. 'I've fed her a line. Told her we're desperate for a baby. She's offered to be a surrogate in return for my help.'

'You're unbelievable, Sheridan Sinclair. What makes you think we can get away with this?'

'It gets her here, doesn't it? Think about it. It would explain why she has to be hidden to begin with, because we'd be passing the baby off as our own.'

'I don't know . . .' Daniel said. 'What if she got pregnant?'

Sheridan shrugged. 'Would it be the worst thing in the world? We could hire a nanny; a baby would get the press off our backs and do wonders for our profile.' She delivered a seductive smile. 'And Daniel . . . she's not averse to getting pregnant the natural way.'

'Bloody hell. You never stop surprising me.' Daniel shook his head. 'But . . . wouldn't you mind? Having another woman in the house?'

'I wouldn't see her. The staff could feed and look after her. She'd be your little pet.' Sheridan had flashed him a wicked smile. She'd threaded her arm through his, drawing him close as she whispered in his ear. 'To be honest, it turns me on.'

If only it had, Sheridan reflected.

'It's not that easy, though, is it?' Daniel had replied. 'It would kill me if I found out you were seeing someone else.'

'It's just a bit of fun. It's not as if you'd be having an affair behind my back. Everything would be under my terms.' Sheridan had turned to him, her face growing serious. 'Do you know what the divorce rate is in Hollywood?' She did not wait for him to reply. 'Over fifty per cent. Throw in an age gap and it's higher than that.

I'm doing this to protect our marriage. If you have Kelly, you won't go looking elsewhere.'

'But Sheridan, I love you.'

'And I love you. Which is why we've got to give this a try.'

'What if she goes to the press?'

'The threat of being sued is enough to buy her silence, and besides . . . once we get her here, she's yours. Who is she going to tell?'

Daniel's face was alight with possibility. It was as if all his birthdays had come at once. 'What about after? I mean, we can't keep her forever . . .'

'We cover our tracks and pay her off. But we can't stay here. Too many prying eyes. There's an apartment in New York with a basement floor. It's ideal.'

'New York *would* be easier for work . . .' Daniel's voice tailed off.

'Exactly. Another reason why we should go.'

'Yes, but another woman . . . What if you hate me for it? It's not worth the risk.'

'You were with another woman last week. How many more actresses will you star alongside?'

Daniel's silence spoke volumes. A tiny piece of Sheridan wanted him to deny it, but he wasn't that sort of man. She knew what he was when she married him, and this was her best compromise.

'You're amazing, you know that?' he said, placing his hands on her face.

That night, they'd had mind-blowing sex. The next day, Sheridan had made Kelly an offer she couldn't refuse.

Now she sat here with Roz in silence, wondering how it had all gone wrong. She never could have predicted that Daniel would fall in love with Kelly, or his reaction when he found out that she had died. Roz was there to make everything better. Sheridan could still claw things back. Because she would rather share her husband with another than have her marriage fall apart.

CHAPTER
FIFTY-FOUR
ROZ
MAY 2019

I didn't have the heart to read this week's update aloud to my baby. I had grown far too close to her. At thirty-six weeks of pregnancy, doing the simplest things took a lot more effort. Eating, sleeping – even breathing, sometimes. I imagined my baby curled up safe and warm in her temporary cocoon. She was at least six pounds in weight and would soon be born. I rubbed the base of my spine as I rose from the table and picked up the letters I had written earlier in the day. I made my way to the bathroom. There was no way I could leave them out for anyone to find.

Tearing up the notepaper, I scattered it down the toilet and flushed. The letters I had written would never be read by their intended, but the small ceremony gave me some much-needed closure. Words of regret had bled on to the page, intermingling with my tears as I said my goodbyes to my mother, to Dympna and to my baby, which was the most painful of all. Daniel had ensured the return of my supplies, including my pencils and pens. But how far would his kindness stretch?

Thoughts of Kelly's final moments filled my mind, keeping me awake long into the night. Did she know her days were numbered? I hoped not. Perhaps Kelly's head was full of dreams for the future: becoming a famous actress, sending money home to her family. Becoming a star.

I had no reason to believe Sheridan's story, but I accepted it just the same. A complication in childbirth had led to Kelly's demise, and there was nothing to say the same fate would not befall me. Sheridan might not be a murderer, but she had stood by and watched Kelly die. Why? Daniel refused to discuss the subject of Kelly in any way, shape or form. I could sense his anguish at the very mention of her name.

Perhaps he loved her, and that was her undoing. I frowned as unanswered questions filled my mind. Why do it all over again with me? Sheridan could have called for help when Kelly started bleeding, but she hadn't. And now it would be the same with me. I realised with some clarity that what I felt for Daniel was dependence, not love. But how did he feel in return? The baby growing inside me was not his flesh and blood.

I combed my hair, then smeared a thin layer of Vaseline on my lips. Sheridan was away with Monica at a charity event in LA. I pulled up the strap on the pretty lace maternity dress that Daniel had loaned me. It was one of Sheridan's, a red number that had been gifted by yet another up-and-coming designer.

The table in my basement room was set for two with plastic throwaway cutlery, and soft music played. Upstairs, Anna was cooking us a three-course meal. Daniel had gone to some lengths in order for me to have a nice night. But my days above ground had ended. He did not say as much, but I knew the trust between us was hanging by a thread.

Dabbing Sheridan's perfume into the curve of my neck, I almost felt human again. Gasping, I placed a hand on the side of my stomach as my baby moved beneath my skin.

'I'll name you Tigger if you keep on bouncing around in there,' I chuckled.

My baby girl was cramped but agile, and it had been a relief when I'd heard Dr Blumberg tell Sheridan that she was engaged, head down. At least she should not have the complication of a breech birth.

My heart skipped a beat as the lift came down. Smoothing my dress, I stood, feeling like a teenager on my first date. I had to get this right. I had to at least try.

'You look beautiful,' Daniel said, handing me a bunch of yellow roses.

I took them with gratitude, inhaling their sweet scent. I wanted to reply that I looked like a whale, but there was no place for the old Roz tonight. 'Thanks,' I said instead, too embarrassed to relay a compliment. Daniel may as well have stepped out of the cover of *GQ* magazine.

'So where are we tonight?' It had become our latest game. Daniel would describe the faraway places he had been to, transporting me into his world.

'We're in The Chequers, back in my hometown.'

Daniel regaled me with details of his favourite restaurant and the food they used to serve. He slid off his jacket and placed it on the back of the chair while I laid the roses to one side. I did not feel like food. I needed to get this over with; my heart was beating so hard I couldn't take it any more.

I took a step towards him. I was barefoot, because Sheridan deemed heels to be a hazard, but my toenails looked pretty in pink. Rising up on my tiptoes, I stretched my arms around his neck. I inhaled citrus and spice, the tantalising scent of his aftershave, as I nuzzled his skin.

'The food can wait,' he said, his voice husky. He slid his arms around my expanding waist.

'OK,' I whispered breathlessly. It was hardly the most romantic setting, a heavily pregnant woman in a basement flat. But it was now or never. Every moment we had spent together had been leading up to this. It wasn't that I *wanted* to sleep with him – I had to. Creating a bond between us gave me my best chance of staying alive. Time was running out, and there would be no use for me once my baby was born.

I allowed him to kiss me, deep and slow, before I followed him to the bed.

'Are you sure?' he said. 'Because if you'd rather leave, I won't stand in your way.'

I suppressed my surprise. It was a trick. He was testing me. I knew what would happen if I tried to escape.

'I want to be here, with you,' I lied, unbuttoning his shirt.

Daniel seemed pleased with my response as a slow smile crept on to his face. 'Really?'

'More than anything,' I murmured, trying to clamber on to the bed. My stomach was not making this easy, and I had no idea how I could turn anyone on in my present state, much less a Hollywood superstar. 'Sorry,' I said, as the mattress bounced under my weight. It was laughable. I was almost out of breath, and we hadn't even done anything yet. I lay facing him on my side. 'I feel ridiculous,' I admitted, as my nerves kicked in. 'Look at the state of me.'

'You're beautiful,' he whispered, but his eyes carried a blank nothingness that drove a shiver down my back. Was he thinking of someone else? Was I here at all? Pushing down the straps of my dress, he leaned in and kissed my shoulder. It all felt so surreal. He was breathtakingly handsome, but there were no fireworks between us, and Daniel seemed to sense my reluctance. The baby kicked, a timely reminder of my circumstance, and my fingers slowed over his belt buckle. I wasn't a princess in a tower, and he wasn't my Prince Charming. He was Sheridan's husband and my captor.

'Woah,' he said, stilling my hand as he placed his on top. 'This isn't right.'

My heart was hammering so hard, I could barely catch my breath. 'What's wrong?'

Daniel shook his head. 'You don't want this, not really.'

'I . . .' I tried to speak, but the words would not come. I watched as Daniel buttoned his shirt, swung his feet on to the floor.

'I'll have the food brought down to you,' he replied. 'It's steak. You don't want it to spoil.'

'No, wait, don't go,' I said, holding my dress to my chest. 'Is it because I'm pregnant?' I needed answers, if only to second-guess what would happen next.

'It's not you . . .' Daniel tucked his shirt into his trousers. His gaze wandered over the room, as if seeing my prison for the first time. 'I can't do this any more.' He bent to pick up his shoes from the floor. 'Leave the dress out for Anna. She'll put it back in Sheridan's wardrobe.' He did not look back as he walked to the lift.

I tried to follow him, but by the time I'd clambered off the bed, the lift doors were closing. I was about to call after him to say he had left his jacket, but managed to stop myself in time. There could be keys in there. How stupid could I be?

I blinked in the dim light, my gaze on the lift display as it showed the lift travelling upwards.

Daniel's jacket felt silky-smooth as I ran my fingers down the side pocket. Empty. Sighing, I watched the lift display signal that it was on the upper floor. Soon he would realise his mistake and make his way down. I had just seconds.

'Please,' I whispered under my breath, praying his keys weren't in his trousers. But as I slipped my hand into the inside pocket of the jacket, I was rewarded not with keys, but a mobile phone. I ran my fingers over it; it was surprisingly cheap for someone of Daniel's calibre. Could I get enough reception to make a call?

The ding and whirr of the lift signalled it was back in action. He was on his way again. I wanted to scream in frustration. Even if I could get reception, there was no time.

It's a burner phone, I thought, having read in *Celeb Goss* of the lengths Sheridan and Daniel went to ensure their privacy.

I jabbed my thumbs over the buttons, texting the one person in the world who might be able to help. One word was all I had time for, but Dympna would know what it meant. Quickly, I negotiated his sent messages folder to delete it. My heart was in my throat as the lift arrived on my floor.

Holding my breath, I slipped the phone back into Daniel's jacket. Taking swift steps towards the sink, I pulled a plastic tumbler from the cupboard as he approached.

'Use the bottled stuff, it's better for you,' Daniel said, taking his jacket from the chair.

'It's fine,' I said, facing the sink wall. I could not risk him seeing my guilt-stricken face. My head raced with worries as I heard him disappear via the lift, my emotions in complete turmoil.

I imagined Dympna's alarm as she read the text. If only I'd had time to think things through. What if she rang Daniel's number? Asked for me by name? I had done everything I could to gain his trust, and now I could have blown it all away.

CHAPTER
FIFTY-FIVE
DYMPNA

Dympna's fingers curled around her armrest as she gulped another mouthful of conditioned air. She couldn't believe her own powers of persuasion. After weeks of nagging her father, he had finally caved in and bought flights to New York. But now her stomach tightened as she looked through the window of the Boeing 777, which was about to take off. Her limbs were rigid, her feet glued to the floor.

'I can't. I need to get off.' Her words came as a sharp whisper.

She had been in such a tizzy since receiving Roz's text that she'd forgotten about her fear of flying – until now. As the plane moved on to the runway, Dympna squeezed her eyes tightly shut. 'Tell them, Dad, please. I need to get off. I thought I could do it, but I can't.'

Beside her, she heard her father's soft chuckle. Felt his strong hand cloak hers and squeeze tight. 'You can and you will.'

'But what if I'm wrong?' she said, between panicked breaths. 'I've taken you from work, given up my job.' She looked at him as if only then realising the seriousness of the situation. 'What have I done?'

'You've opened a strong lead into Roz's case. One we can't ignore. Don't let your nerves get the better of you now.'

After checking her phone, Dympna had done a double-take at the sight of the one-word text. *PICKLE*: their childhood code word. Nobody could dispute that Roz was in trouble, but thankfully she was still alive.

Dympna had agonised about ringing the international mobile number, and had telephoned her father for advice. But US police checks had come back with nothing, and by the time they'd called, they were rewarded with a dead line. Dympna's next action was to get her father to commit to travelling to New York.

'We'll find her,' John continued. 'Have faith in yourself. Now, deep breaths – here we go.'

Closing her eyes, Dympna breathed in through her nose and out through her mouth as the plane ascended. Going to her happy place, she recalled clambering into Roz's bed at the weekend to gossip about who they'd met the night before. But the memory brought a pang of sorrow. Only now did she realise what a huge upheaval this had been for Roz. Her heart ached for her friend and she bitterly regretted letting her walk out of the front door of their flat alone. Whatever she had done, Dympna needed to see her again.

Seamus had said very little on the journey to the airport. She saw remorse in his eyes, but he repeated his assurance that he would be there for her when she got back. Each time he took a short breath, she felt like he was trying to tell her something, but each time his gaze fell to his shoes and the words would not come.

Even Dympna's mother was teary as she'd said her goodbyes. She did not come to the airport. She'd barely come to the front door. Dympna had left her a present on the kitchen table: a letter from the Gardaí confirming her application to join. She tried to imagine starting a new life when she came home. It was something to cling on to. It was hope.

CHAPTER FIFTY-SIX

SHERIDAN

***Celeb Goss* Magazine**
Alex Santana
May 2019
**DANIEL WATSON AS THE NEXT JAMES
BOND?**

Ever since Daniel Craig announced his plans to
retire, Hollywood has been rife with rumors about
which lucky actor will be chosen to play the next
James Bond. Here at *Celeb Goss*, we are rooting for
another Daniel – British heartthrob Daniel Watson.

He is no stranger to working with Bond cohorts, having previously had a great working relationship with
Moneypenny actress Natasha Clarke. Rumor has it
that Daniel and Natasha enjoyed many a late-night
session in the private bar of the hotel where their last

movie, *Justice*, was shot. Daniel Watson, aged thirty-eight, has stated he would love to take on the role of Bond. 'I've dreamt about playing him ever since I was a lad,' he said at a recent charity event. 'It would be the ultimate dream come true.'

Sheridan's eyes narrowed as she scanned the page. She really should cancel her subscription to *Celeb Goss* magazine. She imagined Alex Santana, an arch-villain type, leering as he wrote the piece. She paused to sip her coffee, appreciating the scent of spring flowers that Monica had brought. But her friend's visit was not enough to take her mind off her concerns. The comment about Daniel enjoying 'late-night sessions' with Natasha Clarke was barbed, and Sheridan tried not to let it get under her skin. For once, they had reported something accurate. Daniel *was* on the verge of signing for the part of James Bond. Apart from his family, fulfilling his dream of playing the part was the most important thing to him in the world. The only downside was that he would have to spend six months at a time on set in Alaska. It wouldn't have been too bad if it was New York or LA, but Alaska felt so far away. Natasha made no secret of her admiration for Daniel. A British actress, she was young, intelligent and stunningly beautiful – and soon she would have Daniel all to herself.

Sheridan shook her head as she reread the piece. Daniel was thrilled, of course. He hadn't even consulted Sheridan before accepting the role – after everything she had done to keep him here with her: the risks she had taken, the commitments she had made. She placed a hand over the fake bump beneath her dress. Roz could never replace Kelly in Daniel's eyes. Sheridan's plan had backfired, and she herself was no longer enough to keep him. If he left her straight after the birth of their daughter, all the sponsorship deals she had fought so hard for would fall apart. As for his late-night sessions at the bar with doting Natasha . . . Didn't Daniel realise how bad it looked? It was hardly the behaviour of a family man.

She had hoped the new baby would improve things, but he hadn't even helped her to pick a name.

'Penny for 'em.' Monica's voice filtered into her consciousness. She had been in the bathroom, under Anna's watchful eye. Nobody was allowed to roam freely in Sheridan's house, not even her best friend.

'I should be happy,' Sheridan said. 'Daniel's over the moon, but all I can think about is how it's going to affect us.'

'Quit reading that trash, for a start,' Monica said, her gaze on the report. 'All that guff about Natasha and Daniel. Sure, she likes him, but doesn't every woman with a pulse have a soft spot for Danny boy?' Reaching out, she touched Sheridan's hand. 'He's nuts about you. Anyone can see that.'

'Thanks.' Sheridan gave her a watery smile.

'Is somethin' else wrong?' Monica squeezed her hand. 'You can talk to me.'

Sheridan shifted in her seat, the padding beneath her dress making her skin itch. 'Pregnancy hormones.' She sipped her decaf coffee as Monica stared her down. Her friend wasn't buying her excuse; she needed to come up with something better. She sighed. 'I had postnatal depression after Leo. I'm scared it might come back.'

She remembered how cruel the newspapers had been, how Alex Santana had twisted the knife. Of course she'd looked gaunt; Daniel's sudden act of violence had left her unable to think straight for weeks. It was why she had vowed to put things right. Protect their marriage at all costs.

Sheridan's afternoon with Monica had left her emotionally exhausted. There was only so much soul-searching she could endure. And now Daniel had come home, consumed by his own wants and needs.

'We need to talk.' He patted the sofa, a tumbler of whiskey in his hand.

Shirley Bassey's velvety tones filtered through the ceiling speakers in the living room. It seemed apt, given the topic of discussion.

'If you're going to tell me you've accepted the role of James Bond, don't bother. I already know.' Sheridan pouted as she slid next to her husband. She had poured herself a Martini. It felt good to have a real drink and take off that dreaded bump. Leo was asleep; her entourage had been dismissed for the evening, and it was just the two of them.

Daniel had the grace to look sheepish.

'This is meant to be a partnership,' she said. 'You could have at least discussed it with me. We barely talk any more.'

'I told you they'd shown interest.'

'But not that you'd signed on the dotted line.'

'I'm still waiting for the contracts to be finalised. I've not signed yet.' Daniel paused to sip his whiskey. 'Who told you?'

'TJ called. He presumed I already knew.'

'I changed my burner phone. Forgot to give him the new number.' Daniel swirled his whiskey, his ice cubes clinking against the glass.

Sheridan watched him intently. 'Your agent should be the first person on your list.' She narrowed her eyes as Daniel muttered incoherent words under his breath. 'What did you say?' She said, her frown deepening.

'I thought you'd be happy for me,' he replied. 'You know how much I've wanted this.'

She touched Daniel's hand. 'Honey, I always knew you'd get it. But what are we going to do now?'

'With Roz?'

'Of course.'

Sheridan could barely stand saying her name. Something had happened between the girl and Daniel while she was away. She had felt it the moment she returned. Saw it written all over Roz's face. Had Daniel lost interest now his fantasy had been fulfilled? Had he opened the door, offered Roz her freedom? Had she chosen to stay? Whatever relationship they had, it could not compete with Daniel's lifelong goal of playing James Bond. Such thoughts produced tiny frown lines on Sheridan's face. Botox could only keep them at bay for so long.

'You can't expect me to stay here and look after the baby as well as your girlfriend.' The words were spiked with a jealousy she fought hard to resist.

His jaw rigid, Daniel swallowed the last of his whiskey. 'She's not my girlfriend. She's nothing to me.'

'I know you slept together.' Pain rose in Sheridan's chest as the words took flight. Daniel did not move. Instead, he continued staring into space.

'If we did, you'd only have yourself to blame.'

Sheridan bristled, but she knew better than to disagree. She could not afford to rouse his temper again. 'What happened?'

'Nothing.' Daniel sighed, his voice deep and low. 'I thought it could be like what I had with Kelly, but I've been chasing a dream all this time.' He placed his empty tumbler on the coffee table, leaned back on the sofa and crossed his legs. 'It was all a wild fantasy that got out of control.' He turned to Sheridan, his gaze intense. 'We don't need Roz. Come to Alaska – you, me and Leo.'

Sheridan's lips parted as she inhaled a sudden breath. These were the words she had been longing to hear. She was finally enough for him.

'I love you,' Daniel continued. 'Finding out Mike was here made me see just how much. It's not all these wild fantasies that stop me acting crazy, it's you. It's always been you.'

Sheridan could have cried with relief. 'Do you mean it?'

'More than anything.' Daniel's face broke out in a smile. It lit up his features, like the sun breaking through dark cloud. 'Playing James Bond is as exciting as it gets. I don't need anything else. I've got my career and I've got you.'

'But we're skimming so close to losing everything,' Sheridan replied. 'Roz . . .'

Daniel's smile faded at the mention of her name. 'Get Mike back here. He can finish what you started. End all contact with him after that.'

What *she* started? Sheridan's stomach clenched as he laid the blame firmly at her door.

She opened her mouth to speak but Daniel was still talking. 'The team can run our social media profiles while we're in Alaska. I've made a stipulation on my contract. I want you on set. Leo too.' He paused, allowing the words to sink in. 'You know I love him, don't you?'

'Of course. He's your flesh and blood.'

'Babe, he's *our* son. I know he plays up for the camera, but we don't need a picture-perfect child.' Reaching out, Daniel brushed his hand against Sheridan's cheekbone. 'We've done some crazy shit together, but we need to draw a line under it all.'

'And there's nothing wrong with a bit of role-playing if we get bored.' Sheridan smiled.

'Exactly. Give Mike whatever he wants to finish this.'

Sheridan's pulse quickened at the thought. It was everything she'd ever wanted. But something held her back. 'I can't leave without the baby. Please. Let's carry on as planned. I can pay Roz off, send her home as soon as she gives birth.' But each shake of Daniel's head filled her with dread.

'Keep the baby if you want. But as for Roz . . .' He rubbed his head, as if his thoughts were an infestation. 'There's no way she'll go quietly. I'll leave the details up to you.' Daniel stretched to pick up his empty tumbler and walked to the cabinet for a refill. 'Whatever it takes. You have my blessing. I just don't want to hear about it.'

Sheridan didn't want it left up to her. As usual, Daniel had turned his back on any ugliness in his periphery. But why should she have the burden of disposing of such a young life? She watched as he filled his glass. The promise of Alaska was tempting, but could she live with what she was about to do?

It wasn't as if she hadn't done it before. She remembered the day her mother had tracked her down and threatened to spill the beans. 'I know that baby isn't yours,' she'd spat. 'There are papers who'd pay good money to hear about your infertility.' And Sheridan knew of just the magazine reporter who would revel in the news. A payoff might have silenced her mother, but Sheridan was unwilling to take that chance. Mike had never liked Dorothy and was more than happy to comply. But killing Roz in cold blood . . . Could she be responsible for such a dark act?

'Top-up?' Daniel hung over her, waiting for her response.

'Yes, please.' She handed him her glass. Then again . . . Roz would never leave without the baby. What choice did she have? Mike would do her bidding, no questions asked. It would mean some heavy-duty covering up, but it was nothing that he wasn't capable of. 'I'll do it after the baby is born.' Sheridan took the glass from Daniel's outstretched hand.

Easing himself back on to the sofa, Daniel picked up the TV remote control.

'Let's not talk about it any more. I'm going away next week. Induce her labour and plan it for then.' It was a statement, not a suggestion.

'But shouldn't we discuss the worst-case scenario? What if we get caught?' As she voiced her doubts, she felt the air cool between them. Her time for asking questions had come to an end.

'You know what to do if the police get involved. Deny everything.'

But it was easier for Daniel to deny things when he was walking away from it all.

CHAPTER FIFTY-SEVEN

SHERIDAN

'You asked for my advice and I'm giving it. Ain't my fault if it's not what you wanna hear.' Mike sounded more like a prison inmate than an ex-actor.

Sheridan folded her arms, hating every second in his cheap motel room. Each inhalation brought the stale smell of nicotine, which competed with the stench of beer lingering on Mike's breath. She wanted to go home, to strip out of her dress and shower, but this was not a conversation she could have on the phone.

'Couldn't I ask Dr Blumberg? Don't you think he'll go along with it?'

'Keep him out of it. If he asks any questions, tell him Roz got cold feet and ran away.'

'But you're no doctor. How can you help?' Sheridan slid her long silver necklace between her fingers, wishing there was an easier way.

Mike snorted. 'When you've spent as long in prison as I have, you make contacts. You learn how to survive. I'm sorry, Sherry, I don't like this any more than you, but it's the only way.'

Sheridan played with the tassel on the chain as she contemplated his words. 'But inducing labour. How would we go about it?'

'How do you do think? Drugs,' Mike replied, sitting on the faded fabric arm of the sofa, which had seen better days.

'But what about the labour . . .' Sheridan said, her eyes wide as memories of Kelly came into play. 'What if it goes wrong?'

'Then you call Dr Blumberg. But only if there's a risk to the baby's life.'

Sheridan felt her skin creep as Mike leaned over, felt the heat of his gaze on her skin.

'You'll need a backstory if the cops find out that she was in your home,' he continued. 'Better to have them think she's still alive.'

But something niggled at the back of Sheridan's brain. Something that told her it wouldn't work. She tuned back in to Mike's words, tried not to cringe when he placed his hand on her back.

'Film Roz having the baby, make out she backed out of the deal and you sent them both home. Have her say it on camera if you can.'

'Right,' Sheridan agreed. It always came back to setting the scene. Daniel would not object to having a camera present at the birth, now that he had lost all interest in Roz. But Sheridan would only film what she wanted to film.

'Put a story together,' Mike continued. 'Make the room nice. You don't want marks on her wrists or face. Treat her good. Make her happy. Understand?'

Sheridan nodded. After everything that had happened between her and Roz it was a big ask. But the girl was desperate to keep her baby and go home. Sometimes when you want to believe something so badly you cast aside all common sense.

'Make it a nice moment,' Mike said. 'Buy her a plane ticket home. Dress in her clothes and pose as her leaving the building if you have to.'

'I can't . . .' Sheridan gave a heavy sigh as she recalled the reason for her niggling doubt. 'I covered it up on Miracle-Moms, made it look like *I* backed out of our deal.'

She explained how she'd said she was pregnant, and had then written a reply from Roz's username saying she would look for parents elsewhere in New York. 'What a mess.'

'No,' Mike replied, his hand snaking around her shoulder. 'That makes it easier.'

'How?' Sheridan's stomach knotted at the prospect of what they were about to do. She felt like she was in a maze and the walls were closing in.

'Roz running away with the baby can be plan B, if the cops can prove without a doubt that you held her there. They'll get you for lying, possibly kidnapping, but you can say you had a change of heart and let her go.' He rubbed his bristled chin. 'You got away with Leo. There's no reason you can't do it again . . .' He paused to gather his thoughts. 'OK, plan A: say that you backed out of the arrangement because you fell pregnant. Pretend Roz's baby is your own. You'll have to move fast.'

'But wouldn't the police want proof that I've given birth?'

'Tell them you had a home birth. Get your best lawyer on board. They can't force you to be physically examined – they won't have enough justification, for a start.'

Sheridan nodded. That made more sense.

'After the baby's born, go to Alaska with your family. Disappear for six months. When the coast is clear, come back and do a big promo shoot with the baby. It'll be a whole new side-line for you . . . if that's what you want.'

'What do you mean?'

'If you can cope with what you've done.'

Sheridan could cope. Already, her mind was racing with plans. It could be just like when Bouncer, her dog, died on TV. She remembered how her career had taken off after that. A change in direction refreshed everything. Any lingering doubts dissipated in her mind.

'Yes,' she said, with a renewed sense of determination. 'I'll do it. Get what you need – we'll plan it for next week, when Daniel is away.'

'Leave it to me,' Mike replied. 'Then I'll get that place cleaned up, get rid of the bodies. Make it look like those gals never stepped foot inside.'

'How?' she asked, uttering the question that made her stomach churn. 'How are you going to get rid of her?' They both knew she was talking about Roz.

'Remember Ginger?'

Sheridan nodded, her face grim. Ginger was Mike's favourite horse in the stables they had both attended in their teens. Galloping over some scrub, Ginger had taken a tumble and broken his leg. The vet was called, and the horse was put down. 'Quick and painless,' Mike continued.

Sheridan raised her palm to stop him. She didn't want to hear any more.

His hand returned to her shoulder. 'But we're not talking about a horse, so you've got to make it worthwhile. After this, we won't see each other again.'

'I know,' Sheridan replied.

'And you'll keep your promise. I'm only asking for what we both want.'

'Of course,' Sheridan said, resting her hand on his knee. She knew there was no getting out of it, and Daniel had given her the green light. 'Give him whatever he wants,' he'd said. He wasn't talking about money.

She needed Mike to stay loyal. She had kept him hanging on long enough. She exhaled a breath as his fingers pulled down her zipper. Then she stood and peeled off her dress.

CHAPTER FIFTY-EIGHT
ROZ

'Everything OK?' Sheridan asked, watching each mouthful I consumed.

I nodded, tucking into my cream-laden chocolate cake. The strain of the last few weeks had carved dark shadows under my eyes. Sheridan had been apologetic, assuring me she wanted to make up for all the stress.

'Eat,' she'd said. 'You'll need all your strength for the baby.'

But I viewed each kind action with mistrust. I felt like a pig being fattened for the slaughter rather than the recipient of genuine concern.

My suspicions aside, it was good to taste comfort food again. A couple of days of eating unhealthily would not do the baby any harm. Besides, it was not my diet that was worrying me, it was Sheridan's behaviour. I had not seen Daniel since we almost had sex. Did Sheridan know about what had gone on? She had told me I was there for both of them, which I found increasingly odd. I could not comprehend why someone as successful as Sheridan would want to share her husband. Such questions kept me awake long into the night as I lay, anxious and lonely, in my bed.

I sipped the vanilla milkshake, which tasted like heaven on my tongue.

'This is lovely, thank you,' I said, grateful for her kindness.

It was made all the nicer by the fact that I was having it upstairs in Sheridan's home. Our schedule had been abandoned. It was so out of keeping with how she'd treated me before; she was impossible to second-guess. I watched as Sheridan sprayed the table in OCD fashion, wiping over everything I touched. There was no sign of her entourage, and I'd overheard her saying that she had sent Leo and the nanny to a luxury pony camp for the week. A sudden thought brought a cold slice of fear. Convicts on death row got to choose their last meal, didn't they?

I'd had Braxton Hicks contractions every day this week. Time was running out for me. Sheridan had not asked how I was feeling. She had distanced herself in a way that unnerved me.

'I want to tell you something.' She pulled her chair closer to the table as I finished off my cake. 'It's good news,' she added, taking in my worried expression.

She opened her blazer, slipped a piece of paper from the inside pocket and slid it across the table. Slowly, my fingers crept towards it, my heart pounding as I scanned the writing. A barcode. A flight number. I held my breath. An airline ticket for a first-class flight to Dublin airport . . . and it was assigned to me. I stared in disbelief, not daring to speak for fear of breaking the spell. My name on a British Airways flight home to Dublin. I traced my fingers over the print, tears springing to my eyes. It wasn't happening. It couldn't be real.

'It's a flight home for after the baby is born.' A smile carried on Sheridan's words. 'Go ahead, pick it up. It's yours.'

I struggled to swallow. My chest felt tight with grief for my hometown. I had genuinely believed I would never see it again. I thought about my baby, the little girl she wanted me to leave behind. Was Sheridan really ready to let me go? But surely I had to stay and fight for my child?

'I didn't book a seat for the baby,' Sheridan said. 'Because you'll be carrying her in your arms.'

'What?' I said, finding my voice. I slid my hand into my dress pocket and pulled out a tissue to dab my tears. My chin wobbled as part of me collapsed inside. I had built a wall to protect myself, Dare I believe my baby and I were going home?

'Daniel's going to be offered the part of the new James Bond,' Sheridan explained. 'It'll mean being on location in Alaska. I'm moving out there with Leo to be with him.' She flicked back her hair before delivering a winning smile. 'Happy?'

'Happy?' I blinked away my tears. 'Yes! So happy!' I felt like hugging her, but months of ingrained mistrust kept me firmly in my chair.

'It's obvious you love your baby. It would be wrong for us to keep you apart.' Sheridan's smile seemed frozen on her face as she gushed. She stood, gesturing at me to rise. It was just like the early days, when I first arrived. 'Why don't we talk things through?'

It was strange, walking ahead of her to the living room. I felt like I was walking on clouds, but any moment I could go into freefall. Surely she wanted my baby too much to let her go? From the corner of my eye, I saw her pocket her phone from where she had left it on the sideboard. Had she been recording our conversation? It would explain why she was being so sickly-sweet.

I sat as instructed on the sofa, watching Sheridan's features grow stony as she relayed the terms and conditions of our deal. I rubbed my arms, goose bumps rising on my skin. Spring sunlight sliced through the half-closed curtains, and I was dying to peek outside. I strained to hear traffic, passing music, signs of everyday life. Apart from hearing muffled voices above, life in my basement flat was like existing in a void.

I tuned in to Sheridan's narrative as she took a seat in the armchair across from me. It was a leather wingback; Daniel's chair. I remembered him sitting there, staring into the flames as Sheridan threw the prayer book my way. Not once had he properly acknowledged what she had done.

'Roz. Are you listening?' Sheridan's voice cut sharply into my thoughts. My head was all over the place, half euphoric, half paralysed with fear.

'You were going through the conditions,' I responded. Clenching my fingers, I resisted the urge to nibble my nails. Even my toes were curled within the confines of my slip-on shoes.

'In a nutshell, we give up all rights to the baby and you forget you've been here.'

I nodded profusely. I would have sold her my soul if it meant taking my little bean home.

'Not one word to the police, to journalists or Kelly's family. Speak about us and we'll tear your life apart. Am I coming through loud and clear?'

'Yes, totally.' I cleared my throat. 'I won't breathe a word, I promise . . . on my baby's life.'

My baby. I could have cried with relief. I was so grateful to be going home. I would never complain about my lot again. I thought about seeing my mother, imagined Dympna's face when I walked in through the door. There was nothing I couldn't overcome, as long as I made it to my home soil.

'Can't I go now?' I said, ready to take a flight in the next hour if one became available.

'There are rules about flying this late in your pregnancy. We can't afford to draw attention to you.'

It made sense, but I was desperate to get away before she changed her mind. 'If you dropped me off at a hospital, I could have the baby there . . .'

'Honestly, Roz, is this the thanks I get?' Sheridan snapped. 'You can't just walk in from the street. We've got Leo to think about. I need time to put things into place. We have to be ready should this blow up in our face.'

'Sorry . . . It won't. I swear. I won't let you down.'

But she was standing before me now, her face pinched. 'I'll stop at nothing to keep my family together. But then you know that, given what you saw in the basement.'

A chill ran through my body as I absorbed the implication of her words. She'd said Kelly's death was an accident, but now I was not so sure. She was letting me go. That was all that mattered. I had damaged their marriage and she was taking time out to plaster over the cracks.

'It will be as if I was never here,' I promised, gasping as my baby delivered a kick. Could she feel my growing excitement? I watched as Sheridan moved to place her hand on my tummy, then freeze before drawing it away. Was she really letting us go? That was why she was cleaning the surfaces after I touched them. She was wiping away all traces of me.

'What about *your* pregnancy?' I asked, thinking of other reasons why someone would want to wipe away my DNA. Had she done that with Kelly? Had she told her she was sending her home?

'Let me worry about that. Just . . . just be happy, Roz. You're going home.'

Home. The word carried so much promise. I offered her a smile in response. But there was something behind her eyes that betrayed her. I looked away, not wanting to see it. I could not contemplate anything, except seeing my friends and family again.

CHAPTER FIFTY-NINE

ROZ

JUNE 2019

'You're nearly twenty inches long now,' I said to my baby as I tried to distract myself from the pain. 'You can hear my voice.' I paused to inhale a slow breath as the pain in my back increased. 'And at thirty-eight weeks, you're almost ready to be born . . . Ooh.' *In through my nose, out through my mouth . . . inhale . . . release . . .* Exhaling a low moan, I practised the slow breaths recommended in my pregnancy book. I rubbed my rock-hard stomach, clutching it as I paced. The fabric of my T-shirt was being tested beyond its limits. I could not bear to wear Kelly's clothes for another day and was grateful that Sheridan had allowed me to have some of my old stuff back. My grey tracksuit bottoms still fitted me, sitting snugly beneath my bump. I'd tied my hair into a ponytail, desperate to get it off my face. Braxton Hicks contractions were hitting me with a vengeance. I had been getting them for weeks now, but today the band of pain around my stomach took my breath away. It was too early to go into labour, wasn't it? I wasn't due for another two weeks. But how could I notify Sheridan when I couldn't use the lift? I couldn't believe I had the plane ticket, which I clutched to my chest each night. From listening at the air vent, I gathered that Daniel had left. I had not seen him since our evening together, and he had neglected to say goodbye. Trying to second-guess the couple above me was driving me insane. Sheridan's need for my baby was still strong. I could see it in the way she looked at me, how she monitored my kick chart, scrutinised each and every test.

The pain in my stomach ebbed away. It was as powerful as a rising tide. Daniel leaving always felt like a prequel to something bad – I was vulnerable when he wasn't around. From what I'd heard above me, I had figured out he'd gone on a work trip. Sheridan had kept her voice low as she said her goodbyes.

'Everything will be sorted by the time you get back,' she'd told him, as Daniel said something about Mike. The mention of his name had sent me into a tailspin. This was the man who had dug up Kelly's corpse as if it meant nothing to him. Were they finally disposing of her body? The thoughts of her lying in the room next door had kept me awake for weeks. Kelly was the reason I found it hard to accept that Sheridan was letting me go. If only I hadn't seen her. What possessed me to blow my only chance of escape? I imagined her mother, still looking at her front door, waiting for her daughter to walk in. That could be my mother soon.

The hot-water pipes rattled into life, making me jump. If I managed to get back home, I would call the police and tell them about Kelly. She deserved a decent burial and her family needed peace. I was not the type of person who could let that go. The trouble was, Sheridan knew that. Would they really jeopardise everything by setting me free?

'Ashling,' I said to my bump. 'Your name is Ashling.'

By naming my baby I was making her real. She was mine, and I needed to hold on to that with both hands. Nothing was separating us, and nobody was taking her away.

My stomach tightened as another band of pain wrapped itself around me. The pain was worsening. Why did it feel like a clock ticking down?

Was that what it had been like for Kelly? Thoughts of that poor girl going through a traumatic birth upset me even more. Sheridan had buried her under the floorboards and a few years later, started the process all over again. What sort of person did that? Not the sort to let me go.

'Ow,' I winced, as the pain grew in strength, delivering a warm trickle of release between my legs. These were no Braxton Hicks. This was labour, and my waters had broken.

I opened my mouth to call Sheridan, but fear of Mike stemmed my words. When Mike was around, bad things happened. He was a dangerous man. Staggering to the lift, I jabbed the button, swearing under my breath as it failed to activate without the needed security pass. No surprise there. Low backache kicked in as the band of pain grew. Moaning, I tried the side door, but as I guessed, it was locked tight. *Breathe*, I reminded myself, pushing my panic down. I made my way to the bed, digging my fingers into the duvet as I leaned over the side. Pressing my face into the material, I moaned, soft and low. Nobody was coming to help me. I was completely alone.

CHAPTER SIXTY
DYMPNA

'Sit down, stay there and don't say a word.' Dympna's father's voice was firm as he escorted her to the plastic chair. They were in the building of 1 Police Plaza in Lower Manhattan, the headquarters of the NYPD. The exterior of the fourteenth-floor building looked like an ugly brown box, with row upon row of uniform square windows. The security area felt tense as she emptied her pockets into a tray, and her face reddened as she was rushed through by an armed officer standing at her side. She felt like a little girl as her father did all the talking and met their contact, who escorted them to the office of the Major Case Squad.

The fact she was nervous in a New York police station made her realise how sheltered her life had been up until now. Even in Dublin, everything was ruled by the safety of routine. Joining the Gardaí would open her eyes. So would being in New York. They had been here almost a week and Dympna was relieved to be finally inside the doors of the NYPD. After months worrying about Roz, things were looking up.

Sitting in the side room, Dympna had a good view of her father through glass-panelled walls. She guessed it was some kind of witness interview room, somewhere to put people who came in about a case. She watched as her father spoke with a broad-shouldered brunette who introduced herself as Detective Hartman. The Major Case Squad was the inspiration for TV programmes such as *Law & Order: Criminal Intent*. The real-life department investigated burglaries, larceny and kidnapping, among other things. Dympna had done her homework, and she could not believe that she was here. She slowly leaned forward, pushing the door open an inch. It wouldn't hurt to eavesdrop. Outside, the sudden scream of a police siren made her jump in her chair. As nervous as she was, she could not wait to be part of the police world.

She shuffled to the edge of her chair, straining to listen at the door. There were a dozen officers working at computer terminals in the room where her father sat, with panelled lighting overhead and the scent of filter coffee hanging in the air. The clacking of keyboards and garbled phone conversations contributed to a steady rumble of noise. The atmosphere felt intense, but there was a certain amount of camaraderie too. A sudden shout of triumph erupted from a middle-aged man in the corner who was then heartily slapped on the back by his colleague. Had he had a breakthrough? Dympna wondered. Sent someone down? She was itching to know. But she was aware she was snooping and really shouldn't be here. If it weren't for her father's contacts, she would not have made it past the front door; but thanks to the information Dympna had gathered, at least they were taking their claims seriously. Sheridan's pregnancy had hit the headlines, although there were very few pictures of her so-called bump.

'You're not the first person to raise suspicions about Daniel Watson and Sheridan Sinclair,' Detective Hartman explained, closing a folder on her desk. 'We spoke to them following the disappearance of Kelly Blunt, but we didn't have enough evidence to obtain a warrant for a house search.'

'You've listened to Roz's voicemail,' John replied. 'You've seen the text. Surely you have enough for another call-on?'

Detective Hartman gave John a patient smile. 'We do, and we have. It took a lot of effort just to speak to Sheridan, and she barely allowed officers past the door. We've been here before. We need more evidence to get a search warrant.'

'Forgive me.' John leaned forward, resting his elbows on the desk. 'I'm not trying to teach my grandma how to suck eggs, but have you explored all avenues? What about CCTV? Have you interviewed her staff? Roz mentioned someone by the name of George who was meeting her at the hotel.'

'It's all in hand,' Detective Hartman said. 'I'm sorry I can't tell you much more.' She tilted her head as she registered John's disappointment. 'We receive on average thirty-five missing person reports every day in New York, but many of the subjects are found. The missing person department is working on Roz's case as we speak. As for us, we specialise in kidnappings, which need a lot more groundwork.' She smiled. 'Now I'm the one telling my grandma how to suck eggs.' Her desk phone rang with some insistency and she rose from her desk. 'I've got your number. As soon as I have news, I'll call.'

Dympna exhaled a long breath as her words filtered through. After an all-too-short meeting, Detective Hartman showed them both the door.

As they spilled outside, Dympna threw her hands in the air. 'I can't believe we came all this way for that. You'd think they'd be more respectful. You outrank her, after all.'

'Not in New York, I don't,' her father replied, hands deep in his pockets as they walked through the plaza. 'I've no jurisdiction over here. She's doing what she can. Sounds like it's all in hand.'

'Just because Sheridan and Daniel are rich and powerful, the police have to build up this big case. Why should they be treated differently to everyone else?'

Her father looked down his nose at her, a signal to calm herself down. 'Because regular people can't afford to sue, and . . .' He raised a finger as Dympna took a breath to interrupt. 'AND . . . the scandal of arrest could end Sheridan and Daniel's careers. Besides, the more prep the NYPD put together, the stronger a case they'll have when they act.'

Never in a million years had Dympna imagined the scenario she found herself in. She couldn't have predicted that she'd get on an aeroplane, let alone investigate Daniel Watson and Sheridan Sinclair. She rubbed her freckled arms as goose bumps rose on her skin. The sky was grey and overcast and she felt a sense of impending doom. She followed her father towards the municipal building, her mood low. Frustration had turned to annoyance and she felt like screaming.

Her father was looking at his phone, having drawn up Google Maps. 'Fancy a visit to the 9/11 Memorial? It's a twenty-minute walk from here. It might take your mind off things.'

'But I don't want to take my mind off things. Roz is in trouble. The minute she has that baby . . .' Dympna's cheeks puffed as she exhaled a long breath. 'God knows what's going to happen to her.'

'Darlin', it's not as if they're not looking for her. She's been reported as a missing person. They're reviewing all the CCTV. You never know, she might come home of her own accord.'

Dympna snorted. 'You don't believe that any more than I do.' She paused for thought. 'I don't suppose you caught sight of Sheridan's address in that folder, did you?'

Her father gave her a wry grin. 'I did, as it happens, although she was quick enough to snap it shut.'

'Dad?' she said. 'Can you hail us a taxi?'

Sighing, John shook his head. 'I know what you're thinking, and it won't work. They won't let us inside the door.'

'But we've got to try, haven't we?' Dympna threaded her arm through her father's.

'Aye, that we do,' he sighed, raising his hand to a passing cab.

CHAPTER SIXTY-ONE
SHERIDAN

'Every man is guilty of all the good they didn't do.' It was a saying Sheridan pondered on, as she thought about the people whose silence she had forced. Sheridan had bought both Anna and her granddaughter Juanita's loyalties by paying for Juanita to return to education full-time. Then there was the nanny, who must surely know more than she was letting on; her driver, who was paid over the odds for keeping quiet; then Mike, who had actively encouraged her just to get into her underpants. But George wasn't like that. He was the purest-hearted of all. She hated herself for what she had turned him into. His enthusiasm for life used to rub off on her, and spending time in his company had been a joy. But like everyone who got to know her, he had come to recognise her dark side. She could sense his resentment building for the bind she had put him in. Which was why she kept him out of what she was about to do. Guilt was creeping in, and her actions would haunt her forever. The killing of such a young woman was not so easily compartmentalised.

How could Daniel leave her to meet film producers when she needed him the most? He was childlike in his excitement about playing Bond, but the contracts hadn't been finalised yet. She thought about their relationship, and how he disappeared when things got tough. Yet she knew she would forgive him just the same.

Taking a deep breath, she stirred the crushed tablets into Roz's drink. The sedatives would make her woozy, then with Mike's help, she could administer the injection needed to induce childbirth. Using a glass instead of a plastic tumbler, she watched the tiny pink flecks of powder dissolve. Roz was so convinced she was going home, she would not suspect a thing. Her thoughts heavy, Sheridan gave the contents of the glass another stir. Mike warned her to personally ensure that Roz swallowed every drop. *Quick and painless.* His words returned to haunt her. His gun was equipped with a silencer, and a pillow would stem any mess. But could she really bring her baby into the world, then kill her mother as she took her first breath? A visit from the police had sealed Roz's fate. She could not afford to have her around any more.

Closing her eyes, she took a deep breath as she tried to regain control. *Think of the end-game. Of Alaska.* She imagined the beautiful sunsets and the breathtaking scenery she and Daniel would explore. Her grip on the spoon relaxed.

Absentmindedly, she rinsed it off in the sink. Every inch of her home had been cleaned to wipe all traces of Roz away.

'Ready?' Mike was waiting for her at the lift, his thumb hooked into the pocket of his jeans. Mike was hard. Prison had taken his edges and made them razor-sharp. But she had given him what he wanted and now he was ready to respond in turn. But there was something about his behaviour that was off. She watched the heel of his boot dance against the floor as his leg jittered of its own accord. This was more than nerves. Her eyes narrowed as she met his gaze. It was only now she noticed his dilated pupils, his muscles twitching beneath his skin. 'Son of a bitch . . .' she said. 'You've been using!'

'Just a little something to take the edge off,' he replied. His tone was dark, and Sheridan sensed a shift in mood. 'Are we getting this over with or not?'

'All right,' Sheridan replied. Now was not the time to challenge him. 'Stay in the lift, unless I call you.'

Act normal, she told herself, invoking years of training. This was a set. She was in a leading role. Much of her life had been lived like this.

As the doors parted, she adjusted her eyes. It didn't matter how many lights were switched on; this would always be a gloomy space.

'Roz,' she exclaimed, finding the young woman bent over the bed.

The smile Sheridan was faking slid from her face as she approached, glass in hand. Her eyes fell on Roz's tracksuit bottoms, which were stained and wet. She took in her sweaty face, her wild eyes.

'I'm having the baby,' Roz moaned through gritted teeth.

Sheridan clung on to the glass. This was not part of the plan. 'You can't be. It's not due yet.'

'Tell that to Ashling,' Roz said, delivering another low moan.

How long has she been like this? Sheridan thought. *What do I do now?*

'Here.' She thrust the glass in Roz's direction. 'Have a drink.'

Reaching for the glass, Roz gripped it in her hand before smashing it against the wall. 'I don't want a drink!' she screamed, making Sheridan jump. 'I want a doctor. Take me to the hospital, now!'

Sheridan watched as the liquid dripped down the wall in long pink streaks. A flashback made her recoil. Kelly had lain on this very bed, screaming as the baby crowned. Just like before, Daniel was nowhere to be seen. Kelly had cried for the hospital and Sheridan had cried alongside her, shocked by the turn of events. But she could not risk everything to help the girl her husband had fallen in love with. Bright-red blood had gushed on to the mattress, staining her hands.

Panic rose in Sheridan's chest at the memory of Kelly's death.

'I can't . . . I can't do it again. I won't . . .' It felt as if she were drowning and she couldn't breathe. She needed to call for an ambulance. She had to let Roz go. Fumbling with her phone, she prepared to dial for help.

Heavy footsteps creaked the floorboards as Mike stood out from the shadows.

'You don't need that.' Taking Sheridan's phone, he pressed the button to turn it off. As everything began to unravel, Sheridan had forgotten he was there.

'Babe, trust me. Daniel might have abandoned you but I'm here now. I'll do whatever it takes to keep you safe.'

Roz's face was a picture of fear. 'Keep away from me!' she screamed, backing away from the bed. Picking up a shard of the broken glass, she pointed it at him. 'Keep away!'

'What . . . what do I do?' Sheridan felt like a child asking for her lines. Except that her mother was not there to help her. Mike was.

'Go upstairs,' he said, his voice deep and reassuring. 'I'll take care of this. You don't need to be here.'

It was bad enough losing Kelly through childbirth, but now it came down to it, Sheridan could not allow him to harm Roz. 'No,' she said, her eyes pleading with his. 'Not like this.'

Mike's hand fell on her shoulder and squeezed. 'She knows too much. It's her or us.'

'But the baby?' she said, her breath steadying at last.

'I told you. I'll take care of it.' Mike's hand slid to the waistband of his jeans. 'I'll make it all go away.'

A dry crackle of a laugh passed his lips as he casually waved his gun around the room. 'Haven't I always looked after you? You can't risk keeping her kid. Not with the cops sniffing around.'

That was when it hit her. Mike had never intended to allow Roz or the baby to live. He had used the plan to get down here and finish them both off. She wanted to scream that he was crazy, coked up and out of his mind. But from the wild look in his eyes, now was not the time.

'But look at her,' Sheridan said, turning to Roz. In the grip of pain, the young woman was bent over, still holding the shard of glass in her hand. Sheridan turned back to Mike. 'We can't. Not now.'

'I'm sorry, Sherry, but it's the only way to keep you out of prison.' His jaw remained rigid, his fingers tightening around the trigger of his gun.

Sheridan knew by Mike's tone that the decision was out of her hands. Like it or not, he was taking care of this. She could find herself at the other end of the barrel if she did not comply.

'What are you saying?' Roz said, blood dripping from her thumb as she tightly gripped the shard of glass.

Sheridan's eyes blurred with tears as she watched Roz struggle to stay on her feet.

'Just go,' Mike said. 'It's not fair to drag this out.'

The decision to leave her baby was agonising, but she had no choice. For every moment Sheridan stayed, she was only adding to Roz's pain. They had to put an end to this now.

'I'm sorry,' she said to Roz. Backing away towards the lift, she kept her eyes on her. 'I'll get the doctor. Everything will be all right.' But her words lacked conviction as tears trailed down her face.

CHAPTER
SIXTY-TWO
ROZ

I succumbed to the vice-like grip of my contractions, my legs turning to jelly as I fought to keep upright. I accepted the drink from Sheridan's outstretched hand but had no intention of letting it pass my lips. I could not risk her forcing me to swallow it. From the look on her face, the drink contained more than just vitamins. But I did not realise it was real glass until it smashed against the wall.

During the last hour, my contractions had progressed at a rapid rate. I was still wearing my tracksuit bottoms, unwilling to change into one of Kelly's dresses. I could not bear to look at them. It terrified me to imagine history repeating itself all over again.

I pleaded with Sheridan for help, sweat rolling down my back. Pain was making me crazy. I could not deliver Ashling alone. Then I saw it, a flicker of sympathy in her eyes. But just when I was getting through to her, Mike stepped into the room. His presence was dark and brooding, making the sweat lacing my skin turn cold. I shuddered as I clung on to my only weapon, a piece of glass I had picked up from the floor. Swiping my hair from my face, I begged Sheridan for release.

From the moment I saw Mike I knew that he was there with one intention in mind. Pain rippled through my body as I tried to defend myself. Daniel had abandoned me. Even the staff who I thought were helping me had left me all alone. Nobody was coming. I was weak, emotional and outnumbered.

'Get away from me!' I screamed at Mike. My fingers tightened around the glass and I felt a sharp stab of pain. I turned to Sheridan, watching her mumble to Mike before backing towards the lift.

Mike advanced, his gaze filled with determination. Fear was all-encompassing as the realisation hit me: they weren't waiting for my baby to be born, and they certainly weren't letting me go home. We were both going to die.

'Please, don't leave me alone with him,' I snivelled. 'Please, Sheridan, I won't tell anyone. You promised to let me go.'

Her eyes moist with tears, Sheridan shook her head. 'I'm sorry,' she said, calling the lift.

I followed her gaze to the object in Mike's hand. Horror ripped through me as I realised he was carrying a gun. How could I defend myself against that?

'I'll get the doctor,' Sheridan said. 'Everything will be all right.'

I tried to breathe through my pain. Mike had claimed her mobile phone. He was calling the shots now. All I could think about was my baby, about the life she would not live to enjoy. My Ashling would never draw breath, feel the sun on her skin.

'Please! At least take the baby. She's your little girl, don't let him . . .'

But my words came to an abrupt end as I fought for my next breath. Ashling was coming whether I liked it or not. And now there was a man pointing a gun at my head. His face was stony. Another wave of contractions weakened my limbs.

Mike paused, waiting for Sheridan to leave. The very second she stepped into the lift, my baby and I were dead. As he reached for a pillow, I began to pray.

'Our Father, who art in heaven . . .' Between panicked breaths, I uttered the words.

The words gave Mike pause, and a shadow crossed his face as I asked God to forgive those who trespass against us. But Sheridan turned her back on us both. My time was up. I dropped the piece of glass as the lift doors opened and she stepped inside.

I pressed my face into the duvet and cried out for my child, waiting for the end.

CHAPTER
SIXTY-THREE
SHERIDAN

Sheridan could not listen to Roz's cries for a second longer. As Mike picked up a pillow and held the gun level with her head, the lift doors rolled open. The invitation to escape was one she could not ignore. She could hardly see through her tears, but the moment she put a foot inside, she was forced to retreat.

'Monica? George? What are you doing here?' Sheridan swallowed back her tears, tried to think on her feet as she attempted to usher them back inside. 'Why don't we go upstairs?'

'I don't think so.' In a cloud of heady perfume, Monica pushed past.

Sheridan staggered on her heels at the force of Monica's shoulder barging against hers.

'George!' Sheridan's voice crackled as she tried to drive him back in. But George barely glanced her way as he followed Monica into the basement.

It was too late. They had already seen the gun in Mike's hand.

'What are you gonna do, Mike, shoot us all?' Monica's Boston accent rang loud and clear.

'Help me!' Roz cried, relief flooding her face. 'I'm having a baby. Call the police! Please!'

But as Monica retrieved her phone from her pocket, Mike turned the gun on her.

She raised her hands in the air. 'No need for that, big guy. Why don't ya put the gun down?'

'Throw your phone over here,' he commanded.

Sheridan's stomach lurched. The room had descended into chaos. There was no way out now. 'George.' Her voice was harsh. 'Stand behind me.' If she had to choose, she would save George first.

'Do as she says,' Mike roared. 'Just remember, I've got plenty of bullets for everyone.'

Monica stood, her hands on her hips, her feet planted wide. 'Don't you dare threaten me, you piece of shit. I know what you lot are up to. I can't believe you've done it again.'

'Again?' Sheridan raised her voice as Roz's screams filled the room. Any second now, Mike could turn around and shut her up for good. As for Monica . . . there was no way Mike would let her go. Anyone who knew about Kelly was as good as dead. But the last thing Sheridan wanted was to lose her friend.

Monica glared at her, fearless. 'I know everything about you, Sheridan. What did you call me? *The author of your pain.* I knew I'd unravel the truth in the end.'

'No!' Sheridan said, the blood draining from her face. 'I was talking about Alex Santana. He's . . .'

'Not a he,' Monica finished her sentence. 'It's my pseudonym. Now call off the Rottweiler. He doesn't intimidate me.'

But Mike was in no mood to lower his gun. 'She's a journo? I ain't going back to prison.'

'The police are on their way,' Monica said, her eyes flickering to the side as she exchanged a glance with George. But George hesitated to back her up for a split second too long.

Sheridan shook her head. They had come down here expecting to confront her alone. They had no way of knowing about Mike and the gun – there were no police on their way.

Mike could see it, too. 'You're bluffing. You came here looking for a story – one you could keep to yourself. But you weren't expecting to stumble into this.'

The look on George's face told Sheridan that Mike had hit the nail on the head. Mike's tongue darted between his lips as his finger curled around the trigger. Glancing from left to right, he surveyed the people in the room. Sheridan knew he was a good shot. She had practised with him enough times down at the rifle range when they were teens. She could see he was mentally doing the maths, working out his options. He could take them all out before anyone could reach the lift.

'Nobody needs to get hurt.' George's voice was shaky as he took a step towards Roz. 'Please,' he continued. 'Let me get her out of here before she has her baby on the floor.'

Her face slick with sweat, Roz screamed into her duvet as the latest contraction took hold.

Sheridan looked to Mike for help. Her armpits were damp beneath her shirt, her limbs rigid with the need to leave. The scene felt surreal, as if any second now a director would shout, 'Cut!'

'You're right,' said Mike. 'We need to do something before the baby's born.' Releasing the safety catch, he aimed the gun at Roz.

But George didn't stop, despite knowing he could be next.

'Step away from her, George, or I'll stop your mother's treatment. I mean it! Do as I say!' Sheridan screamed in frustration, a desperate measure to save her friend.

'There's something you should know.' George's tone was flat as he whipped his hand from behind his back. 'My mother died.'

A flash of silver erupted into a deafening bang. The smell of gunpowder filled the air as Mike's body hit the floor.

'You took your time,' Monica said, her relief evident as she scrambled for her phone. 'Guess I should call the cops.'

'Ambulance first.' Dropping the gun to the floor, George reached Roz's side. 'Ahh, my ear – shit, that was loud,' he said, pounding the butt of his palm against it before wrapping his arm around Roz. 'It's OK.' He smoothed back her sweat-drenched hair. 'Everything's going to be OK. Help is on its way.'

Her legs crumpling beneath her, Sheridan knelt with her hands pressed against her ears. But the ringing noise continued, along with the pounding in her head.

Mike's foot twitched as he lay on the floor, his hand outstretched, blood pooling from his chest.

CHAPTER SIXTY-FOUR

ROZ

Relief flooded my system, temporarily numbing the pain. My baby was fighting to be born. New life would prevail despite the horrors around me. I had never been so happy to see so many uniformed officials at once.

'What's your name, pet?'

The paramedic's Geordie accent took me by surprise. She was middle-aged, motherly, another person far from home. 'Roz,' I said, my legs shaking as she guided me towards a trolley.

'OK, Roz, I need you to put your arm around me and edge your bottom on to the trolley so we can get you out of here. Then we're going to pop your tracksuit bottoms off so I can have a quick look.' She took in my horrified reaction. 'Don't worry, we'll cover you up with a blanket first. Roz?' Panic was driving my breath, which was coming far too fast. It felt like my lungs were collapsing, and I couldn't draw in enough air.

Police were swarming around George, confiscating his gun. Another paramedic tended to Mike, placing a mask over his face.

Everyone was talking at once and I couldn't take it in. The paramedic clicked her fingers before my face, making me blink.

'Roz.' Her face was inches from my own. 'Don't mind them. Focus on my voice. Deep breaths, nice and slow.' She laid a hand on my stomach. 'Why don't we get you up here before the next one hits?'

She was talking about the impending contractions, which were coming almost back to back. Once on the trolley, she covered me with a blanket and checked me as discreetly as she could. 'Not long now,' she said.

I groaned as another wave of contractions threatened to carry me away.

'I'm going to give you some oxygen.' She placed the mask over my face, instructing me to inhale. 'Easy now, pet, not too much or you'll make yourself dizzy.' After a few steady breaths, I lay the mask by my side. I cast one last glance over at Monica and George as I was wheeled out. If they hadn't come in when they did, my baby and I would have died.

Shocked faces passed in a blur as people gathered on the street, and the fresh air was as good as any drug as it hit my face. I must have been out of it, as for a brief second, I thought I saw Dympna's face in the crowd. Then a flash of police car lights caught my eye as uniformed officers drew up to the ambulance, preparing to follow us. Sheridan had made so many threats; would the police believe me? All that mattered was my baby. I prayed that she was OK.

'They kidnapped me – Sheridan Sinclair and Daniel Watson,' I said, inhaling a deep breath in the back of the ambulance. 'They've kept me in a basement for months.'

I watched the paramedics exchange glances. It felt like forever before we reached the hospital but in reality, just minutes had passed.

'You're fully dilated,' the ob-gyn said. 'There's no time to give you a spinal block.'

I didn't care. After all I had been through, I was just grateful to be there. I glanced at her freckles and felt a pang as I thought of Dympna, so many miles away. Soon I would be able to call her. We would be together again. Tears of relief streaked down the sides of my face as I heard the strong, healthy heartbeat of my baby. My little warrior. My Ashling.

My body was rigid with tension, and I gritted my teeth as I worked through the pain. I deserved every second of discomfort. It was my mistakes that had led me here. I had almost got my baby killed; the least I could do was endure a natural birth. But the process I was undergoing felt like the most unnatural thing in the world.

A blonde-haired nurse popped her head around the door. 'You've got a visitor. Can she come in?'

'Who is it?' I said, terrified it was Sheridan and I would be dragged back to the basement. It was irrational, crazy – but so were the last six months of my life. What if the police believed Sheridan's account over mine? Would I ever escape the nightmare I had found myself in?

'Her name is Dympna.' She smiled as she watched my face light up. 'From Ireland.'

So I *had* seen her? My fists tightened into knots as my contraction gripped hard.

'Yes,' I managed to squeeze out mid-grunt. 'Let her in.' But I didn't believe it was her, not until I saw her shock of red hair.

'Merciful hour!' she cried, rushing to my side.

I exhaled a low moan, gripping her by the hand. 'I'm so glad you're here,' I said, my shoulders dropping as the contraction ebbed away.

'Me too, chick. I saw them put you in the back of the ambulance. We've been looking for you all this time.' She sniffled, wiping her tears with the back of her sleeve. 'Sorry it took so long.'

'The baby's father . . .' I said, trying to catch my breath.

'It doesn't matter,' Dympna interrupted. 'We can wipe the slate fresh, start again.'

But I was not buying into her sentiment. She handed me a tumbler of water, as if to stem my words. I took a sip, nodding gratefully before handing it back. Soon another contraction would plunge me into a world of pain, and I would not be able to tell her the truth.

'I need to tell you,' I said, panting as I felt it build up.

'Shh now, there's no need . . .'

'There *is* a need,' I said, before inhaling a lungful of air. But they were the last words I would utter before pain swallowed me whole.

'I can see its head!' Dympna screamed at the top of her voice.

'I can't . . . I can't do any more.' Exhaustion washed over me. I'd had enough. 'Make it stop. Please,' I cried, digging my fingers into Dympna's hand as she reappeared at my side.

'Your baby's heartbeat is dipping,' the ob-gyn said, her face serious now. 'C'mon, one big push.'

But my energy supply was depleted, and their voices were growing very far away.

CHAPTER SIXTY-FIVE

ROZ

'She looks just like you.' Dympna pushed back the baby's blanket for a better look.

I cradled my little one in my arms, overwhelmed by a rush of love. At eight pounds two ounces, she was heavier than I thought she'd be.

'Just as well I didn't go overdue.'

I leaned down to kiss her, inhaling her sweet baby smell. She'd emerged into this world just when I'd felt like giving up. Too many deep breaths had left me woozy, and Dympna had given me a stern talking-to to get me through. I was beyond relieved to have her by my side.

'I need to tell you who the father is.' Every inch of me was aching, but I could not carry the burden of the secret any longer. Dympna had travelled halfway across the globe. The least I could do was to be honest in return.

'There's no need, because I already know,' Dympna said in a matter-of-fact manner. Cooing, she melted as Ashling grasped her little finger. 'I'm your auntie Dympna, yes I am, yes I am.' Her voice was as soft and gentle as a summer breeze.

'You know?' Ashling was lying content after her first breastfeed, and neither of us wanted to wake her up. Her face was pink, soft and beautiful. She was just how I had pictured her, with tiny wisps of blonde hair framing her head.

Dympna nodded, finally meeting my eyes. 'I'm coming to terms with it. I know it won't happen again.'

'Wow,' I said, feeling the weight of nine months of worry fall away.

'What's the point in holding on to all that anger and hurt? You're the sister I never had. And I'm gonna make a go of this. We both can.'

I stared at my friend with newfound admiration. How could she be so calm? The betrayal must have hurt like hell, but she was right. It would never happen again.

'And he knows about the baby,' Dympna said, 'so you don't need to worry, it's all out in the open. We'll all work together to give Ashling the best start.' Tears moistened her eyes as her words juddered to a halt. I felt thoroughly ashamed for having hurt the most important person in my life.

'Does your mam know?' I said, trying to imagine the kind of reception I'd get back home.

Dympna frowned. 'No. It's none of her business. If I split up with Seamus it's nothing to do with her.'

It was obvious we had crossed wires. She did not know the truth at all.

'Wait a minute – you think Seamus is Ashling's father?'

'I don't think it, I know it,' Dympna said, an edge growing to her words.

'Then you're wrong.' I wondered how she would react when she discovered the truth. 'I wouldn't sleep with Seamus in a million years.'

'There is no point in denying it.' Dympna's brows knitted in a scowl. 'I've seen how cagey he's been. I did the maths. When I told him you were pregnant he started acting all weird.'

I shifted in my bed, as after-pains ebbed through my body. I needed to clear the air before I could rest. I remembered how I had been unable to meet Seamus's gaze, how he had looked at me in disgust.

'Seamus burst in on us. I begged him not to say anything. I didn't want you getting hurt.'

'How, if he's not the dad?' Dympna punctuated her words with a sigh. 'You don't need to cover it up.' She leaned back in to Ashling. Like me, she could not get enough. 'I'm your auntie Dympna, and I'm going to babysit you all night long.'

'But that's the thing,' I said, as a soft knock on the door signalled a new visitor. 'You're not her auntie . . .' I watched as the baby's father entered, a giant teddy under his arm. My gaze met Dympna's. 'You're her half-sister.'

CHAPTER
SIXTY-SIX
DYMPNA

'Dad?' Dympna said, before returning her gaze to Roz.

John had been in the corridor since their arrival, speaking to the police, filling out forms for the medical bills and allowing Roz to get on with giving birth. Dympna watched a flush creep up Roz's neck as John rested the teddy at the end of her bed. His gaze never left the baby and myriad questions invaded Dympna's brain. This was why Roz had asked if her mother knew. She should be relieved that Seamus was off the hook, but she could not comprehend what Roz had done. Sleeping with her father? How could she? No wonder he had been so willing to fly over to find her. But where did that leave them now?

Feeling like a gooseberry, she retreated to allow her father a better view of his new daughter.

'She's beautiful,' he said, just as Ashling opened her eyes. Blinking, she stretched in Roz's arms, and Dympna watched as her father seemed entranced.

'Her name is Ashling,' Roz said, slowly offering her up.

John took the baby with confident hands.

'She looks just like you,' he said, echoing Dympna's earlier words.

'Dad?' Dympna said again, breaking the spell.

'Sorry,' Roz replied to her friend. 'I wanted to tell you . . .'

'It's OK,' Dympna said, as the news sank in. She could forgive Roz. It was her father who needed to explain.

'Here you go,' John said after a few minutes, gently depositing Ashling in Roz's arms. 'I didn't know about the baby.' He turned to Dympna. 'Not until you told me.'

'What about Mam?' Dympna wondered how she was going to look her mother in the eye.

'She knows. We've been having issues for a long time now. Why do you think I've been spending so much time at work?'

Dympna stiffened. 'So you thought you'd sleep with my best friend?'

'You must have known we were having problems. Roz and I . . . it wasn't planned.'

Dympna drove her fingers through her long red hair, pushing it back from her face. 'Does she know about the baby? What about Diarmuid?' she said, referring to her brother. 'What's going to happen now?'

John lay a hand on Dympna's shoulder. 'We're going to work through it. Keep the family together.'

'Can you see why I had to leave?' Roz looked from John to Dympna. 'The last thing I wanted was to split your family apart. I'm sorry. You must hate me right now.'

'Well, you're not winning any prizes for friend of the year!'

A whine rose from the bundle in the blanket and Dympna felt a pang of guilt. Roz and her baby had been through enough. She didn't deserve to lose her best friend, too. The truth was, a part of her was pleased about having a little sister. It was something she had dreamt of, ever since she was a girl. She just hoped her mother would be OK.

'I'll get over it.' Dympna offered Roz a hesitant smile. 'I'm glad you're both all right.' She did not want her sister's earliest memories to be of her having a hissy fit. 'Here,' she offered. 'Why don't I take her so you can get some sleep?'

'Sleep would be good,' Roz replied, fixing her baby's blanket and giving her forehead a kiss. A sudden flash of anxiety crossed her face. 'Where's Mike? He's not here, is he?'

'No,' John replied. 'He's under armed guard.'

Roz's shoulders dropped an inch as she relaxed back into the bed. 'Don't leave, will you? If I fall asleep . . . don't go.'

Dympna had no idea what her friend had experienced, but she knew her father had been talking to the police.

'I'm going nowhere, chick,' she said, gazing into Ashling's eyes. Usually, babies were kept in the nursery, but her father had explained the circumstances and Ashling was being allowed to stay next to Roz's bed.

Dympna gave her father a look. He had a lot of explaining to do.

'Have the police told you what happened?' Dympna asked as both Roz and Ashling lay asleep. Giving her a sideways nod, John directed Dympna towards the window, out of Roz's earshot.

'Roz isn't the first woman they've kept in that basement. They've got witnesses. There's a reporter. She's been investigating Sheridan for years.'

'Was Kelly Blunt involved?' Dympna said. Her father's expression was all the answer she needed. For the first time, she felt truly vindicated.

'I don't know how you figured that out, but you were spot on.'

In the corridor a trolley rattled past, cups clinking against saucers as hot refreshments were served.

'The timings matched up,' Dympna said, grateful Kelly's family would find closure. 'She looked like Roz and fitted the profile, too. She met a celebrity couple online, spoke about New York and LA, and she was a big fan of Sheridan and Daniel, which is why she was so blown away.'

'Apparently one of the photographers from *Celeb Goss* magazine thought they caught sight of her at Sheridan's apartment. That's when that journalist, Alex Santana, went in undercover. She must have got the shock of her life when she came face to face with Roz.'

Dympna stole a glance into Ashling's cot, grateful her new sister was safe. 'I told you Roz was in danger as soon as the baby was born.' But the expression on her father's face relayed it was much worse than that. 'What?' Dympna said.

John's lips thinned as he gazed out the window. 'I shouldn't be sharing details of the case with you.'

'It's a bit late for that,' Dympna replied tartly. 'What happened?'

'They put a gun to her head while she was in labour. Roz and her baby could have died.'

'You're not serious,' Dympna exclaimed in a harsh whisper, her hand planted on her chest. 'Why?' How anyone could kill an innocent baby and their mother was beyond her understanding.

'Who knows?' John shrugged.

'And here was me, giving her the third degree.' Dympna delivered a sigh laden with regret. Roz was snoring softly now, finally at peace.

Reaching out, John touched Dympna's arm. 'You have every right to be angry with me, but go easy on Roz. She's been to hell and back, by all accounts.'

'I can't believe I have a sister,' Dympna said. She hovered over her cot, feeling an instant bond. She owed Seamus a huge apology.

'She's a determined little thing, all right,' John chuckled. 'All hell breaking loose around her, and she decides to come into the world.'

Dympna peeked at Ashling, her heart melting as she watched her sleep.

'You're safe now,' she whispered. 'Your big sis is looking out for you.'

CHAPTER
SIXTY-SEVEN
SHERIDAN

'I've dug people out of some holes during the course of my career, but nothing like this.'

The gravelly voice belonged to her lawyer, Elizabeth Ross. At almost sixty years of age, she made her living from repairing celebrity reputations and was the ballsiest woman Sheridan knew.

'Have you had some kind of breakdown?' she continued. 'Is that it?'

Sheridan was in no mood to be lectured. Sitting in the police interview room, she was well aware of the trouble she was in. 'How's Daniel? I need to talk to him.'

Elizabeth glared down her thick spectacles, which were attached to her neck by a gold chain. 'You can't. And even if you could, I wouldn't let you. He's laying all of this at your door.'

'No!' Sheridan's hands curled into fists as she rested them on the table. 'He can't be.'

'He said it was all your idea. He thought Roz was there by consent.' She glanced around the ceiling before rummaging in her jacket pocket and slipping out a vaporiser. 'I paid five hundred bucks for this vape, so it better not set the smoke alarms off.' Elizabeth was a chain-smoker, had been since her teens. The evidence of her habit was set in the deep lines around her mouth. She took a sneaky puff and exhaled a stream of vapour towards the floor.

'We were in it together,' said Sheridan. 'He told me to deal with it.' She crossed her legs beneath her chair, her calves aching from wearing flat shoes. Daniel's betrayal cut as deep as if she had taken a blade to her skin.

'Yet he wasn't there when Mike was around.' Elizabeth's mouth twisted as she spoke, her scepticism painfully evident. 'He's denying everything, and Roz backs his story up.' She paused as Sheridan's eyebrows shot up. 'Oh yes,' she continued. 'I've read her statement. She said every time she was with him, he was nothing but kind. He made her meals, took her out, and get this . . . he even gave her his keys so she could leave. On more than one occasion, he told her she was free to go!'

'But Kelly . . .'

'Kelly nothing. Never once did he demonstrate any knowledge of her death. Even when Roz asked questions, he played dumb. Wanna know what else?'

'No . . . yes,' Sheridan breathed through her open fingers as she buried her head in her hands.

'He claims you were having an affair. He had you followed. A private detective has photos of you and Mike in some very compromising positions. How could you be so dumb?'

'He slept with her – with Roz. They had sex!' Sheridan screamed the words, but she knew it wasn't true.

'Not according to Roz. She got close to it but he turned her down. Said it wasn't right, even though she was tugging on his pants at the time. Quite the gentleman, by all accounts. Unlike you, getting it on with an ex-convict in some cheap motel room.'

Sheridan's hands touched her throat as panic rose in her chest. 'I don't believe you,' she said. 'It's not true!'

'It gets better,' Elizabeth continued, her words peppered with vapour as she exhaled. 'Your mom's next-door neighbour saw the report on TV. She's identified Mike as the man she saw leaving Dorothy's address. Now I'm betting your pal Mike is gonna squeal like the pig he is. What else have you been up to, Sheridan? Who else have you tried to bump off?'

Elizabeth was ready with an answer. 'He said he was in love with Kelly. That he was going to leave you for her, but then she disappeared. He's got some lovey-dovey footage of the two of them together. He's got all the evidence he needs. Can you see how much trouble you're in?'

The bastard, Sheridan thought, biting her bottom lip. There was no time for tears now. Despite it all, Leo needed a father. She could not leave him parentless. Her lawyer was right. Daniel did love Kelly, but only now could she see how much. Sheridan took a deep breath as she prepared to give another performance.

'Kelly's death was an accident. She died having Leo. I didn't tell Daniel because I couldn't face it.' The last bit was a lie but it was all about damage limitation now.

'And your mom?'

Sheridan shrugged, holding in a cough as she inhaled the stench of artificial tobacco. 'If Mike paid her a visit it has nothing to do with me.'

'And what about Roz – is she telling the truth?'

'I didn't want to hurt Roz. You've seen the video footage of us together, the flight ticket in her room. But then she found Kelly, and Mike pulled a gun on her. I begged him not to hurt her. I was going for help when George and Monica – I mean Alex Santana – turned up.'

'Ah, the famous Alex Santana. She really has it in for you.'

'And George?'

A beat passed between them, and Sheridan knew there was more to come. Opening her folder, Elizabeth sifted through some of the paperwork. 'Did you know that George was selling stories to Alex Santana all this time?'

'George?' Sheridan frowned. 'No. It was Rachel, my ex-housekeeper. She was the inside source.'

Elizabeth shook her head. 'Shame you're going down. This would make a great movie.' She paused to suck the e-cigarette, locking the vapour in her lungs for a couple of seconds before letting it go. 'It's always been George. He said he tried to warn Roz when she first arrived in New York. He left newspaper clippings in her room about Kelly, and old issues of *Celeb Goss* magazine. He even left her a knife. But he couldn't tell her directly because you were paying for his mother's care. All your staff were indebted to you, in fact.'

'That's not right.' Sheridan stiffened as she was hit with betrayal after betrayal. 'He told me about Roz's note.' She bit her lip. What was she saying? She had just stated she had planned on letting Roz go.

'The famous note in the prayer book? Yeah, he mentioned that, too. He said you were getting suspicious. He told you about the note to keep your trust. But then Monica bumped into Roz in your home and persuaded George to work with her to get her out. She should have called the cops. Typical journo – wanted the story first.'

Sheridan's head hung low. She was so caught in her own web of lies she didn't dare speak another word. But her lawyer was wrong about one thing. Mike would never squeal. The memory of their intimacy would guarantee his loyalty for a long time to come.

She knew she was facing prison, and she was facing it alone. But she would use her time wisely. Monica was not the only person who could write a book. She may have taken her throne, but she wouldn't occupy it for very long. Sheridan would make her regret the day she'd double-crossed her.

CHAPTER SIXTY-EIGHT

Celeb Goss **Magazine**
By Tiffany Matthews
November 2019
SHERIDAN SINCLAIR HELD ON
KIDNAPPING & MURDER CHARGES

It is the crime that shocked the nation, and you heard it here first. One year ago, *Celeb Goss* journalist Alex Santana launched an internal investigation into Academy Award-nominated actress Sheridan Sinclair. An investigation that led to the Hollywood starlet being charged with the manslaughter of missing Carolina waitress Kelly Blunt and the kidnapping of Irish woman Roz Foley. After an extensive police investigation, Sheridan's husband, Daniel Watson, was released without charge.

In another shock announcement, last week's edition revealed the identity of *Celeb Goss* journalist Alex

Santana as Monica Murphy, therapist to the stars. The revelation does not seem to have harmed her relationship with up-and-coming actor Adam Weiss, who announced their engagement last week. Adam recently signed on the dotted line to play the next James Bond. Monica has sold her new tell-all book on her time with Sheridan Sinclair for a seven-figure sum, with movie rights being snapped up after a five-way auction. A Hollywood source says: 'With the demise of #Sheridani, Hollywood is crying out for an exciting new celebrity couple. Charismatic and endearing, Adam and Monica fit the bill.' Here at *Celeb Goss*, we wish our new favorite celeb couple, the #MAdams, all the success in the world.

CHAPTER
SIXTY-NINE
ROZ

It took me six months to settle into some kind of normality. It helped to know that I was getting justice, and that Sheridan was facing trial. My reluctance to incriminate Daniel was not for him, it was for his son. It was for Kelly, too. I still felt a connection with the young woman whose clothes I had worn. What would have happened to her son Leo if both Sheridan and Daniel were locked away? Kelly's mother had no room for her grandson, and I never doubted that Daniel would provide Leo with a good life. Sheridan may have been ready to kill me, but I liked to hope that Daniel had played no part in it. It was some punishment that he had lost his revered role as James Bond.

I heard that George showed remorse, and I was surprised to hear he was the one selling his story to *Celeb Goss* all that time. He was the creator of the 'shit-storm' he told me about – his way of leaking what was really going on. While his mother was alive, his efforts to help me were sadly lacking; just enough to ease his conscience, I supposed. He was not the only one feeling guilty.

Daniel was not allowed to speak to me, but he paid my thirty-grand medical bill in full. The news of his split from Sheridan came as a surprise to everyone.

I was yet to have a full night's sleep without the memory of staring down the barrel of Mike's pistol. I was grateful to George for saving my life, and that of my child. It's a special kind of irony that he did so with Sheridan's gun.

My mother fell in love with Ashling the moment she set eyes on her. It was nice, being pampered and fawned over in a normal way. I felt safe in her home, as long as Ashling's cot was by my side and we had a nightlight on. The gossip set Ferbane alight for a few months, but things eventually calmed down.

'Tea?' Tony said, handing me a cup. His smile was warm, his curly hair in need of a cut. He was a gentle bear of a man and the house felt different now he was around. I felt like I'd known him forever; he had a lovely manner about him. If I were to describe his attitude in a single word, I'd say 'non-judgemental'. It's something that Dympna has demonstrated, too. Her relationship with Ashling was destined to be special, and the information she gathered has helped the police no end. I'm glad she patched things up with Seamus, and have no doubts she'll make a terrific detective one day. John pays weekly maintenance and is keeping his marriage afloat.

Like Dympna, I gained a stepsister. Jenny, Tony's daughter, is a delight. It was hard for her, losing her mother at such an early age, but now she has so many new people in her life.

'Thank you,' I smiled at Tony. 'And not just for the tea.'

'You're coping remarkably well for someone who's been through hell.'

'I hope you're not analysing me,' I chuckled. I was taking baby steps, but getting there. I'd even begun drawing again. It was nice to take pleasure in the simple things, and I would never take my life for granted again. When it came down to it, friends and family were all that mattered.

'Having Ashling here means the world to your mam,' Tony said, as if he were reading my mind.

'I couldn't deprive Ashling of a grandmother,' I replied, feeling like a hypocrite as I remembered I was happy to do so before. 'I mean . . .' I stammered, backtracking.

Tony raised a hand in reassurance. 'No need to explain. Your childhood was the subject of most of your mother's rehabilitation. That day in the coffee shop when you said you were going to America, it almost tipped her over the edge.' He sighed at the memory, shaking his head. 'That evening, I found a bottle of whiskey in her bag. But she hadn't drunk it. She was still fighting.'

'There's a time in your life when you have to stop being a victim. When you have to take back control.' I hadn't realised I had spoken the words aloud until they left my lips. Time in solitary confinement had affected me in so many ways. Back then, I'd spoken to myself all the time, and it had become a habit I needed to shake.

'Your mother told you that?'

I nodded, taking strength from her words.

As he rubbed his beard, the smile widened on Tony's face. 'I said that to her when we first met. I didn't think she was listening back then.' He chuckled, obviously pleased to know she was.

I watched his face light up as he spoke of her, wishing I could find someone who loved me that much. Then I realised I had already found her as my mother returned with my Silver Cross pram. My Ashling. My fighter. My little girl. She would never be a victim. She would keep me strong. I watched Jenny open the door, being careful not to bump the pram against the wooden doorframe. This was my home now, and I was in no hurry to leave. The building blocks of our future: a stable home and good relationships were what my daughter and I could look forward to now.

Flushed from the cold, Jenny's smile was wide, her joy at being an auntie plain to see. Ashling delighted everyone she came into contact with. I exchanged a look with my mother as she parked my sleeping daughter next to me. I saw love there, and it was returned. She was a wonderful grandmother for Ashling, and I had long since forgiven her for past mistakes. I peeped in on my daughter, who looked like a sleeping cherub in her pram. I breathed a sigh of contentment. It was time to look to the future.

I had found the perfect mother for my child.

ACKNOWLEDGMENTS

Launching a book is by no means a solo performance and I am hugely grateful to have such a fantastic team of professionals behind me. To Maddy, Hayley and everyone at the Madeleine Milburn literary agency. Thank you for championing my work.

To my superb editor Jane Snelgrove, a thoroughly lovely lady whose insights have been invaluable. Also, to editor Ian Pindar – your encouragement and guidance have been most appreciated. To the rest of the team at Thomas & Mercer, you are all stars, I wish I had space to name you all! A special mention to cover designer Tom Sanderson – thank you again for your magnificent work.

To the book bloggers and book club members who have supported my work – in particular, Joseph Calleja, whom I was fortunate enough to meet during a trip to Malta recently. Never underestimate just how much your support means to authors, and keep up the good work.

To my amazingly talented author friends, both those on social media and those whom I'm fortunate enough to hang out with in real life. In particular to Angie Marsons, with whom I took my first tentative steps as a fiction author and who has been a brilliant support ever since. To Mel Sherratt, who has been there on a daily basis as we travel through our writing journeys together. Big hugs to you, lady, we come as a pair these days.

To the brilliant Sophie Ransom of Midas PR and to the fantastic libraries and online book clubs who have helped spread the word. To my ex-police colleagues – stay safe, guys, you are always in my thoughts. Also, to my readers, particularly those who have made contact to say you've enjoyed my work. It always brightens my day.

As always, to my family. Thank you for your unfailing love and support.

ABOUT THE AUTHOR

 A former police detective, Caroline Mitchell now writes full-time.

She has worked in CID and has also specialised in roles dealing with vulnerable victims – high-risk victims of domestic abuse and serious sexual offences. The mental strength shown by the victims of these crimes is a constant source of inspiration to her, and Mitchell combines their tenacity with her knowledge of police procedure to create tense psychological thrillers.

Originally from Ireland, she now lives in a pretty village on the coast of Essex with her husband and two children.

You can sign up for her newsletter at www.carolinemitchellauthor.com, or follow her on Twitter (@caroline_writes) or Facebook (www.facebook.com/CMitchellAuthor).

Printed in Great Britain
by Amazon

35677479R00218